**J. California Cooper**

# Some People, Some Other Place

J. California Cooper is the author of the novels *Family* and *The Wake of the Wind* and of eight collections of short stories, including *Homemade Love*, winner of the 1989 American Book Award. Among her numerous awards are the James Baldwin Writing Award and the Literary Lion Award from the American Library Association. She has one daughter and lives in Portland, Oregon.

**also by J. California Cooper**

*Wild Stars Seeking Midnight Suns*

*The Future Has a Past*

*A Piece of Mine*

*Homemade Love*

*Some Soul to Keep*

*Family*

*The Matter Is Life*

*In Search of Satisfaction*

*Some Love, Some Pain, Sometime*

*The Wake of the Wind*

# Some People,

# Some Other Place

*

**Anchor Books**

*A Division of Random House, Inc.*

*New York*

# Some People, Some Other Place

A Novel

*

J. California Cooper

FIRST ANCHOR BOOKS EDITION, APRIL 2006



The Library of Congress has cataloged the Doubleday edition as follows:
Cooper, J. California.
Some people, some other place: a novel / J. California Cooper.—1st ed.
p. cm.
1. African American families—Fiction. 2. Fetus—Fiction. I. Title.
PS3553.O5874S555 2004
813'.54—dc22 2004049349

**Anchor ISBN-10: 0-385-49683-4**
**Anchor ISBN-13: 978-0-385-49683-4**

*Book design by Gretchen Achilles*

www.anchorbooks.com

Printed in the United States of America
10 9 8 7 6 5 4 3 2 1

**Dedicated With Love To**

Joseph C. and Maxine R. Lincoln-Cooper, my parents
Paris A. Williams, my chile
Joseph Randolf Williams, my son I lost
The Great Congresswoman, Barbara Lee, Berkeley, CA
The Dial Book Club of Dallas

IMPORTANT PEOPLE

Cesar Chavez; Noam Chomsky; Rita Hogan, NY; Michael Jurich; Beatrice (Bea) Martin, San Diego; Allison Argo and the Elephants; Lauren Hutton; James Cromwell; Lena Horne, Singer, Actress, Woman; Katharine Dunham, Artist Extraordinaire; Donna Henry, Sister, Oakland; Tuscaloosa College; Tavis Smiley; Deihentics Clay, Cook People; Gustavo "Guga" Kuerton; The Double-Dutch Divas; Daine Goyle, Author; Robert Remini, Author; Eric Nelson, Producer Genesis Awards; George Flemings; Karey Kirkpatrick, Author; Huwaida, Egyptian Woman, Alexandria; Greenworks Pictures; Kyenan Kum; Millie and Susan of Gualala;

*Other Important People*

North Shore Animal League, NY; Animal Rights Groups; Morris Animal Foundation; Animal Planet Patrols; All Animal Protectors.

ESPECIALLY

All twelve million (plus) people who died during the Nazi Holocaust in concentration camps: the many Jews, Jehovah's Witnesses, German conscientious objectors, and Gypsies.

# Author's Note

*

This book really began when I was ill and could only stare at my ceiling for over two years. I kept seeing these houses on Dream Street through a misty yellowish fog. These houses seemed empty, but each seemed full of stories they wanted to tell.

Also in my mind was how every race feels superior to the others, and feels that their race has suffered more than any other. I believe each race IS special, but they all remain equal.

My belief is that though we are all different, seemingly, in our cultures, we all eat, sleep, have children or not, have good habits or morals, or not, etc., we are more alike than we are different. I know we are equal in the sight of God, collectively.

Finally, God has ten commandments . . . for all of us. They are not labeled for any special color; Black, White, Red, Yellow, or Brown. They are not labeled for men or women. They are for ALL. And we all break them in some way. So we are subject to the same weaknesses according to our strengths.

After living with these houses for a long time, they began to tell me their stories. The stories of the people who reached Dream Street. Their struggle to survive, to pursue their happiness.

Unable to handle every race or voice, I saw French, English, African, Irish, Jewish, Chinese, and Indian, always searching for love, or self. One house remained empty. Why? I don't know. This is a story of how these few races of people made their way to Dream Street in a town called Place (as we all want to find a place where we will be happy).

The voice that came to tell me these stories was an unborn child with a stake in the outcome of her mother's and father's survival.

Bear with me. Try the story. I think you may like it. I was fascinated with all the tales. I love looking at life, seeing how people survive in this hard, mostly uncaring world that, Thank God, has pockets of love in it that keep us going, keep us reaching and searching for Some Place like Some People.

Please, please enjoy the quest, the lives in this book. I learned a lot about life and love.

J. California Cooper

# Some People,

# Some Other Place

*

# Some People

*

I have not been born . . . yet. I am not an angel. Nor am I in Heaven. I am some other place. I am going to be born as a human being on Earth. It has taken me a long time to decide to be born.

I wanted enough time, before I made a decision, to look upon the Earth to be sure I wanted to live in such a place. Human beings think their life is very attractive; it is not attractive to me. I'll tell you why. Oh, I have so much to tell you.

One thing helping me to make up my mind is, even after my birth, I will still have freedom of choice. God does give everyone a choice. That is what makes us, even now, almost perfect and it is also what makes everyone born equal. Fate does not control our lives, contrary to the untruths you have heard. You have to make the decisions that will decide and control your life. Believe me.

So, I must make my decision—to come to Earth—the only beautiful planet God has given man to do with as man will, for a while. So far, evidently, for man to destroy. Mankind will have no other. Believe me. Man is not doing very well, do you think? He would be destroying a magnificent creation if he were not to be stopped . . . in time . . .

Mankind has divided Time on earth into seconds, minutes, hours, days, weeks, years, and on and on. But Time is not like that in this place I am in. Can you count Eternity? I have been able, almost in the twinkling of an eye, to look back through time, down upon the world and even at the ancestors I will have, if I decide to be born. Ahhhhhhh, what a huge web has been woven by humans for humans, in which, they say, they are in pursuit of happiness.

I have observed the rich, whom I find hollow, filled with thoughts of gold or money, filled with greed. Greed has driven the soul out of them. They are empty. More than enough is never as good as more than more than enough, because great riches mean Power. And great riches are rarely made honestly. Even so, the rich are admired, even respected and imitated.

I have watched generations of men exploit nations and attempt to destroy other nations using wars, guns, and drugs that pollute and corrupt the mind. They have despoiled and brought slaves from countries unable to stop them or resist their worthless temptations. They have carried and sold weapons throughout the world, causing wars through the ages that killed millions and millions of innocent people. They still do . . . for gold. Yet, they are not always despised by the world. They are honored and revered, even respected, because they are rich and powerful. If they become rich enough, they can become an "aristocrat." Titles are ardently desired in the world. The rich even plot their marriages . . . with gold in their minds and "love" on the bargaining table. When they die, presidents, kings, queens, czars, and others in high places attend their final farewell. Even the poor people they have exploited fill the streets surrounding their grand funerals to pay their respect. Few denounce them. Some are even buried in "holy" ground, pronounced holy by unholy men.

Sometimes the penalty of honesty is that one is thought to be a failure. Honesty is considered a weakness, a poverty of character. Sometimes, throughout all lands, ignominy, degradation, and neglect, as well as hunger and despair is an honest person's reward. There are those few that are honorable: kind, honest, considerate of others, not chasing gold for the sake of gold at the cost of their fellow humans. I have not seen many. Have you? I have observed many, many poor people. Most were used, abused, burdened, and sometimes they, themselves, added more to their own burden and burdened others of their own family and their fellow humans. A painful ignorance. Even violence. Violence perpetrated upon them by the rich and ambitious, and that which they delivered upon themselves. And some of them enjoy the doing of it to others. Why can't humans stop killing each other and every living creation on Earth?

I have seen murderers, liars, thieves, corrupters, the jealous, greedy, and envious. Most of them are the very men people die for. And wars . . . ahhh, wars. They even pray to their "gods" to bless their wars and think the gods on their bloody side; those gods that neither see nor hear or speak. Do they not know that the true God loves all His creation, even those on the "other" side? Even those who call themselves ministers of the Word do not pay heed to the wisdom of God's Words, for they think they can bless the wars! I believe I detest politicians, lawyers, and false ministers of the Bible the most. And, of course, there are those who laugh and say, "There is no God!" then cry for God the loudest when sickness and death is close upon them.

The world has not been such a good place to live in since man was sent from the testing grounds of the Garden of Eden. So much so that there are those who decide to leave Earth, in death, by their own choice and hand. How odd and how cruel life must have been for them. I am made not only melancholy, but sick with the sight of some lives amidst such beauty as could be on Earth. A few people find the beauty which I will seek if I decide to be born. These few people seem to have to go off a bit from the world. They live closer to the naturalness of creation. They are different from the rich, who try to separate themselves. The rich try to build a wall around the beauty they call home, but, too often, there is no true beauty or love within those walls except love of extravagance and gold. When the Time nears for them to die, some try to give some of the riches back to the people. Some try to buy more life, but life is not for sale.

Ahhh, well. Enough. God has a plan and a purpose. God did not create this Earth to be destroyed; God created it to be inhabited by the meek, the teachable, nonviolent, peaceful, loving meek. Mankind has had years, God's sabbath day to make their decisions. And God is not a human, neither man nor woman; God is a God. God will be true to The Word. The promise.

Because Satan is pervasive, I will begin to forget my knowledge as soon as I am born and I will not be able to speak until I have forgotten most of it. I will learn from my parents first. I pray they will know the

Truth, otherwise I will be learning from a world that knows little love or truth and is pompous in its ignorance. If I choose to believe a lie, have faith in a lie, I will simply have everlasting death. There is no burning hell. I will simply not be able to live on a beautiful Earth that has no sin or death on it. Not just a Garden of Eden, but a World of Eden that no man can make. Believe me.

Time, as the world knows it, is short. That is why, if I am going to Earth to live awhile, I must be about my business of studying it and trying to be born in a place where there is a bit of the beauty of Earth remaining to feel and see. Here you can choose if you wish to be born and so I will.

I am alone here, even with others around. Alone. Until I am flesh and blood, I am incorruptible. Satan (yes, Satan is real) cannot reach me until the moment I am conceived, and even then only through my mother and father. He has no real interest in me until I am born, then I am in his domain until I make the next great choice for myself. We understand here, where I am, that the people are the world and the world is in Satan's hands. The Earth is the Lord's, it and the people who choose God over Satan's temptations. God is Love: that is why people are so happy when they have love. Satan knows how to make a love facsimile that never truly satisfies and will, ultimately, be painful. Also, you have to give yourself to God. Satan just takes you, if he can, and some people are so easy to take.

We are surrounded by Love and Wisdom here. But most of us forget within one year from birth. We can only see the past of particular people. We are not permitted to see their future. With birth, changes begin. We are not allowed to speak when we are first born, but we can think . . . and what we know here slowly fades away in the struggle for survival that can, and usually does, begin immediately upon arrival.

That is all I can tell you. I want to remember, not to forget, Satan and his wily ways to help people forget. See, he was the first liar, the father of liars, among all the other things he is. I hope to remember he does not like people to know him or his purpose. He likes people to laugh at the idea of him. He likes to do things God will be blamed for.

He is a master of propaganda. He is so jealous and hates so much; he keeps helping humans create new little false gods and philosophies to take them away from the only true God, Jehovah. (Not the true spelling or sound of God's true name, but humanly close.) He knows mankind has an innate need to worship something above itself. Mankind is always searching. And remember, Satan can look beautiful. Believe me.

An insatiable hunger to know my future mother has made me look back in Time into the lives of my chosen family. I have become a spectator of mankind. Consequently, I have decided to whom I wish to be born. I will tell you a little about the woman who may be my mother and a small bit about her ancestors. These are my ancestors, I suppose, if I hold to my decision to be born to her. I want a good, wise mother who is neither blinded by riches . . . nor steeped in poverty and ignorance. Because, finally, the greatest poverty is the poverty of spirit.

I will tell you, also, about the place, the houses, that led me to my decision. In my search I saw many houses of all kinds, more old than new, and they each had a story to tell. Have you ever looked at a house or place and wondered what tale it would tell if it could talk? Well, I did. From where I am, I could *see* the tales they told. In my searching, I was struck deeply by a town named Place and a street there named Dream Street. With six houses and a store. Fascination and a vague feeling of affinity drew me to look and to listen closely to what the houses had to say.

It was late night or early morning, I don't know, but there was a hazy, vaporous, gray color, like a veil draped over the land there. I was about to return to my place of safety when something held me suspended over this block on the Street named Dream. Something familiar, yet unknown to me.

The trees that lined the street were very old, with gnarled branches, some dead. But within, the tree still lived, with a spirit striving to survive. Both the trees reaching to the skies and the bowed trees bending to the earth had dead shoots still trying to reach for the sky. Water to nourish them was probably coming beneath the ground from the river nearby named Striver River. I do not know the names of these trees, but about them was such a look of sadness, as though they were standing in their graves.

I wandered closer to see the houses better, and saw most of them were blind; still, they seemed to be looking back at me. There was such a deep silence over all. Yet, I could hear the sound of life breathing above the sound of the restless river rushing past. There was about the houses a sense of irrelevance, of bitterness, of hostility and yet there was a sense of courage, even pride. The block surely had about it a feeling of long accumulation of history, of life, of many lives intertwined. A weight hung over the houses as though their history of joy, love, pain, cruelty, melancholy, and foolish memories, even death, had left these houses with a dark dignity. They had a past. Still, I felt a future among them.

But now, they were not living, fully, in the present. Like a cemetery left uncared for, they could have been tombstones arranged on this block. Three houses on each side of Dream Street. Still they were alive, not tombstones. They were scarcely breathing with the lives still clinging to them. I felt the sheer weight of their seeming hopelessness, their faltering strength in their deep silence. But, their strength was holding on, for their undreamed futures, I guess.

I wandered closer to each house, their yards, not just to see, but to *feel* all the houses had to tell me. I wanted to know more. And I could feel, through a hazy blur, my dear mother. How warm even that slight feeling was.

The few flowers struggling to survive, the weed-vine covered fences and gates, the dying moss that fell from the pottery on porches, the wild growths of shrubs, bushes, and vines all reflected the houses there on Dream Street. But, still, they were alive. They were evidence of the life still pulsing slowly, persistently, inside of them.

Two dogs I had not noticed, a small, young gray and a very old brown and white dog, huddled together in the cold beneath the steps of a porch. They watched me, though I had not known they could see me. I have no earthly substance. Yet, their eyes followed me as I passed close to them. I stopped to get the feel of them. They did not move. The feeling of sadness passed from them to me. They were cold . . . and hungry. Too cold and hungry for even a whine or a growl from their throats. I had nothing I could give, so I moved on, my spirit grieving. I felt my mother dear would be here someday.

So.

I wanted to know the history of these houses. I returned often to listen to their tales. But, one thought remained: This Street named Dream seemed to be the loneliest place in the world, as if no dreams, visions, or illusions lived there.

Why? How would my mother get there? I burned with the desire to know the lives of my mother and the people in these houses on the Street of Dream.

The houses are numbered from 902 through 907 Dream Street. Most houses tell the truth about their inhabitants. Some houses lie, but they tell you they are lying. I have known some not to utter a word.

In time, I knew my mother would, one day, live at 903 Dream Street in the town of Place. I learned and will tell you her story and the other stories on that block. I will begin with my mother.

## Life
## Some Other Place

Since Time began, every person, including Adam and Eve, has sought a place to be. Some are fortunate, or unfortunate, to be born in a place where their parents and their parents' parents have had the same place to be all their lives. Yet, usually, people will still seek a place of their own while returning, sometimes, to the first home place as a foundation. All are seeking, were seeking, will seek, a place . . . to be. Some will find their own place some other place.

In whichever place they find, people have changed their dwellings from a cave to a treehouse, farms, cities, urban or suburban and such. They may change philosophies, attitudes, lifestyles, clothes, mates, and all other types of things. But, beneath the surface, intrinsically, human beings remain the same. Like dogs, cats, alligators, chickens, and everything else, with or without a heart, inherently we remain the same.

Evolution is on the outside of mankind. Things they create and can put their hands on. Choices made as humans pass through changes and the necessities of life, come from the inside. Needs. The mind. But people remain always human. Somewhat like water, people are always moving, changing, growing smaller or larger, softer or more dangerous, polluted or clean, and on and on. Like water running toward a place is always water, people are still always human, looking for a place, their place.

I want to tell you the stories of all the houses. They are so facinating to me. But the beginning of this story is about the seeking of a place by my chosen mother, the history of my mother.

# Chapter One

*

Sometime around 1895 in America, Negroes were spreading out and up from the hard past of the poor South seeking food and survival. Among them were a man and woman with four young children: two, three, four, and five years old. The traveling was hard and they were often hungry. They reached what seemed to them to be a large city in Oklahoma . . . and stopped. They had to stop because the mother did not have another step in her feet. She could not bear to drag her children another step.

The husband left them behind, near a small river, as he went to seek a Negro person to get information about a place for his family to sleep a few days and, perhaps, a job. They did not have a morsel of food. He found an old couple who were sharecroppers and worked a piece of land on another man's property. The old couple had only a small room and kitchen they lived in, a small shed for tools, and a mule.

Used to seeing such troubles, even having had them themselves, they allowed the man to bring his family into the shed for the little warmth and protection it offered from the cold nights. The old farmers could not, in their heart, allow the sad, bedraggled, unfed and unrested children go hungry and tired. They took some greens and a few potatoes from their garden. The tired mother wanted to help, but was shooed away by the old wife who cooked for the family, her own memories roiling around in her mind. They had no meat to share. Her two chickens were for eggs to sell.

The traveling family arranged themselves against the walls and on the floor in the farmer's small, and now crowded, kitchen for a meal. Then they were situated in the shed to sleep with what worn quilts and rags the old couple could spare. The old woman grimly smiled and said, "I sewn these here'n quiltes myse'f," as she handed them to the wife. Then the old wife took the two youngest children into her kitchen and laid them down on pallets beside the burning stove to keep them from the cold of the night in the shed. The exhausted husband and the farmer talked into the night about the town and work for Negroes there.

Awakening in the morning to the crow of a rooster, the still tired husband, stiff with cold in the shed, slowly removed the ragged quilt from his self. No need to dress. He had not undressed. The farmer took him, walking, to the white man who owned the land. The white man said, "Your woman can work 'round the house and fields with my wife and you can take that ole barn yonder, close up some of them holes in it, and make a home for your family til harvest. People always leavin', movin' on, so there prob'ly will be a house and some land free 'bout that time and you can move and go to work for yourself. Til then, you can work here for food and shelter for your family."

"Thank ya, suh. Mighty kind'a you."

"We ain't got no lotta food, now, but we share." The white man smiled.

"No pay, suh?"

The white farmer smiled, "Not none as I know of . . . yet. Maybe later on. We got to see what kind of workin' man you are. You want it?"

"I'll take it, suh. Thank you kindly."

So that's the way things went and the husband was able to shelter his family and feed them . . . a little. Too tired and disheartened to move on, the husband thought, "At least this ain't Mississippi!"

Things turned out exactly as the old farmer had said they might after he had introduced his new friend to the owner-boss. When sharecropper people moved out of a little piece of shack on a little piece of the owner's land, the owner let the new family move in it to work the land.

They took the sharecropper job, intending to move on to better things when things got better. But life being what it is sometimes, they ended up staying in that place for thirty years . . . until the husband died from overwork and overworry. They had changed shacks a few times, but they never did get their own piece of land or build their own house as the man and his wife had dreamed of doing; living on their own place.

Their eldest boy moved on when he was sixteen. The next oldest, a girl, married at fourteen and moved on. The next child, a girl named Eula, did the same. (Eula would be my great-grandmother.) The youngest child stayed in the place they called "home" around his mother. He was a little retarded from his mother being undernourished and having babies so close together. In the end the two, widowed mother and retarded son, moved in with a friend who needed the little help they could provide.

# Chapter Two

*

Now . . . Eula was growing up to be a strong, healthy, lusty woman who wanted something else. She had become tired of Oklahoma and "home" when she was about fourteen. During the same time, she became tired of the farming business: harvesting fields, milking cows for milk she couldn't drink, feeding chickens she had to steal to get a bite of, and sweeping yards endlessly. So Eula married a laborer from the oil fields. She moved into a shotgun shack in a near town with her new husband until something better came along. Something better could be almost anything and everything. And Eula wanted something better.

Well, Eula's husband was a go-getter hardworking man for his wife. He was also a brawny, lusty lover. By 1912 Eula had given birth to several children and both husband and wife were tired, near exhaustion, waiting for some job to pan out. Money was, as usual, almost nonexistent. "Something" was always up ahead, beyond them. But life continued on somehow, as it usually does.

Eula gave birth to my grandmother. She wanted a child named after herself so she named one of her pretty children, my grandmother, EulaLee. The family survived, barely. Eula thought everybody in the world was poor except the owners of the oil wells. There were no schools her children could attend. Even white children had a difficult time getting and keeping a schoolteacher. Those few schools which Negro people managed somehow to make arrangements for were too far away. Eula was getting old for those hard, scrambling times and began to feel it. But she was still young enough to dream, so she set her sight on Chicago. "Someday," she would daydream as she washed her family's clothes down at the creek looking beyond the trees, through space. She cooked her family's meals, looking over the crackling woodstove through a hole in the wall at the far horizon. "Something got to come my way someday. I know it's some money in Chicago."

Around 1912 a Woodrow Wilson was marked in to become president of the United States. In 1913 Woodrow signed into law that ominous amendment to the Constitution, the federal income tax laws—even though the U.S. Supreme Court made constant rulings against it, saying it was unconstitutional. He also signed into law the Federal Reserve System, among other things, taxes that went hard against the people. Still does.

Nineteen thirteen was not a good year for the world because, among other things, there was no cure for the Spanish flu, which took so many people from the face of the Earth. Eula lost two children, but EulaLee was one of those who survived. Barely. Eula and her husband wanted desperately to leave Oklahoma, but there was no way. They both did every kind of job they could just to put a little food in their family's mouths. Working for food only. No money available for them. They were stuck in place.

Woodrow Wilson also approved the Underwood Tariff, which reduced duties on foreign importations and, since they competed with American industry, it created greater problems for the common working people. Many tens of thousands of American workers were put out of jobs. Does not that seem strange for an American president to do? Or for any leader of a people to do? Because then, a depression came, bringing with it, of course, huge, widespread despair. With no production for American working people, starvation and much misery became nationwide. It will be done again and again by Earth's leaders the people put into office, or those who just take leadership away from the people. It will be done to all peoples, all colors, all over the world. The *love* of money *is* the root of all evil. Believe me.

Eula's family could not pay their rent, but the owner of the shotgun shack in town did not put them out. At least the owner knew them. He thought if the dilapidated shack was to sit empty, there was no telling who or how many would squat in it and eventually tear it completely up.

Eula's husband worked for a white landowner who gave him an automobile that did not run and had no gas even if it could have run. The husband worked on it a couple of months, finding parts, even stealing parts from cars that were parked and discarded because it took money to run a car, and the previous owners had none. Finally the husband stole some gas. He told Eula, "If we can get somewhere else, maybe East, maybe I could find some work."

Eula's thought was, "Chicago." They started planning their trip to somewhere, maybe Chicago.

In 1914, the government under Woodrow Wilson started a small war with Mexico. (Financed with the new income tax resources.) The war was quickly settled because small nations are powerless against those who control the money. Usually.

Eula's husband was not called upon to enter the military because he had a family and he was Black. And who knew where everyone was, anyway? People, all colors, were scattered all over the country, trying to find work or food, trying to survive. The military call was heaviest among the small middle class, the people who divided the rich and the poor. After them, the poorest people were taken. Both classes seemed dispensable . . . to the governing body.

EulaLee, my grandmother, was growing up through all these things.

# Chapter Three

*

The family started their journey to the East in the faulty car with stolen gas, hungry children, and twenty-eight cents. Sometimes they had to push or pull the dying automobile. When they could, they stole gas in the middle of the night by siphoning it from some rich man's car out too late in a dark place. They were about one-hundred-ninety miles from Chicago one night when the car stopped for the last time. Wouldn't, couldn't, go any farther.

The exhausted, hungry little family sat on the side of the road waiting for the dawn. When it was light enough, they looked around to see where they were. They were in the hills, farming country, cattle country. The good husband, disgusted, stood up from the ground, cold and stiff, took a deep breath and said, "We can't wait for no Chicago! I'm gonna go look for a job." When he returned four hours later, he had found work in exchange for a place to stay.

Thinking of how much she loved him, Eula jumped up, tired and heavyhearted though she had been. She kissed her man, then gathered and hugged her children together for warmth. She was trying to smile at life in the midst of her feelings of love for her husband and her children. She thought, "Well, we all together, goin on our way somewheres." She turned her face to the landscape again, and really looked around herself. She thought back to her parents and where she had come from and all she had been through. Then she sat back down on the ground and cried.

EulaLee petted her mother, Eula's back, as the little girl looked off into the surrounding space listening to a rooster crow somewhere off in the distance. It was full of hazy purple hills and trees, green and pretty against the pale blue sky. As young as EulaLee was, knowing hunger, depravation, and desperation, all she could see around herself was space . . . empty, empty, hungry space.

In 1917 EulaLee was ten years old and the little family was still there, living and working in that area. They were able to do a little better with money when a war was struck up with Germany.

Pacifists all over the country were crying out for Peace. They were called subversives and "The People" were told that Germany had started a war against all mankind, etc. Though many, many people fought against it, conscription began. Motion pictures were made showing Germans raping underage girls and other horrendous things in American households. The draft age for men was lowered from twenty-one to eighteen years: Of course, they could not vote or go into bars or other sundry things, but . . .

At first, the newspapers were angry at these things. But soon, strangely, they were silenced. The day of the freedom of the press seemed over. All males between eighteen and thirty began to register for the draft.

Most newspapers and radios applauded and many women stood with proud eyes watching their sons march off to war. Heroes. But, later, when their sons and husbands and brothers returned with no legs or no arms . . . or dead . . . there was a new and different knowledge in the air. Of course, it was the same as in any war. All wars. That is why God hates all wars, He does not bless any side, contrary to earthly teachings and beliefs. He will not bless death and greed. God is Love.

But the time for peace was not yet. In my limited vision, in some chaotic space, there was an angry man in Europe. His name was Hitler, and he was taking his place in a long line, following, among others, Attila the Hun, Genghis Khan, Napoléon, great false religious leaders and too many others. He waited for his turn to begin.

All of this happened while EulaLee was growing up. The family was too poor to have a radio or newspapers and none of them read well anyway. Not one of the family members had proper schooling. They did not know the world that was taking shape around them. But they heard of the money that could be made in the new plants for the making of instruments of war . . . in cities like Chicago.

Older than her actual years, the mother Eula thought of Chicago and smiled at the old dream. Time and circumstance had bent and broken some of her ambitions. Now, her ambitions were for her children; she wanted to find a way for them to go to school and learn to get out of poor, pitiful lives.

The couple had only two dollars in savings from the housekeeping work Eula had done for the last two or three years. It was not enough to move the family. The good father asked his boss for the loan of a mule for a trip into town for a few days extra work and, in the middle of the night, the family packed a small wagon with their meager belongings and set the smallest children on it. Walking beside the mule the family started to Chicago . . . again.

Again, they did not get far. They gave out, walking. The mule, alive but slavering from the constant heavy pulling, gave out pulling about one-hundred-twenty miles from Chicago.

The father walked on, alone, until he found a place for his haggard family, again, in exchange for work and a few dollars. They lived that way for a few years, until he found a small piece of land with a three-room shack on it and an outhouse in back. All the children, no matter how small, worked to pay it off. So they had their own home at last . . . about ninety miles from Chicago.

# Chapter Four

*

One night the good father, always tired, sat outside of the little shack beside the doorway listening to his family finding places, making places, to sleep. Someone was trying to make the old stove cook the turnip greens they had found "along the road."

He sat there listening to his family, looking at the sky, trying to pray, but wishing he was dead at the same time. Desperate times seemed to live in his life. Lies told to him when it was more than important to know the truth, and even having to lie, sometimes, his own self. "Why I got to have to lie just so my fambly can live?" Poverty. Poverty. Poverty, any which way he looked. He couldn't find a single reason in his mind to take another breath. It was his family that made him want to run, run, run away. But, it was also his family whom he loved that made him stay and kept him alive.

They never did get any farther. Doing whatever work the whole family could find, they lived on in that shack for several more years.

At around fifteen years of age, EulaLee got pregnant looking for love. The way these things happen when you are tired, disgusted, poor, and in need of a little warm bit of love, even a little excitement. Imitation love, at fifteen years of age, looks like what you think real love is (and may be) and is welcomed into arms that are empty of everything else.

Eula, her mother, had always found some little church to go to in the places they settled. So EulaLee was married by a minister. She smiled as she listened to the words of the minister and thought of how things were going to be better for her own new family. A rooster crowed somewhere in back of the church as the new husband and wife kissed to signal the completion of their wedding vows.

For some reason, in some way, EulaLee's husband took her thirty miles closer to Chicago, but it was still sixty miles away. In a village-type town called Tweenville, he was able to find a better job because so many people were leaving the country farms to move into the cities that the remaining farmers needed help.

After a few months EulaLee wanted to continue on to Chicago with their little savings. The husband, with his strong young back, worked hard those few months and saved his money. But instead of taking her to Chicago, he paid down on a little land with many trees on it. He cut some trees down and built his own four-room shack for his family.

He cut a few more trees and made their bed and a cradle for the baby. He smoothed the cradle down to a smooth satin finish so it wouldn't scratch his child. He even carved designs on it. He made all the furniture for his home, crude, but hand-carved beautifully. Furniture making became like his own business since people liked what he did and ordered from him. In another time, with an education, he could have been an architect or great furniture maker. But, times being what they were, my grandfather was uneducated except for very rudimentary knowledge. He only knew enough to "get by."

EulaLee had to settle down then. She still wanted to go on to her mother's dream, Chicago, where the money was. They never did move, though, because soon another baby was on the way. Well . . . when you are young, even tired, and you want to feel better, I guess, when you turn over in bed, who do you turn to? Going on sixteen years of age, EulaLee had one child in her arms and one on the way and that pattern did not change for fourteen years.

There weren't many people in the area who could afford to keep the young father busy enough to work at his furniture business steadily, so he always worked for someone else in the harvest fields. Hot work, sometimes. Cold work, winter times. Hard work, each and all times.

Over the years, some very lean years, what with a new baby every year or two, the father, my grandfather, was slowly broken down in spirit and backbone. The same as EulaLee's body was wearing out. The house fell into disrepair and was not fixed in time to keep more damage from occuring to it. More food, more medicine, more clothes for children, more everything was needed. Catching up seemed impossible. EulaLee's husband began to take drinks of the cheap liquor offered to him during the day to help him ease his mind. He had been ambitious, now he was tired . . . just tired . . . all the time. He had his own little piece of land and he could make the crude furniture, but he just couldn't seem to get where he could make a living working for himself. He began to despair. No matter the money he took home, it never helped much anyway. So, now, he bought liquor for himself.

Life is sometimes conceived through overbearing circumstances, but seemingly necessary choices. EulaLee and the good father now dreaded the very thought of having another baby. Another mouth to feed and back to clothe. But warm, pulsing, alive blood will have its way. Early mornings, as their own rooster was crowing to announce the new day, the good husband turned to his wife and she turned to him, losing themselves in the warmth of their familiar bodies and their good love for each other. On one such morning, they conceived Eula Too, even as the rooster was crowing. Eula Too, my dear mother.

Nine heavy months later, EulaLee gave birth to her third little girl, her fifth child as a rooster crowed off in the distance. Thinking of her mother, the first Eula, she mused, "I don't want no Eula Three." She frowned down at the baby girl in her arms, who frowned back at her. She named the child Eula Too. After herself, of course, and my great-grandmother.

A year later Eula Too was removed from the cradle to make place for her new brother. For a while she slept in the bed between her father and EulaLee, then, soon, she had to give that place up to make room for her younger brother when the next new baby was placed in the worn cradle.

Eula Too eventually had fourteen brothers and sisters. There were nine children left at home after her older brothers just left one day and the sisters hurried away to some marriage, seeking the bluebird of happiness or just anything except the crowded poverty at their house. If they had to live in poverty, they wanted to make their own.

When Eula Too was five years of age, EulaLee looked around for some help and seeing Eula Too said, "Come on here, girl, do somethin' with yourself! You got to learn how to be a woman!" Eula Too began standing on chairs stretching her little short arms to reach for and fix oatmeal cereal, hold babies trying to soothe them, change ragged diapers, then take the diapers down to the creek to swish them through the water trying to wash them. She washed daily because several of the children still wore diapers. When she was eight years old, she was doing all the weekly washing. As the eldest child remaining at home, she became EulaLee's helper.

EulaLee needed the help, badly, because the years of constant childbearing and the lack of proper food and health care had left many sore and sick places in her body. She was often in pain. She would think to herself, "If that man come near me one more time with that thang pointin' at me, I swear I'm'a take my scissors and cut it off!" But she didn't. She knew her man had no other joy. In fact, it was the best thing they had together . . . besides the children.

When Eula Too was fourteen years old her mother called to her, in the midst of trying to rock a baby to sleep, saying, "Eula Too? Come in here when you finish that. I'm gonna teach you to sew. You need to know how to make baby clothes and how to mend things." Eula Too's throat suddenly tightened around what felt like a rock stuck in it and tears came to her tired eyes. "I don't want to know, Mama."

"What you say?" EulaLee was shocked at the first denial she had ever had from Eula Too. "You bett'a come on in here and do what I tell you!" But, no matter how EulaLee tried, nor how long, Eula Too was never able to learn to sew. She refused to learn and was finally left alone to go about the business of cooking, washing clothes, keeping wood and water in the house, and caring for the new babies. As the younger children became older, a few of the ones that were not trifling helped her. When Eula Too was not too tired, she made them help her. Often she was too tired to fight with them, so she just shooed them outdoors, preferring to do the work herself.

The children all seemed to love their mother and father, but they did not, all, love or even like each other. They had too many arguments or too much envy of little things another would make or find. Childish fights were a daily occurrence. Each had a different personality and mind. I guess it prepared them for the world they would have to live in.

But it was not an unhappy home all the time. Sometimes everyone had fun playing games outside. Kick the can, hide and seek, red rover, blind man's bluff, and hopscotch. They had a dog or two which were better fed than they themselves were with everyone feeding the dogs their scraps. Cats came and stayed awhile, then left as silently as they had come. They couldn't fight the dogs for food. Kittens, handled roughly by too many hands, left, preferring to be on their own. But they were a family. Eula Too had made those who were able go to school because her dreams for herself were of going to school.

The father worked almost all the time, so he could offer little assistance to anyone. He just tried to keep some kind of money coming in to feed his family. EulaLee, in the beginning, tried to keep the house nice, clean, and neat and to cook good, hot meals for him. Didn't have meat too often, but plenty beans, rice, and vegetables. Eula Too tended the small, irregular garden with the halfhearted help she could get from her siblings. One little sister, Earle Mae (pronounced "Early"), seemed always to be by Eula Too's side and always ready to help her. Sometimes, after a hard day's work, the good father helped her the most.

As Time passed and more babies came, Eula Too had to take over the housecleaning, cooking, and washing. She sometimes thought, "I do everything but have these babies." Since she was young and still small, the housework suffered. Eula Too could not get the younger children to help much, except Earle, and she was not able to clean properly. None of them, not even Eula Too, had been taught exactly how. EulaLee knew how, but, by now, she was too tired to teach anyone anymore. The older boys and girls had learned from their mother, but they were scattering, reaching out looking for a way out or already gone. A few came home, now and then, to find something to eat or a dry, safe, free place to sleep.

The kitchen table was always sticky from unwashed hands reaching for whatever food was there. Caked pots and pans waited unwashed on the stove seemingly forever, but actually only until it was time to cook again. Eula Too brought in water to heat and wood to burn in the stove and washed the dirty dishes she needed to use. Still, more dirty dishes seemed always waiting in a basin to be washed. Dirt was in the corners and in the cracks and ground into the floorboards the husband had lovingly placed. Smoke from the woodburning stove clung to the once-bright ceiling and walls. The little house that had once been such a joy became drab and dreary. Inside, in EulaLee's world, the house became a dismal, depressing place to live in. Outside, in the father's and his older children's world, times were, as usual, dismal to live in.

# Chapter Five

*

In time, besides falling into disrepair, the barren brown earth around the little house was packed down, beaten hard and smooth by the feet of running, playing, careless children. It was littered with trash and broken homemade toys or toys already broken when they were given as gifts from someone their father worked for. The father's dream was rotting, putrefying.

Eula Too's favorite dream was of going to school. She tried to keep up with all her chores and still sneak a few hours a week at the school her siblings were allowed to attend for free, as long as they sat in the back of the classroom. The teacher told them, "You all are too raggedy and dirty, so sit all the way in the back."

Eula Too wanted desperately to read. But the hours she could steal for school were, sadly, few. She tried to live up to her mother's needs. One day she heard EulaLee tell friends, "My Eula Too is my standby! She my best helper I can count on. I'm'a keep that girl with me always! I don't think she got a whole lotta good sense, but she keep these kids in line 'round here. She don't need no more better sense than that. And no schoolin'! I'll take care of her. I know these boys and some'a these grown men round here is tryin' to get up under her dress, but I done 'splained to her 'bout babies and things. She don't want none. So there." Eula Too stopped washing the dishes and scratched the back of her neck with wet fingertips as she pondered her mother's words.

One day, when she had managed to steal away from home to go to school, the teacher took pictures of the little scrawny class. Eula Too tried to stay out of the picture because she looked so poor, dress so ragged, hair not really combed, sticking out every which way. She wanted to just die. But the picture was snapped and, later, her brother stole one and, laughing, brought it home for her to see. She waited until he had forgotten about it, then took it down by the creek to hide.

In the course of time, Eula Too found one friend whom she loved for several reasons. Miss Iowna Hart was a retired Negro schoolteacher. Miss Hart had been in love but never married because of unwritten laws. Such laws, in early times and in the times of depression, ruled that if you were a woman and married you could not keep a teaching job, but had to let it go to a man who was considered a more deserving person of the job because, married or single, he needed the money. Qualifications had nothing to do with it.

Eula Too visited Miss Hart's home an hour or two, when she could escape her own house, whenever her mother and the younger children were taking naps. The teacher's house was closer than the regular school and she could make it back and forth from home in shorter time, before EulaLee missed her. In the beginning she went to learn reading and writing.

One of the reasons Eula Too loved to visit the teacher was because it was so quiet, so peaceful at her house. Miss Hart loved to teach reading and arithmetic. She was not very old, in her late thirties, but worries that had beset her life caused her mind to weave in and out of her many thoughts at unexpected times. Yet she never, never forgot the rules of reading and arithmetic.

She also knew and loved the Bible. Her parents had raised her from it. She often thought, "Ahhh, You have helped me through this hard life, God. Without Your wisdom I don't know what I would have done!"

Miss Hart sometimes called Eula Too, Mary Jane or Sally Ann or some other child's name from the past that slipped into her mind in the midst of a lesson. But that did not matter to Eula Too. Eula Too answered all names and kept learning.

I can tell you this: Many years ago, Miss Hart's family had owned several acres of woodland and had cleared and farmed some of it. Her father had built a comfortable little home on it to raise their son and daughter. Miss Hart's parents worked hard to educate both of their children. Daughters, at the time, were prepared more for marriage, but the mother had pushed her daughter further into a good solid education, sending her far from home to relatives in good places for education.

Iowna Hart, a good, appreciative daughter, had come home often to see her parents. After her father died, she went home to see about her mother at every opportunity. Iowna taught school in the city where she graduated from teaching college. Her brother taught there also. After many years her brother died, but his widow was a city wife and had no pleasure in the country and no intention of going to see about any inheritance her husband might have there. She told her friends, "As it is, I barely made it out of the country! I'm not going back there to no dusty roads, dirt fields, and rocky hills!" And she didn't even look back or think about it again.

Miss Hart didn't want her mother living alone in her old age, so she gave up her city teaching job. She was tired of the politics of working with the system then enforced upon Negro people. She went home to be with her mother on the free, fresh land that she loved. She received a very small pension after a few years of fighting for it.

In especially hard times, Miss Hart had to sell the family land, a piece at a time. First some of the trees were sold. Then her mother, already old, got sick and then, sicker. They sold a few acres to pay medical bills. When her mother died, a few more acres went to pay for a "decent" funeral. She was closed in, but she kept an acre of trees surrounding the house. The trees flourished and formed a jungle-park around the house. She had them fenced in. Iowna Hart planted dozens of flowering plants within that fence. Lilacs, sweet peas, roses, wisteria, and anything with color, which she loved. She also loved flowers with scents, like honeysuckle; she could open her windows and smell on rainy days and sunny days alike. Her apple, pear, apricot, and plum trees were often heavy with sweet, juicy fruit. When she planted anything, she could hear her mother saying, "Don't never spend your money and plant nothin' you can't eat or get some 'nother benefit from!"

Iowna Hart loved and cared for the wild, colorful garden so everything in it grew bountifully for her, each in its season. It brought the beautiful birds to sing for her. She had two glass doors that opened out into the magic-like garden. Open or closed, they let the garden in the house and her mind, out. She loved the smell of wet earth, the look of flowers glistening with rain as she sat before her little fireplace and knitted, crocheted, read, or just stared at the beauty outside. She loved the look of the snow in winter as it fell softly on her magic garden. She would glance through her windows, enchanted, at the wonderwork of God. She thanked God for the blessings as the good smell of her meal wafted around her. After her small dinner she would read the worn books (no money for new ones) as the fire crackled quietly, until she fell gently to sleep with her cat drowsing at her feet, her dog near the fireplace.

It was to this wonderland that Eula Too came for peace and learning. Miss Hart was getting on in years, and her acquaintances were sick, dying, or already long gone to some city. She welcomed the sad-faced, yearning, hungry-eyed Eula Too into her world. She loved to teach. She welcomed her to sit at the little round wooden table (held back from the selling times) with an almost transparent (from washing), old white cotton tablecloth that her mother had embroidered, placed on it. She always offered Eula Too a cup of hot chocolate made from real milk served in delicate, time-worn, pretty cups. The white dairy farmers in the area gave Miss Hart creamy milk and butter. They liked her; she had known their own old parents. She had a few chickens she would never eat that roamed the garden freely. "Good fresh fertilizer and keeps the pests off my flowers and give me good eggs too!" she smiled as she spoke.

Eula Too loved all the books Miss Hart had. Especially the Bible that Eula Too knew Miss Hart had bought new with her hard-won little bit of money. They talked about the Bible often: the beautiful language, the perfect wisdom. "Some people say the Bible is full of myths that are not true. But don't you believe that, Eula, they just don't want it to be true. You meet somebody who does not like the Bible, you be careful with them. It's the only book in this world I know of that tells you to love everybody and that has to be a good thing because it is the lack of love that causes all the world's problems. I'm going to give you one, when I can." Eula's love of the Bible wisdom began during that time and remained throughout her life.

Miss Hart loaned Eula Too some of the other books from time to time, which Eula Too hid until she could take them, in her quiet time, down to the creek near her own full and noisy house. She also loved the learning. When she managed to visit Miss Hart it was as though she had left a tearing, rampaging space of her life, a storm, and come into an enchanting, entrancing, magical world of light and peace. Miss Hart was rich, to her, although of all the riches in the world, Miss Hart had only beauty and peace. Two of the most important of riches, after all. God's gifts. Beauty, from the one true, just God, can be shared by all. Peace . . . you have to earn.

The only other quiet magic place for Eula Too was by the creek. The land sloped upward from the creek and there were large rocks with grass around them and a few wildflowers. She could feel the life beneath the grass moving around her. The life of the Earth and its tiny, even microscopic inhabitants buzzing, running, scuttling, flying, crawling in their daily quest for survival and procreation. Breathing just as she was. She imagined herself an Indian maiden, living free in beautiful forests. In the shadowy shade of the trees she listened to the birds calling back and forth. She listened for the magnificent silence of peace she craved. Even at her young age. My grand, poor dear mother.

Eula Too's best times at the creek were at dawn when her father was getting ready to leave for his job and everyone else was asleep. It would be quiet, with only sounds of the wind, the birds, and the water flowing in the creek. She would go to get water for the awakening of the household for the day, getting ready to prepare their breakfast and clean the latest baby. She stretched the time at the creek as long as she could.

On hot nights in summer, she would go to the creek when she could. Mindful of snakes, she would wrap herself in a blanket and go to sleep listening to the singing gurgle of the creek as it flowed its way down the hills. Eula Too would be dreaming of another life. But she was limited by the fact that she knew no other life. She dreamed of being old Miss Hart.

*I loved my mother so much, even though we had not yet met.*

Eula Too had a sort of superior intelligence and a strong integrity for which I am supremely grateful. She loved her family and tried to do for them all. She especially loved her mother, but felt a sadness for her inside that love. "I will never, never, never have babies," she would think to herself. Eula Too carried a weariness beyond imagining inside her growing, thin, underfed, overworked body.

Eula Too was able to make it to the school more often, though her mother would scold her for "leavin' me alone here with these kids." She spent more time at Miss Hart's, also. She could let out a breath without thinking of the next thing she had to run and do for a sister or brother. During this time she became closer to one of her younger sisters, Earle Mae, ten years old, who was a quiet, sweet, and sensitive child. It was thought Earle Mae was stupid because she said so little, but she was not stupid, she was thoughtful and liked to observe the life around her. Earle Mae was Eula Too's favorite sister and friend. "I'm goin' to take her over to Miss Hart's house one day and give her what I have there."

One day EulaLee told Eula Too she needed some things from the grocery store before the husband came home. "You gonna have to walk down that hill to the store and get 'em." Eula Too said, easily, "Sure, Mama."

EulaLee smiled tiredly at her daughter, saying, "God was sure good to me when I got you. You was born to be useful. Born to be my helper. Go on now, go on."

Eula Too loved going to the little town where she could take her time looking in the windows of the small stores. Once she had crossed the railroad tracks that were halfway to town, her mind came alive. Other sights, other people, new dreams to gather to take back to the creek with her to think about.

Eula Too had just turned fifteen years of age. She was going to be long of body, but not too tall. Her breasts were just beyond first budding, showing promise of future fullness. Her hips were still slender, but well-formed. Her skin, good skin, was dry and flaky from lack of care. The skin of her hands was callused and cracked. Her fingernails were split, cracked, and blackened from grime no matter how she washed them.

She was not a talkative person, didn't smile too much, but that was because she was always thinking and her companions were mostly children younger than herself. She moved slowly but surely, with direction, wasting no movements. Eula Too did not read how to do that; she learned it the hard way. Still, her movements held quiet grace. She had a bronze skin color and a ripe pink, beautifully shaped mouth. Her dark eyes with their heavy lashes were remarkable, but no one had ever remarked about them. She wore her dark hair in braids, and she was comely. Eula Too did not know all that about herself.

This day she put on her mother's frayed shoes (she was fifteen now) and pinned the sacred dollar bill secure in her pocket as her mother spoke. "Don't be stoppin' nowhere talkin' to no stupid boys!" Eula Too laughed at her mother's words. As she walked, she touched the lump in her pocket often; it was money. She had never had a nickel of her very own in all her fifteen years of life. All the years she had ever known, or even heard of, were Depression years. All poverty years.

It was a darkened, cloudy day that threatened rain. Eula Too wore the old raincoat Miss Hart had given her on another rainy day. She walked slowly to the store and, more slowly, window-shopped. She stared long moments through the dirty store windows, but after a few raised eyebrows and smirks from the lazying salesclerks, she finally was on her way home, swinging the small bag in her hand. She reached the railroad tracks and slowed. Her heart grew sad because the tracks put the little shabby town of dreams behind her and put the shack she lived in, full of screaming children, in front of her again.

Eula Too began dragging her feet after she crossed the dreaded tracks as she rested the bag she carried on her hip. About that time a car passed her with a man driving, slowly, past her. He slowed more as he crossed the tracks going into town, then he turned the long, polished black car around and came back. When he reached Eula Too, he stopped. She looked over her thin shoulder at him with a natural bit of wonder. The man rolled down his car window and smiled as he nodded his head at her.

He held the smile as he said, "Mornin'." He looked up and down the road quickly, then back at Eula Too, who was still walking slowly and looking at the silly white man. Still smiling, he asked, "Looks like rain, don't it? You gonna get yourself wet! Got far to go?"

She had no experience that would make her afraid of the smiling man. Eula Too spoke in her normal way, softly with a kind of song in her voice, "Just up over the hill."

"Would you like a ride up the road over the hill?"

Eula Too hadn't ever thought anyone would ever ask her anything like that so she didn't know what not to say. She looked at the shiny, long, black automobile (the man was a chauffeur on his way to Chicago to pick things up for his employer) and it looked like a real dream. So she said, "Yes, sir, I would." She crossed the street, clutching her bag and got into the car beside the man as she thought, "I'm gonna ride in a real car."

Now . . . it was a time of depression over most of the world at that time, and though Eula Too didn't know the difference because it had made no new or real difference in her life, her father knew. She had heard him talk. "There just ain't no money nowhere." So when somewhere up the next slow mile the man offered Eula Too two whole dollars for a little piece of her self, Eula Too said in surprise, "Two dollars!?"

The man had his own family to support, but he was, among other things, a thief and he worked as chauffeur for a rich man, so he had a little money to spare. He also knew two dollars should have seemed a lot of money to a little Negro girl. He misunderstood the sound in Eula Too's voice because he worked around people who complained and negotiated all the time, but still spent a great deal of money. So he raised the price one dollar. "Well, then, . . . three dollars, but that's high as I can go, darlin'," he smiled.

There is no doubt Eula Too was a virgin because she didn't ever want any babies like her mother, but she did want that three dollars. As he put the money in her hand and turned off the main road, she asked, "What do you want me to do for this three dollars?"

"It ain't nothin' much," the man smiled at her. "Ain't gonna hurt you none. I know that!"

She answered, "Well, if it ain't nothing much, okay."

This man had a problem. He had been unable to penetrate a woman for some time. His wife laughed him off and he was too embarrassed to go to a professional prostitute and, perhaps, have her laugh at him too. So he planned to just rub hisself on Eula Too.

When Eula Too understood what he wanted, she was a little stunned. She was used to "that" going on all the time in the settlement she lived in. She could not believe people paid hard-earned money for it. Money! She made a few quick, uninformed decisions; she would do it, but would not take her little ragged panties off. She didn't call it "sex," but, she knew about sex. This was her privates, and she was ashamed of the ragged, homemade panties also. He was excited, and he didn't care if they were off or not. She was able to keep her virginity intact and keep the three dollars, too. Then the man drove her close to her turn in the road going up the hill to her house and dropped her off at the bottom of the hill. Eula Too walked up that hill counting the three dollars, over and over. Hers! Her own! "Mine! And wasn't nothing hurt."

Eula Too took her package into the house to her mother, then she rushed over to the creek around the large rocks. She wrapped her money in a small brown paper bag then dug a hole between two rocks that looked just right and buried her money. Then she stooped at the creek and washed herself and her panties.

She wanted to give some of the money to her mother; she could say she found it. But she knew EulaLee would take it all and it would disappear without a trace. She would be back where she started . . . with nothing. So Eula Too hid it away. "Mine," she murmured under her breath.

Now when Eula Too sat on one of the tree stumps in the yard thinking, she was thinking of that money and how she got it and ten thousand things she was going to do with it. She also thought about how to get some more.

She went to town a few times, lingering, but the man didn't come along no matter how slow she walked. Then . . . the third time, the man came along again. He was a normal man in most all his ways. Many, many men all over the world lived as he did. But, in this, he just wanted to be body-close to someone who didn't laugh at him. Eula Too didn't know there was anything to laugh at and since he didn't hurt her, he never even heard a snicker from her.

This time when he offered her three dollars, she was already in the car. Going. She was amazed he would give her three dollars *again*. "Three dollars! Again?" she breathed.

The man misunderstood her tone again and said, "Five dollars then! But that's as high as it ever is goin' to get, little missy!"

When he dropped her off this time, he smiled as he asked her, "How often you come down to this little town, darlin'?" Eula Too shrugged, clutching her five-dollar bill, "I don't know." The man patted her on her thigh and Eula Too moved her legs away from him. The man laughed softly at her as he said, "This is Thursday; come next Tuesday 'bout the same time."

Eula Too jumped out of the car, said, "Okay," and walked on up the road to her house . . . after first going to the creek to add the five dollars to her other money. Her step was a little lighter by the time she reached home. She was counting the days until Tuesday.

Life and work continued as always at her house and by Tuesday she was worrying her mother about what she needed from the store. Something was always needed, so Eula Too got her chance to go walking slowly to town.

She met the man, as planned, but this time he had brought a friend along. "This my good friend, darlin', you be nice to him, too, and you can get yourself . . ." But Eula Too was gone. She didn't know why, but the other man being there made her feel confused and dirty. Miss Hart ran swiftly across her mind for some reason. She would not get in the car. She ran off in the direction of her house. The man drove to catch up with her, but she kept moving. She wouldn't stop and talk. As the car rolled along, he called from the car window, "You be here Thursday and I'll be by myself." He knew. And his grudging heart respected her, even liked her.

The next Thursday he gave her another five-dollar bill. From then on, each time she met him he gave her a five-dollar bill. Her only thought, "He don't hurt me!" The meetings went on, and Eula Too's savings grew.

She had begun taking Earle Mae to the creek with her because Earle was quiet and loved to watch and hear the music of the birds in the trees and the little creek rippling by. She never took her money out, though. When Earle wasn't with her at the creek, Eula Too would sit and squeeze the bag with her money in it and dream. She lingered longer at store windows, dreaming of owning the dress or shoes of the week, but she didn't buy. She even began stopping at the small bus station in town and watching the people get on or off the bus. There were very few either way. Somehow this added to her dreams, though she could not explain why.

She did spend some of her money for a few gifts for Miss Hart: tea cakes to go with the hot chocolate, or tea when there was no chocolate. She bought chocolate, sugar, and flour and they made cookies together. Or tea cakes. A medium-size bag of chicken feed or something small Miss Hart could use and could not exactly afford.

Eula Too had taken Earle Mae to meet Miss Hart and they had liked each other. Miss Hart just liked good children, smart children. Earle could go over alone now to learn to read better. "Don't bother Miss Hart too much. You shouldn't wear your welcome out," Eula Too explained. But Miss Hart liked Earle Mae and her name. She smiled as she smoothed Earle Mae's hair, "Your name sounds like a beautiful spring morning! And being early is a courtesy, a smart way to be! And May is one of the loveliest months!" Earle Mae had never liked her name before; now she turned her cute, little face with the pretty, shining eyes up and smiled brightly at Miss Hart.

One day Miss Hart told Eula Too that Earle was artistic and could draw very well. "It's a shame that child cannot have good lessons, better than I can give her. She can draw trees and birds just beautiful. We just don't have any colors. We can make red or green from plants, but she sees more than those few colors, I know. Poor colored children. Never enough of anything for them."

Next time in town Eula Too bought Earle Mae some crayons and a colorbook and some plain white paper. She took them to leave at Miss Hart's house. Earle Mae already loved her escape to Miss Hart's house. It was all she dreamed of. Now . . . she had a dream. But, of course, the coloring book could not last forever. So she learned to trace over pictures and make her own coloring books.

**I**t had been three years since the last baby had been born and Eula Too and the mother were both grateful for the peace and rest. Eula Too breathed a sigh of relief each time she knew her mother was having her monthly period. EulaLee was glad because her body was ill. She had grown fat and sluggish from having to eat to provide milk for nursing. She was sick and tired in mind and heart. She could find no real interest or pleasure in her life because now any dream at all was over . . . past . . . gone. For all her young and vital life, there were only children. Now she would only be a wife and a mother in what was, to her, a Godforsaken piece of dirt, the land. She blamed her good husband for all her "misfortune." "He shouldn't of never stopped here and paid our money for this here land!"

EulaLee had also reached a point in her life where her love for her husband and even any happiness she might give him had dwindled down to almost nothing. She looked around her and hated the house. She was so sick of children! She was still hurt and disgusted at the sight of her children in their patched clothes and split shoes . . . or no shoes. These were the children she had planned such good things for when she was younger. When they would have been in Chicago. There wasn't even any way for them to go to a real school where they could really learn something to take them out of this hole full of nothing. "And I am aging before my time!" She laughed an ugly laugh at herself. "My time! Shit!"

One morning soon after she had these thoughts, EulaLee called Eula Too to her. When Eula Too looked at her mother she could see the anger mixed with tears on her mother's face as EulaLee said, "I'm pregnant, again!" She looked as though it was someone's else's fault.

Eula Too stared wildly at her mother with her fifteen-year-old, already-tired eyes. She stood there, silent, twisting her hands together.

EulaLee screamed at Eula Too, "Again! Got-dammit!"

The look on Eula Too's face brought the mother to abrupt attention. She saw something in that look that was terror-stricken. Then Eula Too's face took on a savage and fierce look that was strange to EulaLee. It was like someone fighting for survival suddenly sinking down into loss and failure. EulaLee was shocked at that look on Eula Too's face. She misread the look and said, "I'm the one havin' this baby! Not you! What you lookin' like that for?" She forgot that Eula Too had helped raise all her siblings.

Eula Too just turned swiftly around and ran out of the room, then out of the house. Once outside, she stopped just as abruptly and looked around her as if from a black emptiness that was screaming inside her head, blinding her eyes.

As if for the first time, with nothing to compare it to but Miss Hart's home, Eula Too saw, through a tearful haze, the poverty around her with stark clarity. Over the years, shacks had been built near her own house, crowding the hills. She saw the chicken pens and hog wallows, broken fences, leaning clotheslines. The children, most of them unwashed and ragged, running around everywhere. She saw the tired women that happened to be outside at that time tending something that needed to be done, just as she was usually doing. They were dressed, dirty or however clean, in hanging, mended, faded dresses. Dresses like her mother's and her own, worn, like everything they owned. Eula Too saw and could no longer take the seeing.

"Another baby," she thought, frantically.

She heard her mother calling her, "Eula Too! Eula! Come here, girl!" She turned her face in the direction of the creek and swiftly made her way to her "thinking" place. Her place of peaceful self.

Eula Too was crying soundlessly as she dug for her money and unwrapped it. She counted, again, the wrinkled bills: one-hundred-twenty dollars. It had seemed a large amount just last week, but . . . today it seemed small. She thought quickly, removed a few bills and replaced the package back in its hole. It was Tuesday, and she was going to town. "He" was coming today!

She didn't go back to her house. She walked directly to the little town and bought more paper for Earle. Flour, sugar, tea cakes, and a special small box of candy for Miss Hart. She carried her packages to the place she usually met the man. She didn't even know his name, nor did he know her name. While she waited, she took a piece of the paper out and wrote her mother a note:

*Dear Mama,*

*I have to go now. I am tired. I'm going on my life. If I stay here with you, I will not love you the way I should. The way I love you now. You will hear from me. Your child, Eula Too. Tell my daddy I said I love him too.*

Then she decided to tell her daddy, herself.

*Dear Daddy,*

*I am leaving here, but I am not leaving you. I love you very much, but I got to go. I will see you again. Love, your Eula Too.*

She would leave the notes with Earle Mae to deliver them when she was gone. Eula Too sighed, "Gone."

When the man came she asked him, "You be going on your way to Chicago Thursday?"

The man looked at her from the corner of his eyes. "Yes, I am. I got to go two times a week. Why you askin', darlin'?"

Eula Too looked down into her lap. "I want to borrow a ride from you. I want to go to Chicago when you go."

The man turned his head to look directly at her, saying, "I ain't got any place for you in Chicago. I don't even stay there myself. I just come right back after I pick up some business papers. So you can't go with me."

Eula Too shook her head, said, "I'll get off when we get there. I'm . . . gonna stay."

"You gonna stay? You mean we won't . . . meet here no more?"

"No, sir. I got to go away."

The man turned his gaze through the windshield and was quiet a moment, thinking. Then he turned to her, saying, "That's a mighty dangerous town, that Chicago. The Depression still hangin' on to everybody. You know anybody there? Anybody you can go to?"

"No, sir. But I'll find a job and learn to stay there long as I can."

The man looked thoughtfully at her from the corners of his eyes again. "You gonna need money. You been savin' that money I give you?"

Eula Too looked down at her hands, twisting in her lap, and intuitively decided this man should not think she still had the money. "No, sir. We poor. We had to use it all up." Well, she had her packages of food, so he believed her.

"Wellll, I'm goin' on Thursday, if you sure you want to go."

Eula Too looked him full in the face for the first time, ever. "I'm sure."

"Well, then just be here."

He had his usual way with her, but he only gave her one dollar. Said, "I'm short today. This all I got. But, Thursday I'll have a little more. 'Cause you gonna need money in Chicago, girl. You might not find a job right away as you think. I got a few friends. I might see what I can do for you."

First, Eula Too took the packages belonging to Miss Hart to her. She told her she was leaving as they hugged. When Miss Hart kissed her good-bye, she said, "At least I still have Earle. But, listen here, Eula Too, you are a smart girl, but you are still a girl, a child, with no real experience in life except around people you know. You, please, remember . . . there is a different world of people out there. Everybody will not be like you. They will not think like you think. Some will not be like anything you've ever known. Keep your mouth shut, your eyes open, and your business to yourself. Don't be quick to make friends, wait to see what they are. And remember, someone smiling at you won't mean they like you. Chile, you think you have been struggling to survive here in this place with a small group of poor people, but you ain't seen nothing like surviving in a big city full of thousands and thousands of all kinds of poor people with strange ways and things to make money with. Depression is still in this country, especially with colored people. First thing people are going to think when they see you is not what a nice girl you are, but 'Wonder how much money she got! What she got I can use!' I don't have any money to give you to help you. But I got this Bible I told you I was going to give you. When you need some peace, and love, you can find it right in here. And, Eula

Too, if you ever need to come back, you can come back to me, here, in this house, and make yourself at home. Anytime."

Eula Too cried, silently, her loose shoe soles flapping, as she ran home to find Earle Mae. "I got one whole day to get ready to go." There wasn't anything to pack because she didn't have anything. But she had to find a way to hide her money where no one could find it as she traveled to a new job.

She took Earle to the creek, showed her the hiding place for money and gave her ten of the crumpled dollar bills. "Hide this money, right here. Don't give none to nobody. You keep it hid 'til you need it for somethin' special. You hear me? Save it! God willing, I will come back to get you once I get me a job and a place to stay. And you keep going to Miss Hart's and learn all you can. Read all you can."

Earle Mae nodded, tears shining in her eyes. "I'm gonna miss you too much, Eula Too. I'll go to Miss Hart's every chanst I get! Please don't forget us. Please don't forget me."

"I can't forget you. I love you, all of you, but I love you more. You my best sister." They hugged a little more and cried a little more. Then Eula Too went to all the little places she had hidden things she had bought for the trip. A new pair of panties, her first brassiere, and a new pair of socks. "I'll get a new dress to get a job in when I get to the city."

Eula Too hardly slept on Wednesday night, waiting, praying, dreaming of Thursday. Early Thursday afternoon, with a rooster crowing in the distance, when she ran down the hill and the road, her feet flying to a new life, she found the man waiting for her. She had worn her raincoat; it was the only coat she had and it had deep inside pockets, one on each side. She had pinned her money, ninety-five remaining dollars, at the very bottom of the pockets, a little on each side.

She carried a little paper bag that held one of Earle's colored pictures, folded, her Bible with Miss Hart's address on the back, a rock from her creek, and a few leaves from her favorite creek tree she had sat and dreamed under. She had all her new underwear on. She washed and gave her old ragged clothes to Earle. "'Cause I'm going to a new city!"

She was so happy to see the car she didn't notice that the man was not alone. There was another man with him. When she really saw the other man, she hesitated a second or two, but Chicago was on her mind. She thought, "Maybe somebody else had to go there, too." So she hastened to the car.

The man got out and opened the back door for her, smiling and saying, "My friend and me are goin' to sit in the front and talk. You can just stretch out and be comfortable in the back on that blanket I done laid out for you, 'cause we got a long ride." He noticed the little paper bag and decided, since she had no purse, "Maybe she really don't have no money saved." He was frowning as Eula Too got into the car and he closed the door. He got in the driver's seat, smiling cheekily at his friend. They drove away. "Goin' to Chicago." The crowing of an already distant rooster fading away.

The long black automobile moved smoothly along as if it were eating up the road. Eula Too watched in amazement. Her eyes were full to brimming with tears of joy, even elation. She had never before ridden in the car for hardly more than a mile. She turned her wide-eyed attention to the view outside the window. She had never been even this far from home before. Her vision of the future chuckled, burdenless, in her happy heart.

For a long while she watched as they passed little villages or towns and the lonely looking farmers' houses as the land stretched out before her. The flatlands and the hills beyond them. Here and there a ridge of trees stood, lovely to see. Lonely looking cows standing, staring in the direction of the road, seeming barely to notice the cars passing on it. Then a small forest, in its beauty, passed swiftly. Time passed that way.

The men had been talking softly. Now she noticed they were drinking, now and then, from a bottle they passed between them. Every once in awhile the man would raise his voice and call out, "You doin' alright, darlin'?"

She always answered, "Yes, sir."

Eula Too dozed off in a light sleep once or twice. Awakened by her head falling and hitting the window, she would quickly look up the road to see if she could see the city coming up. They had been driving a long time at around thirty-five miles an hour, which seemed fast to Eula Too. Outside the window the landscape was the same. Dreary. She felt for her coat, laying in her lap, so she could pat the pockets to be sure her money was secure. It was. She smiled a little, singing in her mind, "Goin' to Chicago!"

The sky darkened as time passed. The car moved a little slower. The empty liquor bottle was replaced with a new, full one. Eula Too was feeling stifled with the smell of liquor and smoke from their cigarettes. She didn't know a thing about opening car windows, but tried the shiny brass handle on the door. It moved and the window rolled down a little. She held her nose up to catch the fresh air. There was no city in front of her, so she settled down to sleep again.

The car bumping along caused her to wake from her sleep and when she opened her eyes, they were off the main road, slowly moving down a seldom-used road, like they were looking for something.

"Are we close to Chicago?" she asked as she yawned.

The man laughed, not his usual cajoling laughter, but with a more menacing sound in his joy, "Oh, we real close now. Just about there."

Eula Too slowly leaned back in her seat and wondered what Chicago was doing along this forlorn road. But she didn't relax to go back to sleep again.

The man finally pulled into an opening in a nest of trees. He turned to her and said, "We got to use the toilet. You want to go to the toilet?"

Eula Too did want to use a toilet, but it was too dark in these woods and she didn't want to get out of the car. "I'm gonna wait."

As the men walked off, laughing drunkenly, she heard the man say, "I ain't gonna mess up that car. I can't." The new man answered, "You already got a blanket on the backseat!" Voices fading away, she heard, faintly, "Yeah, but she kick her foot out and break somethin'. . ." Then the voices were gone.

Eula Too became frightened. She knew the foot they were talking about could be hers. Was hers. Oh, Lord, she wanted to get out and run . . . but run where? In these woods? Back to the main road was at least a mile or, maybe, two. Her mind was racing, "What he gonna do make me kick my foot out?" She thought of her money. "They want my money!" She quickly rolled up that old raincoat into a tight ball and stuffed it behind her in the roomy corner of the seat and pushed it down as far as she could. Then she heard them coming back. They didn't get back in the front seats, one on each side, they opened the doors to the backseat. Where *she* was.

Now . . . for whatever mysterious reason, whatever contempt or hate or rage might have been in the first man's mind and heart, he didn't mind hurting, or letting someone else hurt, Eula Too. He knew she was still only a child, really. But in some Godless, muddy, corrupt, slimy, putrified pocket of his brain, he was mad at Eula Too because, as bad as it could turn out to be, she did have a future. "And," he thought, "real sex is in her future." He had none. And one day, he knew, she would understand about him . . . and laugh at him. And . . . she had taken his money; and . . . he didn't feel he had ever gotten anything for it . . . and . . . and, though it was not her fault he could not get erect enough to fully have sex, he hated her for it. So, he had decided *someone*, *anyone*, would get some of her body. "That bitch think she smart!" he had told his "friend." Eula Too had no idea that she and the first man were not, at least, a little friendly. He had always smiled at her as he handed her his money.

As he opened the back car door and leaned in, she tried to smile at him through the tears of fear running down her face. She wanted to remind him, somehow, that they were friends. Eula Too certainly didn't want to pee now, but her fear pushed the urine out, a little at a time. Her thoughts swirled through her mind. One question repeatedly, "What are we doing here?" *She didn't exactly know, but . . . she knew.*

The "friend" man smiled as he leaned over her, stepping into the car. "We gonna have us a little party." A sob broke through Eula Too's heart and she began to cry. Now his smile was sullied as he said,

"Ohhhh, you ain't scared of me, are you? We done this a whole lotta times. Now, just you lay back in that seat and open them damn legs for me, darlin'."

In the grip of fear, Eula Too, sniffling, thought, "Well, he never has hurt me before . . . and he is taking me to Chicago . . . and he is gonna help me find a job." Yet, she was terrified. She did as he told her.

When he was shoving her legs wider, she raised her head to see where the other man was. "Is he gonna watch us?" The "friend" man laughed. "Turn your back, Ja . . . Man."

The new man laughed as he pretended to turn his back to them.

Again, Eula Too raised her head and asked, "Can he walk a little ways off . . . so we be alone?" Her body had stopped trembling so intensely all over. She wasn't too afraid of the man she knew. She laid back with her legs wide open when, out of the clear and starry night, suddenly the man slapped her, hard. "He ain't got to go nowhere, you little bitch! Now, shut up! And open them legs wider!" Abruptly, he pulled back. "No! You take them pants off this time!" It would be the first time without the panties on.

Eula Too cried from the bottom of her terrified heart. Snot, tears, and spit were smeared over her stinging, pained face. She pushed the little brand-new panties down (first new pair she'd ever had), but she held them tightly in her shaking hand.

The man couldn't do any more than usual, but this time it made him angry and, since he knew no one would ever know, he raised up and slapped Eula Too several more times with his open hand. Then, his excitement at what the other man was going to be able to do rushed him to a better climax than he usually got by his lone efforts.

He was crawling off backward when Eula Too looked, through a blur of tears, behind him at the other man standing there with what looked like a stiff arm coming from his body. Eula Too had seen her brother's privates, but she had never seen one hardened. She was not dumb; she was inexperienced.

The new man lunged into the car pushing Eula Too's knees apart. Eula Too was still a virgin, and now fear and terror made the inside of her as dry as old bones in a desert. He raised his body up and plunged down, hard. His face smiled, teeth glittering in the dark as he forced his grievous, unconcerned, painful self into her tenderest body. If possible, she was crying even harder from the savage attack and the excruciating, careless pain. It was as though he hated her. Did he love his mother, his wife, women? Why did he hate Eula Too so? *My poor mother.*

The man was tired of her crying, so he raised his body up and hit her with his huge, hardened, callus-knuckled fist until he felt his body crushing through the young, innocent canal of her body. She screamed from the pain assaulting her soul. Then the new man laughed as he pumped and smashed his penis into her. Over and over and over again, he plunged; he plunged until he climaxed from the mixture of her tears, pain, screams that charged his own hidden thrills and hatreds. At last, finished, he wiped hisself on Eula's dress. He placed his large hand hard on her bruised, throbbing, inflamed stomach and heavily pushed himself off, grinning at his friend. "Let's wait a few minutes. I can do that again. Man, she tight as a chicken's ass! I can do that stuff again! This the kind'a lovin' I love!"

But the "friend" man, jealous of the other man's deep, bloody success, said, "No. We got to go. You done had enough already." They argued a bit, but the driver was getting ready to go, so the other man pulled his pants up, laughing, but angry he had to stop making "love."

Eula Too curled up in pain, past crying, whimpered softly into the cushion of the sleek seat, while they finished the drive to Chicago, about thirty minutes away. They reached a little bridge set in a craggy part of the road and pulled over to the side and set Eula Too to the side of the bridge. With curled, tight fingers, she had pulled her rumpled raincoat behind her. They had searched her bag for money and found none. The "friend" man pulled a dollar from his pocket and dropped it in her bloody lap, saying, "You a bigger fool 'en I thought!"

As they drove away, the "friend" man gave a strained little laugh from his, somehow, still unsatisfied chest, and said, "That fool gonna sure have a hard time in Chicago with no money but that dollar!"

Then they concentrated on trying to feel satisfied because they had "outsmarted" a child.

Painfully, Eula Too tried to straighten her clothes as she lay there on the ground. She tried to straighten her bloodstained legs so she could get up and try to walk. The dollar bill floated from her lap to the ground, the wind making it skip lightly a few paces away. Eula Too forced herself to catch it and crumple it tightly in her hand. "No, I'm going to keep you. I'm going to put you in a frame and keep you all the days of my life, so I don't never forget about people." Stopping every few steps to gather more strength or ease the pain in her little body, she began to hobble up the road toward the bright lights of the city. She made her way slowly, tightly clutching her raincoat with the pockets holding her money, the tail of the coat dragging behind her painful, weary body.

# Chapter Six

*

She had been christened Elizabeth Eve Fontzl, but Time and circumstance had led her to change the name her proud parents had given her to the more fancy "Madame LaFon." No one ever called her by a first name. The last man to call her by her first name, who had made possible her present circumstances, was dead. She would love no other.

Madame LaFon had been beautiful as a child, unexpectedly so, because her parents were plain, ordinary-looking people. They were good people, hardworking and clean, of, perhaps, French, German, and English descent. But their daughter was exceptionally beautiful as a baby and as a young woman. She was their only child. Elizabeth Eve had been born in a small town named Placeland, sometimes referred to as Place. She had grown up hating the small town as all her young friends did. There was nothing there to compare to the places in the magazines she read at her friends' houses.

Her family lived in a neighborhood with different nationalities that could be called middle class in Placeland. They lived on a corner of the block, with a river running along behind all the houses on their side of the street. Elizabeth liked to play with the Negro children next door, the Greens. Mr. and Mrs. Green were also hardworking, clean people raising their family. One of their children, Marion Green, was the same age as Elizabeth so they had much in common. Each liked boys, clothes, movies, and both were intelligent and liked books. They were friends, though they did not socialize away from their homes. Their goals were not very different. Marion wanted to go on to college after graduation, but her parents couldn't afford it. Elizabeth had graduated from high school with good grades, but her parents were not able to send her to college either.

Marion's two brothers, Robert and Calvin, helped her ward off boredom. Elizabeth was the only living child of her parents, so there was nothing much to occupy her mind at home. She was bored with dull, dull Placeland.

Because of her boredom, Elizabeth searched for things to bring some excitement into her life. Well, there is always love and romance. That was all her girlfriends talked about. Because many young men, even from small towns around Placeland, were in love with her looks she had never worried about romance. Still, Elizabeth was a lonely person for several reasons, not the least of which was her beauty. For one thing, other young women didn't want her around their male friends.

Pursuing romantic excitement, finally, Elizabeth went further than just light petting and kissing an enamored admirer, like most of the girls of her set did. Well, he was a nice, handsome young man. She became pregnant, as did a few other young ladies: They, however, got married to their beaus. Elizabeth didn't want to marry her beau. She saw him as a weight to hold her in Placeland. She wanted to get away. Go to college . . . or something.

When Elizabeth became pregnant, Marion Green was already working at a domestic job, but still trying to find a way to go to college. The two young women became closer somehow. Each of them was caught in a morass of life they could not seem to get away from. If one of them would get too disgusted or disheartened and cry, the other would hold her and try to soothe away the fears and tears.

Elizabeth's parents, the Fontzls, almost went out of their minds with fear at the news of the pregnancy. Fear of what, they did not know. Lost pride? They wanted her to marry. She didn't want to marry. "I don't want to have to stay here in Place all my life! I want a decent home when I have my baby! A decent husband I love!" As they argued and talked and talked about what to do, seven months passed and the baby was born. At home. With a cheap doctor.

The baby, a girl, was dead when the inexpensive doctor finally delivered it. The breathless, small, pitiful body was buried in her grandparents' backyard under a tall poplar tree near the river that flowed at the back of their house. Elizabeth wouldn't let anyone help her dig the grave or lower the small coffin except Marion Green. She cried all the while she worked. Elizabeth wasn't Catholic, but she buried a cross at the head of the burial mound, along with her still flowing tears. "Well, a cross is connected with God," she sobbed. She had seen and felt the helpless, hopeless tiny lifeless being she had given birth to. It made her love deeply, though late, the child who had depended on her for its life. Now she loved her child even more, no matter how her fate had once seemed tied to the little unlived life.

Elizabeth's parents, the Fontzls, had also suffered a loss. They thought they would ignore and hate the little fatherless baby. Now the child was gone, and they would never have a chance to do anything with the baby. Now, instead of reviling their daughter for getting pregnant, they loved their lost grandchild. But Mrs. Fontzl blamed Elizabeth for the loss. There was something unexplainable about the antipathy between mother and daughter.

After Elizabeth lost her child, it was to Marion she went most often for solace. Marion, kind and thoughtful and patient. Marion was wise in her youth because her mother, Mrs. Mary Green, was very persistent in trying to teach her children about life. Especially her girl. Because Marion knew Elizabeth's feelings in the whole matter, she encouraged Elizabeth to go somewhere she could be on her own and get a job.

In the end, Marion Green didn't get to go to college either. The money just wasn't there. So she married Fred Bridges, the beau she loved, and they began to raise a family. Then, Marion dreamed big dreams for her children's future instead of for herself.

When Elizabeth Eve got her strength back and felt in good health, she left Place looking for a new place to be. Her mother screamed at her as she went down the front steps, a small suitcase in her hand. "You are a fool! You're gonna get filled up with babies again! Don't look to us for help when you do!" Elizabeth heard her mother and thought of the inexpensive doctor and her dead baby.

She went straight to New York. At first try she got a job in a millinery shop, modeling and selling hats. She did well because her face could wear so many styles beautifully.

The old friends didn't see each other for several years. They wrote each other maybe twice or so. Then, because Elizabeth moved so often, her letters were returned to Marion and she stopped writing. The friendship had passed its immediate need and, though Elizabeth thought of Marion Green when she was most depressed and lonely, she could not always afford even the stamp. In the end, the friendship was left to wait in Placeland.

Elizabeth didn't go back to see her angry mother until her father died and she came home for the funeral. Elizabeth didn't stay home long because her mother was full of regrets and recriminations. "I have nothing in my life! You killed your child, my grandchild, and now you have killed your father from all his worrying about you! You never gave us nothing!"

Marion had two children by then and didn't get the time to see Elizabeth except for a few brief hugs and talks over the fence. Years passed.

Among her newly made friends in New York there were the kinds of women who realized Elizabeth was an attractor of men. They were plain and unattractive, so they often asked her to join them on their nights out. During these times she met and trusted a few men, letting them take her home to her little one-room apartment. Of course, she had been raped, twice, because though she did not want sex, the men did not believe her. A single woman, living alone? No family? The second time she was forced against her will, she became pregnant again.

Elizabeth listened to the foolish and mixed information given to her by her new friends and went in and out of dark alleys looking for someone to give her an abortion. How could she afford this tentatively loved, but unwanted, child, in her poor, working condition? She did not love, nor want, the father of the child. She hated him.

After a botched and wretched abortion, she was given ten minutes to lie on a much-used and dirty couch, spotted with blood. A sheet was thrown over her and a rough, weary voice said, "Ya got ten minits, kid, then you got to get up and get outta here!" After what seemed more like five minutes, she was shown—pushed, shoved, still bleeding—to a door and outside into an unforgiving and cold-shouldered world. She, nauseated almost to oblivion, struggled, clinging to blurry unseen walls. She tried to stay on her feet in the street, to find an unaffordable taxi. Her silvery blond hair blowing wildly in the wind attracted a taxi that took her to her room, her home. The driver, a kind older man, helped her into her room, but he had to leave her there, bleeding. He was afraid she might die before he could get away. He had no money, no time, and no information as to what she should do.

She lost her job. In Time, she survived. She did not go out alone with a man again for a few years. Now she was really afraid of what might happen. Work was all she knew. She realized how little she knew about life . . . real life and men. But she was young and pretty and, in Time, loneliness and youth changed her mind.

She felt she had had more than her fill of men and sex and "love." She knew a little more about life, but the blight of poverty with its lack of joy, and the excitement of the Jazz Age brought so many lifeless people together who had nothing but themselves to share. Not even hope for the future. Music offered so many women to the jazzed men of the time, who were everywhere. And poverty, of course, offered nothing. *Satan has accomplished his purposes well.*

In those times, when she was let go from a temporary factory job or some such, she absolutely did not know what to do. Jobs were so hard to find.

She had a friend, a rather fast woman with many men friends who had fairly good taste and loved to buy clothes. The plan just came to Elizabeth (*unsolicited, the way the devil works*) to visit her friend and borrow something to look for work in. Shame and embarrassment stopped her from asking. She planned, and when she visited her friend she excused herself, going to the bathroom nearest the bedroom. She took, from the bedroom closet, a wool dress and grabbed the first pair of plain, dark shoes she could reach. Then she went back into the bathroom and wrapped the dress around her body under her own dress as best and flat as possible. She put the shoes in her purse, thinking, "I hope that gin has her high enough not to look at me closely." In dread, she didn't stay around to visit but a few more minutes.

The next day, bathed, brushed, and polished as much as possible, she dressed herself in the wool dress, added a stolen fresh white collar and went out to apply at several of the best department stores in the city. Female employment interviewers did not like her beauty at the interviews. They did not hire her, besides, they had friends in need.

Tired, becoming despondent, the dress becoming crinkled and tired-looking too, she decided to make one last try at one of the very best, richest stores. There, she was finally accepted by a man who placed her in the perfume department at the glorified store. The manager put the beautiful young woman in that department because he thought her beauty should be surrounded by beautiful scents and lovely designer bottles and that she would enhance them.

It took no time for men to notice this lovely vision of a woman. She kept in mind her rapes, so she declined all offers. This was noticed by management and they mentioned it, in passing, to owners. Owners mentioned it, in passing, to dinner guests or business meeting associates. "Imagine . . . a beautiful 'good' girl, alone in New York!, not looking for a rich man! Or any man, it would seem!"

It had not been her intention, but this unimportant news, meant for amusement only, reached the ears of the right man. The man went to see such beauty and virtue for himself; not to encourage it but, perhaps, to possess it.

He was a married, older gentleman, but, alas, his heart was lost from the moment she held a perfume stopper for him to smell the scent and smiled up into his delighted eyes with her golden-green eyes. It was not as though he had never done this type of thing before, but it had always been just for fun. He did love his wife. But, with each refusal from Elizabeth to his invitations, he grew to respect her and love her, too. She began to trust his manners and his gentle speech.

After several months of an empty purse and fast food at the cafeterias, Elizabeth accepted an offer of dinner from the kind, older gentleman. "I'll be safe with him, he's older," she thought.

And she was safe with him. He took her on a long drive to a lovely estate in Long Island, not too large and not too small. He had servants serve her, quite extravagantly, with excellent food in a gracious and tastefully furnished dining room. When they finished their meal, he took her into an exquisitely furnished drawing room where they warmed themselves before a merry fireplace. Over brandy-filled snifters, he told her the entire estate belonged to her.

She was taken aback. "I can not afford such a place as this."

He smiled as he took her hand. "It is all paid for. All of it. It is yours, my dear. My very dear." And so it was.

Later, he had her quit her job because it interfered with his plans. He wanted her to take business trips with him and be able to see him whenever he wanted to see her. He paid handsomely for the privilege.

Traveling with him, always, was his very trusted Negro valet, Burnett. Burnett was the only Negro her lover ever allowed close to him. He did not particularly dislike Negroes, he simply thought them inferior; Burnett, he thought, was a different kind of Negro. In time Elizabeth came to know the kind, gentle-mannered, honest Burnett and developed respect and admiration for him also.

Living in a metropolitan city, Elizabeth had learned to love the many types of houses and interior decoration. She was always in fear she would end up poor, on the streets and dependent on the mean streets again. While with her lover, she acquired a villa in Southern Italy, a large apartment in Paris, France, an eight-room apartment in New York, and of course, her estate in Long Island. She worried him, pleasingly, to pay every house off so she would not owe anything on anything if "you should leave me for another pretty woman," she would smile up at him. She could not say "die" to an old man.

He argued that would interfere to the detriment of his tax portfolio. She smiled, pleasantly, "Then you should give me the exact amount of money to be put away if you should leave me."

He sighed heavily. "You have furs, jewels, expensive, beautiful art, and many things my own wife never asks for."

She smiled at him, then turned her face away. "Your wife does not have to ask. Do you want me, darling, to sell all my cherished memories of you to have to hold on to the precious houses you have given me? If you should leave me?"

He threw his arms up in defeat. "No. But stop saying, 'if I should leave you!' I will never leave you." His arms reached out for her. She hastened into them.

She put her lovely arms around his neck and said softly, "I cannot live, peacefully, without knowing what you gave me really belongs to me . . . and me alone. I want no one to be able to come take even one exquisite memory of you from me." She laughed lightly, "Your tax lawyers are very smart; they can work it out for . . . us." She kissed him sweetly because she really did care for the fine old gentleman. Moments later, she smiled and said, "Take your hand off my thigh, my darling, until you have made me happy . . . too."

"I will never leave you, my sweetest girl in the world," he whispered into the curve of her neck.

He did get two of the new homes paid off. The one in Paris and the apartment in New York. The Long Island house was clear before she had moved in. Two weeks after those things were completed, he suffered a heart attack and died. He did, indeed, leave her.

She grieved in her New York apartment. Many visitors came, male friends of his; almost all of them wanted her. She was gracious as she accepted their gifts, but she truly did grieve for him. She gave them nothing in return for their handsome gifts. He had made it possible for her to have choices in life. There would be no other as he was, for her.

By then she knew many of the older and younger bored, rich men. They were her friends now. And she knew many women, some of whom struggled to survive and some who did not have to struggle to survive. Some of the women were beautiful in their own way. Appealing to men. Now those women, who could also be called "ladies" and carried themselves in that way, she introduced to a few of her male friends. That was how it all developed.

Over the years she had become a madam. She sold the house in Long Island, bought a fine estate of several acres in Chicago, and moved there. The house in Chicago was of gray stone with green ivy crawling over it, surrounded with fine old trees. The intimate gardens were well kept by excellent gardeners. The house had a long driveway that led through the broad, tree-lined lawns in front of the house to the rear, where there was a large garage partially hidden by many trees. This was where her visitors' cars were parked when they came to see one of the four "ladies" who now lived for most of the year with Madame LaFon.

She chose the women very carefully. Her house was a private house for private parties. There were no large gatherings of frivolous groups. No outsider could come to her house and sit and wait. Each of the four women had her own apartment with a sitting room, small dining room, and bedroom. Dinners were prepared by chefs who would have been welcomed in the richest mansions and served by impeccable servants. Madame paid handsomely for all the interior decoration.

At the time in the United States women did not have many or any of the important rights allotted to men. Woman were in colleges and universities in the smallest numbers. There was not much a woman could do except marry, which was the strongest reason why so many women looked for a wealthy husband. Or a smart husband, because if she had any inheritance, by law, he was the one decreed to handle it without any concern for her wishes.

Women could not buy land of their own. They could only do certain types of work, and so were not trained to be much other than housekeepers, cooks, teachers, or farmers. There have always been a few exceptions to the rule. Some women, with determination, found ways to accomplish what they wished for and dreamed of. Many failed. Some, for money to survive, turned to prostitution, for which society castigated them.

Only one of the women in Madame's house, Rita, spoke of going to college. Rita was also taking on the responsibility for a sister's child, one living parent, and her own future. Madame LaFon liked Rita the best of all. Lana and Viola, two others, were just having "fun" at a job unusual for them before "settling down to a 'good' marriage." They laughed at Rita, saying, "Oh, dear me! We never want to see a book again!" Melba, the fourth and last woman, didn't laugh at Rita, but only spoke to her in a lowered voice when Lana and Viola were not around. "I would like to be a real doctor or even a nurse. I know I could be a nurse!" But no one made a move to go to school, not even Rita. Nights of fun were too long and full of bootleg gin and Champagne.

Madame LaFon did not suffer fools at all, if possible. The cost for a night was fifteen hundred dollars. And the men paid it. *During the Depression, investors in munitions plants had a great deal of money from the wars they fomented around the world. Money was plentiful from other related things like oil, railroads, shipping lines, and such.* Madame kept seven hundred dollars of that money, a tidy sum. And so it had gone these last ten or so years of her life.

Now, even in her early forties, Madame LaFon was still petite, maybe five foot two or three, with a charming, youthful-looking figure. The silvery blond hair that hid the gray framed a piquant, alive, and still beautifully planed face. Soft, gleaming, mature curls floated to her shoulders. Her lips were well-shaped, small but full, with a natural pink glow. Her golden-green eyes, luminous with heavy dark lashes, reflected golden lights. She had intelligent eyes. Amused eyes. Madame was often amused by the human race. But at the right moment, if you caught her off-guard, her eyes, in their depths, might be sad and morose.

Her skin was, still, naturally smooth, an off-white color like the beginning of a suntan. A French color, perhaps. Or perhaps just age. Her rounded hips and thighs with gently plumped buttocks were shown tastefully in her chosen clothes. She shopped in Paris or Madrid each year, taking a girl or two along. She did not always like to travel alone. They paid their own way, however.

She had instant entry to every fashion salon. Some of the richest men from France, England, Switzerland, and America were her customers when they came to Chicago. She lived very well. After all, she had once been the mistress of one of the richest and most powerful men in the world. She had learned well. That is, how to live well.

**M**adame LaFon was taking the ladies out for a drive and dinner on this Thursday afternoon. The chauffeur of her Rolls-Royce took them for a long drive through the countryside to see the changing of the seasons reflected in the trees and hills along the road. In the early evening they stopped at one of Madame LaFon's favorite restraurants away from the city. They enjoyed a sumptuous meal with a fine light wine and a few hours of gossip and general women's talk. Darkness was upon them as they exited the restaurant, got into the automobile, and prepared to go to their house. Everyone in the car was full and content with the food and the lovely scenes during the ride.

(*They were not taken out to be shown off. Madame did not like notoriety. Her clients did not like notoriety. There were never naked women running around her house.*)

On their return home the chauffeur used the same road Eula Too had been abandoned on. Madame was remarking on how early it was getting dark when her sharp eyes saw a girl stumbling against the thick concrete shoulder of the small bridge overpass. She spoke to her driver, "Slow down, Paul. Pull to the right a little." He did as he was told. "Slower!" The chauffeur turned his head to gauge the traffic, which was light, then slowed almost to a stop.

Madame would not ordinarily have stopped for a stranger on a lonely road, but she noticed something special about this stranger. It was a young girl clutching something in one arm and holding her stomach with the other arm. The girl leaned against the cold concrete and tried to pull herself up to walk on, but she stumbled again.

"Drive closer" came the word from Madame.

As they drew closer, she could see the dark, dried blood down the inside of Eula Too's right leg. She knew these signs and knew the pain on Eula Too's face.

Madame didn't call out to Eula Too. "Pull over by that girl, but stay behind her a little," she told the driver. When they were as close as possible and Eula Too, in fear, was trying to run, Madame got out of the car. She never trusted others to do very important things for her. *Right.*

She walked slowly, speaking softly, to Eula Too. "I am a woman. I won't hurt you. I am a friend." Then she touched Eula Too lightly on the arm which clutched her raincoat to her breast. Madame looked at the unraveled braids with crumpled leaves and dirt in them. She moved ahead of the girl slightly and saw her eyes, still terrified, in shock, but determined. She saw terror, and she also saw strength in Eula Too's face. She asked, "There are no houses out here. Where are you trying to go?"

Everything was confused, muddled, uncertain to Eula Too. Something in the gentle voice made her stop her anxious, shaking body. She tried to focus her staring eyes as she moved closer to see Madame's face. A sob escaped her bloody lips as she turned to the strange woman, saying, "I don't know, mam. I've got to find a job."

Madame almost laughed in wonder, but she stopped herself and asked, "What happened to you? You are in no condition to ask anyone for a job. Someone beat you. Who beat you?"

Eula Too started to speak, but instead of words, a small moaning scream came out of her mouth as she leaned down toward the cold concrete to steady herself. Madame recognized the scream, and the pain in that scream.

Eula Too managed to say, "I don't know, mam. Some men . . . I got a ride . . . to Chicago. Thought he was . . . a . . . friend." She turned her head in the direction of the black emptiness of the distant land, saying, "We . . . they turned off the road . . . an . . ." Eula Too's body bent over from a knife-sharp pain. When she straightened up, she told Madame, because she was afraid of everyone now, "Go away. Go away, please."

At those words Madame seemed to know something she had needed to know, so she took Eula Too's arm, saying, "I will not go away. I will take you home and get you some help. I am your friend now. Don't worry. You will repay me. And you will get to Chicago."

Paul, the chauffeur, placed Eula Too in the front seat of the car between himself and Madame. Safely in the car, Eula Too near fainting from pain, sheer relief, and gratitude . . . and fear. She clutched her fear and her raincoat tightly in her arms, looked through a haze, first at the chauffeur, then at Madame's eyes and, giving up at last, she fainted as if dead.

# Chapter Seven

*

Madame's heart was distant and even cold to the world in general. Memories from her past made her a reserved and cynical woman. But, in her heart was also a compassionate empathy for the helpless when she remembered the times in her life she had been helpless. She trusted no one, completely, except her dead lover and her old neighbor, Marion Green, from her youth.

This distrust of people, her reserve, made hers a very lonely life. There were times, despite her rich house and furnishings and bank accounts, she was so lonely and felt her misery so deeply it was as though a heavy dark fog enclosed her. Keeping her separate from the joy in life she thought she should have. Didn't she have all the worldly things people said would make a person happy? Did they lie?

Madame wanted to be closer to her own mother, who now lived alone in Placeland, but the mother was filled with scorn for her. Scorn made from jealousy and resentment. She wailed or screeched, casting blame on her daughter for her own misery. Elizabeth had somehow succeeded, contrary to her mother's dire predictions, leaving her mother to her empty life. A life she persisted in choosing.

When Madame would visit her mother, taking gifts of fine clothes, jewelry, even a fur coat, she would belittle the gifts, throwing them on the floor of her closet as if to spit in her daughter's face. When Elizabeth was gone she would take them out, fondle them, and brag to her friends about them. Elizabeth always placed money on the kitchen table when she was leaving. Mother always shoved it aside, but not too far. Madame guessed, but did not really know her mother's thoughts. And, even without closeness, she did love her mother. Elizabeth needed her mother. She kept returning to Place and her mother, seeking to fulfill that need.

When Eula Too came unexpected into her lonely life (which is a hazardous situation), Elizabeth, known as Madame, took Eula Too into her home. She told herself, "It is for Marion Green, my friend, that I do this."

Eula Too was carried into the house unconscious, with Madame quietly giving directions to her servants. "We will put her on the first floor, near my rooms." She called for her housekeeper, "Bettyl! Greta!" Alarmed by the unusual, urgent tone, Greta came almost running. Madame said, "Call the doctor. Tell him he must come immediately. I need him."

Bettyl answered, "Yes, Madame," as she turned to do her bidding; at the same time, she watched ahead to see where they were taking the new person.

Now, each woman living in this house had her own personal maid paid for by herself. Madame kept a general housekeeper to run the house and all the maids smoothly, Bettyl Knoll. Bettyl was sister to Madame's personal maid, Greta. Each fancy lady had her own small apartment on the second floor, while their personal maids and the other servants had their rooms on the third, or top, floor. Madame occupied the first floor, which included the living and dining rooms, a library, and a social room with a liquor bar. The kitchen and pantries were also on the first floor, in the rear, where all the deliveries were made. Far enough away not to disturb Madame, but close enough for convenience. So all of the first and lower floors were her "home." Her personal maid slept in a room just near enough to Madame's own bedroom to be able to answer her calls quickly and yet far enough for Madame to retain some privacy. This was the room where Madame directed her chauffeur to take Eula Too.

The other women stood grouped around the staircase, eyes wide, lips parted in wonder at the goings-on over a Negro girl. Melba, the blond one, asked, "What is she going to do with her? I won't work with a Negro. Why she is almost still a slave!" Viola, the pretty, plump redhead, said with a soft laugh, "Why? Are you afraid she will take your men from you?" The other two women, Lana and Rita, laughed derisively, each with their own secret reasons, at Melba, but they all felt the same as Melba.

Melba had a narrow, hard face with high cheekbones, a narrow long nose, and brown eyes with no warmth in them. She had some breeding, taste, and a certain elegance and she was clever. She never discussed her past. She did not like or want any children.

Viola was very pretty, slightly plump, and rather short with no loss in beauty. She was, appropriately, very stylish. She had tiny feet and hands, and very white skin she loved. Her face was round, soft, dimpling almost constantly in her cheeks, chin, and around her mouth whenever she smiled with her round pink lips. An up-tilted, dainty nose set in naturally rosy, blooming cheeks. Soft waves of red hair falling over a low forehead caught fire from any light. She was usually sweet and charming. She really did not give much thought to her words: She neither liked nor disliked Eula Too. Among a million other things, she wanted children . . . someday.

Lana was golden-haired with a small, but exquisitely built figure: a little too slender, but very chic with impeccable style. Graced with lovely, slender legs she knew how to use from the time she learned to walk. She was usually unconciously remote to her visitors. An adorable face, exquisite in its perfection. She was a great liar and schemer and would steal, but only if she could get away with it. She did not give Eula Too a thought.

Rita stood slightly apart from the others, watching Madame. She was not pretty in a conventional way, but was strangely attractive. She had lustrous, rich black hair, but her nose was too large, her mouth too full. The blue eyes set in that face were brilliant, deep, and beautiful with long lashes. They seemed to take a person's mind away from everything but them. Her figure was not too shapely, but she knew how to dress to her advantage. She moved her eyes from Madame to Eula and mentally wished her Godspeed in getting better.

Madame paid no attention to the women as she spoke to Greta, "Prepare your room for this girl. We will put her in there temporarily until I can think of what to do." She led the way to the room, saying to no one in particular, "Has the doctor been called?"

Greta's eyes were wide as she stared at Eula Too lying in the advancing chauffeur's arms. She started toward her bedroom, looking back with disdain at the Negro woman with the dried blood on her skirt and legs. Reaching her room, she spoke to Madame as she snatched the lovely fresh spread from the bed, "I have just changed the sheets on my bed!"

Madame answered her without looking at her. "Good."

Greta thought Madame did not understand her. Her tone was desperate. "But they are the good sheets, not the best of course, but the good sheets from your closet!" She turned to leave as she said, "I can hurry and get some old sheets from the employee's closet."

Madame lifted her eyes to Greta. "Why?" She turned to the chauffeur, Paul, saying, "Put her in that chair, Paul. We need to bathe her." She turned back to her maid, "Greta, run some water in the bath."

"My bath?"

Madame was bending over Eula attentively. "Your bath and your bed. You can sleep on a cot in my rooms until we decide what to do with her."

Greta was sure Madame did not understand. "But . . . but, Madame . . . My bed. These sheets. These are proper sheets! She is a Negro! Madame."

"These sheets look fine, Greta. I can see she is a Negro."

Aghast, Greta said, again, "But this is my bed! Where I sleep! And . . . she is a Negro, Madame."

Madame finally gave Greta her full attention. "These are all my rooms and furniture . . . and sheets . . . in my house. And she is a Negro as you are white. So?"

"But she is a Negro, from . . . from Africa. A nigger!"

"Where are your ancestors from, Greta? And do not use that word in my house again."

Greta did not give up. "But we are from Europe. We are white people. From many years! And my own son was born here, here in this country."

"I daresay her people were here earlier. So, probably, was she born in this country. We are wasting time. Has the doctor been called? Even if he has, call again; see if he is on his way. Then run the bath. Warm, not too hot. And put good towels out for her."

The maid, confused, angry, and alarmed to give up her precious room, turned to leave, thinking, "This is *my* room. The first fine room I have ever had. I know that nigger has never had one like it and she does not deserve it with her colored skin and kinky hair. Blood all over her. Nasty! Proba'ly fightin' over some man! Humph! To sleep in my bed and bathe in my bathtub. Madame is surely out of her mind. Well, I will never sleep in it again after that one!" But even she knew she was lying. She rushed off thinking of disinfectants and soap.

Madame was thinking, "I must call the maid service in the morning. Greta is losing her mind, questioning my decisions in my own house."

The bath was prepared and taken in the comfortable, but not lavish bathroom, while Madame folded back the sheets on the bed. When Eula Too was settled in the bed, the doctor, finally arrived, attended her. He examined her, shaking his head. Finished, he said, "I do not think she is ruined for life, but you can see it was a vicious rape. Put a hot-water bottle on her stomach. See if she can take a good long warm douche. She has been torn a bit, but she is young and she will heal. She should rest perhaps a few days. She should then be able to be up and around." He looked up at Madame, "She does not do . . . your regular type of work, does she?"

Madame gave him a fleeting contemptuous glance, shaking her head, "No."

The doctor looked back down at Eula Too. "I thought not. I believe she was a virgin before this happened. Unusual for Negroes to be virgins."

Madame looked at him, again with contempt and disgust. "Do you say that because you think they are born deflowered? Or because you missed that moment of study in medical college?"

The doctor, obtuse except in matters of money, laughed those words away.

While they were talking, Greta listened eagerly and was disappointed that Eula Too had been a virgin. It did not fit her image of Negroes. "She'll be up and back out! I know Madame will not have such as this in this fine house. This is not really a house of whores, which is surely what that black girl will be after she is put out. Those people live like animals! She does not belong here with refined people like we are!"

Madame turned to look at Greta to tell her to give the bruised girl a shallow, warm douche in the morning, but seeing the look of hatred on the woman's face, decided she would give Eula Too the douche herself. She sighed, thinking of all the bother with hatred and jealousy in the world. She looked down at Eula Too, wondering about the pitiful young girl.

They had had such a struggle taking the paper bag and raincoat from the girl, even in as much pain as she was. She would not let go of them. As Eula slipped in and out of consciousness, they had cajoled, pulled, tried to distract her. But even when her mind was in darkness, she would moan softly, saying, "No, no. I'll hold my own stuff."

Madame spoke in a low, stern voice, "You can't undress or take a bath with those things in your arms," even as she thought, "Something is in that bag she is afraid to lose."

Eula moaned, "It's all I got."

Madame snatched the coat away at the moment Eula least expected it. Eula tried to rise, but was held back by the pain. She growled a moan deep in her throat as she tried to get up, to take it back, but the pain hit her stomach and black spots danced before her eyes.

Gently Madame said, "Look, you will see where I put them." She opened Greta's closet and pushed the few clothes aside and hung the coat far to the wall. "See?"

Fully awake now, with desperate tears in her voice, Eula said, "My money . . . it's all I got. I have to get to Chicago."

Madame nodded her head. "Ahhh, I thought as much. How much is it?"

Eula Too's eyes moved to Greta then back to Madame. She gave up. These strange people . . . Miss Hart had warned her . . . Now she was naked and helpless, so she whispered, " 'Bout ninety dollars."

Greta, eager with glee, thought, "At last! Now this will show Madame what a fool she is to take a thief in our house." She bent to Eula with rigid eyes and asked in a hard voice, "Did you steal it?"

Aching muscles tightened in Eula Too's throat and tears filled her eyes, "No . . . I worked for it . . . for a whole year."

Madame patted Eula's thin pitiful arm, "Do not cry. Do not worry. It will be safe with me. What is your name, dear?" Greta straightened her body as it filled with hatred that now included Madame.

The second shot the doctor had given Eula Too was for sleep, and her head, very heavy, dropped back down on the pillow. She tried to keep her eyes open but began to doze off as she said, "Eula Too." A moment later, as Madame and Greta were turning to leave, Eula raised herself up and tried to get up. "I want my things . . . here with me."

Madame gently pressed her down again. "I have told you . . . they will be safe with me. Do not worry. Rest. Get well. Sleep." The anaesthesia was working and Eula Too lay back down, her head falling to the side in sleep. Madame watched her a moment, and Greta watched Madame, then they left the room.

*I was in pain for the little, pitiful woman who would be my mother. I thanked God that someone with a kind heart had come along to help her. God did not send the helper, but it was love from Him that led her heart to help. How blessed we were.*

# Chapter Eight

*

A few hours later some inner compulsion forced Eula Too to open her eyes. She was not fully awake, but her mind tried to understand her life-situation at that moment. Her hands groped over the crisp, fresh sheets she had never before slept on in her life. Her mind took the time to feel them in wonder, and even pleasure, but did not linger on them long. Her body felt a little better, but she was sore and parts of her body throbbed numbly in pain. Her eyes longed to close again. But, in her need, she forced them to stay open.

Fingers lingering on the touch of beauty, she carefully, slowly, turned back the covers. She pushed and pulled her body up until she was standing. She waited a moment to steady herself. There was less pain, but pain still.

Her face flooded with perspiration as step by step, pitifully, she made her way to the closet. Never having had one, she struggled to open the closet door, reach for the hangers until, finally, getting her hands on her coat and into the pockets where her money was pinned. Sweat pored from her brow from the strain of the labor it took to get the safety pin out. At last it was done. She fell against the closet door, closing it. Then, taking small, throbbing steps, she made her way back to the bed. Breathing heavily from some weight she felt pressing down on her body, she pinned the money to the inside of the borrowed nightgown.

When that job was finished, she looked at the bedside where Madame had shown her the bag would be placed. "I am so tired. Very tired." Her arm felt so heavy as she reached for her bag and pulled out the Bible Iowna Hart had given her and placed it under her pillow. Sweat was running down her face, which was twisted from her labor.

Her body was grateful when she fell back to the pillow. She fell instantly back to sleep, her brow damp from her exertion.

One of the shots the doctor had given Eula Too had been strong enough to ease her pain and make her sleep for at least twelve or fifteen hours. Madame waited until her maid, Greta, mumbling angrily, had gone to sleep on her cot in the hall of her sitting room. After midnight, Madame went quietly into Eula Too's room and into the closet for the raincoat. She felt the pockets for the money the girl was so concerned about. The pockets, inside and out, were empty.

Madame quietly closed the door to the closet, turning to look thoughtfully at Eula Too lying there asleep. She then moved to the bed and put her hand slowly under the pillow and brought out the Bible. She leafed through it, finding nothing. She put it back. She felt Eula Too's forehead and was startled at the dampness.

Knowing the girl was sound asleep, she rolled the covers down carefully, slowly, then she ran her hands lightly over Eula Too's body and felt the packet. She unpinned it and the money fell into her hands. Madame counted the money: ninety-five dollars. She felt like crying for the girl, knowing how long it must have taken to save the money. She did not believe Eula Too had stolen it. "Ninety-five dollars! Who would this girl know who has ninety-five dollars?"

Madame pinned the money back to the gown where Eula had first pinned it and left the room wondering why she was so concerned about a Negro stranger with problems, while she herself did not need to worry about anything.

She had already completed all her usual bedtime rituals, brushing her hair, using the expensive cream on her hands and feet. She almost smiled as she pulled the covers over herself. "I am getting old. And Marion Green is getting old, too!"

Eula Too had awakened off and on during three days. In the first twenty-four hours they had wakened her for her medicine and to force-feed her soups and drinking water. She had fallen asleep again almost before they made her take a last swallow. Eighteen hours later they did it again. Feeling her aching body, the rape assualted her mind, making her turn her face away from the horror back to sleep again. Madame gave her the medicine.

After three days she awakened fully. She was not just sleeping from the pills, her body was resting from her years of constant work, constant care for others, and no real rest. She lay still in the bed, remembering the night she had left her home. She faintly remembered the bath she had been placed in. The warm water, the gentle hands. Her mind smiled. "Water inside a house! Water in that great, big white bathtub!" (Her first ever.) "Sweet, pretty water. Sure ain't like my little spring I bath in. All that water in one place. So big and white. And so warm. Right inside this house!"

Her eyes opened wider as the bed and room she was in became clearer. She looked at everything, all shining and golden, with such sharp vividness it became painful to her eyes. "A mirror over a wide dresser with drawers with golden, shiny knobs on 'em. And all them pretty bottles and figures on it! Miss Hart would sure like them."

Her gaze moved to the lovely pictures hanging on the walls, but she was distracted by the sun shining through the parted, clean, white drapes. The shaft of sunlight filtering through the trees outside the window fell across the bed and hurt her eyes. She lay back and closed them against the glare.

She reached under the covers to feel the packet pinned to her nightgown, then turned to reach for the paper bag that held her sister's picture and a few leaves from her secret thinking place, the spring. Her body didn't respond as quickly as she was used to. Her arm was still heavy with fatigue from fighting her rapist. Her whole body was weary from just two days of being out in the world on her own.

Eula Too cried out in her mind, silently. "Where am I? What am I doing here? Who are these strange people in this world? I got to get away from 'em. I'll . . . I'll take my money and go back home." She thought a moment. "Maybe I could just go on to find a job in Chicago. I can find something."

She began to push one weary leg out of the bed until her foot touched the floor. She sat up, her body slow and stiff. After resting a moment she pulled her body up until both feet were on the floor. "I got to get out of here and find me a job!"

As she moved her body she began to gather strength and even felt a little better. Not her normal self, but better. "Whoever these people are, they sure been kind to me. I got to get on my way and not bother these people no more."

When she reached the closet door to get her clothes, her knees buckled weakly and she reached for something to hold on to besides just the doorknob. There was nothing, and so she slid to the floor. She couldn't understand why, but *I* know it was the medicine. She crawled back to the bed, pulled herself in under the covers, started to cry softly, then fell asleep again, whimpering as she slept.

**T**hat evening Madame came in to see Eula Too as the home nurse was finishing helping Eula eat something. She touched Eula Too's brow and checked the bed to be sure it was clean and smooth. Madame had done this several times each day during the past three days, but this time, she sat down to talk since Eula Too was now wide awake.

She smiled at Eula as she spoke to the nurse, "Change her gown again, please." Then she said to Eula Too, "How do you feel?"

"I'm much better, mam."

Madame thought with some pleasure, "It seems she has some manners," as she spoke to Eula, "We have been very concerned about you. But, you do look much better. I'm glad you feel better." She said to the nurse, "Would you please leave us alone for a moment." When the woman was gone, she asked Eula, in a gentle way, "Do you want to tell me what happened?"

"No, mam. I don't want to even think of it. I remember . . . most all of it, but it feels too bad to me to think of it." With a small, sad smile, she said, "But I sure do thank you all for helpin' me."

Madame looked at her for a moment, without smiling. Then she said, as she rose from the brocaded rose satin bedside chair that Eula had caressed with her eyes, "As I have said to you before, I am glad to be able to help you. Sleep . . . rest." Madame left.

Eula Too could not know, or imagine, the things that went on in the huge mansion on the second floor, away from Madame's rooms. So, later that same night, when she could hear nothing stirring and the house was quiet, Eula Too, just as quiet, got up and found her old clothes. They had been washed, starched, and ironed by the nurse because Greta would have nothing to do with anything belonging to Eula Too. All the evidence of "that" night was gone. The small top drawer of the dresser was the first Eula opened and the only things in it were her brassiere and panties. She dressed, pinning what was left of her money to her underwear. She put on her thin raincoat, which she knew would not be of much help. Even with the sun out each day, she remembered it was very cold outside, especially at night. "Well, it's what I got is mine!"

In the drawer of a small desk Eula found paper and pencils. She wrote a note to Madame: "I cannot pay you for all you done for me, but God knows I will pay you what I owe you after I get my work. I cannot pay you for a doctor and all right now, but thank you." She signed her name at the bottom of the sheet of paper and wrote, "And good by."

Eula had counted and divided her money, took fifty dollars of it and placed it in the envelope with the letter, sealed it, marked "Mam" on the envelope, and placed it in her place on the pillow. Then, very quietly, she started sneaking out of the room to the hall outside the room. She did not know her way in this house so she followed, on tiptoe, the light that led her to the elegant entry hall and the front door. She stopped, in awe of the tall, wide front door with two small sparkling glass panes that reflected the low lights left on at night.

As in the fairy tales she had read at Miss Hart's, the doorknob looked as though, if you turned it, you would go through such a door to a great and magic wonderland! Barely moving her body, she reached out for the golden knob and, turning it, she opened the front door. It was black night on the other side of the door that Eula Too stepped into. Out!

The open door caused a small ringing, like an alarm clock, to go off in Madame's room. At first, Madame drowsily thought it was just one of the guests from upstairs leaving, then it hit her mind, "They don't go out that door!" Madame was up instantly, calling for Greta.

When Madame reached the front door and opened it, she saw Eula way up the drive, almost at the gate to the road. She called out "Eula!" Eula Too started to run in a wobbling, stumbling way like a baby animal learning to flee.

Greta was right behind Madame. When she heard Madame call out for Eula Too and saw the little figure running away, her heart leapt in gladness. "I tole you! I tole you! She has stole something of ours! I know it! I know it! That little ni . . ." She remembered Madame's warning. "Dirty little black thief!"

Madame had no answer for Greta. Instead she ran in her nightgown through the cold night to catch Eula Too even as the thought ran through her mind, "Am I crazy! It's cold out here! Does she have something of mine? Why am I doing this! Let it go. I can buy another of whatever she has taken!" But, she didn't stop; she ran as best she could until she caught up with the stiff and half-drugged Eula Too. Shivering from the cold, but holding tight to her raincoat, Eula reluctantly let Madame lead her back to the house to the bedroom she had been using.

Madame knew Eula had no bulky places on her body where she might have hidden anything she could have stolen, still she glanced quickly around the room to see if there was anything missing, thinking, "I don't see anything missing, unless Greta left something in here. And I know she would have complained already if the slightest thing was gone." She saw the envelope and picked it up.

Madame loosened Eula's coat and called for Greta, who was hovering nearby waiting to hear whatever was said. When Greta showed herself, Madame said, "Would you get us some tea, please?" Greta, flushing with anger, went away to fetch the tea, muttering to herself as she did, "Tea, she says, for a blackie this late in the night! Well, I'll just make my own self a cup too!"

As she opened the envelope, Madame, catching her breath a bit, sat down in the bedside chair. Eula slumped and breathing hard, sat stiffly on the edge of the bed as if she were waiting to escape again. Madame read the scrawled note then just looked at Eula for a moment. Her breathing slowing to normal, after her run, she said, "You are a foolish girl."

There was only silence as Eula looked down at her lap, not looking sorry at all, just defeated.

Madame continued, "You are, also, not well."

"I feel better."

Madame sighed, "You are not well . . . enough."

"I got to be. I got to go."

"Where?"

"To Chicago."

Madame sighed again, "You're in the Chicago suburbs now."

Eula looked up, surprised and, thinking of her mother, pleased. "I am?"

Madame looked at the innocent face smiling in wonder at her and liked Eula Too even more than she had before. She counted the money in the envelope and shook her head slowly. "And . . . you are in a safe place here. The Depression is still here for many, many people. The streets of Chicago are full of all kinds of starving people who don't have any money. They might not be dangerous people when they are full of food and working, but they haven't been full and working for a long, long time now. You could be killed for the money you have." Madame sighed deeply. "People are dangerous because they have children starving, in some hovel if they are lucky, and perhaps a thin wife waiting for a husband to come back with *something*. Anything. They fight, many steal, some will kill. You do not really want to go out there."

Eula Too leaned toward Madame, "This here Depression been in my life all my life. We ain't hardly ever had enough to feed everybody.

Beans, beans, beans, potatoes, potatoes, potatoes is most all we had every day. That ain't new to me."

Madame leaned toward Eula Too, "Evidently, most surely, you have not seen what I am telling you about or you would not have this money you have." Her look was expectant as she said, "I am not going to ask you how you 'worked' for it."

Blushing and ashamed, Eula Too told Madame how she had acquired the money because she didn't want Madame to think she was a thief. God hated thieves, and Madame would too. She ended by saying, "But he didn't never put nothin' of his in me. 'Cause I didn't want that 'cause I don't want no babies, and I ain't never done nothin' like that anyhow."

Now it was Madame's turn to be silent, looking at this young innocent, dumb girl, as she thought of the women up her own stairs making many hundreds of dollars.

Eula Too broke the silence by saying, "But I got to go. I got to get started making a livin'."

Madame shook her head, "We are going to see about that. Be patient."

"I can't. I'm all alone. And my money won't last too long."

Madame stood up with the envelope still in her hand. "I'm giving you back what you gave to me, and . . . I'll give you a job making ten dollars a week helping me around here."

Eula's eyes filled with tears as she said, "You will give me a job? Here? In this house?"

Madame nodded as she said, "Yes. I must."

"But . . . mam . . . I didn't expect . . . You done already helped me so much. I prob'ly would have died out there by myself, sick as I was."

"How do you expect to find a job? Your face is still swollen a little. That blood clot in your eye. He really beat you, didn't he?"

Eula Too's voice sounded soft and in pain. "He sure did. But, when he did, I was so scared, I didn't blive it. I had so much pain I couldn't feel it all."

"Eula Too, that is why I don't want to let you go out into the streets of Chicago. There are many men just like him . . . and poverty has made some women like him, also. I mean the beating. You have only a little money; you can't go far on that money."

"Well, I learned a lot since I been here at your house. Baths and food and all. I can find somethin' to do . . . to put a roof over my head."

"You need more than a roof if you are going to have a future. How old are you?"

"I'm young, but I'm old enough, fifteen. And right now, a roof is more important than the money."

Madame shook her head slowly, "The most important thing in this world we are in . . . is money. Without it, there is no future. It takes brains to be happy. Brains get you the money, then you make the happiness."

"Well, I heard my daddy say you all got you a good president so we all could be equal and then . . ."

"Do you really believe that? Politicians will say anything. Your father believed them. Politicians lie. They are men. Human. Flawed. Always smiling and lying. I know many of them. If you stay here, you will meet some of them."

Eula wiped her eyes with her hands and asked, "Doing what, mam? I'm tired of housework and baby work. I want to learn somethin' new. Somethin' what will make me have enough money." Thinking of Earle and her mother, she added, "I got teeth troubles, they ache all the time . . . and . . . that man made 'em hurt more."

Madame nodded, saying, "Good! Oh, not that you have dental problems, but that you want to learn."

"So . . ." Eula waited, then said, "What would I have to learn to do in your job?"

Madame laughed as though to herself. "We have to take time to see what you can do. What do you want to learn? What do you like to do?"

"I like to read, but that ain't no job. I can write. I like to be 'round flowers and trees, but that ain't no job. I like animals, all of 'em. But that ain't no job neither."

"So! You can write and you like to read. What do you like to read?"

"Well, I ain't been 'round too many books, but I love 'em, and I ain't had much time to go to no school. I just had a teacher friend, is all. Like you been a friend." Eula Too leaned toward Madame again, "What we was talkin' about before? Happiness? Is this house and stuff yours, really yours? Is it your happiness?"

Madame sighed, smiled, and stood up to leave. "Well . . . I'm happy enough. Now, I must go. I am tired." She handed the envelope to Eula. "You get some rest yourself. And let me tell you something you remember all your life: Never, never, no matter what you have, never give anyone else more than you keep for yourself. Never. Give away as much as you want, but you must come first or, in the end, you won't matter at all."

"More than you even give God?"

As Madame went out of the room, she turned at the door and said, "I've had enough experience to know that the God you are talking about does not exist. People who claim they speak for God are usually asking for themselves."

Eula Too answered, "God won't ask. God is a giver. The Bible says so. Only people ask."

As Madame left the room, she said, "And remember, people are not usually givers. You be careful with your Bible. It says a lot of things that cannot be proven. Only a fool would believe there is some great God."

Eula softly said, almost to herself, "That is what faith is for. Maybe only a fool would not believe it. I believe it."

Madame's parting words were, "Well, I don't want to hear it. You keep your Bible to yourself, dear." The door closed and she was gone.

# Chapter Nine

*

Madame was surrounded with people she did not trust or, sometimes, even like. Her feelings about Eula Too confused her. She was usually very careful with strangers. When she went to bed that night, her last thoughts were, "Eula and I do not have much in common, but I like her. She is pitiful with her trust. And, I think, she is honest. She is even still innocent. I want her to stay. What is ten dollars a week to me? She will be a breath of fresh air in the house. In any event, we shall see what we shall see." As she drifted off to sleep again, she thought, "She is thinking of giving God something, and she has just been beaten up and could have died out there. I guess that is what they call faith." Then her mind closed off her thoughts and she slept.

Eula Too was overwhelmed and in awe at the very thought of living in such a huge, beautiful house. She thought of her old home, her family still living in their poor, miserable conditions. She got up to look out of the window and saw the light of the dawning sky moving between the trees and through the leaves. Instantly the sight of nature's work and the sounds of a few early birds lifted her feelings. "She has trees and birds! Now I will learn the names of the birds."

She turned to look around the warm and friendly room with its beautiful pictures, flowing drapes, clean, crisp sheets, and pretty, colorful spread covered in what seemed like full, live roses. Then she thought, "And I will have books!" She hugged her recovering body, "Oh, God, I hope I get to stay and work here."

. . .

*Some other place in America, around this time, a child was born to a mother who could not afford to keep her. Her mother named her Lona, without a last name. She left her at a place where many such children were abandoned, usually because of poverty, by mothers and fathers who could not feed the new, small, hungering mouths. But, they left small hungering hearts that may never be full or satisfied. Lona will seek a place to be. I will tell you more about Lona soon. In some other place.*

In Eula Too's new position of "helper," the fresh air, regular meals, rest, and just plain peace helped to heal her body. Her mind slowly covered over, but did not forget, the rape. Her skin was a rosy bronze, her eyes clear and light. She had always just brushed her hair back with her hands, but now she had a real brush and comb. Still, she couldn't seem to get it to look right, so she tied it up in a scarf Madame gave her.

Madame decided Eula would, of course, need some clothes. She thought carefully about what Eula's duties would be. Madame did not want her to have a maid's uniform because others might imagine they could take advantage of Eula. Finally she had her dressmaker come in to take measurements of Eula for two black broadcloth dresses, elegant in their simplicity and style, which could be worn with white collars and cuffs when desired. Another dress was charcoal gray with long sleeves, and another of bronzed yellow silk with demure lines. All complemented Eula's color and the almost straight shape of her body. Madame bought Eula underwear of both silk and cotton. Madame looked forward to throwing away the sad, cheap underwear Eula had been wearing during the rape. She also bought Eula the first pair of shoes she had ever owned (*the first shoes she had ever owned!*) to complete the softly severe, but solid, wardrobe. *I don't even have to tell you,* Eula was out of her mind with wonder.

Madame didn't quite know what to do with Eula's tight, curly hair, soft and nappy. After talking with her permanent Negro cook, Dolly, and Madame's own hair stylist, Eula's hair was, at last, in neat French braids, accomplished by a professional. Eula was very proud and pleased. She could not pass a mirror without turning to look at herself with a hesitant, huge grin.

Eula Too spent most of her time, now that she was up and around, in the library going through books, most of which she did not understand. Those she could understand, like Flaubert and de Maupassant, she read hungrily. Madame watched her, pleased, and one day she came into the library and said, "I am not sure just what your job will be, but you just might look around and find things to do when you feel up to it."

Eula did look around. Sometimes she would try to help the observant, friendly but reserved, colored cook in the kitchen. Greta had been trying to persuade all the household help that because Eula Too was colored, she was useless and might steal. She left "colored" out when she spoke to the cook, Dolly. Dolly looked at Greta in her knowing way and said nothing beyond slamming a pot on the stove. Greta departed. She didn't like the colored cook either, but she thought Dolly was at least in her rightful place, the kitchen.

Now, none of the household help really liked Greta. Her job so close to Madame gave her some power which many times made her a tyrant. She was mean, arrogant when possible, contemptuous always, and overbearing. She had been in America only ten years, but felt more American than people with a different hue to their skins. Surrounded with the material things bought with Madame's money, Greta felt far above "common people," as she said.

The Negro cook, Dolly, and her husband had a room on the place. They had sacrificed to buy their own small house years ago. Their oldest daughter and her children lived there, and they went there when they needed to get away. Dolly had been working for Madame for at least eight years. Her husband was hired last and was one of the several gardeners there.

Times were hard, the Depression was not going away. They had not saved much because of trying to help their needy family. And Dolly had sense enough to know there was nothing to steal in the kitchen when you were already being fed well. But she did not want any problems with Greta. "That Greta most likely a dangerous liar with some power." Dolly did not want Eula in her kitchen because the girl *was* colored and might know or learn her own cooking secrets. White Americans who owned America did not like colored folks, so, sometimes, Dolly didn't like them either.

"You go," she would say to Eula, "I don't need nobody in my kitchen confusin' me. You go. Go outside. Find a little piece of ground and work on that."

"Maybe I could clean somethin' for you? Or put somethin' away," Eula asked again.

With hands on her hips, Dolly said, "Don't you understand? You go!" But, even as the cook said it, she thought of how Madame must like the girl to keep her and she was not sure whether Eula Too was going to end up upstairs with the "ladies" or not. Also, she had heard from the ladies' maids that Madame had stopped them from giving her their own work to do. To be safe, she added as Eula stepped out of the back door, "Maybe tomorrow, maybe next week, chile. Maybe."

Eula, feeling much better physically and like her old self again, ready to work, loved the beautiful grounds surrounding the mansion. The Irish gardener frowned at her when she showed up at the gardeners' shed. Greta had talked with him, too (but not Dolly's husband). Also, the Irish gardener was protective and jealous of the gardens he cultivated. Didn't want anybody watching him to notice he only worked just enough for things to seem well done. In a hard voice, he asked, "Now, what you going to do? What can you know about a fine yard and gardens like these? I ain't got nothin' for you to do out here."

His unfriendly and mean attitude was not lost on Eula Too, but she remembered what Madame had told her. So she said, "I really like flowers and things and you got all this land out here. I'll just pick the weeds and things like that. I won't get in your way."

Eula Too picked up a trowel that was lying close by. He moved toward her to say, "I'm gettin' ready to use that." Then, he thought, "I can't pick up everythin' she picks up 'cause she may stick around to see if I do use 'em, and I ain't gonna do no much work right now." So he let her alone.

Eula moved away, looking over the landscaped yard, patches of all different types of flowers and all the glorious colors around the base of the trees and filling the wide spaces between them. Most of them were filled with weeds at the base. She chose a pretty spot to do her weeding. Soon she had a few piles of weeds and leaves. The colored gardener, who had been keeping an eye on her, brought her a sack to put everything in.

The Irish gardener, already friends with the colored gardener, decided it was really helping him to have her cleaning weeds and debris from the flower beds, except she stopped to stare off into space and daydream a lot. Still, she worked. He finally decided to forget about her and, after telling her about a few ways which would help her and the plants, he went on about his business.

Eula Too loved to learn and as the sun shone down warmly on her, she thought, "How wonderful it is to sit in the sun 'round all these beautiful flowers and these big ole tall, strong trees and listen to the wind and all the birds. I miss my little creek, but it will still be there when I go back." She bent to pull up a mean, tight weed. "If I ever go back."

The women upstairs did not pay her much attention after they learned about the black dresses, the braids, and the low-heeled, made-for-comfort shoes. "She is just a maid after all," they thought. They did not bother to like or dislike her. A few of their maids decided to give Eula their mistresses' underwear and lingerie to wash. Eula Too, her arms deep in warm water and puffy suds, unusual to her, did the washing well and without comment. When Madame found out she asked Eula, "How much did they pay you?"

"Oh, nothing. I don't mind. I ain't got nothin' else much to do, so I don't mind helpin' 'em."

Madame frowned, "It is not wise when you wish to save money, as you said, for you to work for nothing. They are all making money. Why should not you?"

"Well . . . they are nice to me."

Madame shook her head, "You mean, I think, they do nothing mean to you. But that does not mean they are nice to you. What do they do *for* you that is nice?" She watched Eula for a reaction. Then asked, "Or, perhaps, they are not mean or unkind to you because they plan to use you for their little purposes in the future?"

Madame continued studying Eula a moment then said, "Eula, I notice you observe people and things, but you do not know what you are looking for. Shouldn't you . . . wouldn't it be wise to ask yourself *why* people do or do not do certain things."

Confused, Eula Too shook her head in uncertainty and raised her shoulders in an "I don't know" gesture, as she silently looked at Madame.

Madame allowed herself only a slight smile. "In other words, Eula Too, it is very good to observe things, but it gets even better for you when you think about what you see."

Eula shook her head slightly, then said, thoughtfully, "But, Madame, I don't know what all to think yet. When I wat . . . observe people, I am learning about the person I am looking at. I guess I am slow 'bout learning, but I don't forget whatever I learn."

Madame nodded in understanding, but said, "Eula, I don't want to say anything to hurt you, but the man who drove you to Chicago . . . You knew him, watched him for some time, didn't you? Still . . . *that* happened."

"I couldn't learn that from watching him. But, I lost my good sense. Miss Hart shown me from the Bible about strangers. Strangers are very dangerous. Mankind, that means women and men, is dangerous. But I didn't remember it in time."

"I know how that can happen; what you wanted to do got in the way of what you ought to have done." Madame shook her head in sadness for all the people had that problem. For some of her own memories, in fact. She returned her focus to Eula Too, saying, "I was a stranger to you, Eula. But I was not dangerous to you. The point is, that he had shown you what his interest was in you. So that was doubly dangerous. That is what you should try to see, what you should look for, when you observe strangers. All people, as a matter of fact. Even people who say they are your friends. Where their interest lies. Then you ask yourself what it has to do with you."

Eula Too nodded as she turned her head away. "Yes, mam. I will always remember that. I'm gettin' more careful now." At that moment she proceeded to wonder what Madame's interest had to do with her.

Madame smiled as she patted Eula's arm. "You are doing much better, but be more careful when you are speaking, about those *ings* I keep telling you about."

Madame did not speak to the maids about the matter, but she sent word to the ladies. "Anything you may have in mind for Eula Too, ask me first. Or, better yet, other than being friendly and kind to a young lady in my care, do not have her in your minds at all unless you wish to give her something."

Most evenings when Madame was not having guests for dinner, or after such dinners if she was, Eula would sit near Madame's feet while they talked. Eula would talk about her day, her thoughts, and the books she had been reading from the library.

Madame loved music, especially the jazz music that was new to her. She had a Victrola and records. When Eula had discovered the black, shiny discs and the sounds they made, she was amazed and almost delirious over the fact that such a silent thing, when you held it, could make such sounds of music. She could listen to records for hours with smiling pleasure. She almost wore the records out. Only books held her attention as strongly. She took a book or two to bed with her every night.

Madame tried to show her what dance steps she knew, which were quite a few because Madame loved all things alive with life and, sometimes, went to halls where live musicians played. Dolly, the cook, had a son who was a musician. Sometimes Madame "dressed down" less rich and went to hear Negro musicians play the new jazz and the old blues.

Madame and Eula laughed together as the music blared out and they pranced and trotted over the floor. Greta, jealous and angry, would steal peeks at them and scuttle away muttering, "I bet that Madame got some Negro blood in her. Makin' a fool of themself over that nigger music! Both of them nothin' but niggers!" But Madame had no Negro blood in her. She just liked good music.

Madame also thought of Eula Too's real needs and the fact that Eula would be bored, at her age, with nothing to do but piddle in a garden. She had been making some tentative plans in her mind for Eula, but had waited for the girl to rest and heal. Now she decided to proceed with her plans.

She had turned over the apartment in New York to the valet, Burnett, when her lover had died. "I'll never live there again." She did this even though her lover had left Burnett a very tidy sum of money in his will. "For many years of faithfulness, industry, and honesty," it had read.

Madame had thought, "Burnett deserves a fine place to live in, he has earned it, and they would never allow him to buy an apartment in that building. I will give him the deed and he can live there because they think it is still mine." She had never regretted her decision. Burnett and Madame remained friends. She could even stay there on her trips to New York if she wished. Burnett had excellent servants, but he allowed no one else to look after her.

They kept in touch, talking every two months or so. When she missed her lover and was down in the dumps, saddened by her loneliness and wanting to feel near her dead lover, she called Burnett.

Now she made a telephone call to Burnett. The old friends talked warmly a moment or two, then she asked him a favor, "I would like you to come stay with me for a month or so. I have someone I would like for you to meet and help."

Burnett answered with a smile and a question. "Help? Me? There? Tell me more about what you want. Please."

"I would like you to take someone in your hands whom I think I have plans for. I also need to know what you think of her. You know so much more about people and things than I."

She heard soft laughter as Burnett asked, "Her? What could I possibly tell those ladies?"

She smiled into the telephone as she said, "They don't have sense enough to listen to you. I'm talking about someone else. A young girl I want as a friend. A friend . . . I wish to trust. A friend . . . I want. I am too lonely now, Burnett. I have no one."

The laughter ceased. "When do you want me to come? I won't be entirely free for a few days, but I will come."

Gladdened laughter sounded in Burnett's ear as Madame said, "Fine! Good! And I think you will enjoy this yourself. Give her one week and we will see what you think. Then, maybe, you can go home quicker than four or five weeks. You can go home anyway, every weekend if you want to. I hope you do come, my friend."

They said their good-byes and she sat back in her chair in anticipated satisfaction. Burnett hung up his phone and stood there a moment, wondering what the call meant. But, he liked and respected Madame. She had been good to him, even when he didn't need it. So, he would attend to his immediate business and go.

Burnett arrived in due time driving his own automobile. Eula Too happened to be outside on the grounds working a patch of flowers. Sometimes she looked for the hobos the Depression had spawned. They came hesitantly onto the grounds to ask for some work in exchange for something to eat or some money or, even, a regular job. There were so many of them, younger even than she was, and many old ones.

Eula always tried to get some food for them from Dolly. Dolly always found a little something to give. She told Eula, "Girl, you can't feed the world 'lessen you ain't gonna have nothin' left for yourself!" Dolly began to like Eula because Eula was different from Greta; Eula cared about the hungry, the poor.

. . .

*In the world the years before the 1914 war were considered golden days or the good old days to most people, even though most people had been poor. Certainly thoughout the world. Nineteen fourteen is considered by many scholars to be the last "normal" year in the world. In 1929, the stock market crash hit everyone very hard, bringing most people and everything down with it. People in America and other rich countries had been playing with life like a game in the Roaring Twenties. But there was nothing more real than the Depression. Bread lines. No employment. The country was starving. Men left home on the railroads . . . trying to help their families survive. Many families were destroyed by the poverty. The Great Depression bewildered everyone. It lasted until December 1941. World War II. Most colored people in America could tell no difference in their life before or after the Great Depression. That is what my mother, Eula Too, lived.*

Now, as usual, Eula Too had been weeding the garden and was stopping her work to sit on the lawn in the shade of an old, wide tree. She was staring into space thinking of her mother, her family, and how they were living. She was almost ashamed to be living as she was while they were doing without everything. "And Mama was pregnant, too." Eula's eyes filled with tears which she was wiping away with the back of her hands when she saw the shining car driving up the road to the house.

When the driver stepped out of the car, Eula was amazed to see a well-dressed Negro man. Eula had, by now, seen well-dressed white men, even a priest, coming to have dinner with Madame, but she had never seen a Negro man well-dressed anywhere at all. Try as they might, the preachers in the churches her mother had taken them to had never looked anything like the tall, immaculately dressed man walking across the lawn in her direction and smiling at her as he waved.

Though he was smiling, Burnett looked closely at Eula Too, studying her as he got closer, and said, "Well. Good afternoon, young lady."

Not only had Eula never seen a Negro man dressed so well, but she had never dreamed one might have a car . . . and look pleasant, too. Most of the Negro men she had known were bent and frowning under the burdens on their backs. "And he talks so different, too!" she thought as she smiled back at the man. She remembered a phrase from one of the books she had been reading, "Wonder of all wonders!"

She held her head down as he reached out to shake her hand, then she held her hand out to him, smiling slightly, thinking, "I am so glad to see somebody colored like me 'sides Dolly and her husband!"

Burnett said, "I didn't mean to interrupt your thoughts. It just looks so beautiful out here, and here you are, in the middle of it all. I don't have it like this in New York. I had to say 'hello' to you." They stood silent a moment, looking into each other's eyes, trying to find something in the other they could recognize. Finally Burnett said, "I'm going in now to see Madame, little lady. I am sure I'll see you again. Soon." With those few words he smiled his good-bye and, turning, walked to the house and went in through Madame's private entrance. The entry was opened without his even having to knock. Eula noticed. So did Greta.

In her private sitting room, Madame opened her arms to welcome Burnett. He accepted the embrace, only slightly stiff, but he smiled down at her seriously as he said, "Well now, Miss Madame! You look exceedingly well."

Madame showed joy at seeing him, "Sit down, sit down. Let me get a good look at you. You look very well yourself. Are you still feeding all the hungry people you can? Did you see my young lady out there in the flower beds?"

As Burnett removed his coat and sat down, he said, "There are still so many hungry people and still no jobs. Mr. Roosevelt is doing an excellent job for the people, though. And Mrs. Roosevelt, too! Yes, I believe I did see the little lady. She is the only little brown flower out there." He laughed. "I think she is nice looking, healthy, and her face shows some intelligence. But, I am interested in knowing what you have in mind."

Madame smiled approvingly. "Well, right to the point, as usual."

Burnett sat down, mannerly, with his back straight and legs crossed, waiting.

Madame cleared her throat softly, then said, "Well . . . what I have in mind is your taking Eula Too in hand. I want her to be taught social graces. Etiquette. A bit of the elegant ways of life. Your manners are impeccable, Burnett. I want her to have manners like yours."

"Eulatoo? Is that her name?"

"Yes. It's a story you will probably hear."

"You know, you can teach her those things yourself."

"My manners are not as deeply ingrained and . . . refined and relaxed as yours are."

Burnett nodded his head, smiling ever so slightly, saying, "Thank you, Madame. But that isn't true." Then his face became serious as he said, "If I may ask, since I am being asked to contribute, what do you have in mind for this little girl? This young lady with no experience."

Embarrassed at his slight reference to her being a madam, she laughed softly, because she knew what he meant. "I know you know I have never knowingly placed any woman in any position that would lower her in the eyes of others or take away any chance she might have to do something more . . . beneficial to her life. You, of all people, know I didn't ask for this . . . job. I fell into it because I knew the type of rich man who would worry me to death to take my dead lover's place and I did not want anyone to do that. I thought getting those men a substitute would be quick and simple. I hadn't planned on regular employment at this. It is the same with the women who have lived here. From the beginning *they* asked because they thought it was glamorous. There was the Depression. Now most of them just need the money. And they are the best of their, temporarily, chosen profession, and I don't believe they would remain in this profession if it was not in . . . these types of circumstances."

Burnett, understanding, nodded his head slowly.

Madame was encouraged to continue, "Another thing, I was left with some fluid cash, but I don't know where this Depression will lead. Did any rich person, now broke, know? Money is money and it doesn't just talk, it sings opera to this world. I am not . . . greedy. I'm just, shall we say, being careful?"

Burnett tilted his head slightly, saying, "So. If I might ask again, what is your interest in Eula? Why are you doing this for her?" He sighed in soft exasperation. "What are your intentions for this girl?"

Madame sat forward, softly, but with intensity she said, "Burnett, I am growing old. My mother is old and sick and seems to hate me. I am so lonely, sometimes I just cry. You are my only old friend. I trust you, not only because I know the man I loved trusted you, but because I know you for myself. If my mother should die, then I won't have anyone even remotely connected to me . . . but you. And you are getting old too, my friend. I need to have someone. Someone I can trust to follow my wishes."

Madame leaned back, thoughtful for a moment before she said, "Yes . . . I have this house, and others, but who wants to grow old and die of loneliness? All of my friends who come to have dinner with me are now truly old. Soon . . . who will come to visit me? Many people who know me from the past think of my house as a whorehouse, even though it is not, in the true sense of the word. Assuming some new people, new friends, might come, they won't want to be seen coming to see an old madam of a whorehouse. I would be more alone. And I like life around me. I like youth and life. I don't want to just sit around with my money and watch myself grow older with death hovering over my head."

She looked, beseeching, into Burnett's eyes. "So I will have a friend. Eula Too. Perhaps she will have children, and I will have them to plan for and do things for." Madame looked away from his penetrating eyes. "I will not be alone."

Burnett leaned back in his chair as, with a little bitterness, he said, "Like a trusted servant?"

"Not like a servant. Like a friend."

Burnett waved his hand to sweep away the bitter thoughts he had. "And you think this Eula . . . Too, a stranger to you, might be this person you need?"

Madame leaned back, a little less intense, and said, "I know I have not known her long, but I am not a complete fool. I see things in her. Honest things. Kind ways, an alert mind. She loves to read. She can write. She can think. We have to help her to know what to think about. In the meantime, if she has even half the manners you do, it will prepare her better for life. It's not just for me. I want her to join me in some of my dinners. I can discuss things with her afterward. As a companion she will be stimulating. Not old and boring. The only problem might be that she speaks of her Bible so much! And believes it!"

Burnett nodded in agreement. "That may be why you are making such a connection to her. Why you trust her so and are doing so much for her."

Madame sat forward again, but her voice was still soft. "I am not doing it all for her. I am also doing it for me. I am afraid I am a little selfish, Burnett. But I still say, it is for her benefit."

Burnett shook his head no. "You are doing it all for you. She is being helped in the process. And I can not deny that she needs everything you will do to help her." He sighed and leaned back in his chair. "You have thought of everything except what she might want to do. Life is short, but life is long, too. Life, love, children, a man or men are coming into her life. She can not be expected to . . . cleave to you. That is for husbands and wives. You may lose everything you are investing in Eula Too. There is no guarantee on anything in life except death."

Madame just looked at him in silence for a few moments, then, "What in life is not a chance? Who knows anything? As you say, the only sure thing in life is death. But I can try to plan, can't I?"

"Why do you not choose one of the ladies who lives here, whom you know already?"

"Because they think they have learned all the 'tricks' of life. They are not dumb, but they are just slick. Not smart. They would do it for the money that may be involved. There would likely be no real caring or friendship involved. I think they are too slick to be happy. Several could already have married and gone on to better things and didn't. And another thing, while they are smart, to an extent, before long they will begin drinking to be able to do their job." She leaned forward, her voice low, "Except for the nymphomaniacs."

She leaned back, nodding her head like a child and continued in her normal voice, "And the alcohol will tear down their beauty and their personalities." She sighed deep in her breast, sadly saying, "Some will turn to drugs to forget what they are doing, or because they find a man who wants to keep a paying thing, a whore. A man who will get her to use drugs until she needs them, then she might, will, have to work on the streets. She will, then, probably have two drug habits to support while her marketable assets, her very life, are wasting away." Madame leaned forward again; however, this time she did not lower her voice. "Her man would be the biggest drug." She sat back, rankled, "Without their youth and looks, they will no longer be in demand. They will, perhaps, become shoplifters, pickpockets, and even drug peddlers. Or eke out a living in dark saloons of the poorer neighborhoods."

She sighed, sadly. "Usually their families don't want them back. It is pitiful. Being a whore is a very poor substitute for real living. Perhaps a few will save their own money and make their own plans, and they will come out of this life trying to buy a new life. But very few have sense enough for that. I have been a mistress, but I have never been a whore. I have never been involved, and I do not want to be involved in their personal lives."

Now Burnett sighed, a deep breath of relief. His respect for Madame remained intact. "Well, Madame, you have already decided these things or you would not be going this far with plans for Eula Too. I am, now, glad you asked me."

"I am alone, Burnett. Who does not need a wiser head to guide them? I am fortunate I have you as my friend."

And so they talked for another hour or so about their plans before

Burnett rose and asked, "Well, is my room ready? Will I have to speak with that dreadful Greta of yours?"

Madame laughed, "No. Except to tell her what you want."

Burnett stood, "Good. I'm going to locate a more personable employee for you. There are hundreds of people, well trained, out there starving to death, who would give anything to have a job such as this. Lodging and meals!"

Madame knew Greta was standing somewhere close trying to hear what they were talking about. She said to Burnett as she rang the bell, "Well, Greta does keep everything and everyone quiet and running well. But we shall see."

When Greta did come to the room, she had indeed heard the last words and decided they were a compliment to her from Madame. She smugly thought, "My position is assured!" Feeling secure, the thought flicked across her mind to think of new ways to pilfer more food for her unemployed husband back in the dreary room they called home.

Madame lifted her hand to Burnett and called to Greta, "Greta, show Mr. Burnett to his rooms, the ones that look out over the most beautiful parts of the gardens."

Burnett had not stayed overnight since Greta had been hired several years ago. Greta looked at "Mr. Burnett" with wide startled eyes as she nodded her head in assent. "Yes, Madame."

As Burnett was leaving the room, Madame said, "Mr. Burnett, I would like to know what you think of her as soon as you have an impression. I intend to trust her with money. Going to banks and carrying cash to pick things up for me. Also, she will hear many private, important things when my own old friends come to visit me."

Greta was beside herself. Her mind was whirling trying to think of who it was Madame was talking about with this . . . "Is it me? Will I be handling money?" She looked quickly over her shoulder at Mr. Burnett who followed her through the golden oak wood hall of splendor that gleamed under several small crystal chandeliers along the way. "I will be nice to this nigger man because he must be important to Madame. But I'm not going in that room with him. He is not goin' to rape me!"

Greta was not afraid to receive parcels from Negro men at the back door, as she often did, but this was the only one who had come beyond that back-door limit.

When they reached the rooms Mr. Burnett was to occupy, Greta turned and fled. Mr. Burnett shook his head in amusement and went in to rest until dinner was announced.

When she was alone, Madame reached for her telephone and dialed a number. She intended to leave a message for another friend of hers who was a fine teacher, Mr. Leane. He was very poor, even as good a teacher as he was at the university. The Depression had brought everyone to some state of despair. Bad, hard times. She knew of other teachers tutoring in fine houses. This man was in much need of money because he was trying to support his family. Mr. Leane returned her call immediately.

"She is a Negro."

Mr. Leane did not hesitate. "She could be a striped two-headed person, Madame, and I would still die to have the job."

"You haven't asked the pay?"

"I will take anything. I have nothing."

"It will only be for about six months. She will need the basics: math, English, I think. You will decide when you have met her. When can you come? A week?"

Mr. Leane almost gasped as he looked down at his worn clothing hanging limply from his thin body. Several years of real poverty had stripped him of everything except the remains of one suit and one set of cheap, used underwear given to him by a friend. "You mean, I'm going to live there? At your house? To dine there? Food?" They both laughed a little. Madame because she understood the times; Mr. Leane laughed because he was happy for the help to his survival.

"If possible. If you decide—"

"Oh! Madame, it is assuredly possible. I will be happy to come and teach the young lady all I know."

Madame laughed softly, "We won't have time for all that. Good! Make it in a week. Your room will be ready."

Madame sat back, sighed with some satisfaction. Then she thought of her mother. "She could be my dearest friend, if she would let us be close again. If she would love me again. Perhaps I can go see about her during these next few busy weeks. Oh, I wish she would come here to live," she sighed again. Then, "On the other hand, maybe I don't want that."

All things were running smoothly at the house. Mr. Burnett and Mr. Leane took up most of Eula Too's day. Greta was helping her sister, Betyl, assure the efficiency of the household help, including the upstairs ladies and their maids. Madame took a deep breath and relaxed. During this time she decided to go see her mother.

When she arrived in Place, her mother, as usual, was full of accusations, recrimination, and invectives between bouts of crying. Madame and her mother were both miserable. Madame wanted to give love and was being hurt by her mother whom she felt was supposed to be close to her, love her. She was in despair. She was torn between staying in Place to make things better with her mother or to go back home.

One day, in the midst of one of their arguments, she said, "Mama, I love you. Leave the past in the past. What happened to my baby was not done to hurt you! It happened without any assistance from me! I was the one who lost my baby. I felt the pain in my heart and my body." She tried to step close to Mother Fontzl. "Mama, we are all we have. You have me, I should have you. We should be closer, not further apart."

The mother, miserable because she wanted her daughter to love her, didn't think clearly. Her tired mind was in the confusion old age can sometimes bring. Almost from birth she had been bewildered by life. She had no imagination that could help her see beyond her immediate vision: herself. And, too . . . she was jealous of her daughter, Elizabeth. The obvious symbols of success. Money. None (that she knew) of her dire warnings to Elizabeth had come true. She did love her daughter, but that love did not keep her anger from growing. Nor did that love stop the hatred that was always simmering in her empty breast long enough to receive the love her daughter brought to her. Though, somewhere in the recess of her mind, she knew her daughter loved her, that did not count to her. She would not move her mind out of the mangled, imagined past.

Madame's mother lived in that past with some comfort, while her daughter supplied the very things that kept her comfortable. Mrs. Fontzl's thoughts to herself were, "She owes me everything!" She cried out to Madame, "Don't give me anything! I don't need nothing of yours! Slut! Baby maker! Baby killer! You murdered your own child! We was poor when you were born, but I still gave birth to you!"

Mother didn't think about how she had never been hungry during the long Depression. She had spit no food out that she cursed and condemned. And she gave only a little food away to her friend and neighbor, Mrs. Green (Marion Green's mother), whom she really liked. Poverty does strange things to a person's mind. But Madame kept her mother from poverty.

Whenever Madame spoke to her mother of her love, Mother answered, "I'll never be close to you! You don't know how to love . . . and be close to anybody! You wasn't close to your own child!" Then a thought cut through all the mire in her mind as she looked at her own daughter. Her voice lowered as she struggled to say, "I do love you, Elizabeth, but I'm scared to love you too much." The good thought that had pierced her mind fled as the memory of her buried grandchild fought its way back. In her renewed fury, her voice raised again. "You bury things! You ain't here with me . . . and that child you got laying in the ground outside! You don't love nothin' but your own self!" Then she slammed her bedroom door. Gone, only for awhile.

Madame Elizabeth stood outside her mother's door. Like a child, a little girl. Heart-wrenched. Sobbing.

Later, in her bed, Madame cried long into the night.

When Madame was leaving the next morning to return to her own home, Mother came out of her room and suddenly grabbed her own child and held her. They were both in tears. Her mother crying tears from the past: the same, old, self-constructed, destructive past. Over the years, each time Elizabeth left, the mother was more afraid than ever that she would die and never see her daughter again. She did not know how to do a simple thing: believe the words and actions of her daughter. Old, rusty thoughts, emotions, feelings left in an aging mind can warp it. Make it tear down bridges to others, build dams where there is nothing to fear. Fighting, holding back what is most needed.

## Meanwhile

Solemn, serious, and in awe, Eula Too glided through her new life as in a dream. Listening, learning, questioning, laughing, and sometimes crying in frustration as new words and worlds crowded into her mind. She was happy! "How will I ever know how to pay Madame back? The blessing of all this?"

The last thing she did at night before falling into exhausted sleep was say, "Thank You, God, from the bottom of my heart." And she meant it, because she knew it was not just "luck," it was a Blessed opportunity. "And thank you, too, Madame."

*Unfortunately, being where she was, Satan was now interested in her. He owned almost everyone else living there and all the visitors to the ladies. Sometimes, when he hears words about "blessings," he just laughs and laughs. He is a master at disguising life.*

As Eula performed her duties, she would look at herself in a mirror, thinking, "I am learning! I have a new friend. Two! And I have a bath every day in that glorious hot, wet water. My hair is so nice, so clean and pretty. I am pretty! Oh, God, I am happy." Every now and then she felt a little dizzy from all the excitement in her life.

Mr. Burnett was very proud of Eula. She was, indeed, an innocent child turning into a very bright young woman almost right before his eyes. After he had gone home to New York, they spoke on the telephone often. She brightened his day and he welcomed her calls. One day, when he was answering one of her questions, she said, "All these things make my head so dizzy, I feel sick. But it goes away because I am happy." They laughed together about it.

Thoughts nagged at Eula somewhere in the back of her mind. Nights, when all was quiet, they stole into the front of her mind to be the last thoughts before she dozed off to sleep. Sometimes they woke her from sleep, completely. They were about her sister Earle, and her mother, her father. She didn't worry as much about the others.

*My mother thought of her mother as an old woman, but EulaLee was not yet thirty years old. And EulaLee had eleven children. She would, perhaps, probably, most likely, never get to fulfill her dream: Chicago. Can she be blamed for making no other choices, or is it . . . she had no other choices she knew of? Or just . . . were there actually no choices for her?*

# Chapter Ten

*

Madame returned to her well-run home and settled back into her usual routine. "I can't think of my mother all the time. I would go crazy. But, I must think of something to do! She should not be alone."

Soon after her return, she was speaking with Eula Too about her duties when Greta came rushing upon them, saying, "Madame! We have a emergency! Viola! Viola has tried to kill herself! Commit suicide! She is . . . with a baby. Pregnant! Her maid found her early this morning, but she wouldn't let her call on you! The maid didn't want to disturb you either! Bettyl found out and sent me to call you to come. I didn't want to disturb—"

Madame moved quickly, speaking as she sped toward the upstairs. "Are you a fool, Greta? I want to know, immediately, whatever happens in my house!" Striding quickly toward Viola's apartment and tightening her robe as she spoke, "How can I rest? What was that fool Viola thinking of? Herself, of course!"

She forgot Eula, but Eula followed on her heels. Madame suddenly stopped, turning to Eula. "Go . . . study. Read. Do the books!" Eula bowed her head and went back to her work, worrying about the woman, Viola, whom she hardly knew.

When Madame reached Viola's apartment, Rita, Melba, and Lana were all trying to soothe and quiet Viola. They stood aside as Madame approached the bed. Viola was vomiting and crying at the same time as she screamed "I want to die! Leave me alone! Oooooh, God, oh God!"

Madame sat on the bed, which was tossed and soiled, drenched with tears. Viola quieted a little as Madame took her hand. She could see the woman was very ill from whatever she had done to herself. "Call the doctor, Greta! Bettyl!" She bent to Viola, "What is the matter, Viola? What have you done to yourself?"

Snot mingled with tears as Viola said in a weak, angry voice, "I'm pregnant! That's what! And I know who the father is: Lionel! He always says he wants to take me away and we live together until he gets a divorce from that conniving wife of his . . ." She vomited again, wiped her mouth with the back of her sticky hand and looked up at Madame with tear-filled, hard, sad eyes.

"When I told him, he told me he didn't want a baby and I would have to get rid of it. That you would handle it again! This is my fourth pregnancy," she screamed. Then she cried. "I . . . I want my baby."

"Yes, yes," soothed Madame as she turned to Greta and said, "Have you called the doctor?"

"No, Madame. I waited until . . ."

Madame looked to Bettyl, the head housekeeper, "Will you do as I ask and as any fool could see is necessary? Immediately!"

Madame turned her attention to Lana, "You, help Greta and Melba straighten this room and clean this woman and the bed." She grasped Viola's unsteady hand, "Quiet down now. You will be alright. You may lose Lionel though. You believed him? You should know better. The lies he tells you are as good as the lies you tell him." Madame made the point by looking at the other ladies standing there. Rita had already gone back to her apartment. Madame sighed, "Use protection. Around his penis and around your minds!"

Greta returned, nodding her head. "He is coming immediately."

"I pay him enough." She turned back to Viola, "I will return after he is finished with your . . . operation, if it has gone that far. How many months are you?"

"Two or three . . . I forgot to count," Viola whimpered.

Madame rose to leave, "Always count. Too far and you could die." At the door she turned back, saying, "One more time. One more time with all this drama. One more pregnancy, and you will have to leave this house." Then she was gone.

. . .

Time seemed to fly for Eula Too between her lessons with Edward Leane, her duties, and her new friendship with the cook, Dolly. She really liked Dolly's son, Lester, the musician. He brought records for Eula to hear and they would dance. He liked touching Eula and dancing slow with her. In her youthful inexperience she became enamored of him. He encouraged her by asking her, often, to go out with him. In an exciting voice he would say, "You got to be there! You got to hear these fellas in person! C'mon! I'll show you some things will flat-out make your mind grow!" He smiled and leaned down toward her with the two teeth missing on one side of his mouth. "Make your fine body grow healthy, too!"

Dolly tried to discourage the visits. She knew life and she knew her son. But, she needn't have worried. Madame knew Dolly's son, also, and any dates were forbidden with words couched in soft denials of that freedom. "You are far too young. Remember strangers? We will go out one night soon after you have learned all you can learn from Edward. We will go out to hear first-class jazz. Lester will only take you to . . . dumps! And you are above that now."

Eula had been at Madame's house about three months when she began to feel sick every morning. Even having to vomit. Usually rushing to her classes, which were almost all over, she did not give it much thought. She did not think of her mother's morning sicknesses. What had happened to her in the rape didn't seem, to her, to be able to make a baby.

One morning, when Eula did think back, she could not remember having a menstrual period since she had left home. She became alarmed and decided to go see Madame. She did not want to ask anyone else. "Besides, Madame has a doctor," she thought.

Madame had an arrangement with a doctor who took care of all her ladies. Especially if they happened to become pregnant: "Get rid of the baby" was the rule. Usually, they did. If they didn't, they had to leave. She replaced them without hesitation. Even ladies who were her favorites. They thought she hated babies.

Eula Too was in her third month when she went to Madame. She walked, slowly, from her room through the beautiful halls made from beautiful woods, past the tapestries and paintings. She felt alarm that she might have to leave this dream house. "Well, I can not, will not, go back to my mama's house. But what will I do?"

When she reached Madame's door, she hesitated. She took a deep breath for courage. She knocked lightly, as she had been taught. Hearing the tinkle of the little bell Madame used to signal entry, Eula Too opened the door. Each time Eula entered these rooms she was struck anew. One entire wall was a huge mirror that reflected the richness of the room and doubled the impact of the beautiful shimmering satins and silks.

Madame, in a fluffy satin and lace bed jacket, sat in the middle of her bed surrounded by the latest fashion magazines. She frowned as she looked up, but smiled when she saw it was Eula Too.

"Oh, Eula! Yes? What is it? I was not expecting you. Has Edward Leane gone? We must celebrate the end of your studies. He gave me very good reports of you. What would you like for a graduation present? I'll give you a gift."

Eula sat down slowly, her face troubled. "I blive I have to talk to you about somethin'."

Madame smiled. "You have not learned to say *be-lieve* yet? And how to complete all *ings* at the end of a word?"

Preoccupied, Eula sighed and answered, "I thought I did."

"'I thought I had,' would be more correct. Well, you haven't. Try harder. Apply yourself." Her mood had changed. The smile was gone. "I have plans for you. I have spent quite a sum of money on you." As she looked at Eula's downcast face, her mood changed again, her voice softened, "What is it, Eula?"

Eula sighed, "Madame . . . I think . . . I don't know . . . Something is wrong with me. I haven't had a . . . period since I . . ."

Madame said softly, "A cycle."

"Since I have been here."

Madame thought a moment, then said, "You went through quite a shocking experience, Eula, perhaps that is why." She reached for her telephone as she said, "I'd better have my doctor have a look at you."

In a dull voice Eula said, "I'm . . . throwing up."

"Vomiting? You're vomiting?"

"Yes, mam. Two days in a row."

"Oh, my dear! That sounds like baby talk."

Eula looked up to see Madame's face, "Like baby talk?"

"Like you are going to have a baby."

"But . . . I haven't . . ."

A frown turned Madame's face ugly as she said, "But he did," pushing her magazines aside to reach for the phone. "I guess I'll call our Doctor Spill. He will know all about a baby."

Later, the old, handsome, richly dressed, illegal abortionist spoke with distaste of the brown girl he had had to examine. "She is pregnant. About three months I estimate. I don't like to handle these people. If I have to do it, I'd better do it as soon as possible. She is pretty far along."

Madame, thoughtful, shook her head, "No . . . no. I haven't decided that. I believe I will let her have the child."

Doctor Spill, surprised, looked at Madame over his glasses, waiting for an explanation. But none came.

Madame tilted her head, still thoughtful, and said, "No, you don't have to prescribe anything. She is only just getting healthy herself. I'll have my own doctor look at her for the term of her pregnancy." Doctor Spill left, taking bruised feelings with him.

Eula went back to her room entirely bewildered and perplexed. "I do not want to have that man's baby. I just got to where I can see some kind of future for myself. What will I do with a baby. What is wrong with Madame? She knows I don't want no baby. Any baby!"

When Madame returned to her room, she brushed the magazines angrily from her bed and flung herself across it. She looked up, as if toward God, and said, "I have lived . . . lived . . . lived and I am tired. Even of all the money. But I can not give it up. I have only lived over the top of life, not in it. I have not lived real life since I lost my child. What is all this importance of money and fucking about? Not life. Only love is life. Love between men and women, people. And babies. God? Are you really there? I no longer have love. Except I can buy anything I want. But I do not want anything. Except love . . . And love is lost to me. I want someone to call my own. Friendship is Eula. I have Eula. She has God . . . And a baby to come. I am lonely . . . so lonely. Who will ever love me . . . again? One thing I want now. We will have a baby. God, if you are there, please help us."

*One of Satan's strongest desires is for humans to have problems. He hates Love. Hatred empowers him. Love is his enemy. In passing he heard Eula Too. He heard Madame. A little tragedy in the making . . .*

*I understand Madame's reasoning. But however good a reason is . . . it is not an excuse.*

*The baby is not me. I am glad.*

# Chapter Eleven

*

The pregnancy that disgusted Eula Too only changed some of Madame's thoughts about Eula's future. Two days later they had occasion to talk again. Madame leaned back in her bed and reached for a cigarette. She only smoked in her room, privately. Also, to her, smoking made women ugly. Her smoking in front of Eula was a large step in her comfort in the friendship and her plans for the girl.

With a brooding look on her face, Eula Too was looking abstractly through the bedroom windows. Her mood was apprehensive as she looked from the original oil paintings of nature on the walls and then, outside, to nature's original work. She was thinking she would have to leave this haven, this new world.

The cigarette smoke curled around Madame's face as she thought about the future. "This baby." But, Madame was not frowning with displeasure. She looked at Eula with a faint smile on her face. "We shall have the baby."

Eula, surprised and disgusted, was speechless. "I know," she sighed at last.

Madame stubbed her cigarette out in the crystal ashtray. "I have been thinking. For a long time I have been wanting to do something with the basement. And I want you close to my apartment, but I need Greta close also." Then, as an afterthought, "I'm going to replace her . . . soon."

Eula didn't smile; she just shook her head no. "I don't want to have this baby. It's not my baby . . . it's his."

"It is in your body. I will start immediately on plans for the basement."

Eula was not understanding. "How soon must I leave? I'll pack my things, unless you want me to leave 'em."

"Leave them? What are you talking about? Leave?"

"Well, I know you won't want me here having a baby."

"But, don't you understand? I want you to have this baby."

"His baby."

"Your baby, too." She turned her head slightly, looking at Eula from the corner of her eyes. "A child is a blessing."

"I don't want this baby. I am young. I can have other blessings."

Madame looked directly at Eula, "You don't know what will happen to you in your life. You may not have another chance."

Gently, Eula answered, "Then I will have none. I didn't ask for this chance."

"You will be . . . all alone in your life."

"I don't care."

"You will. You cannot kill a child. It will be a great loss to you."

Eula thought of Miss Iowna Hart's words and how she was alone. Speechless for a moment, because all the words confused her, Eula stood up to leave and opened the door.

Madame persisted; she almost sounded desperate. Her voice battering Eula, she said, "You have been here almost three months. It is too late to abort the child. Don't worry. I will help you. I have already made calls to contractors to began designing new quarters for you to raise your baby in. They will start immediately."

Eula slowly turned back and sat down. She looked at the woman she had learned to admire, even love, and trust. She was bewildered and confused, but firm, as she said, "I don't want this child. I don't think I should have this child. I . . . hate its father. I might hate this baby."

Madame crossed the room to Eula, raising her from the chair and taking her in her arms, saying softly, but firmly, "You can never hate your child. I know you; you have no hate in you. We will love this blessing. You will see. Now, go to the kitchen and order something good you would like to have for lunch . . . and then rest . . . and read.

Do anything you like. Be sure and take the pills the doctor left for you. We must build this baby up."

Eula sighed deeply and turned to go. The last thing she heard Madame say was, "Trust me."

*Oh, fateful, sometimes true, but most times dangerous, ominous, untrustworthy, overused words. "Trust me."*

Lester had been dropping by more often to see Eula. Dolly, the cook, had told her son several times, "I done told you to stop coming by here botherin' that girl. You keep yourself in this kitchen! Don't even think about going nowhere up in this house! Stay where I can see you! Or go outside! And don't stay long!" Banging a pot or two, she added, "I don't know why she let you bother her noway!"

He had asked Eula several times about going out with him. He always found a way to put his hands on her or pulled her outside where they could talk alone. Eula was impressed with his big talk of success with his music and the famous people he knew. As he stroked her young, strong back, he tried to talk a hole in her ear. He really wanted to get to one of the white ladies. "White meat and money, too!" But they hardly looked at him when they happened to come into the kitchen and he was there. Other than being Dolly's son, they hardly knew he existed.

When Lester heard that Eula was pregnant, he backed off. Way off. "It wasn't me, Mama! I ain't had nothin' to do with that woman no kinda way!"

"I know that. Now, you stay 'way from 'round here. You can't find time to make a dime and even if you did you wouldn't give me a nickel! So you not gonna mess my job up! I work hard! And I intend to keep my job. I been here twelve years and gonna stay longer. I respect Madame. You stay 'way from here, 'less you want to see *me* 'bout somethin'!" Lester was leaving as she spoke.

. . .

Carpenters, electricians, plumbers, and interior designers soon transformed the basement into a two-bedroom apartment. There was a spacious bedroom with a tiled fireplace and its own large bathroom. One wall on the garden side was of glass, with patio doors, just as Eula had, hesitatingly, asked for. A second bedroom with its own bathroom. A lovely sitting room with a small brick fireplace and ample shelves for books and a Victrola! The small kitchen and pantry completed the new quarters.

Greta was so glad to get her old room back (which she fumigated), she even helped the cleaning girls clean the place after the workmen were, at last, gone. She helped Eula move her clothes (enviously, she wiped her nose on as many as she could). She also moved books into Eula's new abode (with disdain and suspicion because she knew colored folks couldn't read and, if they did read, they didn't understand a thing white people had written!).

Eula moved in, crying a little in her happiness. She thought of Miss Hart as she looked out of the glass wall, with the lovely drapes on each side, at the closeness of the trees, flowers, and birds, and stopped crying. Still a young person, she momentarily forgot the baby and just enjoyed the peace and beauty of her *own* apartment. One of the first things she did was get a frame and place the dollar bill in it that *he* had thrown at her the night of her rape. As she hung it on the wall in her bedroom she thought, "I'll never forget!"

"Why, if Mama and Earle could see me now."

She thought of the money she had saved, plus the money she had never spent even when she walked through some of the grand stores to pick up Madame's orders. She remembered their circumstances and her joy receded. "I'm going to send them some money through Miss Hart."

She had begun to show during the last few months and now she was big with child. Some nights, before she fell asleep, she would hold her stomach and cry softly. Her heart confused her: She didn't want her baby while, at the same time, she loved it.

. . .

*Adolf Hitler was ravaging Europe. The Japanese bombed Pearl Harbor. The United States was at war. It was felt by quite a few in America. The mothers and fathers, the wives and children of* all *sides were the great losers of fathers, sons, brothers, and husbands in the World War II. Satan was so thrilled he could have died, but God's purpose was not completed, it was not time for Satan's end . . . yet. He had more wars to help men create and he looked forward to it with relish. Wars, famines, turbulence of hate and fear, pestilence, oceans of tears and mountains and canyons of sorrows.*

Time passed as Eula did shopping for Madame in Madame's favorite stores. She handled all the banking and attorney errands for Madame and, still, kept Madame company. Madame was glad when Eula seemed happy. But sometimes, in the middle of one of their discussions, Madame would become jealous of the baby when she would see Eula, absentmindedly, gently rubbing her stretching stomach.

*A female child was born around this time and named Ha. The parents were poor farmers eking out a living in the beautiful land of China. The father did not want the new daughter. One of the reasons was because she would be of no help in the fields he had to work for his landlord. A male child would have been a blessing. As the mother, Peony, watched him, he lifted the clean little rag-blanket and looked at the tiny baby girl, spat, and walked away. The mother, exhausted and fearful of her husband, pulled her little daughter closer to her own warm body and nursed her with breasts that already looked dry. "You shall live, my little Ha. Your father is a good man, but he is a poor man. Your mother will make you live. I am your mother. Now, suck. Suck hard. We shall laugh at ole ugly life."*

*Ha would, in later years, seek a Place in Life. I will tell you more.*

Eula gave birth in her new apartment in due time. Exhausted after thirteen hours of labor, she looked down at her little baby. She could still feel the pain in her body. It felt as though her body had been raped again by the baby of the same man who had raped her the first time. Sweat lay like a blanket over her face and body. There was hatred in her heart as she cried out, "I will never have another baby again!" Her only memory of sex was of rape-sex. As she tried to take a deep, labored breath, her voice dropped, but repeated, "Never."

*I cannot see into the future. But . . . then, how will I be born?*

It was a girl. Madame pronounced her name to be Jewel, as she cooed and tried to soothe the crying baby. She could not stop hovering over the peach-colored baby and smoothing, with a gentle hand, the head thickly covered with smooth, black hair.

Time passed. As Eula nursed her baby for the first nine months, she wondered how to keep up with her duties and still take proper care of Jewel. She spoke, weekly, with Mr. Burnett. He knew the way Madame felt about the new baby. He told her, "I am sure you will have nothing to worry about. If you do, you let me know right away." Madame told her, "Don't worry. I can do some things and Greta can do some things. We will be just fine. Feed the baby!"

Bettyl, head housekeeper and Greta's sister, had left Madame's employment a few months after Jewel was born. She married and went to work where her husband was employed. Madame had not replaced Bettyl yet, but had divided her duties and power, temporarily, between Greta and Eula until Eula could do more.

One morning, about a month after the birth, Greta decided to visit Eula's apartment. She envied Eula having a baby she would not have wanted for herself. "I want to see this new little ugly, black baby."

Eula had been sitting beside the huge, nature-filled window, nursing her baby. Her eyes glowed from her now rapidly growing love for Jewel. She smiled as she looked down upon the little body with the hungry mouth nursing at her breast.

As she nursed her baby, she was thinking how Greta could and would create more problems for her in the new position. "I know that woman still does not like me because she is jealous of Madame. I know she wants this apartment for her own self! I don't want to lose my wonderful apartment."

At that moment Greta knocked and, without waiting for an answer, entered Eula's apartment. Eula turned her head toward the sound, thinking it was Madame, as usual. But it was wide-eyed Greta.

Eula, with narrowed eyes, watched her come forward and look at the baby. Greta's eyes opened wide, gaping at the baby, whose skin was almost as light as her own.

Eula looked up at Greta, forgetting her usual self-control. Suddenly she wanted Greta to see the hatred *(which came from fear)* which had been boiling in her almost from the beginning of their meeting. Eula could not help herself. Her quiet, dark eyes brimmed with her hatred and fear. "I must protect my baby, too," she thought.

She stared at Greta with grave detestation. Greta stepped back from that look, saying, "I . . . I wanted . . . to see the baby. Such a . . . nice baby for you. The father . . . I . . . I . . . must get back to work." She left, quickly. Eula breathed again. She had been holding her breath.

**M**iss Iowna Hart had walked to the little village-town, Tweenville, to call and tell Eula, "Child, your poor father has passed away: He's gone." *Ahhhh, the poor man, my grandfather, who had been so tired so long, had died.* Eula cried, hard, until Madame reminded her it would affect the baby's milk. She held her tears back, sniffling, not knowing that suffering would affect the baby's milk anyway. But, suffering begins early: Life is life.

Eula did not resent her father for dying; she had loved him. But, she did not know how she could leave for the funeral, take the baby to that horrid place and still take care of her duties for Madame—duties which expanded every week. She was now, partially, overseeing the ladies' apartments, the main house, and her own house.

The new duties did not bother her. The ladies, for the most part, seemed very interesting. She had been wanting to get a closer look at them. Two, Melba and Viola, preferred Greta and said so to Eula Too. "It is nothing personal, dear, it's just that she knows what we like and don't like, already, so . . ."

Rita, one of the remaining two, was very interested in Eula Too because she had never known a colored person, closely, other than the cook, Dolly. And she didn't really know Dolly. She welcomed Eula, and because she did, Lana did also. Rita asked Eula, "How did you get a name like Eula Too for heaven's sake?"

Eula Too laughed, "It's a long story, but I will tell you sometime. It's not very interesting though. You can just call me Eula," she smiled. "Now. Greta will do most of the overseer work upstairs. I will just be here if you should need someone when Greta is busy at something else." The two ladies glanced sidewise at each other and lightly laughed together, as though they knew something Eula didn't.

Now . . . she had to leave Chicago. She was so tired from handling the accounting, banking, and shopping duties, plus taking care of Jewel; nursing, washing, and cleaning. "But," she thought, as tears filled her eyes, "that's my daddy. My father. And I sure am going to go see that he gets a proper burial."

She didn't even discuss it with Madame. After she was packed, she went to see her and said, "My father has died. I have to go. I will call you, if I have a chance. If not, I'll be back as soon as possible."

Madame stared at her, saying, "Leave the baby. Leave Jewel here. She is only nine months old. Too young for travel. She's almost weaned. I'll just have Dolly make a milk formula. Greta can help watch Jewel."

"No, I can't do that. My family has never seen her. I need to see my own mother, and she needs to see my baby. So . . . I'm taking my baby with me."

Finally, resigned, Madame arranged for Paul, the chauffeur, to drive Eula to her old home. "Wait for her and bring her back." But Eula told Paul, "No need you waiting around here. I'll call when I am ready." And so it was.

. . .

People stared at the limousine that was trying to drive up the narrow road toward the several small houses that included Eula's old home. Finally, the automobile could go no farther so Eula stepped out to walk, holding her baby, smiling widely at her family. She had not known she missed them so much.

While Paul was reaching for Eula's suitcase, Earle recognized Eula and ran screaming with joy toward her. When she realized Eula was holding a baby! her joy increased for some reason. She was certainly used to babies, but this was Eula!

Earle took the baby from Eula's arms even before she hugged Eula. Eula was hugging her though. Earle was thinking, "My beloved papa is gone and just look what heaven has sent us. Eula!" They walked the short distance to the now lopsided house, with Earle holding the baby, kissing and cooing to her.

EulaLee, slowly, came through the battered doorway to see what all the commotion was about. She headed, carefully, for her big, wooden chair her late husband had built for her great bulk. All her upper teeth were gone, so a toothless smile slowly grew on her face. She stared at the limousine Eula had come home in.

As Eula Too came closer to her, she stared at her clothes, stockings, and shoes and her coat. Her eyes took in the suitcase. She thought, "A suitcase! There must be more stuff in that!" She looked back at the limousine. "What has that girl been doin'?"

Eula Too was opening her arms to hug her mother even as she was crying for her father. She held EulaLee tight. When she stepped back to get a good look at the mother she loved, her heart broke for the things she knew her mother, in her lazy ignorance, had been through. She moaned, "Oh, Mama," and took as much of her mother as she could back into her arms.

EulaLee loved Eula Too, that was her child, but she had so many children to love, and so many needs, her attention went to other things. She wanted to ride, for the first time since their running-away trip in the broken-down automobile, in that long, black car Eula Too came home in.

Over Eula Too's shoulder, the mother watched as Paul shut the trunk and the doors to the car, then backed, carefully, down the hill. Away from all the hands reaching out to touch . . . just touch, that beautiful automobile. He thought to himself, "I know why she ran away. She had to!" In fact, he had run away from a home similar to Eula Too's. Poor times for everybody that had not already been rich. The new war had made a big difference though. Paul now made plenty of money with his sidelines and tips from the ladies upstairs for small favors.

"I sure wanted to try an' ride in that car," EulaLee thought to herself as she watched the big, shiny car back slowly down the narrow road. Unashamed, she looked at the real, medium-sized emerald ring on the finger of one of Eula Too's hands, and a dusky gold band on the other hand. "Real gold!" They were Madame's gifts.

Now . . . EulaLee greatly missed her husband. She even loved him more, now that he was dead. And gone. "Who gonna take care of me now? All these here grown-ass children ain't worth a damn! Only one of all them been gone done ever sent me a cryin' dime!"

Eula Too helped her mother through the little lopsided door into the house, so they could talk in peace after she put her things down. Earle was fending off the eager hands, but she couldn't hold the baby, show the baby, and keep the ready hands away much longer.

After the greetings and hugs to her brothers and sisters still at home, and then to the little ones who were new to her, Eula Too sat down. The group gathered around her as she opened a bag and tried to find a gift for everyone. She couldn't. "Well, I'll go to the store later and get something for those I missed!"

EulaLee quickly and happily thought, "Money. She got some money."

After awhile EulaLee beckoned Eula Too away from her siblings. Earle took little Jewel from Eula Too's arms as soon as she had finished nursing. So Eula Too followed as her mother led her into her own old bedroom.

EulaLee heaved herself on the now slumping, scarred bed so lovingly handmade by her dead husband. She said, "I need to talk to ya."

Eula looked down upon the ragged, food-smeared blanket and sadly thought of how she had been living while her family suffered.

"Girl . . . Why, no, how you got all these things? Where you get them clothes? And who car is that?" Before Eula Too could fix her mind for the answer, EulaLee continued, "You ain't one of them womens what sells their body for money . . . are you?"

Eula Too laughed as she thought of the ladies at Madame's. "No, Mama."

"What so funny?" She waited. Eula Too didn't have an answer. So she continued, "Well, I see you got that baby. You married? Where the daddy?"

Quickly saddened, Eula Too answered, "No, Mama. I'm not married."

"Then whatever you did was a sin, Eula Too. Where the daddy?"

Sighing, Eula Too answered, "Well . . . it wasn't my sin, but . . . yes, Mama. And I don't know, and I don't care, where the daddy is."

"Well, you got money for all these here nice things for yourself. If you ain't no loose woman, didn't he give it to you?" Her tone changed, became harder as she tested her control over Eula Too. "But why can't you help your family more? You knew we was strugglin' tryin' to keep up with things. Food. Chilren. Your father killed hisself for your family."

"Yours and his family, Mama. You have more children than I do. You have a grown son, Jesse, here now, and—"

EulaLee inturrupted, "Ain't no work here. You always knew that! 'Sides, he's lazy."

"Then let him go where there might be work. There is a war going on and they want everybody."

"Most all your brothers and sisters done gone. These few 'round here now . . ." She stopped, thoughtfully, then said, "We got one boy, Tommy, your father taught him 'bout that furniture makin' and he do that. But these white folks ain't payin' nothin', you know that!"

"Then let him go somewhere to school, or work as a helper in a furniture factory job. If he is as good as Papa was, they'll be glad to give him a job."

EulaLee looked at her namesake child, thinking, wishing, she had learned more about her daughter when she was home, how to control her more. She was the same way with almost all her children after the third one was born. She said, "What you gonna do? Send all my children who is still at home . . . tryin' to help they mama . . ." She paused to let that sink into Eula's mind, "away from me? Leave me here all alone, scuffling with them last few younguns?"

"Mama, I was just trying to—"

"Eula Too, I don't need no help thinkin'! I need money. We all need money! Like what you are spendin' on them clothes for yourself! Who that car b'long to that you came here in? How come you don't offer me to come live with you? Where you livin' anyway?"

"Chicago."

"I gave you that idea to go to Chicago! Why don't you do your own duty by me and take me there? Take care of me, your mama?"

Eula Too looked at her mother and remembered: "Mama was not always like this. Mama was nice, in the beginning. Babies and troubles have done this to her. Life, I guess, just life and ignorance." She said to her mother, "I did my duty to you when I was here, Mama. I raised about eight or nine of your children, my sisters and brothers, for all my life 'til I was fifteen years old."

EulaLee interrupted again, "That mean you finished helpin' me?" It was hard for her to cry because she was so glad to see her child who had run away. But, she squeezed out some tears, partly real, partly just needed for Eula Too. "Your daddy gone now. Gone on 'way from here. Done left me. I ain't got no help but your brother, Tommy."

"I've been sending you money from time to time, Mama."

"Why you got to send my money through somebody else hands? You don't want me to know your address? Shit! Earle got to be the one bring it to me from that ole lady. 'Sides, it ain't enough! You don't have to spend all that money on yourself. You could send more here to home." She waved her fat fleshed arm around, "Look at this here house! It's fallin' apart! It's nasty . . . dirty. We can't get it clean no matter how hard we try. It's just old and done for. I ain't got no clothes even. We just can't do no better."

Eula Too raised her voice over her mother's loud lament. "Mama, Mama, you used to do for yourself. You made some of the clothes for yourself and us. A man, my daddy, is lying in that funeral home 'cause he worked himself to death for a bunch of kids. You don't even know where all of them are to tell them he is dead. He did all he could for you . . . and for them! You laid there and had so many babies, let him make so many babies, you ran me off. Tired! Women around here know some things they can do to protect themselves from having so many babies." She shook her head, sadly, and lowered her voice. "Now you want my help. More of my help. 'Cause you say you couldn't 'help' yourself. You could have taken in sewing during every nine months you waited for a baby to be born. Daddy got you a secondhand sewing machine from the man he worked for. You could have learned to knit, crochet, and then sold things. To help him. Miz Thompson, just cross this thing you all call a street . . . she did it!"

EulaLee was hurt. She knew some of these things were true. She had had dreams. She looked around herself and saw the reality. For real. She had thought, many times, "How did I get here in my life?" And now, her own child had told her, and she knew it was mostly true, but, "Eula Too don't know it all. She ain't lived it, yet."

She said to Eula Too, "You are my chile and you gonna sit up here and talk to me like this?"

"Mama, I love you. But . . . don't I have anything coming to me from you, except giving me birth and a lot of years of hard work? I'm all alone now, except for a helpless baby. I need my money myself, still I send you some every month. Mama, I got a future. And I'm going to keep it. I want to keep going to school. I want to be more independent."

"You go to some school? At your age? Are you that dumb? And you got a baby, now!"

"That baby is why I have to go to school, maybe college. I have to be independent! I have to raise that baby." Eula Too got up to hug her mother, lovingly, because she knew there was so much more to her mother's life than just learning to knit, sew, and crochet. There was the daily survival that didn't always have anything to do with money. "I love you, Mama. But you have got to help a child love you sometime. If I had stayed here . . . I'd be hating you by now. I'd have no life . . . for myself or for my baby. Probably have no job either."

"As my child, as my daughter, you got to share—"

"Mama, as I used to hear you tell other people, 'You made your bed . . . now, you have to lie in it.'" She hugged her mother again and softly said, "I can't take you with me. You have eaten yourself out of many things. You are too . . . large. You are not well. You used to have a good mind. I know it. But the thing you used to do most was have babies. Daddy is gone and you are older, so even that is not left for you to do. But, I bet, if you really thought about it, and talked to Miss Iowna Hart, you might be able to come up with something you could do to help yourself make . . ."

EulaLee saw where all that was leading, and she didn't want to hear it. All her hope in life was gone. There was, now, only fear for the future. She had spent her life on a job that did not pay retirement. (*Very few jobs did at that time. Poor people struggled . . . forever, 'til death did them part from this cold earth. Until Franklin D. Roosevelt.*) She said, "That's alright! My son is gonna help me."

Eula Too shook her head and held her mother tighter, "Don't take Tommy's life, Mama. He will not like you, one day, maybe. He may realize his life is passing away . . . over another person's mistakes. He can help you some, but . . . let him go away and learn to be more than a babymaker and an alcoholic. Daddy finally turned to that, you know, in his misery. Besides, Tommy might get a good wife one day and she may take him away from this forsaken place, somewhere to make a life. Like you and daddy started out to do in the beginning of your life together."

Thick furrows appeared in EulaLee's forehead as she thought of her daughter's words. She did, truly, love Eula Too and all of her children. They were all she had. She thought of her dead husband and the early hopes and dreams they had dreamed together. Real tears began to quietly fall over the rims of her eyes. A sob caught in her throat as she rested her head in her daughter's arms and thought, "Oh, God, You know I do need some help. I wisht I had'a remembered to be wise in my youth. But, God, I'm so glad she is wise in hers."

Eula Too was a saver of money. She saved all she was paid because Madame's house accounts took care of food and, of course, her lodging. In all the months she had been there, she had saved a tidy sum. She was able to raise her father's burial ritual up from a wrapped body placed into the ground, to a decent coffin in a sunny sometime, shady sometime grave with abundant flowers. Some people came who had had no intention of attending. "I got to see if what I heard is true!" Even a tombstone was paid for with delivery promised in a few weeks. EulaLee, in her new dress, was pleased and proud among her friends.

Miss Iowna Hart was at the funeral. She looked a little tired, but she looked well. She was very happy to see Eula Too and know she was alright.

After the funeral, she saw the baby, Jewel. She held the baby a moment, saying, "This baby is beautiful. I hope she will be as beautiful on the inside as she is on the outside, like her mama." She looked over the baby at Eula Too, "I know she is going to have a good education!"

She handed Jewel to Earle, who was always hovering near Jewel, arms reaching for her. She asked Eula Too, "Will I have a chance to talk to you while you are here, dear?"

Eula hugged her, saying, "Miss Hart, I have been here three days and I have been on my way to your house every minute of that time!" They laughed and hugged again. Miss Hart noticed Eula Too's voice and diction. "Well, like you wrote, you've been doing something right. I'm glad you told me about Jewel. But, how did a baby come into the picture so fast?"

Eula Too opened her mouth, but Miss Hart stopped her. "Hush. Don't tell me now. Wait until you come to see me, then we can talk over some tea. You did a lovely, wonderful thing for your father, Eula. I'm proud of you like you were my own daughter, child."

"I feel like your own daughter, Miss Hart. You were an important part of my birth into a new life."

That evening, when Eula Too could get away, she left her family, with all their friends eating the food she had provided and some they had brought. She went to see Miss Hart, smiling as she followed the old worn path to her favorite teacher and friend's house.

The tea had been prepared and they sat in the comfortable kitchen eating Miss Hart's delicious tea cakes. Eula had been bringing her friend up to date on all that had happened to her since she had walked away from her old home. Miss Hart had alternately *ohhhh* and *ahhhh*'d, sighing for what her young friend had endured. "Eula Too, Eula Too, Eula Too . . . Well, you have been blessed, child. You have come through all that and met a good, kind friend. You have a baby, Jewel, but that is not the worse thing that could have happened on that road to Chicago. Do you thank God?"

"Every day for every thing. I have not forgotten what you taught me, Miss Hart. And I read lots of books. I try to read the books that will give me, teach me, some wisdom. The longer I live in this world, the more I know that you need to know all you can in order to make it in any way livable. I know some people survive without reading a single book, but knowing things about life can put you ahead of the things in life that can come up and ahead of the games that some people seem to have to play on you. Knowing the experiences of others can, kind'a, prepare you for what might happen to you."

"That's true, Eula. And, too, you may think that house you live in is a nice, beautiful place to live in, but, child, it is still nothing but a whorehouse. You remember what I showed you in the Bible; bad associations spoil useful, clean habits! Stay far away as you can from them people! Unless you can help them. Because there is something about life they do not know or they would not be there doing what they are doing! I know times were hard. But, they were hard for everybody! And, Lord knows, women didn't have but a few choices in this man's world, couldn't hardly own nothing nor be nothing but a wife! A glorified housekeeper and babymaker! And that wasn't too glorified either! For any woman, any color, but I'm not especially speaking of the rich. A poor woman, or even middle-class woman, couldn't hardly get into a college to learn nothing that would make her independent! Unless it was to be a teacher, and that didn't pay enough to make nobody independent; it barely, very seldom, kept you from paycheck to paycheck! But, some women made other choices, did something else with their lives. It can be done. You can do it!"

"I plan to, Miss Hart. I'm saving every cent I can. I don't know what I am going to do, because I have the baby now, but I will think of something! I've got a good job and I can plan while I decide what I want to do."

Miss Hart sighed, shook her head, sadly, and said, "I have to say this to you, Eula Too. Try to hear me out. Now, I know you are living in that beautiful house and all the ladies there look beautiful to you. You have told me how the land is full of trees and flowers, birds, squirrels, and everything else; that is beautiful, too. But always remember, Satan does not catch people by showing what he really is. People do just what Satan does; make a thing look so good or feel so good, 'til you can't believe there could be harm and pain in it. But there is!"

Miss Hart took a sip of her tea and looked at Eula Too to see if she was listening. She asked her, "Am I boring you or bothering you talking 'bout these things?

Eula shook her head no, and said, "Miss Hart, the longer I am in this world, the more I realize I need all the wisdom and good sense I can get."

So Miss Hart continued talking, "I'm just going to say this and I will be through, dear. The Bible says Satan looked beautiful, but was evil on the inside. He was a liar and a stealer of lives! He makes his things *look* beautiful. But once you are hooked, you realize the whole truth; it is ugly and unhappy. When God created Adam and Eve and she listened to Satan and disobeyed God, and Adam listened to her and disobeyed God, they suffered. No more paradise. Then they had

Abel and Cain. Now, listen at this: Four people on earth, and the first two made wrong choices, the third one, Cain, was a murderer because of envy and lack of love. Abel was trying to do God's will and he was killed because of that. It is just like in today's world."

Miss Hart came to the point. "I'll be straight with you, from my little experience: Pussy is imperfect. It may be good as from can to can't, but people get killed over it. Die about it! Will kill for it! Women can sell it because it is so good! Satan takes such an advantage of that kind of danger. Even if you are not selling it, you can die about it. Let a woman or a man be married, and you just watch and see what their husband or wife does if they find out their married partner is going to bed with somebody else!

"Now, child, you are living and working around all these different emotions and possibilities. Around human beings, Lord, anything can happen and usually does. You just remember, Satan sets people up for bad, evil things to happen to them. Don't you make any quick decisions. Wait until you see more of the world! You will see everything I just told you! And watch out for the liars! They are dangerous to themselves and everybody else around them. There are no white lies. Just some lies are not as dangerous as others. White lies are seeds that may grow to be big dangerous lies!"

Miss Hart sighed and reached across the table and placed her hand over Eula's. "I know I talk too much, but I don't have the time I used to have to talk to you." Eula leaned toward Miss Hart and clasped her little hand.

Miss Hart smiled at her young friend, saying, softly, "I wish you could do something about little Earle. She is talented. And she is smart! She is cute and it's no telling how long she can hold out against all the male eyes that are thinking on her. Can't you take her with you? So she can go to a real school? Isn't there some job for her near where you are? Not with the ladies you work with, but a little maid's job somewhere else? Or something? With you there, I wouldn't worry so much about her. These boys and men around where your mother lives, some of them are dangerous to little blossoming girls."

"I've been thinking of that, even before I came back here."

Miss Hart smiled at Eula with love shining from her eyes. "Good."

"I need someone who will really love Jewel to take care of her so I can do my work faster and better. I have my own apartment, like I told you, and I have plenty room for her. I'm going to ask Mama when I go home, because I have to leave here very soon. In the morning, I hope. This evening, I'm going to walk down and call for Paul to come get me."

Miss Hart leaned back and laughed softly, "Lawdy Jesus! Girl, you got a car you can call on! There is nothing like the future in your life." Her body jerked forward, "But don't *ask* your mother; you better *tell* her, because she will not want Earle to go away. She wants all her children to stay around her and help her."

They talked another hour or so, Eula trying to learn what problems Miss Hart was having, to see if she could help. "Oh, I'm alright. Times just changing, that's all. The older white farmers were my friends, always kind'a good, was kind to me. But their children, the younger generation, don't hurt me, just could care less about me. Those that didn't leave for the war have gone away to college or to the cities to learn another business. Farmers didn't fare well at all during the Depression. Those that are still here, remained behind to tend the dairy business or their pa's logging business. They want me to move, to release my hold on this last acre of my land. They say it's sitting right in the middle of their big-business land."

"What will you do?"

"What can I do? Where else would I go? That little bit of money they're talking about wouldn't take me nowhere. Besides, I know my acre is worth more than they are telling. I pray about it. I know some of them aren't trying to really hurt me, but you can't tell what Satan might tell them to do one day! When colored folks got something somebody else wants . . . well . . . you know."

The two old friends sat and mulled that over together for a while. Eula knew Miss Hart was talking about it as if it wasn't much to worry about, but she also knew Miss Hart was scared. She knew that teacher retirement check sometimes didn't come. They wanted to stop sending them at all. Miss Hart didn't like to talk about it.

When Miss Hart went to get Eula's coat, Eula Too slid some money in the sugarbowl for Miss Hart to find when she was long gone. "I've got to remember to send her some money every month, so I can be sure she eats!"

They hugged tightly in the entryway, because they did not know how soon they would meet again. Then Eula was gone.

Eula Too took the long way around so she could do some thinking as she walked. She walked all the way down to the little drugstore so she could use the phone. She dialed Madame's private number. With a tired smile in her voice, she said, "Madame? I am tired and weary and ready to return." Madame said nothing except, "I think it will take Paul about two hours to get there. Be ready: he does not want to wait . . . there."

When Eula returned to the house, the visitors had all left. The youngsters were fighting over the food left on the stove and table. Hiding it for later. Earle was lying on her pallet in the corner of Mama's room with Jewel asleep in her arms and Mama was sprawled across her bed.

Mama, EulaLee, was laid back, smiling, thinking of how she had entertained the neighborhood and church in her own home. "They ain't never had that much food, good food, at their house! They gonna always remember me for that!"

As Eula Too sat on the bed, her mother raised her head to see who it was. "So, you decided to come back from the ole lady's house? You stayed a long time! We missed you. I needed you here. I thought you were only gonna stay a minute or two."

Eula Too took the deep breath she always seemed to need when she spoke with her mother and said, "I had to make a call, so I can get picked up and taken home."

"Home? This your home!"

Eula Too waited a moment, as she reached over to take her

mother's hand, then said, "I might as well tell you now. I have asked Earle to leave with me. I have a little job for her to help herself, and she needs to go to school."

EulaLee struggled with her weight, trying to sit up in the sagging bed. "What you saying? You talked to Earle? Earle don't make no decisions 'round here! You can go on an' do what you want to, since you gonna do that anyhow, but you ain't takin' none other of my children 'way from me!"

"Think of Earle, Mama. She could get out of this . . . place. She could find a new place in life. Decent, clean, a future. A better life."

EulaLee tightened her lips, then said, "She can find that 'round here. You don't know what's gonna happen!"

"Yes, I do and you do, too."

"She too young to leave home!"

"You were fourteen when you left home and got married. I'm going on seventeen, but I was fifteen when I left here. Earle must be fourteen now, so she can decide. I am her sister. I'm not going to let anything happen to her."

EulaLee sneered, said softly, "You couldn't help yourself from gettin' that baby. And you ain't like me; you ain't even no Mrs. yet!"

Eula Too stood up, a little angry at her mother for fighting a dumb battle. "She can stay here with you and with your other children. That's what you got around here. Or she can go with me with my one child and get an education and make a life for herself better than any she will ever get here! Mama, why you make me talk to you like this?" She turned to Earle, saying, "We talked about this. What do you want to do? The car will be here in two hours. I'm going to be ready to go."

Mama and Eula Too watched as Earle gently lifted the baby, Jewel, off her arm so as not to wake her, then got up, saying, "I ain't got no clothes to pack. My back is my suitcase. I just got a few pictures I drew and a plant from a seed me and Miss Hart planted. I want to take them with me. But that's all." She turned to EulaLee, saying, with finality, "I'm going, Mama."

EulaLee gasped, groaned, waved her arms, and gave up.

Soon, people crowded around the pretty, shiny car when the limousine moved slowly up the narrow road to them. Amidst the crowd, Eula Too was holding Earle's hand, leading her to the car. Finally, she took Jewel from Earle's arms and pushed her gently into the car. Earle looked back over her shoulder at the empty chair her mother usually sat in. They had said their good-byes already, but still . . .

EulaLee didn't come out. Everything was over anyway. She was in her bedroom, counting the money Eula Too had pressed into her hand as she was leaving. They thought they understood each other. Eula Too understood her mother better. Being greedy was not why EulaLee caressed and held tightly to the money as she tried to think of a place to hide it. And she didn't want to hold Earle back, she was just afraid. Afraid she might need her. Or afraid she, herself, would end up alone. She was poor. And she had wiped all her choices out, except two: pride and try.

*Money, to the poor, becomes sacred. To be without money in this world is too dangerous. Money is, sometimes, your only protection. If you have no God, it can be even worse. It can, finally, come down to what a human will do to get some money and what they won't do for money. Choices. Some people sneer and laugh, calling people stupid when humans call on God, but they would do better thanking God that some humans believe in God. Think! What would the world be like if humans didn't know about loving their neighbor. And about the shalt not kill. All of the Ten Commandments, in fact. Take them from the world and all you have left are killing fields and hate. The world seems full of hate. Satan, the great propagandist, the very first liar, with his representatives that have lived on earth since Cain. He has seen to that! There is a fine line that separates sinners from Satan's representatives. One has a chance. The other is lost. Learn why, if you have opportunity.*

# Chapter Twelve

*

Earle moved into Eula Too's apartment with such silent ease people hardly knew she was there for the first month or two. Her eyes and mouth were agape at the wonder of such a life. For anyone! No one had ever received her like Madame had before. She forgot Miss Hart momentarily. She tried to control her enchantment and gratitude. She pressed her hands to her breast lest she explode. She even had her own bed. A real bed. A beautiful room with her own bed! Ahhh, the beauty, the beauty of it all!

Eula ordered some not too expensive, but good, clothes for her right away. She insisted Earle take a bath every day. But, there was no need to worry about it, Earle loved the water, a whole tubfull of her own, in the room right next to the clean, blue and yellow bedroom she slept in. Every day, she said to herself, over and over, "I live here! I live here! This my room! Lord, Jesus, You are good to me!"

Things settled down, and during the day Earle took care of Jewel and read the books Eula gave her to study. During most evenings, Eula studied with Earle and gave her little tests. She brought art books down from Madame's library for Earle to study. The next time Eula was sent to the city on an errand, she bought art paper, pencils, and paints. "I don't want her to get bored or get interested in anything else here."

While Eula was gone, Madame had started building a stairway, narrow and circular, from the upstairs down to Eula's apartment. Madame liked Earle, so far. At first she had worried about her precious art books, but she saw how Earle revered art and was in such awe of the books; Earle washed her hands before handling them. Madame also watched her with Jewel.

Earle paid a bit of homage to Madame, too. "I live in a very nice white woman's house, but it's my sister I work for! And my sister pays me!" She was always asking Eula, "What more can I do?" The answer was always, "Just keep doing what you are doing. You really are a big help to me. You'll learn what to do to help yourself if you keep studying!"

When Earle asked Madame, "Madame, mam, is there somethin' I can do for you? Some work?"

Madame answered, "Just keep taking care of our baby like you are. That's good enough. I see you like art. Someday I may take you to a real museum. Your little drawings show talent. We might get an art instructor for you. You can't go off to school, because we need you for Jewel." But Earle didn't want to go off to school. She thought she hated school. She wanted to stay right there in that house.

Earle met and liked the cook, Dolly, and Dolly liked the bright-faced young girl. They became friends, talking softly in the kitchen before the house awakened. Earle wasn't sure how to feel about Lester, Dolly's son. He liked to tease her, play with her even after his mother warned him to stop. And Earle didn't like the look in his eyes when he bent down to look in her eyes, but soon decided he was harmless as long as she was inside the house.

Some afternoons Earle opened the patio doors and took Jewel out in the buggy for a walk in the garden. On one of those occasions she saw two of the ladies in all their brilliant color. In their gorgeous spring frocks of fluffy pinks, blues, and gold, they resembled butterflies come to life as women.

The ladies saw her and the baby buggy and strolled over to see the baby. They looked the baby over, and Earle looked them over. She was in awe of all their beauty as the sun shone down upon them, creating a brilliance that seemed to, pleasingly, hurt Earle's eyes, which were unused to such brightness. They didn't say much to Earle, except "Hello" and "May we see the baby?" The dark-haired one, Rita, smiled at Earle, saying, "What a lovely baby!" Then they strolled away, their heads close together, their voices nearly hushed.

Earle called after them, "Where do you live?"

They turned and, again, the brunette, Rita, said, "Why, right where you live. Upstairs. I may come down to visit the baby soon. My sister has a baby about that size." Then Rita turned back to Melba and they continued their stroll, taking the air.

Earle began to take the baby out for walks every day, sitting on the lawns, watching for the ladies. In this way Rita, Viola, then Melba, came to know and like Earle. They gave her little things of beauty they were ready to cast off: a compact, handkerchiefs, silk underwear, scarfs, and such. Madame knew about the meetings and the gifts, but she didn't give it too much thought. "What harm can that be?"

But she did not trust the red-haired Viola. Viola was always saying, "I get bored sometimes just sitting around looking at your beautiful yard. Why don't you give me something to do for you? I can be of some help, perhaps." Madame always refused Viola's help, as she wondered what the manipulative woman was after. She told Eula Too to watch Viola, "And all my other property as well."

Eula watched Viola, closely, for a while, but the ladies always played with Jewel when she was outside on the lawns. Only Rita came to her apartment to bring gifts for Jewel or Earle. Rita liked to talk about her own sister and niece she was supporting. "They don't write or send me pictures of the baby until they need something, but at least I know they are there and love me."

Eula liked the quiet, mature, dark-haired beauty, Rita. In time, knowing that Earle and Jewel were alright, she didn't mind Rita making friends with Earle. Viola had soon lost interest and that pleased Eula.

Eula knew she had better tell Earle the truth about what happened upstairs. She finally did tell Earle the basic truth of what the ladies did. That seemed to intrigue Earle even more. She stared at the ladies when she saw them, wondering.

At the next opportunity, when they were settling down for bed one night, she asked Eula, "Why do such beautiful women do things like these ones do?"

Eula took a moment to think about the answers Madame had

given to her. She, reflectively, answered, "Why does any woman, not just beautiful women. Everyone is beautiful to someone." Little, new furrows on her forehead appeared as she tried to express her thoughts. "For some of them . . . it must be an escape from thinking. They don't have to decide anything for themselves. Someone will see that they eat and dress as long as they lie there and let someone . . . use their body." After a moment's thought, she added, "I think that is Viola."

She looked up to see Earle's intent gaze on her face, then she continued, "Some, just for the money. Maybe some are put out of their families, sent off anywhere to get them away. Maybe they just don't want her around. She gets in their way. Something. I don't know. I think that is Melba. Except Melba really likes the . . . job. The sex." Her voice betrayed the amount of thought she had given to the question for her own self. "Then, sometimes they have a sort of emotional poverty. Many have a poverty of intelligence. Just don't think at all. Some do it from a lack of love. Family, like. They just keep trying to find it in the things they know are lies. So, they have lack of hope for any other kind of future. I think that might be Lana, but it really could be any of them. Lana loves clothes and sex, but, maybe, they all do." Eula raised her hand and pointed at Earle, for emphasis, "But when they do become a prostitute, even a rich one, they have no protection from the law. All they have is their youth . . . and that is fading, diminishing every day." As if an afterthought, Eula said, "I do know they have a very hard time on family holidays: Christmas, New Year's, Thanksgiving, times like that. They feel real lonely even with all the things Madame plans for them."

She looked intently at Earle because she wanted her to understand the losing side, the bad side. "What it all adds up to is a poverty of spirit. No spiritual food, no real love. I think that might fit Rita. Their spirits grieve. So they accept things in any way they can."

They were quiet for a time, thinking. Then Eula sighed and said, "So that's the only way I can think it. I don't know why. So don't get excited by what it looks like they have. They don't have it." As an afterthought, she added, "This is the last time we are going to talk about those ladies. For your job, you need to learn more about babies. Now, my dear sister, get some rest while you can."

Eula left to go and check on her work. Earle sat there thinking about Eula's words. She believed her, but she was still entranced by the ladies. She thought, "I want to paint them, these beautiful women, someday. These poor, rich, beautiful women. Why don't they get out of it?" Then, duty called at the sound of Jewel's cries. As time passed, Earle forgot about the ladies for a while, although, when she saw them in the gardens she always enjoyed seeing what beautiful things they were wearing.

**M**adame, finally, invited Eula Too to one of her dinners. Eula dressed in her simple but elegant black dress. Her jewelry was a pearl necklace and earrings. She was nervous as she stood beside Madame as Madame inspected the table arrangements for the night. She always had a caterer for her affairs; it was too much to expect Dolly to do. Besides, Madame always had a menu that was time-consuming to prepare, and extra servants were needed who would know how to serve her world-traveled and worldly guests.

There was a fire burning in the bronze-colored Italian marble fireplace spreading a warm glow over the dining room. Drapes at the windows were shimmering rose and gold in the light. The Aubusson carpet was beige with dim and muted colors of gold, scarlet, deep green, and blue. The polished golden wood gleamed from the Italian dining chairs. A few small, fragile tables were placed around the room, with crystal and silver lamps on them. Small, delicate marble statuettes were scattered around the room carefully, bathed in the soft light from the small, dimmed, crystal chandelier hung in a beige ceiling with gold molding.

At Madame's dinners there were seldom, if ever, any other women. This did not disturb her guests because they were not interested in anything they did not already have, except more money . . . or power.

Tonight there were three guests: two bankers and a priest. All of them were old. One, Mr. Grugult from Germany, had a medium-sized, bending body with a large, nearly bald head, with a few gray strands clinging to it. Another, Mr. Crekle from England, was very thin, with dyed brown, wispy hair combed over his narrow head. Both were impeccably dressed. The priest, Monsignor Dali from Italy, was dressed in an expensive, tailored, black frock. They were amiable together, but did not really like one another. They were old friends Madame had met traveling with her, now dead, lover. They had always been charmed by Madame and also enjoyed the exchange of ideas on these occasions. They knew Madame always had interesting guests.

The guests had been told of Eula Too before this dinner, but, really, did not expect to see her there. However, they were sophisticated gentlemen of the world and could indulge their hostess and her strange whim. "After all," they thought in general, "Negro people know nothing and have nothing to do with our businesses. They hardly know the English language so she will not even understand any private matter we might speak of." So they accepted and seemed to welcome her company, then, almost immediately, forgot her. This did not disturb Eula; she preferred to listen, unnoticed.

The meal was served by excellent hands that discreetly and quietly placed and took away the different courses of an exceptional meal, almost without notice. Eula Too was amazed at the variety and flavors of things she had never eaten before, even in Madame's house. Madame had schooled her on table manners and tools, so she was safe from embarrassment. Near the end of the meal when Eula was getting full, her attention shifted from the food to the conversation.

Mr. Grugult was saying, "That country found a devil for the people to hate. It won't be long now. Other countries will soon follow in their hatred. Arms dealers are getting orders from all over the civilized world. And such wonderful new inventions for destruction!"

Monsignor Dali spoke, drily, "I thought I had heard of a few countries that were speaking of disarmament."

Mr. Crekle laughed softly, saying, "Don't be silly. We have orders from Britain, France, Japan, Germany, and others. Enough to keep the munition makers in England and America busy for a few years; if they have that much time. They have been working days and nights. Some, a few people in Washington, are wondering why all the industry is going on in the munition business right now."

Mr. Grugult laughed in pleasure, "We shall see that all the . . . unarmed countries begin to see the light and start to arm to 'protect' themselves from any advances. We must keep 'peace' alive." He laughed again, stammering in his glee. "The politicians holler 'Peace' with their lips and reach for the money with their hands and votes. In every country." He turned to bow his head to Madame. "Your political countrymen are particularly good at it, Madame. Some strong men in your Congress and Senate put up a good fight to try to keep a president who will not question their agenda."

Monsignor Dali said, "Sometimes they are quite fortunate. Their agenda is also the president's agenda. You have a difficult time, sometimes, getting rid of the liberals and radicals. I can name a few who have been screaming to high heaven. They must be in your way in some places. They actually speak of the 'public welfare' and they love the new 'Social Security' your crippled president has put in place. Other . . . politicals . . . will try to break that over the years, and they will one day succeed." He turned to Mr. Crekle, saying, "There are small leaders among the people who are against any war, all over the world. They are tired of dying for some world leader or corporate financial market." He laughed softly as he said, "Almost the same entity." He patted his smiling lips with a napkin. "But America must rid itself of this education for everyone. One day, in the future, the new educated intellectual will cost you your military power. Even, God forbid, all your power. The church may not always be able to control the masses."

Mr. Crekle smiled as he said, "One day we will have a world trade market, then workers cannot make any demands, not even with unions, because workers will be easily replaced. I told you not to be silly. The proper words in the proper places and anyone who does not see reason, our reason, shall find themselves in a miasma of slander and ridicule. Our people own many newspapers and transmitting stations. We have the right people in the right places."

Mr. Grugult nodded his head in agreement as he said, "We will have no interference. The lower classes, if I may use that phrase to refer to the workers of the world, do not have sense enough to see even what is before their faces. They love to hate, anyway. They love to fight. Napoléon knew what he was talking about when he described mankind and wars."

Mr. Crekle agreed, "I have yet to see any man, in war or not, refuse an offered victim. Killing seems to be in human blood, even more than animals." He turned to look at Monsignor Dali, saying, "Churches benefit very well from wars, Monsignor, don't they? They stay full of widows and mothers praying for their dead. Your offering plates and coffers must be running over now."

Chuckling, Mr. Grugult said, "Not just your church either, Monsignor. All churches are busy, on every side, working for the Lord as they rake in, and hoard, the money."

Monsignor Dali was about to chuckle in agreement when his eyes fell on Eula Too. Her concentration and her frown in understanding of what they were saying disturbed him. He waved his hand lightly, saying, "Well, and enough of this talk. We have not heard much from our hostess, nor her delightful little guest, Miss Eula Too! What an interesting name. I would like to hear more about how you got that name."

Eula did not want to be singled out; she had planned to be quiet and unobtrusive, but now she leaned forward and asked the Monsignor, "I thought that peace was the point for the world; wasn't it, isn't it?"

He smiled a beatific look at her and replied, "Child, peace is the main hope of all mankind," then turned his attention to the others. He felt he had satisfied the unimportant child. She was colored anyway, a backward race. She would not have been allowed in his particular church, his parishioners would not allow it. What could she possibly know about anything?

Still leaning forward anxiously, Eula pursued the answer. "But, don't people put their faith in you, I mean the churches, to help us get that peace? What about God? Aren't you supposed to be doing His work? Doesn't the Bible tell you to hate the very things you all are talking about? You talk as though you are glad of the war."

Annoyed, they all looked at Eula Too. Mr. Grugult was a church-going atheist and was amused at the Monsignor's discomfort. He smiled as he waited for his answer. Mr. Crekle was irritated that "this stupid girl had even been invited to sit at table with gentlemen so far above her. She should be clearing the dishes, not asking questions she has nothing to do with!"

Monsignor Dali, vexed, answered with the same beatific smile on his face and finality in his voice. "My child, God will decide everything. We cannot always understand His ways. We cannot believe every word in the Bible. Most of it is only fable or myth. Written by men for men. We, you, must be content with what we have. The Bible is sacred because people love it. It must not be questioned by any but the highest scholars. So I am unable to give you sacred answers." His manner dismissed Eula Too. He turned to Madame, saying, "Your dinner was delightful, as usual." His next words were significant. "I hope you do not plan to extend your guest list, so that I will be able to enjoy the fruit of your culinary expertise again."

With the same smile he had bestowed on Eula Too, Madame smiled on him, saying, "I always enjoy my guests, all of them, and as long as I enjoy your company, you shall be invited to enjoy ours."

And so the tone of the conversation changed. Soon the dinner was over. Eula Too excused herself and left Madame to entertain her guests, alone in the library, with cigars and brandy.

Later, when Madame asked her how she had enjoyed the evening, Eula answered, "I thought you said they were bankers. All they did was talk about war and money and the right and wrong leaders of the world. I don't think they want peace for the world."

Without her usual smile, Madame answered, "I want you to know what is going on in the world. To know how this world is run and who runs it."

Frowning, Eula said, "But they were bankers. I thought they would talk about stocks and bonds and savings."

"Eula, bankers, people who handle the money of the world, are in many other businesses. Deposits from small depositors are not enough. They give small interest and use the money as collateral to make huge interest for themselves. Wherever money can be made, there the bankers will be. War is one of the biggest, most important ways of making money. War is often a business . . . for some people. It can send stocks up or down. War can give you more power . . . more oil, more gold, more labor, more markets for investment. Some people are not content with their own country's markets. They want the world markets. Bankers are businessmen. To them, life is a business. The richest and smartest ones control politicians so they can control laws. Most politicians have studied law, are lawyers. They, with their laws, control your life. I want you to know that. With what they know, and what they control, they can even decide who will win a war. They lend money to countries to buy the tools of war. They can even decide who will be the president, or even king, emperor, premier of any country. They invest heavily in munitions, war tools, and airlines. Some even own them."

There were other dinners with different guests, but Eula Too did not really enjoy them. She spoke to Madame about her feelings.

Madame replied, "Everything you need to do, in order to live, to survive, might not be enjoyable to you. But, the quality of your life will depend on what and how much you know. All the major powers in the world are in this war. It is the most destructive war ever waged. Men and women, even some children, are in this war. Old and young. Cemeteries are spreading all over the world. It is an important war in that it will decide the type of life the world will live, how we will live. You don't have to come to all of my dinners, but you must come to a few. I will choose the right ones for you. I need someone to talk with, about the things we learn. I happen to like living in my style. I intend to keep it that way."

Eula Too nodded, sadly. "Yes, I can see. First the Depression changed America and now, this World War II will be making the world we have to live in. I know it is serious, but I do not like to hear people talk like people are dying for them. For their riches and the power they want. The people dying don't mean anything to them."

Madame looked gravely at Eula. "Those few who know about upstairs want to visit our ladies, but I will not let them. Greta, the fool, thinks this is a common whorehouse and that we should make some of the money the war has brought. Soldiers, even generals and captains, are not welcome here. The war and hate will not enter this house any farther than the dining room. We will have peace and joy in this house as long as possible. After all," she smiled, "we are raising an innocent child."

When the war finally ended, the world could hear the wailing of widows and mothers, the brotherless and fatherless people. Amid the joy of winning the war, medals were given to many generals and leaders of that ilk. But truly the real heroes of the war were those who did not return home. And those who had tried to prevent the war.

In the next few years Eula was able to get about more since Earle was there for Jewel. Earle had private teachers for art and music, and she had Dolly and, sometimes, Rita for company. She was happy. Jewel was growing into a lovely, but terribly spoiled girl. She played her mother and Madame against each other. She usually got her way.

Madame took a trip to Europe, taking Eula Too with her, to see the designer fashion shows and the ruins left by the war. They traveled by ship and Eula was astounded by the extravagance, luxury, and waste. She saw that there were people starving in America, in Europe, in the whole world!

Her life had changed. Oh, all the luxury and expense was still part of her life, but she was no longer in awe of these things. She had seen things in her travels, and even in the house she lived in, that made her know many things were terribly wrong with the world. She saw and heard from Madame and her guests, and even read that no one seemed happy, or even satisfied, anymore. People, those who made the major, weighty, influential decisions, filled their own lives with money and whatever pleasures it pleased them to have, while they dallied, played, with other people's lives. With many smaller wars, with heavy taxes, with heavy laws. With burdensome lies. The whole world was changing as many, many people stood by or cheered for their taskmasters and executioners.

The world was lopsided, upside-down, topsy-turvy. Right was becoming muddled with wrong; good was becoming muddled with bad. They were saying, these hollow, uselessly vain, decadent intellectuals, "There is no God. We, the entire human race, are an accident! Forget a God that never was more than a figment of some idiot's imagination!" And the world began to lose its footings. Its balance. Its brilliant future . . . again. These were the kind of thoughts Eula had as she fell asleep nights. She did not understand, exactly, but when you know what is right, you can easily see what is wrong.

When Madame planned her next trip abroad or in the Americas, Eula Too told her, "I would rather not go, just leave me to stay here and take care of things for you. Besides, Jewel is getting older. She almost thinks Earle is her mother." She laughed because it wasn't true, but it softened her words to a frowning Madame. Who could argue?

Once Eula said, "Why not take Greta? I'm sure she would love to go!"

Madame answered with light scorn, "Greta can never fit into my world. Her world is too small, and her mind does not grow. She is not learning anything new except new ways of reaching for more money."

But soon, even Madame, growing older and feeling more alone, began to tire of even the thought of such long trips. She didn't wear the clothes she had from the last few seasons. She did not want any of the other ladies to accompany her. The trips slowly faded from her mind and life. She stayed closer to Chicago and to Place, where she went, each time with trepidation, to see her mother.

# Chapter Thirteen

*

*From my vantage point there are a few important things from the past that I will tell you:*

*Around 1913, with the ratification of the Sixteenth Amendment to the Constitution, the government was able to tax the incomes of the People. North America's population was, it was reported, around 125 million people; annual income was around $700, for those who had jobs. The tax revenues to the government were believed to be just over 25 million dollars that year. Later, starting in 1929, it is reported, there came to be what was called the Great Depression.*

*By 1931 and 1932, it was reported, almost ten or fifteen thousand banks had closed and nearly 20 million people were unemployed. Franklin D. Roosevelt became president of the United States, developing a "New Deal," which really helped even the poorest people in America. Around 1939, the full impact of Adolf Hitler moving into his worldly place began with wars. America began to arm herself for war, creating much-needed jobs for Americans. The government decided to start taking tax money directly from paychecks in 1943; with the ratification of the Sixteenth Amendment to the Constitution, which was begun in 1913, around another war. World War II started in Europe around 1939, as planned by the greedy and powerful in the world, including The Great Munitions Industry; and came to America, as planned, in 1941. Seek knowledge of the heads of Munitions Companies and who is on their boards. Some names will be hidden. Very carefully.*

After the initial excitment of the war ending, people began to think of new opportunities to make money. Many people made money from war jobs that were extended, and general, related businesses. The making of the instruments of war would never stop again.

During this time Madame still refused to open her house up to any new circumstance. "I do not run a whorehouse!"

The old, steady gentlemen friends were still enamored of their ladies and continued to frequent the residence, even bringing new friends of theirs as allowed. To other ladies, of course.

Greta was handling the upstairs now, so all the ladies and their maids looked to her for their needs. Greta made very good money in wages and tips, but still she stole when she could. She and her husband no longer lived in rooms or small apartments. She had bought them a small house of their own. She tried to get it in her name, alone, but her husband was careful to be sure his name was on it also. Still, she was very proud. And secretive. She never told Madame about the house.

During the war when soldiers were everywhere, Greta's husband had tried to get her to open, as he said, "a real whorehouse for all these soldiers! We got to do our patriotic duty for our boys fightin' for us!" He wanted to come see where she worked, wanted to see the women, but she wouldn't let him come to Madame's. "We do not have a whorehouse like such as you know them. This is a decent house where ladies meet their beaus!" His only answer was "Bullshit! I know a whorehouse when I hear it!" Greta nearly hated her husband, but she was so busy making money she took no opportunity to meet anyone else.

Madame removed Greta from her room downstairs to as good a room upstairs with a sitting room for her office. "To be near your work." Greta was sick at heart and almost wanted to die. She felt the move upstairs was a step beneath her. She had threatened to quit, but only to her husband.

Her husband threatened her in return, "If you quit, we will have to part ways." He didn't say he would move from the house they owned together: What he wanted to say was he would put her out instead. But Greta's work paid too well. He kept almost all the money he had made in his wartime job. It had paid him more than he had ever made in his life. He had a nest egg that Greta didn't know about. Greta had a nest egg of her own he didn't know about.

Greta and Eula Too were always amiable with each other. Eula seldom thought of Greta anymore. Her mind and hands were always busy on some list or accounting book, hiring or firing some household or yard help or just trying to find time to rush down the little stairway to be with Jewel and Earle.

Greta thought of Eula Too every day. She was jealous of Madame's affection for Eula, of the lovely apartment downstairs she did not have to share with anyone, of her travels with Madame, and even, as she said, "that ugly white-nigger baby. A Jewel, ugh! A stone she shall be around her mother's neck one of these days!"

Another year or so passed slowly, as things seemed to degenerate up the stairs from Madame. She noted one day, "The ladies are getting older, but they don't seem to be getting better. They are not progressing in any way; they seem to be regressing. What are they doing with their income? I know they have a good one. I know Greta helped them sneak young lovers in during the war. I didn't bother about it because I know they get tired of old men sometimes, and I knew the young men would soon be going away."

Eula leaned back in a satin chair and thought about upstairs. Things seemed to have been running smoothly. Greta seemed to keep all the ladies and their maids satisfied. Some things had changed; music was heard now, sometimes, all the way downstairs. Madame liked music, but did not like it to interfere in her own day unless she had turned it on. Eula said, aloud, "This new radio . . ." Madame waved that aside.

Eula continued, "All the ladies have changed gentlemen friends one or two times. Their early lovers are growing older or getting sick. Still, the older men visit sometimes, just to reminisce, I guess."

Madame leaned forward from her bedroom desk, saying, "But the money is changing. The ladies seem to be as busy . . . The bills from upstairs remain the same, or more, but, the income money has changed. It is less now than it was six months ago." Madame shook her head in bewilderment.

Looking intently at Madame, Eula said, "Melba would like to bring in the military; generals, captains who are still around."

Madame shook her head, "I will not become a whorehouse."

Eula was glad because she already had enough to do. She yawned as she said, "Well . . ."

Madame held her hand up, counting off the fingers, "Greta gives the money to you? Every night, or early morning?" She frowned, thinking, as she waited for the answer she thought she already knew.

Eula nodded as she said, "After she gets it from the ladies, she gives it to me. Mornings, sometimes, middle of the night, sometimes. She loves to wake us up, banging on the door, at three or four o'clock in the morning."

"I don't hear her. Why don't I hear her? Your door is not that far from me."

Eula looked seriously at Madame. "Because she does not intend for you to hear her."

Madame leaned back in her chair, thoughtfully, saying, "Tell Greta I want to see her. Soon."

Eula found Greta talking to Melba and gave her the message from Madame. When she turned to leave, Greta made an ugly face behind her back. Eula could hear Melba laughing with Greta as she moved down the hall.

"I don't have to take orders from that monkey!"

Melba grinned at Greta as she said, "Perhaps you better; that was an order from Madame."

Twenty minutes later, Greta knocked on Madame's door and heard the bell ring for her to enter. "Greta, how are you?" Madame didn't wait for an answer. "I wanted to see you about the music upstairs. Tell the ladies to keep it turned down."

"Yes, mam. That's prob'ly Rita."

Madame was busy a moment with a few papers on her small desk. "Oh, yes, before I forget. Are they ordering more drinks lately?"

Greta looked confused for another moment. "No, mam. It don't seem so . . . to me, anyway. Why do you ask?"

"Eula says the liquor bills are much higher than usual."

Greta scoffed, "Welllll, I don't know. I give her the money, and, I guess she gives it all to you."

Madame took a minute to casually ask, "You guess?"

"Well, I don't know, Madame. I give it to her. I don't know what happens to it after that."

Madame took another moment to ask, "What about the money the ladies give you from their income?"

In earnest, Greta said, "Same thing. I give it to Eula, just like always, like you told me to do. Except I don't see you . . . and I can't watch her 'til she puts it in your hands, Madame."

With a confused look on her face, Madame asked, "Why would you have to 'watch' her?"

"Well . . . You know . . . I don't know. But, have you been downstairs to her place lately?"

"Have you, Greta?"

Greta blushed, saying, "Well, yes. One day I was looking for her, to give her some message from the girls, and the money, you know? I forget what message, but it seemed urgent at the time. But I know what I saw: She has bought that little girl of hers one of everything in the world. That child has everything! And her sister, too! She has a different dress or apron on every day! Now, I don't know, but I'm just tellin' you, Madame."

Madame looked as if she was considering the idea of Eula stealing. "Thank you, Greta." She smiled a friendly smile, "How are the ladies, Greta?"

Greta's face brightened, "They're just fine, Madame. Always fine. Except maybe, for Rita. She always got something wrong with her. If you want my advice, Madame, if I was you I would let Rita go. She would be easy to replace with all these beautiful young girls who are in this business since the war." She looked eagerly at Madame, but getting no response she wanted, she said, "Oh, yes, I believe that Lana is thinking of getting married to that friend of hers whose wife finally died. She seems awful happy lately. You know, she has seven gentlemen, and she has tried to give three to Melba and two to Viola."

"How?"

Greta laughed, "Oh, by Lana inviting Viola or Melba to her dinners or in for drinks." Greta caught herself, and trying to look surprised, said, "Oh! Maybe that's why the liquor bill is higher! Extra dinner and cocktails! Socializing. The men drink a lot of dinner wines."

"Mmmm hummnn. Are the gentlemen changing ladies, as you and Lana planned?"

"Well, slowly, mam. But they are; because the gentlemen are older now, and the ladies are still pretty and the gentlemen don't want to start all over, some strange place. They already know Viola and Melba."

"What about Rita?"

"Well, mam, Rita don't always act so . . . congenial, to the gentlemen. Nor, for that matter, to the other ladies either. I'm telling you, Madame, we would have a happier place if Rita was not here."

"Since when has that been happening, Greta? I know Rita is a very private person, but I have never known her not to be congenial in business matters."

"Well, I don't know, Madame. I can only report what I know."

Madame lifted her hand, slightly, in dismissal, as she said, "Yes, well, let me know. More often. Every evening, Greta."

As she was leaving, Greta hesitated at the door, "I tell Eula every evening when I give her the money. But I guess she is too busy to get the time to tell you." She turned to leave, but turned back once again, "Oh, Madame! Christmas coming and all, the ladies have already shopped, wrapped, and I have mailed all the packages to wherever they told me to. They don't have no thank-you letters from nobody yet, least, Eula didn't give 'em to me. You know all the gentlemen, 'cept for Lana's, are not going to stop by here on New Year's night and it is going to be like a funeral parlor up them stairs! They are always sad and crying then. I better order up some special things and liquor for 'em for that night! Alright?"

Madame smiled, saying, "I'll order it, maybe get something special for them and have Dolly, or maybe a special chef, cook something extra delicious for all of us. Dolly sorely needs a few extra days off. So, thank you, Greta!"

Later, Madame said to Eula, "Go upstairs to get the money, for a while. Talk to the ladies a little. Especially Viola and Rita. Before this week is out . . . No, wait until the holidays are over. Next week, I want the ladies to write on paper what they give Greta, and give the note to you. Don't tell Melba next week when you tell Viola and Rita, wait until the week after. When you are upstairs, have little quick friendly talks, innocent conversations with all of them. There is something I need to know, and I don't want them to think you are prying. Also, call the agency and request a chef for two weeks, live-in. Give Dolly a much-needed rest. We will pay her for her vacation."

Eula liked telling Dolly about her paid vacation. Dolly didn't want a vacation until she learned she would still receive her wages. It was the first full two weeks off she had had in at least seven years.

When Dolly next spoke with Earle she invited her to come spend one of the holidays with her family. She didn't know whether to feel sorry for Earle or not, seeing that Earle had everything she would have wanted for herself. But Dolly knew Earle was lonely with only the company of an old cook, a young child, her sister, and a prostitute in the only life she had at the moment. Except for the times, the few hours, she sneaked out to hear music with Lester. Dolly watched her son, Lester. "You better get that girl back here in time, and I can tell by lookin' at her whatever you done done! So you better do right!"

. . .

Everything went smoothly for Eula with the ladies, Viola and Rita, until she told Melba to start writing down the amount of money she gave to Greta. Within an hour, Greta came rushing downstairs, knocking, to speak with Madame.

"Madame! I think something is going on here. Eula is asking the ladies to put what they make down on paper, and they are very upset about it!"

"Thank you for telling me, Greta."

Later, Madame said to Eula, "It is just like I thought. There is something going on with Melba and Greta. Did anyone complain to you the first week, before you asked Melba?"

"No."

"Eula, I want you to continue visiting. Tell them I want them to pay you for each bottle of champagne or any liquor they order from you."

The incoming money got better, much better.

Next time Greta reported to Madame, she said, "Well, Madame, that sure was a good idea to see what was happening, giving Eula those extra jobs. Even if she don't like it."

Madame answered, "Yes, I think it was a good idea, Greta."

Madame might have dismissed Greta and even Melba. But it seemed under some control for the moment and Madame had other things on her mind. Her mother was not doing well, she was sick. Madame had heard from Mrs. Mary Green, the neighbor who kept Madame's number for emergencies. "My poor Mama. We are no closer. I love her and she won't let me take care of her. I am going out of my mind!" Madame screamed inside her brain.

Eula continued making quick, friendly visits on the ladies upstairs. When she went in to see Madame three or four weeks later she had to tell her, "Viola has a pimp, Madame. She was sneaking him out of their private entrance when I was up there early this morning."

"A pimp!?"

"He didn't seem to be a stranger to this house, either, Madame. He threw me a very nice, big smile as she was pushing him out the back entrance. I asked her private maid how long he'd been visiting here. She said, about a year!"

Madame was shocked, and her face showed it, "A year! Damnit! I have been lax and my house is getting away from me! Why hasn't Greta told me? Does she know? I hate pimps! They are thieves of the worst kind; they not only steal the money they take from the girls, they steal hearts and break them, and they steal lives! They are the bane of a woman's existence!"

Eula nodded, saying, "Greta knew. But the worst part . . . and I had to give her maid a small raise for her to tell me this, he actually lives here, more than half the time."

"Then when do her appointments come? How or when can she entertain them if he is here that much?"

"Madame, he has even slapped her around, beaten her sometimes. Very quietly, apparently."

Madame was outraged. "In my house! Beaten her! What are you saying, Eula?"

Patiently, Eula repeated, "I'm saying Viola has a man with her most of the time and he eats and drinks and lives here. He even slaps her around. In this house. And, she has, in this past year, been pregnant twice. Remember when she was sick twice?"

"Someone is always sick upstairs. No one mentioned abortion. I did not call the doctor."

"He gets rid of the baby by punching Viola in the stomach, until she is vomiting and bleeding. He ties her mouth so she cannot scream. She helps him; they do it together. But I think he makes her do it. She wanted children someday, and she loves him. It would seem she would want his baby. Anyway, Greta calls the doctor when they are finished. The pimp leaves so the doctor won't see him. That doctor of yours, conveniently, only sees the signs of her being knocked about. Viola pays him not to tell you."

Madame placed her head in her hands, shocked, ashamed, and pitying Viola. At the same time she was angry with her. "Can a person not trust anyone? My own doctor I pay a ransom! Besides, being in my house, why does she stay with him? And why hasn't one of the other women said anything to me . . . or to you?"

Eula waited a moment before answering, "Maybe they thought they sent word to you." There was nothing else Eula had to say. They were both silent as they looked at each other and thought the same thing.

At last, Madame said, "Greta will have to go."

But Eula said, "Or have better control on the whole situation. Because if Greta goes, I am going to end up doing some of that work upstairs, and I can tell you right now, dear, I do not have any plans for going upstairs, unless I am visiting Rita."

Madame started to object to Eula objecting, but didn't. Instead she said, "Well, let's make some plans to control my money. I'll talk to my lawyer. Also, she is a good producer of money, but Viola will have to go. How can she work if she is beaten? And he could kill her, accidently, one day, and I know he will walk away from her and leave me with police problems."

"He never hits her face. He wants her able to keep working and making money."

"Her face isn't what is going to kill her. Eula, why, after all this time, have you not made a personal friendship with even one of those ladies so she would tell you when things are going wrong up there?"

Hesitantly, with thought, Eula said, "Rita and I are friends, but Rita does not like to tell anything on the others. She does not tell me, but I can feel that the other ladies do not like her very much. She gets along with Lana, but Lana is indifferent to what the others think, and I think that's why."

Eula shook her head, sadly, "Rita did tell me Viola, confused by her problems, went to Rita's room one time and Rita talked to her about everything, but she told Rita, 'I don't care! I love him!' Then Rita said to her, 'He's just going to gamble or drink or sniff your money away!'" Eula shook her head, again, "Viola said, 'It's not my money. It's his money!' And Rita said, 'It's your body, though,' and the answer from Viola was, 'That's his, too!' And Rita said, 'That's a little too dumb for me and too much for me. Close my door behind you as you leave.' Then Viola shouted at her, 'You're no better . . .' But Rita told her, 'I spend all my own money on myself or my family back home where I can go when I need to. I have no intention of being a . . . this all my life. I'm going to a home I paid for! You said you had no intention of staying in this business when you first came here. Well, you better start saving your own money!' Then Viola started to shout again, so Rita got up, led her to and pushed her gently out, slammed, and locked her door."

A few days later, when Viola's man heard she was going to have to move from Madame's house, he really beat her, even her face. The doctor had to hospitalize her and tend her carefully to save her face and try to heal her. Her arm was broken and had to heal. She was in the hospital for at least six weeks. Her man had the nerve to sneak in to eat her food from the tray.

Madame had to let her come back to the house to convalesce. The silly woman, Viola, had called her man to let him know where she was. He began sneaking in, again. Madame's lawyer had a lawman wait in a maid's room for the boyfriend to come creeping, slinking in again. He was arrested for trespassing and put in jail.

When Madame, at last, said good-bye to Viola, she had a long personal talk with her. Told her to go back to her family. "You are still not well, Viola. It will take a long time for your body to heal. Go to school, learn to type, learn any good thing for your own money and your own self."

Viola went back to her family, which was not a poor family. She was welcomed and stayed there awhile. Then, one day, she left to find him. She lived on the streets, making a little money and looking for him. She developed consumption. TB. With no money and no care, and still trying to pick up a man, any man, for a few dollars, she became sicker. She died. Her man had known she was out on the streets. He heard about the new girl, among the many other new women, because she had had some vestige of class. Other pimps were trying to "catch" her for their stable. When he saw her, of course he recognized her, if only from the marks he had left on her. He had known her when she was fresh, so he knew, now, she was very ill. He avoided her. He knew when she died. He did not even come to the funeral. He took his new woman out to dinner, paid for, of course, with his new woman's money.

That left Melba, Lana, and Rita at Madame's grand house. They, each of them, believed they were too smart about life for anything like Viola's fate to happen to them.

Melba seemed to be the leader under Greta. She controlled Greta with promises and money. Rita continued to be reserved and private, keeping most of her confidences to herself. Infrequently, she would share them with Eula Too, whom she had come to respect.

Madame did not replace Viola.

Lana finally left to marry her old gentleman lover. She did not love him or even like him very much. She couldn't, because all she could really think of was herself; clothes for herself, jewels for herself. He was, simply, a way out. From old habits, Lana was a person who lied unnecessarily and a petty thief of things that would already, by her marriage, belong to her. Yet and still, she made him feel happy because she was young, compared to him, and beautiful to him. She tried to give him what he needed, the way he needed it. He smiled when he thought of his good wife.

His family would never understand him. They did not smile when they thought of her. Though they were pleased she was not ostentatious. They had quiet, secret meetings with their attorneys to ensure the safety of his inheritance. And their money.

*These are success stories to Satan. He has laughed since the beginning and still laughs at his fools. He wrongs those who do wrong for him. He does not love, or even like, anyone.*

Madame did not replace Lana. "I'm tired," is all she said.

Melba had a few female friends she wanted to "help." She pushed Greta to persuade Madame, or Eula Too, to allow her friends to work in the house, saying, "The ole bitch can get more money to stuff in her bank accounts!" But Madame always told Greta, "I will not have whores in my house." And Greta would not ask Eula Too.

. . .

Eula was glad, because her life was changing. She was still young but was far from being the young person who had come into Madame's house. Her jobs, now, required less of her time. She could be with Jewel, who was pretty, smart, and healthy. Enjoy her more when she came home from short vacations with Madame. She would be able to see and help Earle more. "We need to go to our mama's house too. That will be good. Maybe some of the other kids will have some get-up-and-go in them." She was so busy with everyone else's life, she did not see that her sister Earle's life was changing, also.

Earle Mae had been a wonderful help with Jewel, making it possible for Eula Too to be of more assistance to Madame, who really didn't do much in the way of work. Though Madame made many things possible for Eula and Earle Mae.

Jewel had grown up to be a lovely looking child. Madame seemed to love her and was always buying her beautiful things to wear. Jewel was pretty, adored, pampered, and spoiled. Her petty mean ways were not noticeable to most people because usually Jewel had her way and whatever she wanted. It was different when she did not get her way.

Jewel had a mind different from her mother and aunt's. She could be quite ruthless for a child, lacking any sign of charity, gentleness, or kindness. She was abusive in tone and action when denied anything she demanded. She lacked humanity of thought and spirit. Eula Too was blinded by her love for Jewel and was too tired, distracted, or forgiving to see the danger implicit in Jewel's ways. Jewel felt superior to everyone except Madame. With Madame, she felt equal.

Madame secured the best tutors for Jewel and managed to get her prepared to enter the best schools for young women and, then, college. Jewel grew more comfortable, feeling invulnerable and confident about herself in her mind. But she relied on herself for nothing. She took responsibility for nothing. Everyone "owed" her. She thought herself unassailable and felt abused when her will was not done. She felt affection for Earle, but considered her a mere mean servant. Earle took no mess from Jewel, but Jewel was secretive and deceitful, and so she found ways around her aunt. Even at her young and innocent age, she always wanted money. "I want money and riches like Madame has!" Madame and Eula smiled at her and knew she liked gifts. Earle knew it for what it was: greed. And Jewel knew she would have money, by any means necessary.

For the last four or five years Eula Too had begun crying for no apparent reason. She did not understand why. Didn't she have everything? It could be a sudden burst of tears or just silent crying with tears streaming down her face when she was alone. She shook off these episodes and kept going.

Earle, with her duties cut down, was exploring the world close to her. She met the Negro gardener and chauffeur from the estate next door. She liked the chauffeur; he knew more and had more money to spend than Lester. When he told her about the life he knew in Chicago, she got excited about the things happening in the city. She began letting him take her out to see the "real and fantastic life" out there. But she never forgot her art and her music. Everything Earle saw or learned, she applied to her main interests.

Madame had taken Eula Too to see the great musicians when they came to Chicago. Usually in sedate surroundings because Madame's male friends, others she sometimes dined with, were very staid and conservative. Sometimes when Eula insisted on taking Earle with them, Madame would say, "Then let's go where the real music is! Paul can be the man with us." Then her chauffeur would gladly go with them to a few good Negro jazz clubs.

Duke Ellington, Louis Armstrong, and young Dizzy Gillespie were a few of their favorites. Madame knew the people she saw needed money as much as anyone else. Even more. But she was particularly delighted to be among relaxed, real, joyous people who were not talking about wars, money, and death.

Eula Too had looked into many inviting eyes on those occasions. She was confused by her own feelings. She wanted to meet and know some of the handsome, sharply dressed young black men smiling at her. But, also, there was such a deep fear in her of being close to any man. Except Paul, because Madame, or someone, was always with her when Paul was around.

Now, in a way different, more focused than Eula, Earle saw the great musicians: Duke Ellington, Fats Waller, Billie Holiday, Louis Jordan, Eubie Blake, Noble Sissle, Charlie Parker, Dizzy Gillespie, Erroll Garner, Louis Armstrong, and many others. She heard multicolored loud jukeboxes, went in juke joints, fish-houses, nightclubs with blasting music and loud, boisterous, colorful crowds.

She ate chicken-an'-waffle breakfasts or bar-b-que ribs with steaming beans and potato salad or cole slaw, or crispy, fried chicken cooked to a fare-thee-well taste. Sometimes she ate while watching the sky lighten as the sun came up with the good low-down, weary blues from weary, but able, musicians. She would welcome the new day with her mind, body, and soul. Then, inspired, she would go home to her oil painting or to practice on the old piano she had acquired. She was getting quite good at both.

Madame cautioned Earle Mae about the danger "out there" with strangers. But Earle said, "I appreciate that, Madame, but this little piece of life I have in these walls ain't telling me nothing. Anything. I'm gettin' older. I'm a woman. And I'm gonna do something else! I want to be an artist, to paint and draw. I want to learn to play the piano that I love." She smiled at Madame as she said, "You all are good to me, but there is more to life than you." Madame noticed she did not say "more to life than you *all*."

Earle had met many people as she saw the nightlife in Chicago, and she had met several men she liked. She was trying to see one especially, but times were difficult, unless you lived in the city. Earle said to Eula one night as they were preparing for sleep, "You better plan something. Jewel is mostly away at school, and I want to go to school for what I want to do in my own future. Jewel does not need me here like she did when she was small, and you just want to keep my wonderful company." She smiled at her sister, but said, "So I'm gettin' ready to get on away from here. There are plenty things in Chicago besides this! and I want to go!"

Eula, anxious, answered, "Earle, you're too young! Don't you like living here? Don't you have everything you want? We have a home here. Madame gives us everything. Food, a lovely house to live in."

Earle had an answer for that also. "I like Madame and appreciate all what she does. And this is alright, but, Eula Too, this ain't all there is. And this is still just a whorehouse to me. I want to go outside to school . . . or somewhere. And while I'm talking, let me tell you, you don't have much of a life either. This house is your whole life, Eula. Well, it ain't . . . it isn't mine."

**M**adame wanted two things. She wanted Earle to go before she lured Eula Too away with her talk. She also wanted Earle to stay because Eula needed someone she loved near her. So, first, Madame bought Earle a piano and hired a teacher for her. That took care of matters for a while. A year or so passed as Earle happily and diligently learned. Then, Earle's young man friend told her of an art school in Chicago she could attend that would not take all of her savings. In a short time, Earle was raring to leave the suburbs for the city. Eula, who was sending money to her mother and Miss Hart, took from her reduced savings and added to the money Earle had saved and let her go. To the City . . . To Chicago.

Eula missed her sister and her daughter and felt it all the way down to the suffering beat of her own little, lonely heart. The crying fits happened more often. She bore her pain in silence, on her wet pillow, at night, alone.

Jewel seldom wrote Eula except to ask for something. She wrote more to Madame, asking for even more things . . . and money. But

Earle wrote to Eula Too of her weekly adventures. She wrote, excitedly, of seeing Joe Louis, a world champion prizefighter, at one of the nightclubs. She wrote of different things she was learning and even bought or sent books Eula had not known existed. Of course, Eula had the enormous selection of European and American authors in Madame's library. She could choose any book she wished, but Madame didn't have the new American books Earle sent.

There came books by Zora Neale Hurston, Langston Hughes, Countee Cullen, James Weldon Johnson, Richard Wright, Jessie Faucet, James Baldwin, and more. Negro magazines! Eula begged Earle for more and sent money for them. The view of other Negro lives astounded her! Negro thoughts written down! And to see a book! a real Book that a Negro had actually written! A Negro just like her! Eula Too was knocked off her two steady feet. She began to want to go to Chicago, but she couldn't. Jewel needed her to be here. Madame needed her. She had responsibilities. People, her mother, Miss Hart, and, sometimes, Earle. Earle worked little jobs, but rent and food took most of her pay. She needed money for her art lessons and supplies. Eula Too never forgot how faithful Earle had been nor for how long when she had needed her for Jewel. She was sending her mother and Miss Hart money each month. Now she added Earle to her list of responsibilities. She was always trying to save money for her future; still, she managed to help the people she loved. Eula would think to herself, "What future do I have other than Jewel anyway?"

# Chapter Fourteen

*

Madame no longer asked Eula Too to come to every dinner she gave, but one afternoon she announced she was having guests for dinner and would like Eula to attend. "One of my guests is bringing a friend of his I do not know. I would like a little company of my own at the table."

Eula had several new dresses Madame had bought for her, and she was bored since Earle was no longer with her. "I'll come, but don't you get tired of those old, greedy men who talk of nothing but money and how clever they are?"

"I have my reasons, as you know."

"Madame, you are not an old woman. You should have younger men around you sometimes."

"I'm too old and tired to think of younger men," she laughed softly.

Later that evening the caterers came and performed their magic with table settings, food, and flowers. The atmosphere was set by candlelight and a fire busily flaming in the fireplace. Madame welcomed her four guests and served them martinis or their aperitif of choice. As the usual niceties were observed, Madame had an opportunity to do some observing of her own; she looked the new guest over. He had been introduced as Elton J. Gross.

Mr. Gross was tall and slender with a full head of chestnut-colored hair graying at the temples, which complemented his hazel-green eyes. A brilliant flash of smile came often enough to let you know he was quietly personable. Reserved enough for one to know he was a thoughtful, deliberate man. His manner and dress were flawless. He seemed American and European at the same time. Here was a man who had been educated and had traveled extensively and well.

Mr. Gross was the friend and guest of Mr. Hoewl of Switzerland. The other guests were Mr. Beek, an Englishman, and Reverend Smith, an American. With an eye on Mr. Gross, Madame introduced the men, who were strangers to each other. Eula had met Mr. Hoewl before, but the others were new to her. Mr. Hoewl first cast a friendly look on Eula, then looked resigned.

Eula was pleasant to the gentlemen, but was already bored. She gave her attention to any person speaking, but she was listening to the background music and thinking of Earle, her mother, or Jewel. She heard snatches of the conversation and she laughed or smiled at the proper time. She was practiced, having had to do it so often.

She noticed Mr. Gross was usually looking at Madame, no matter who was talking to the table in general. She observed Madame's subtle glances at him, lingering at times. Then, hearing something interesting, she would give her full attention to the speaker's words.

Mr. Hoewl was saying, "Your problem is going to be the middle class. It is invading all parts of life in America now, more and more. They want to have a say in everything. That is why it is best to keep vulgar people with their bad taste and worse virtues and morality down with the lower classes! They even want to involve themselves in politics! That is what comes of education. Free education of all things. Your leaders better get rid of some of the education they pass around like bread rolls, and keep the vermin in their places. I say!"

The smiling Reverend Smith answered him, "In our great America we have laws. For instance, the income tax laws. Those laws will prevent any citizen from keeping new wealth, because the taxes will increase eventually. Inevitably. The tax law will protect those who are born to wealth, rightfully so, from the low order invading their realm. The stupid middle class all over the world."

Mr. Gross laughed softly as he said seriously, "You will never stop the middle class in America. They vote. You have elections in America. And they know that if they have a class system here, as they do in many places in Europe and Asia, it will mean the end of their preferred type of freedom."

Mr. Hoewl laughed at the very idea. "You give the common people too much undeserved credit for thinking!"

Mr. Beek spoke, "The political system here in America has so many holes in it. There are no laws, that they enforce, against libel. You can say anything, lies or whatever, about your opponent. And nothing seems to disqualify a person from running for office. Money has the advantage over any poor man running for an office. You can buy the presidency, if you have enough money."

Mr. Gross looked at Madame, who, of all things, blushed. He said, softly but clearly, "But what is money for if not to buy what you want?"

Eula Too, without thinking, said, "Surely, money is the lowest value of a man." She could feel Mr. Gross slowly turn his face to her. Her brown skin blanched beneath its surface, but, still, she continued speaking. "What of character? Honesty? Love for the people who depend on you? There are truly wicked, evil, greedy people with money. In fact, in history, those are, especially, the types of people who make the most money. Because they will do anything without concern for any other human being. Superficial. With no truth in them. They are dangerous people to lead a country . . . just because they have more money."

Though Reverend Smith understood her words perfectly, he chose to obtusely nod his head in agreement and direct the conversation in a safer direction. "Even 'society' is a money-based proposition. Any plebeian with enough money can make it in 'society' with only token resistance. I've seen it over and over. My parishioners are some of the richest in the world. A poor man cannot come to my church."

(He was speaking to Eula, who understood that.)

"So I have seen new rich of almost any background among my church members."

Eula had one last thing to say. "Most men, so I have read, are liars. Even in their spirits. Many men, people, hate the truth. Nevertheless, the truth does not depend on man's love. Nor fear man's hate." She looked directly at Reverend Smith and said, "Mr. Smith." She was silent for a moment, then said, "There really is a God, you know."

He had only ignored Eula Too, but now his eyes pinpointed her with instant hate. But, master of deceit that he was, he laughed congenially, and said, "I have labored long in my chosen service to God. I have earned the title 'Reverend.' I am not refered to as 'Mister.'" He thought, "That will put this poor, indulged urchin back in her place!"

Eula Too wanted to stand and leave, but she knew Madame would consider that very ill mannered, unless there was good cause. She remained seated and, as she picked up her dessert fork, she smiled at the man who liked being called Reverend. She said to him, "Respectfully, sir, I do not revere you, so I cannot call you 'Reverend.' I must call you 'Mister,' in respect for your age, instead."

Mr. Hoewl, who often ridiculed religion, smiled obliquely at Eula. Mr. Beek, who thought God was a wonderful tool when you needed one, was aghast. Mr. Gross looked down at his creamy dessert and applauded Eula in his mind. The Reverend Smith was speechless, but his thoughts were those of the Ku Klux Klan.

Madame smiled faintly, saying, "That is what we love about America, we have freedom of speech. Even if it sometimes interferes with our so-called manners." She knew Eula wanted to leave so she said, "Would you gentlemen like brandy with your cigars, a good bourbon or excellent scotch?" And the dinner was over.

Later Madame and Eula laughed congenially about it. Madame said, "Eula, if you don't want to come to dinner again, I will not ask you, dear. I didn't know you felt so strongly about some of the guests."

Eula answered, "I would like to hear someone talk about 'loving your neighbor' sometimes. Good things. I get tired of hearing people making the whole world ugly and hating people. Because that is what they do; they hate people! Even people of their own countries. Many American politicians too! They seem to have no country but the country of money! They would like all the world at war all the time, just to sell the oil, guns, tanks, bullets, chemicals, airplanes, and all things made for war! They hand out bombs, then hand out care packages that do not begin to solve the problems they have created. Big power is dangerous. But I don't want to talk about those things right now."

Then she smiled more deeply at Madame. "I notice you and Mr. Gross had plenty to say to each other with your eyes. He was a really handsome man!"

"Yes, he is. But I'm too old for romance now. Just look at me! I have let years go by without a tinge of regret or desire. But I am interested in . . . his conversation. He has a way about him. I liked him. But what could he see in me? He certainly has more money than I do." She sighed, happily, "But we have made plans to see each other again. I gave him my private number."

"Good for you, Madame. You need more company than me."

Madame looked sharply at Eula Too, then the conversation went on to other things and life continued, as usual.

# Chapter Fifteen

*

One day in the life of this house, Eula Too listened to Madame speak as she lay across her silk and satin bed stuffs. "I like going out with Mr. Gross. He is very gentle with me, and complimentary. His manners make even the least important meeting we have seem . . . wonderful." Then she looked at Eula, saying, "Do you know, it is as I thought, it is planned to have many little festering wars all over the world? A small class of very, very rich people want very, very much power and control over the people of the entire world! They are going to turn America, because she is the richest country, into a business corporation that they will own."

Eula nodded as she said seriously, "What I have learned is the poor always depend on the rich and the rich always see that it remains that way. They control our incomes and the costs of our living. One man, I cannot remember which, they are all so alike, he said that jobs control the economy for the poor, and that they are planning to send most of our factories and businesses somewhere else where the people will be glad to receive a few cents, whereas now, Americans are demanding sufficient pay for their labor. They certainly do not like unions, the common (as they call them) people joining together and fighting for their rights. They are taking over our whole government. They own all the money, Madame!"

"Yes, they do. I think it was President Wilson who first warned the voters of America never to permit a strong centralized government in Washington."

Eula's laughter held no humor as she said, "People rather go to a baseball game or a fashion show than listen to someone telling them what is happening in their country. They think the Constitution and the Bill of Rights will do all the work they should be doing. Those things are only on paper, and politicians are making amendments to them every day."

Madame listened to Eula Too with pride. Then she fell back on her bed, yawning, "Oh, I am tired of all these matters. I may not even live to suffer under their plans. I have enough to think about. I will never have a real love life again. And my mother is a constant worry to me. She is getting worse, and I may have to go care for her, live with her for a time, since she won't leave Place. But this time, I want you to come with me. I won't leave this house with Greta, alone, watching over it. You know that."

Eula Too waited in silence, listening, thinking.

Madame continued, "Oh, you will still receive the same pay as ever. I know your mother is sick and they all cost you money." She looked at Eula and said with a bit of sarcasm and irony in her voice, "And you still send money to that friend of yours, Miss Hart."

Eula Too slowly nodded, saying, "Yes, I do. I plan to continue as long as I am able. She is to me what you say I am to you, a necessity."

Madame sat up, waving away her thoughts, saying, "Well, I pay you enough, but you send . . ." She waved those thoughts away, too. She said, instead, "I want Dolly to remain to look after the house. But we must decide how to tell Greta, Melba, and Rita that they must leave and when."

"Alright. When?"

"Give them a month. Exactly. No longer."

Eula rose from her seat as though she was very tired. "I will inform them today."

Madame lay back down on her bed. "Good. And I will call my mother in a moment or two. I have to gather my strength before I call her."

As Eula Too was leaving, she turned back to Madame, saying, "I have heard from Miss Hart. I believe I will have to go to my mother. She isn't doing what that doctor I send to her tells her to do."

"Aren't your sisters and brothers there to help?"

"Yes. But she is my mama to me. And I don't know what they really do. When Miss Hart tells me something, I know there is some reason she tells me besides the obvious one."

Madame sighed, "Families. They say they are about love, but they seem to be more about problems."

Eula turned to go, saying, "It is about both love and problems. I guess the love helps you to take care of the problems."

Madame sat up again, "If you leave you must be back here before they leave, Greta and the ladies. I don't want to have to deal with them."

"Then let Dolly deal with them. They know her and pay attention to what she says. I hardly take time off, and this is my mother." She sighed, feeling the tears threatening to come, she wanted to leave, be alone. "It probably won't take long. I don't like to be there, even though I stay with Miss Hart."

"Well, tell Paul to drive you there when you are ready. Then hurry back, please. I do have to go to Place to see about my mother and that woman I hired to take care of her."

The tears suddenly rushed back to wherever they had come from. "Then we understand each other. Our mothers are important to both of us."

Madame, sighing again, made no answer.

Eula softly closed the door.

Eula Too went, without delay, up the stairs to speak to the ladies. She went to Rita first because they were friends. They had developed a bond because both could be trusted. Rita had respect for her own word and maintained her dignity, her self-esteem. Things had not changed upstairs; Greta and Melba still did not like her. Eula Too did like Rita.

Rita took the unexpected news quietly. She smiled, "Thank you, Eula." She asked about Jewel and they spoke of a few other mundane things before Eula left to tell Greta. When Rita closed the door to her apartment, her first thought was, "What am I going to do now? How much money have I saved? What has my family done with the extra money I sent them? Well, anyway, I can go home because I have sent them the money to pay for that home. And I still have a friend or two. Maybe one of them will put me up in an apartment of my own . . . for now."

Greta already knew because she had been listening to them through the small opening of her door. Her eyes grew large with speculation. She had quite a bit of money put aside now, stolen and earned. But, she had no life. She was married to a man who did not love or respect her, and she did not love or respect him. "This house has been my life! They are taking my life from me after all I have done to keep things going around here!"

Though she tried to control herself, the loathing in Greta's eyes showed as she looked at Eula Too. "Are you going to have to leave, too?"

Eula did not like to give Greta any firm answers about herself. "I'm not sure yet."

"Not sure yet?" came the flat voice.

"No."

"What will happen to your beautiful apartment in the basement?"

"This is Madame's house; that is her apartment."

Greta smiled, "Ahhhhh." Then, "But your daughter, she will be coming back here. Do you have only thirty days also?"

"I'm not sure yet."

"No. You will tell Melba, please."

"Greta, I think it is your duty to tell them first."

"Certainly. I am still working, no? I am still getting paid, no?"

"Yes, for thirty days. Now, I have to go speak to Paul."

"Yes, yes. And I must go speak to Melba," Greta said, nervously, as she hastened away.

After Melba's lover had gone for the evening, Greta and Melba talked, as they sipped Madame's Champagne, deep into the night, until the early dawn. Melba was the only one really worried; she had only a very small nest egg. She had thought Madame would be there for her forever.

Greta was trying to think of a way to put her husband out and move Melba in to continue making money. But she knew her house was in no way a fitting place for luxurious, clandestine meetings. She also knew Melba was drinking far too much. Drunk, too many times. "But," she thought, "that may be to my advantage. She does not necessarily need to have the same kind of man she is used to. Soon the only kind she will be able to get will be ones who will think they are in a mansion when they come to my little house. I will keep her supplied with gin and wine. No more Champagne; too expensive. I must think how to do this thing."

Eula did not understand why she still cried so often when she was alone. The tears would come suddenly and, most times, would dry up just as suddenly. "I do not feel sad. I am not worried. I miss my daughter and my sister, but that is no reason to cry. I hear from both of them. Jewel has started college in that ritzy place Madame chose for her. My God, how time flies."

Eula placed her hand on her breast, shaking her head. "My mother is sick with diabetes, but I send her money for what she needs. My dear friend, Miss Hart, is taken care of, but she is getting too old to be alone in that place no matter how pretty her special place is. She is too old to keep everything nice like she used to. But, almost all my savings seem to be spoken for. And I am getting older, God. In this beautiful house. Right here in my beautiful home . . . where I do not have a life for myself."

Then she slowly pulled herself up to go tell Paul, the chauffeur, to get ready next morning to take her home to her mother.

# Chapter Sixteen

*

Over the years Eula Too had had the old house that belonged to her mother repaired, improved, and added a room in the little space of land her father had bought for his family. It still didn't look much better, but EulaLee now had a decent-sized room with a new bedroom set with a larger bed for her bulky body to lie in comfortably.

Several of her grown children were there to attend her and to eat and sleep at no cost, thanks to the money Eula Too sent her mother. The few who had gotten on with their lives, trying to do better, were there sometimes, bringing food and medicine for their mother. Earle Mae was among them as often as possible, sitting in a chair beside her mother's huge bed.

EulaLee was dying.

Eula Too arrived with the automobile filled with things she knew her mother liked; perfumes as well as the fresh, new, pretty sheets. One look at her mother and Earle's faces and she knew that death was in the room with them. She felt her heart filling with anguish and guilt. "I should have been here more. I should have done more. Helped her stay on her diet." She looked around at those who were parasites, her siblings, thinking, "I guess there are always some in every family. Lord knows, I tried to help those I could."

EulaLee was, gradually, regaining her consciousness when Eula Too came into the bedroom. She smiled, weakly, at her favorite daughter, opening her lips to speak, but no sound came. She felt so tired, so tired.

Earle moved out of the way, and Eula Too slid into the chair as she reached out for her mother's hand, clasping it in her own. EulaLee turned her head slightly toward Eula Too, saying, with a small, tender smile, "Earle Mae . . ."

"No, Mama, it's me . . . Eula Too."

EulaLee's eyes dimmed within the frown that moved over her face, whispering, "I want my mama." Then she dozed in unconsciousness for several moments. When she opened her eyes again, she asked, whispering, "Where is my man? My husband?"

Eula Too did not want to say the word "dead," so she said, instead, "All your children are here, Mama. See? Here is Earle Mae and your sons, Lester and Lionel. And there is Betty and Charlesetta and Jimmy and Lillian . . . almost all your children. We love you, Mama." Tears began to fill Eula Too's voice and eyes, but she did not want to cry before her mother lest she alarm her.

Then EulaLee focused her eyes on Eula Too. Everything and everyone else in the room vanished. Earle moved closer to the bed, reaching for her mother's arm, but EulaLee's eyes remained focused on Eula Too as she whispered, softly, "I'm fixin' to die . . . ain't I?"

Still holding in her lap a pretty package, a pretty gift, for her mother, a sob broke through the tightened lips of Eula Too.

"I already know it," whispered the mournfully smiling mother. "I ain't 'fraid of it. I wasn't never 'fraid of nothin'. Just for ya'all. Ya'all so small . . . tryin' to grow." She moved her head closer, in the direction of Eula Too. "You a special kind of woman. 'Cause you a kind woman. You ain't mean."

Tears spilling from her eyes, Eula Too was treasuring the words of her mother . . . until she realized what her mother was about to ask her. She spoke softly back to her mother in a broken, tear-filled voice, "All your children could be special, Mama."

But EulaLee either didn't hear her or didn't want to. "You look out for my chilren, Eula . . ." She had to stop and try to take a deep breath, then she continued, "Eula Too. Don't you let 'em be hungry and do without."

The tears remained in Eula Too's eyes, but her voice grew stronger as she spoke to her mother, "Don't you give me that to do. Don't you try to put me back where I was. They grown. They can do as well for themselves as they want to. I will not pay for anything but education . . . and not all of that." Still holding her mother's hands, as EulaLee's eyes, buried in a bewildered frown, followed her, she stood up. "Don't you put that grief on me, Mama. I am not you. You will not send me to my grave. I have my own child to look out for. I will do anything for you. I would die for you. But only you. I tried to save you. I cannot save all of them. Do not ask for the things that will kill me, Mama. I work for money; I did not inherit money. I am not you."

EulaLee's mind escaped into a swirling tunnel of darkness and unconsciousness. But, she did not die yet. In a few moments, her mind struggled to reach the light again. Sweat streamed from her body as her eyes strained to see Eula Too's face again. She gasped, her slack mouth gaping open as she tried to speak . . . and couldn't. She was a woman unable to move, drowning, sinking. Her eyes dilated, a tiny flame flaring within them, as she stared at her daughter in silence. Eula Too was looking into her mother's eyes and could almost see when the smothering waves of death flowed over the tiny flame and took her mother away. Eula Too stooped, quickly, and screamed to her mother, "I love you! I love you, Mama!," as though her mother might hear her, even faintly, as she sped away from this life. EulaLee did hear a rooster crow, way off in the distance. She heard it crow, dimly, once more, then fade away with her life.

EulaLee was too large to be carried to the funeral home and then the church and then back again, near her home to be buried next to her husband, so the funeral was held in EulaLee's bedroom in her house.

Her preacher preached and all her church sisters came, as well as Miss Hart and a few other people Eula Too did not know. The coffin had been made by EulaLee's own son, Lester. There were several funeral wreaths around the gravesite. A beautiful blanket of white roses from Madame covered the casket as it was lowered into the ground.

Her children cried as if the end of the world had come. Well, it had for some. Though others of them hadn't seen her in years, they loved her. A few hadn't come, but perhaps they hadn't heard she was dead yet.

When the family gathered in the little old house after the service, Eula Too told everyone they could have the house she had put so much money in. "Just live in it if you have to, but don't tear it up or down. Don't make a gambling joint nor a bootleg joint out of it. That is why I am giving it to the women in this family. Live here, if you have to. Your brothers deserve a temporary roof over their heads sometime, so let them have a temporary roof. Lester works, so he can stay as long as he likes. But, you other brothers who have been laying around on Mama, you need to get on out in the world and find a way to make yourself and your family a living."

Later, Lester told Eula Too, "I want to go somewhere where I can make a decent living and build my own house for myself. I don't know no place no where. So I'm asking you to keep me in mind when you see a place I can be and have a chance to be happy like you." Eula Too smiled wearily at her brother, nodded her head as she thought, "Maybe I look happy to you, but I *ain't*, brother. I want a place just like you want, for my own self."

Her weary dispirited body took her to Miss Hart's little house with a few gifts she had brought her. On the way her thoughts were "Lord, I need time to grieve. I need to be alone with my thoughts of my mama. I need to think of Jewel. I need to think of myself."

Through all her little troubles and fears, Miss Hart was still smiling. Her brother was long dead and his children were with his city wife; they would never come to see about her. They might not even know she existed. The smile wasn't as bright, but it was still there.

Eula never forgot Miss Hart and sent her money every month, but, now, she could see Iowna Hart was alone and lonely. Before she knew how she would do it, she said, "Miss Hart, you hold on girl! I'm going to send for you. I'm going to take care of you. You are not going to be alone the rest of your life. I have some plans!" (She had no plans for even herself.) "And you use that telephone I had put in here and call me when you are feeling lonely! You hear me?"

The gratitude, the love, the thanksgiving that shone from Miss Hart's eyes filled even the air in that little house the weeds seemed to be taking over. (Sometimes fear and being alone, unhappiness, drain all your energy away. Any zest for life fades away.) As she hurried back to her family house, Eula Too was embarrassed because she had opened her mouth and did not have a plan. "Well, I sure am going to make one. I almost owe my life to Iowna Hart." Her grief for her mother was set aside until she could embrace it and cry out the way she felt inside.

Paul, the chauffeur, came to pick her up at the arranged time. She and Earle left together. Eula Too was thinking, "Earle can get to Chicago from my house and I will just go home."

Almost immediately, as Paul turned onto the highway toward Chicago, he said to Eula, "Madame is not in Chicago. I have taken her to Place, to her mother's house. She was already planning to go, but the nurse staying with her mother called to tell Madame to come as soon as possible. Her mother is having medical problems, and the nurse has problems getting her to take her medicine or eat or do anything. So, Madame's already gone. She wants me to take you there as soon as you can go. So, grab a few things to pack, if you need to do that, then we can start right away. It's a two-hour drive, and it is going to take us about an hour and a half to get to the house as it is. So, what do you think?"

Eula, fatigued and weary physically, and drained emotionally, felt as though she could collapse at that very moment. She thought, "I am so tired, so tired. But what do you say to a friend? I want time to grieve for my own mother. I haven't had time for all this to sink in. But, she must need me. She has never taken me to Place before. And what am I paid for except to be there when she needs me? I have to find the strength to go, somehow."

Earle watched her, as Paul peered through the rearview mirror at Eula, waiting for the answer. Eula leaned forward toward Paul, saying, "Of course. I will just run in and get a few changes of clothes, check the house, see if there are any messages from Jewel, and then we can go."

Still thinking of and grieving for her mother, Earle Mae made a disgusted sound with her breath and sadly asked, "Paul, will you be driving through Chicago city? Can you drop me off there?"

Because he and Earle were friends, Paul apologetically replied, "No, we're not going into the city, but there are a couple of places on the way where you can catch a bus or a train. Not far from Chicago. Take you about forty-five minutes. Okay?"

Earle tried to smile, "What can I say? That's better than walking." She looked meaningfully at Eula as she said, "And I sure will be glad to get back to that little room I used to call a dump. It looks really good to me now. Nothing but my own stuff in it, and I have peace and a little quiet. Home. I can do what I want to do in it. And I have to catch up on the civil rights news. Black people are fighting to be *all* free, Eula Too."

"I keep up with that too, Earle."

Earle decided to just say what she felt whether Paul was there or not. "Don't Madame know our mother just passed away? Don't she know you have some life of your own to take care of . . . without her in it?" Eula turned her head to look out of the window and did not answer.

It was quiet and somber in the automobile. Eula Too was thinking of peace and quiet as well as of her mother, when Earle interrupted her thoughts.

"Where was Jewel? Why didn't she come with you?"

"Oh, she's in school, studying, and I didn't want to burden her with Mama's death. She never did like going to Mama's anyway. She hated it there. I haven't even told her yet."

"What kind of child do you have? No, not 'child,' Jewel is almost a grown woman! Seventeen going on eighteen. Don't she know about death?! It could happen to her, you know. She don't know nothing about love, Eula. You better stop treating that girl like she is somethin' special! She is just a human being! And not a very nice one at that! Sometimes she acts like she is inhuman, so greedy and inconsiderate of others. No matter what they do for her. She never writes me, and I raised her the first ten years of her life, even if you were there! You better let her learn about life! And love! Mama was her grandmother!"

"I couldn't keep her from it. Life teaches everybody anyway. She is going to learn about love, Earle."

Earle retorted in her quick way, "You need to learn about love at home first. Well, without your help, it will be the hard way! And aside from sending people some money, you don't know nothin' much about it either." Glancing at Paul's back and lowering her voice, she added, "She worship that Madame too much, too. You ain't raising your child; everybody else is."

"Oh, Earle. Do we have to talk about that now? I don't feel like arguing about anything. Money is the only way I have to show love, anyway. And I don't have enough money reserved to take the time to do anything else."

Earle gave a tsk! with her tongue as she turned her face to the window, saying in a lowered voice, "You and all that 'proper' talking and your 'beautiful' apartment in somebody else's house on your 'beautiful' job! You still ain't living in nothin' but a whorehouse. Everybody fucking upstairs, all over your head, and you don't even know what sex is all about. You ain't got no love in your life, Eula. No love but family love. Listen, sister, I love you, but I know you are not happy and haven't been happy since I've known you. You need to do somethin' about that. Somethin' for yourself!"

"You so smart, Earle, just tell me who is happy? You need to read more and learn about life! Nobody is happy!"

Earle shook her head as she looked into her sister's eyes and said, "There are some people, red, yellow, white, black, and brown, who are happy. Not a lot of them, I'll grant you that, but some people have found their way on this earth and you don't always find the way in a book like all those books in Madame's library. I found it in the Bible! It's the only book I know that gives answers instead of a lot of questions and it's the only book I know that urges people to love and not hurt each other! Every other book I ever picked up, even in Madame's library or the public library, was somebody talkin' 'bout what they think and most times they can't prove it or they end up with a question! 'Cause if they thought so much and even put it in a book, and if they were right, this would be a much better world! Words! Just a lot of words! Don't know where they come from! Do they come from the heart? Or do they come from that wicked ole brain? Words supposed to make you civilized! Well, even civilized people, especially 'civilized' people, sometimes, kill people too! Not always with a knife or a gun. Poverty, and I have lived and seen poverty, is killin' people, too! It ain't just killin' black people either. It's killin' a whole lotta colors of people! This is a cold-blooded world, if truth be told, and you better be very careful, 'cause there ain't much 'love' in it that ain't fading away 'bout the same time it's beginning. Usually after it's done got what it came after!"

Paul pulled into the driveway of Madame's house. Eula turned a sad look to Earle as she reached for the door handle. "Are you coming in, Earle?" Earle shook her head no, saying, "You only gonna be a minute, aren't you?"

"Yes, I'll only be a minute. Get my bag for me, please, Paul."

She ran toward the house hearing Earle hollar from the car, "Tell Dolly hello for me, tell her I'll call her later."

When Eula Too entered the kitchen Dolly was stirring something at the stove with a kettle steaming and pots boiling. She turned to Eula with a frown, preoccupied in her mind.

Eula hugged her and started downstairs to her apartment. Dolly spoke in a serious tone unusual to Eula. "Eula? I think you better stop and talk to me a minute." Eula, sighed, tired, thinking it was something about Greta or something upstairs. She sat her bag down and stood still to listen.

Dolly put one hand on her hip, "How are you doing? I know you grieving. Mothers is hard to lose. Just remember, time takes care of everything, and it will take care of you." She motioned for Eula to take a seat at the table, but Eula shook her head no and said, "I can't, Dolly, I have to run right back out again. Madame has sent for me."

Dolly shook her head in wonder, "I know Madame is important 'round here, but she ain't in that Bible you love. You better stop and take a breath in your life." Dolly waved her thoughts away, saying, "Well and all, that ain't none of my business, but I need to tell you somethin' 'cause I can't take care of everything 'round here." Eula sat down and listened.

"You know . . . white folks is strange," Dolly began. Eula interrupted her, saying, "Everybody is strange sometimes, Dolly."

Dolly nodded sagely, "Yes, that's true. But, there is somethin' strange happinin' upstairs here. Now, I cook and Greta has the food taken upstairs to the ladies. Well, ain't but two of 'em now. And when you left here, just a few days ago, Rita was feelin' fine. But two days later, she don't feel so fine and when she happen to come down here, she don't look so good either. I ask her what is wrong with her and she say, 'I don't know, Dolly.' Well, I got my own thoughts about that Greta and her mean ways. I don't blive she mean to kill nobody, but if she mad at you, she just might want to see you hurtin' a little bit. I also know that accidents can happen. So a few days later, when I ain't seen nor heard Rita, I climb them stairs and go to her room. Honey, the chile was almost green. I mean green!"

Eula was tired and didn't want to think about anything but her dead mother, but she was alarmed. Dolly did not have an overactive imagination. "What happened? Did Greta call the doctor?"

"No. She actually smiled at me and said 'It will pass. Rita always puttin' on.' So I called him. He came and gave her something, but I told Rita, don't eat any food upstairs anymore. Come down here and eat and if you can't, I'll bring it up to you. So I been payin' Lester to come by here twice a day to run them stairs for me and take her a tray. Don't worry, I watch him. He ain't got but a minute to do it, then he got to hurry on back down here, 'cause I know he been dyin' to get up them stairs. And Rita too sick, anyway. She better now, but I need you to make a way so I don't have to keep all this worryin' up. I like Rita."

Eula thought a moment, while Dolly went back to stirring her pots. Then she said, "I will give you back the money you paid Lester. Get him to move Rita down on this floor to Greta's old room and leave her food to eat when you take off to go home. I don't have time to take care of everything now, but I will definitely have my mind on it and so will Madame. I'll run up to see Rita before I leave. Now," she stood up to leave the room, "I'm going to have to hurry."

As she rushed down the stairs she heard Dolly's words, "Your daughter is downstairs. She rushin' too." The words had just registered as Eula went through the wide-open apartment door thinking, "Jewel is at college studying for her junior year." Then she saw Jewel setting a suitcase down near the door.

Eula Too's eyes lit up and a weight seemed to lift from her soul at the sight of Jewel. Her first thought was to reach out and hug her daughter, then she saw Jewel's face. Jewel had hoped to get in and get out before her mother's return. She cursed Time in her mind as she resigned herself to having to speak with her mother.

"Hello, Mother. I had to get a few things. I'll have to come back because I can't carry them all this time."

Eula Too was overwhelmed with the pace of things happening around her. Everything seemed so sudden, so harsh. She dropped her arms. She was used to Jewel not acting like a loving child. Madame always said, "She is just reserved." Eula asked, "What . . . Why did you have to come get them? I would have sent them to you. You can't need that much that fast. Jewel, my mother, your grandmother is dead and has just been buried today."

Jewel took a firmer stand with her feet. "I'm sorry, Mother. I didn't really know her. As to my things, I want everything! I may never come back here again." She shrugged, "Unless it is to see Madame."

Eula tilted her head as she asked, "What are you talking about, Jewel? What do you mean, you're not coming back here? This is where we live."

"No. This is where you live. In a whorehouse! I've known the truth for years, but I had no way out. Now . . . I do. I am engaged to marry a fine young man who will be a doctor soon. A doctor! You hear me? I could never bring him or any of my friends home to visit me or meet you. Another thing I know is that I am 'supposed' to be illegitimate and you were supposed to be raped."

The sneer on Jewel's twisted face was ugly, and painful to her mother. Eula had never even dreamed her daughter, Jewel, felt the way her words sounded. Jewel continued, "I know, from the way your 'family' is, that my father was probably stupid and illiterate and lived in filth like your family. I don't blame you for running away, I'm glad, grateful really, you ran away from that hellhole."

Eula stepped back, knocked off balance by the barrage of hurtful words spewing from Jewel's mouth. She tried to speak, "Jewel, I had no control over . . . I never knew your father. It is you and I who are together. You are my daughter. I am your mother. I love you."

Jewel laughed with ugly hateful sounds Eula Too had never known were in her child. The laughter stopped abruptly as Jewel said, "Love? You love money! You loved me because you knew Madame loved me and I will probably get all that old woman's money!"

Eula Too's mind shrank back further as she tried to understand the ugly face spewing ugly words at her. All she could think to say was, "I am your mother. I love you, Jewel."

Jewel picked up her bag and started toward the patio doors, where Eula could now see a car loaded with clothes was parked. "I'm going now, Mother Dear. *MISS* Eula Too. I'm going to be a *MRS*. And don't you try to contact me and complicate my life! Just leave me alone. I don't want any part of your life to interfere with my opportunity for a new clean life. Madame has given me enough money to hold me until I am married."

Jewel looked back as she closed the patio doors, "By the way, Mother Dear, you'll be a grandmother soon, but you'll never see it." She laughed as the door slammed closed.

Eula Too stood still in wonder, full of all kinds of grief . . . and love. Grief for her own mother, love for her own child, as her child, Jewel, got in her car, slammed her car door, and drove away from her.

As Eula Too, dazed, stumbled to her bedroom, her eyes searched through tears for the little frame on her wall that held the dollar bill from her rape. She had framed and kept it to remember the pain and never go through it again. All she could think was "Life. Life. Life."

There was no time for tears, no time for thought, no time for Rita, no time for herself. "I don't want to think. God, help me. Help me. Help me find some place where I can be quiet, and alone, 'til I can get myself together. Dear God, please. Help me. I've got to go, one more time, to Madame, then I'm going to get away to myself, God. I've just got to, God. Or I'll die." Then the tears came anyway.

Finally Eula Too got into the car with Paul and Earle. She didn't say a word and, instinctively, Earle read her mood and didn't disturb her. After driving an hour or so, Paul began pulling over toward the train station.

Earle placed her hand over her sister's and leaned over to Eula Too, saying, "You are not all alone, Eula Too. I can see in your face something bad happened in your mind. You are confused because you are not living your own life, Eula. Use your own mind for your own self! You got some of your own money, I know it."

Aghast at her sister's words adding to a load she already carried, Eula asked, "How can you say that? What makes you so smart?"

Earle placed her hand on the door handle as she said, "Because I know. 'Cause I been kind'a livin' and learning on my own. 'Cause I'm kind'a happy. 'Cause I'm doing the things I love—my art and my music. And I got a man who kind'a loves me more than I love him, right now anyway. 'Cause I'm living my life. My way. And I thank you for all the help you give me to help me do that. But, I have just decided, I don't want no more help from you. You need help yourself, dear helping sister. I have also decided I'm going to go south and march with the Reverend Martin Luther King people. He is doing good things with his 'help.'"

Paul pulled to the curb as Earle pulled the door handle down and reached for the little traveling bag at her feet. She got out of the car smiling at Eula with love, saying "I love you, Eula Too. I'll write soon . . . and send you another book or two!" With reddened eyes from all the crying she herself had been doing, Earle laughed her bright laughter as she said, "You can count on that! I love you, fool." Then she was rushing into the train station, away, and Eula was left in the backseat, alone.

Eula wanted to cry out for Earle or get out of the car to grab her sister and hold her a moment. But the traffic was distracting with its blowing horns, and . . . Madame was waiting. So Eula Too sat back in the seat and, looking out of the window, thought about her sister's words all the way to Placeland. The Place she had often wondered about. The Place Madame had run away from. She rolled the name around in her mind: "Place." Shaking her head sadly. "Lord, I sure do need *some* place where I can rest and get my mind together."

*My birth is to be there. In this Place! Those are the houses I told you about. I know the stories of all those six houses and that grocery store! My mother is going to be there! But, where is my father? Who is my father?*

# Chapter Seventeen

*

From the highway, in the distance Eula could see the sun sparkling on the roiling dark blue-green water of Striver River. Finally Paul turned off the highway on the turnoff to Placeland. Eula, in mental and spiritual turmoil, was lured away from her painful thoughts. The car glided across railroad tracks and past a good half mile of beautiful tall trees in shades of green, silver, and blue. He turned left on Dream Street before he reached the little bridge spanning Striver River that led into town proper. He drove directly to Madame's mother's house at 903 Dream Street.

Still stunned from the last few days of her life, Eula forced herself to sit up and see what she could of the town Madame grew up in. There were only houses and one small grocery store on Madame's block. She thought, "It looks . . . kind of poor. Middle class, I guess, and lower middle class, if there is such a thing here. But it looks friendly and clean. It's a nice little town, I guess, but where is the town itself?"

As if he had read her mind, Paul said, "There are some very rich old families here with fine houses, but they live farther inland from the river. I think they wanted to get as far away as possible from the industrial section and the railroad tracks they knew, in advance, were going to pass through here near the river." He laughed softly. "I think they realized their mistake about this prime river property later. But, by then, people had bought this riverbank land, cheaply, and built their homes on it. This is a pretty place, most of the year. You have to follow that road that goes over the bridge to get to the downtown section where all the stores are."

Paul slowed down as the car neared Mrs. Fontzl's house, saying,

"I'm not going to stay here. You can call me when Madame is ready to go home. I'll check to see if there is anything she wants before I leave." The car pulled up to a dreary gray house in the middle of a large yard with the Striver River flowing behind it. Eula thought, "Dream Street, huh? That's all I need," and reached for the car door handle.

Madame had been waiting, watching for them to arrive. She rushed to the front door, opening it. Her arms reached out to welcome Eula, who could see Madame's eyes were red-rimmed and sad. As Madame ushered them into the house, she spoke to the chauffeur first. "You can go, Paul, I won't need you. Nurse Santi will get whatever we need from the pharmacy and I have a car here that Eula Too can drive, should she need to. Thank you so much, Paul. We will be calling you. If you have to go anywhere and won't be at the home number, call Eula and let us know."

She turned to Eula, "Oh, come in, come in, Eula. I'm so glad you've come. Perhaps you can handle my mother better than we can. She wants the nurse to leave, Nurse Santi. You'll meet her, she tries to be so good to Mama. Prepares such good things Mother won't eat. I can't handle this all by myself anymore. Come on, I'll show you your room."

She was so upset she picked up and carried Eula's bag all the way to the room, talking as she led the way. "Mama does not eat, no matter what Nurse Santi prepares for her. I stay in the room next to her and I hear her stirring around in the night, knocking things over. Screaming at me, sometimes, but she won't let me in. She locks me out! She believes every bad thing that ever happened to her since I left home is my fault. I don't know what to do anymore!"

They reached a small, but cozy, room. Madame dropped Eula's bag as she looked around the room, saying, "I have tried to improve things here, really fix them up, make everything pretty for her, but she never really lets me do much. There was just too much arguing to go through to get anything done."

Eula, understanding, nodded as she said, "Why not do some things now, while she is sick and locked in her room."

Madame tightly clasped her hands together and answered, "You don't understand. She would fly out of that room, then, and raise holy hell."

Eula patted Madame's shoulder, saying, "Isn't that what you want her to do? Come out of her room?"

Madame stood there, discouraged and heavyhearted, then a pathetic smile appeared on her face. She reached her arms out for Eula and held her, laying her head on Eula's shoulder. Finally, she said, "I knew. I always knew, you were the one, my friend. You make things so simple, so easy, so real."

Eula patted her back, briefly, then moved to unpack her suitcase. "Listen, honey, I'm just too tired . . . too tired, to think of anything better right now, but I will. When you feel calm enough, you sit down with some paper and write and draw out what you might want to change around here. Just little things to begin with. You might start with that yard. That river in back of your yard makes the whole place just beautiful! Do that first, then we'll see what to do next. Alright? I'll see what I can do for your mother. Alright?"

Madame put her hand over her face as she said, "Your mother! Ahhh, you have just lost your mother. Oh, Eula, I don't know what to say. What can I say? Did the flowers I sent get there on time? They kept calling me back because they couldn't find the house. Oh! Eula, you know I am so sorry. All my sympathy goes out to you and your family."

"I know it does, Madame. Let's not talk about it right now. I'm saving it for when I can rest and think. I haven't had time to really think. I didn't see her often, but at least I knew she was there. I'll be alright . . . in time. Has Jewel called?"

"No, she hasn't. You know I have hardly thought of her this past week. I have had so much on my mind. But, no, she hasn't called. Well, she must be alright, because if she wasn't we would have heard from her." A sound from the room next door caused them both to look at the wall dividing the rooms. As Madame turned to go, she said, "See! She's moving around in there, but she won't come out! She needs her medicine! She needs to eat!"

When Madame left the room, Eula sat down on the narrow bed and reckoned on her space in life at that moment. She needed something to make sense. "I wish I knew some place I could go and just rest. Just rest and think . . . get myself together. I have to put that at the top of my list: I have got to find a place for myself, all my own, away from . . . everybody, but Jewel. For a while."

She thought of the money she had been able to save, stealing it from herself, and all the responsibilities she had taken on over the years. Twenty-something thousand dollars. "That's all I have to show for all my years of work." She shook her head sadly. "Lord, I know that's more than a whole lot of people, but, Lord, so much money has passed through my hands, I should have more saved." She stood up, thinking, "But, I'll be alright, Lord." As she left her room to go to the kitchen, she thought, "Lord, I'm thinking so much more of You since my mother died. I'm so glad You are there."

Eula met the nurse, Miss Santi, who was a bright, pretty, tan-skinned, middle-aged woman. She moved sprightly and efficiently among the trays and bottles of medicine on the counter in the sparkling clean kitchen. She was smiling, but worried, as she took measure of Eula Too.

When Madame left the kitchen, Santi turned from the counter to Eula, saying, "Mrs. Fontzl does not have long to be here in this world if she does not eat and take this medicine the doctor says she has to have! And Mrs. Fontzl's daughter has her own problems with her mother. I'm at my wits' end trying to balance my work between them. But I have to concentrate on Mrs. Fontzl eating and taking her medicine. I'm glad you are here. Mary Green, the next-door neighbor, is her friend and tries to help, but even she can't make her take her medicine. And she is old and sick herself. She will let Mary Green in, but she won't come out! until I am asleep or out of the kitchen. Now that you are here, maybe I can concentrate on Mrs. Fontzl."

Madame's mother had been sick a long time. Perversely, she had hidden it from Madame, or Elizabeth, as she called her daughter. She thought she was punishing her daughter by not telling her. Now Elizabeth was there. As pain held her body in sharp, long, clawing grips, she thought, "Let her be in pain like I have been in pain!"

On this morning, when she heard someone called Eula, arrive, the pains were more harsh than usual. She panted, grateful as the latest pain receded. "Eula. That's who she is always calling on that telephone." After a moment, when her breathing was regular again, she turned to reach for a bottle of pills she had hidden "to fool them," but the small container was empty. She was suddenly desperate. "I know I have another bottle in here." She searched the room with her eyes. "There it is, on my dresser." Mrs. Fontzl was happy, for a moment. She knew she could not get up easily or go far.

She started to call for Elizabeth to send for Mary Green, but she remembered the door was locked. Her mind blanked out in the midst of another pain. As the pain left her body it seemed to take with it a veil, a cloud from her mind. Her reasoning cleared to a reality and she wondered, "Am I going to die?" Frightened, she looked at the locked door. As another pain bore down through her fragile, exhausted, body she thought, "My daughter is on the other side of that door. Why did I lock that door? My daughter is not going to hurt me. Why did I lock that door?"

Then the veil returned, a mist that clouded her mind. She was snarling, "Because I hate her!" but it hurt to snarl. It hurt her face, and it hurt her heart. A dark, deep loneliness almost of the grave filled her body with a different kind of pain. "I am alone." She began to cry. The mist cleared from her mind once more. "I don't hate her. My child. I don't hate her. I . . . love her. My own baby. All that I have . . . I owe to her. I have nothing."

In her tortured, disturbed mind, something broke through and, for the first time in years, she thought of her daughter's face, her tears, her pleadings. The Mother's heart tried to beat stronger, to race back into life. She wanted to hold her daughter and tell her she loved her. "Everything is alright, Bethie. Everything will be alright . . . now. We will be together now."

The Mother willed her body, covered with sweat, to move, to turn out of her bed. She fell, with a soft thud. Soft, because she was so thin, so small. Elizabeth, ever listening, heard the sound and ran to her mother's door, asking, "Are you alright, Mama? Mama! Open this door. Mama?"

The Mother tried to crawl, but could not move fast enough for a heart that was urgently urging her body to be still. But her will said, "Move!" She reached out to her bedside table and pulled the covering cloth off, the lamp and small bottles came crashing to the floor. Then she fell back, spent, exhausted, to the floor herself.

Elizabeth pounded on the door. Eula Too came rushing to the sounds of distress, taking Madame into her arms and quickly taking in the situation. She hollered to Santi, "Where is a hammer? Are there other skeleton keys around here?" She turned back to Madame, "Don't panic on me now! Go!" She made her voice calm, saying, "Look for a skeleton key."

Santi handed Eula a hammer. Eula turned away from Madame as she said, "I'll try to open the hinges with the hammer." She looked back at Madame, "I'll get this door open, so help me!"

Elizabeth was gone, rushing, searching for keys. Saying out loud, "Keys! Mama, where are the keys?!"

Eula Too was trying, with some success, to hammer hinges out that had not moved in thirty or forty years when Elizabeth came rushing to her with a handful of skeleton keys. "They were in the highboy!" She pushed Eula out of the way and, fumbling, tried one key, two keys, and, finally, the third key turned the lock. It was the sweetest, kindest sound she thought she had ever heard in her life.

Crying out as she flung the door open, Elizabeth, the daughter, rushed to her mother, lifting her before anyone could move to help, by herself, back onto the bed. She smoothed her mother's hair as she asked, "Her pills?" She held the Mother to her, making soothing sounds as she asked, "Where are your pills, Mama?"

But Santi was standing there, pills and a glass of water in hand.

The Mother had given up trying. Hope was gone. A wasteland of loneliness filled her dying body. For she realized it had been a waste not to use every minute she could to love her child. *The mind is kind, sometimes. It will forget, for you, the things you cannot bear. Also, sometimes, it will bring things back to you, when you have forgotten them, and least want them. But, now is not the time to think of that. A woman, a Mother, is dying.*

Madame Elizabeth sat holding her mother, soothing her with the soft, tender sound of her voice, lovingly brushing back a wisp of dry, gray hair, delicately kissing the beloved brow she could now kiss freely, compassionately. She had longed, for so long, to do this, but not in this way. Madame knew, almost, that her mother was dying.

She had taken her medicine without a whimper. Then they tried giving her warm soup, tea, warm milk with a piece of toast soaked in it. Even warm eggnog. "For strength," Santi said as she tilted the cup to Mrs. Fontzl's slightly blue, parched lips.

Eula Too watched them, the Mother and daughter, and she thought of her last minutes with her own mother. She cried without knowing she cried. When Madame looked up, she thought Eula was crying for her and her mother. Eula Too was deeply sorry for Madame's mother, but she was crying for her own mother, her own self. "Who will come save me?" she asked God. *I wanted to cry out to her, to my mother, "I will," but could not.*

The tears Eula was shedding, in her heart, were for her own mother. "Why didn't I move away? Buy a house? Give my mother a place where she could be happy, and I could take care of her myself? Be with her?" She had forgotten, for the moment, why she had not done that. Her mother had had an entourage. A family that would not let go. Or was it she, the mother, who would not let go?

Mrs. Fontzl, as she lay dying in her daughter's arms, tried to tell the child she had given birth to and who had begged her for these words for years, how much she did love her. She tried to lift a frail hand up to Elizabeth's face, but no longer had the strength. She could whisper though, "I do love you, Elizabeth. My daughter, Bethie. I love you, my Bethie. I love you."

"Shhhhhhhh," Madame Bethie cautioned. "Save your strength." She said this, while at the same time longing to hear more . . . more. Her heart was feeling so happy, so happy, even as she feared she was losing her dearest on earth. "Save your strength, Mama. We will talk more, when my doctor gets here and makes you well again."

She placed her finger, delicately, over her mother's lips. The Mother lifted a weak, but loving, hand up to hold her daughter's finger. As she looked at her daughter, she murmured, "I love . . . Don't leave . . ." and breathed out her last breath. Her eyes were open, still staring at Elizabeth, until the nurse, Santi, closed them.

Elizabeth cried with joy for the love, with relief that they had become friends and a family before it was all over. But with frightened tears of pain and anguish that her mother was gone. Gone, before all they could have done together had been done.

She turned to Eula Too.

Both Eula Too and Santi tried to console Madame, but there was no consolation for the suffering, devastated, broken middle-aged woman who had had everything she had ever wanted, but her mother. When her own doctor arrived, he gave her a sedative and she slept, in her mother's bed, eyes and cheeks still wet with tears.

Santi helped Eula Too with local arrangements from the information Madame had given Eula. Mrs. Fontzl's body was taken away while, after a sedative, Madame slept. The Waiter Funeral Home was the best in Placeland. Neighbors and a small group of church friends Mrs. Fontzl had made over many years began to call and were directed to the funeral home for information. The minister of her church was consulted.

At last the house was quiet. Nurse Santi sat, staring at the medicine trays and dishes on the counter. She was truly sorry for old Mrs. Fontzl and, of course, for Elizabeth Fontzl. "She must have been a beautiful young woman because she is still a good-looking woman now. I wonder why she never married? She never even had any children who could comfort her now. She has no sister or brother either. Lord, Lord, Lord. I guess You let a person make their own life, but the life a person makes sure can get cruel on you." She shook her head in sadness.

Eula lay, spent, on the bed in her room, staring at the ceiling. "Lord, this is too much death. Too much grief. I can't take anymore now. And what am I going to do when she wakes up? I still have my own grief, and I am going to have to deal with hers. Lord, help me, please." She wanted to sleep, but sleep would not come.

The room became shadowy as the sky darkened. Eula had barely moved, still staring into space, when she heard the scream from Madame, in the next room. She jerked her body up on her feet and rushed to Madame's call.

Eula entered the room, searching the wall for a light switch, but discarded the thought when she remembered the lamp beside the bed. She bent to pull the little chain and, when the light came on, Madame was sitting up, staring wildly, searching with her eyes. Relief flooded her face when she saw Eula Too. "Eula Too! You are here! Oh, Eula Too! Hold me!"

Eula quieted her with calming, caring words as Nurse Santi got the sedatives the doctor had left for Madame. When Madame lay back down again, she still stared at Eula Too. She reached for Eula as the tears streamed down her face. Eula reached back and, sitting on the bed, pulled Madame into her arms and just held her until the sniffling stopped. A long time.

Nurse Santi had cleaned and cleared the kitchen and, with nothing else to do, she told Eula, "I'm going to go lie down and rest. I'll be right here if you need me. Just call for me. I wonder should we have let her sleep in her mother's bed. In that room? Well, too late now." She yawned and shook her head, saying, "I'm really tired. I know you are, too. You're a nice person, Eula Too. I know you just come from losing your own mother. Lord, have mercy on you." She yawned again. "Well, I'm sure tired. So, good night, child."

Eula, still sorrowful, smiled a little as she said, "Thank you. But, Santi, I'm as old as you are. I'm in my thirties. How can you call me a child?"

Santi smiled sadly in return, saying, "You know . . . We are all children when it comes to pain and sorrow. Not many can take it, and I don't think any of us really understand why it happens to us. Some people don't survive it. But, thank God, most of us can. Well, good night . . . child." She chuckled as she moved down the hall to her room.

Eula Too was so tired. "I have to get some sleep myself because tomorrow is really going to be hard on all of us." She looked down at Madame's head in the crook of her arm. "I think she is sound asleep. Maybe I can leave her now."

But Eula had hardly moved a muscle when Madame's eyes opened wide, her grip tightened on Eula's body, and her lips parted in distress and indignation. "Don't leave me, Eula! Hold me, hold me. Get under these covers, get in this bed and hold me. Get undressed, get in bed, and hold me. Put your arms around me. Now. Please. I need you. Please."

Eula gently twisted her body away, saying in a low voice, "Let go of me." Madame held on, tightly, until Eula said, "I'll be right back."

Madame watched the empty doorway, feverishly, until Eula, dressed in her nightgown, returned. She lay back, never taking her eyes off Eula, as Eula pulled back the covers and moved her body into the bed.

Madame's face relaxed a little. She leaned over Eula and pressed her lips, hard, on Eula's head. Madame moved her body over, giving Eula more room. Eula moved into the space Madame had made for her. Madame wrapped her arms around Eula, placing her head on Eula Too's shoulder. She clung tightly to her. Throughout the night, in Eula's own restless sleep, she heard Madame whimpering softly in her sleep. Eula would cradle the distressed body closer and pat her back until Madame rested quietly again. Throughout the night.

*There was love in that bed with the two women. One was fearful, lonely, dependent, desperate, and searching. The other was fearful, dependent, desperate, lonely, and possessive. Each was lonely without the other. Each was lonely even with the other.*

*Sex . . . had nothing to do with it.*

# Chapter Eighteen

*

*I have told you this tale has its beginnings in many places leading to the houses I saw and told you of on Dream Street, to this town called Placeland. I cannot see the future, but I think this is where I will be born. My mother has just arrived here.*

*Most of the inhabitants of Placeland call it Place. This is not a large town, the population is mainly older people because most of the young people leave after high school or, getting old enough, seek some other place. Place is large enough to have two banks and a few small but adequate department stores. There are two shoe stores, one for the elite and high middle class, one for the general working middle class and poor. It has a few good restaurants with the same distinctions, several cafés, and numerous small drinking places.*

*The post office is situated almost in the middle of town near the courthouse, a place where people meet and pass time in friendly conversation. A block or so from the post office are two large markets, across the street from each other, in unfriendly competition. Several small grocery stores are scattered throughout the town and suburbs for convenience. The one pharmacy is large and contains general notions departments and the only bookstore in town. The hospital is nearby.*

*The Striver River separates the main business section from one of the slightly smaller, poor or middle-class sections, sometimes called Otherplace, where Dream Street is. People who work in town can drive or walk over the short bridge across Striver River. There are no businesses in Otherplace, except for two small grocery stores about two miles apart and one little bootleg liquor house.*

*I love the Striver River. It is a full, swift-flowing river fed by many creeks, underground springs, and other inlets. It flows clear and glittering through the town, full of flitting and jumping fish. It nourishes its banks so the earth is rich with everything growing lush and abundantly there. Pine trees, spruces, willows, and many other beautiful trees with a multitude of colors and smells. They are home to a variety of beautiful birds and shelter many small creatures.*

*There are places where the river widens and becomes shallow with rocks so wide you can cross over on them from the town to the other side where Dream Street sits in front of the woods. On one side of the bridge road, a few houses are scattered throughout the miles of woods. On the other side, farther along a dense strip of woodland, is the small railroad terminal.*

*The woodland gives an impression of broad depth, yet the highway is just beyond at the base of the hills. The hills seem to stretch miles and miles away, following the river's course. The train station, two miles from town and about a mile up the river, transports people and goods in and out of Place. For the young-at-heart and the seekers there is a big little city, Elysee City, full of the latest exciting things, about forty minutes away by train.*

*In the summers the river land smells of cool, sweet, wild scents of sap, earth, leaves, stones, wild ducks, fungus, and various other natural odors. Birds and wildflowers abound and make their home there. Though it is a clear, sparkling river, it is muddy and swampy near its banks. All the living creatures that thrive and survive on the Striver River can be likened to the people who, from their own inlets, trickled into Place or Otherplace.*

*Otherplace houses had been built along the river before the moneyed townspeople realized the shoreline property's worth was much more than they had imagined. At first they thought placing the workers across the river was close enough and far enough for any division necessary. But the town was too small for much segregation of rich and poor, black and white, yellow and brown. People lived everywhere. The size and style of their houses was an indication of their money . . . and the degree of separation.*

*There are not many rich people who move to Place. The founders grew rich after they established the foundation. The hardware store family, the Places, have sold all the lumber used in Placeland from the very beginning. The first family of bankers, the Winters, loaned the money to buy the lumber and held mortgages on the buildings. One old contractor and his sons, the*

*Evans, held mortgages, or have, on most of the town. The old dairy and egg farmers, the Goodes, were here from the beginning and are very, very well-to-do.*

*These first families who came seeking a place, found and named it Placeland. Their children, grandchildren, and even some great-grandchildren had grown up in Place or came back to their home base. They had long forgotten, if some of them ever knew, why their ancestors had been seeking a "place" in the first place.*

*Sometimes when musing over the waterfront land wasted in Otherplace, the wealthy wished their forefathers had had foresight enough to see the advantage of even more potential income and, of course, a view. They lived farther inland where their forefathers had looked at the never-ending land, thinking to buy more of it in the future. It was the only direction to go if the town expanded. The railroad depot was built in Otherplace because it was near the highway, thereby seeming to condemn the railroad side of the town to the poorer residents and industry.*

*Across the bridge from town, in Otherplace, one of the two streets was named Strong Street and our street was named Dream Street. Just as the river at its back door received its flow from all the inlets to it, so did Strong Street and Dream Street receive those whose less-than-monied life brought them to it.*

*The houses on Dream Street are not ugly so much as just old. Their paint is fading away, their wood decaying, their bricks holding, but loose. Windows that won't open in summer and, once opened, won't close in winter. The houses will be fixed "one day" because the people here want to keep their property up, when possible. These are two-story houses with basements. Madame's family, the Fontzls, are at 903, the Greens at 905, and 907 has been vacant for a while. Their backyards face the business center of Place and sit above the river. The river runs some one hundred feet behind the houses on the odd-numbered side of Dream Street, creating a naturally beautiful backyard with the lush green growth of all those bushes, trees, and wildflowers I told you about, filled with birds and small animals.*

*Across the street, on the corner of the even-numbered houses, there is a small grocery store owned by an Asian man, Mr. Henry Lee at 906 Dream*

*Street. Mrs. Maureen Iris McVistin, a widow of Irish, Hebrew, and English descent, lives at 902, on the other corner of that block. She survives on a small pension her Irish husband left her. The house is paid for but she has to live very frugally. At 904, the middle of the block, lives a Black schoolteacher, Mr. Lamont Heavy, with his invalid wife, Odearlia.*

*I tell you of these people because my mother, Eula Too, is going to meet them.*

The nurse Santi followed Madame's instructions and took care of all preparations for the funeral, which would be in two days. She had one of her cousins, Jean Collins, come to help her comfort, calm, and bolster both Madame and Eula.

The house was full of both their griefs, but everyone, even Eula Too, catered to Madame. Eula nursed her grief when she was alone in her little room at the back of the house, facing the river. Gloom filled the house like a heavy fog, and everyone kept their voices low with respect for the dead.

Though she certainly understood, finally Jean was weary of moving through such encompassing sadness, so she called for her husband, Jerry, to come and help them out. He had a wonderful sense of humor, as well as respect for the dead, and soon the house lightened up a little among those preparing for the wake. There were no visitors to interrupt anyone so Santi was able to keep the house running smoothly with their help. A caterer would bring most of the food.

Santi spoke to the house in general, "We don't need a lot of food because I don't think that many people are coming. I don't even know if everyone knows yet. To tell the truth I don't even know who Mrs. Fontzl knew."

Jerry spoke up, "Her church will know. The minister will tell them."

Jean answered him. "The funeral will be at the funeral home. The minister is helping with the contacts. The wake is going to be here tomorrow night."

Santi said, "Let me go ask Eula to ask Elizabeth about this again to be sure."

After Santi left the room, Jerry asked his wife, "Why does she have to ask someone else to ask somebody else something?"

"Because Elizabeth cannot be disturbed now. Eula Too seems to handle everything for her."

"And who is Eula Too? Eula Two or Eula Too? Where did somebody get a name like that? Eula number two!"

"Hush, Jerry. She is a very nice person."

"I don't question that, I just question where she got that name!"

"Hush. It is not yours to question. Her mother named her."

Santi returned saying, "Eula says someone will go around the block and tell the neighbors. I don't think Mrs. Fontzl went out much because she was alone and didn't like to go out alone. So Eula will take care of it."

**M**adame lay on the bed in her mother's room staring at the ceiling. Eula Too was restlessly trying to nap in her room. She was trying to think of nothing, but everything kept forging through her mind. Her mother, her daughter, her life swirled around in her head almost at the same time. "I already called Burnett and Earle. He is old and sick and she isn't coming." Burnett had told her, "You are a caring and wise friend. She hasn't needed me in years." He wryly chuckled, "She won't need me right now. I'll see her later, when I can get away from my loving relatives, who are trying to be the nicest so they can get the mostest!" He laughed again, because he knew most of his relatives loved him as much as they did his money; if they hadn't, he wouldn't have let them near him. He knew quite a bit about people.

Eula turned over on the bed and looked through the windows at the darkening sky. She thought, "So much. So much going on in life now. I do not have time to think about myself, my mother, nothing. I have to think about Madame and the funeral. I have to think about a wake for Mrs. Fontzl, and Madame is no help at all. Well, I guess I'll be the one who will walk up this block and let her neighbors know. Tomorrow. Tomorrow I will do it. I need to get out of this house anyway. I need to be away for a while."

Eula stayed in that room until Jean and Jerry had prepared dinner and served it to Madame. She ate in the kitchen, glad for the opportunity to lighten up the atmosphere with low laughter at Jerry's mild jokes. They were glad to see her smile. Then she went back to her little room and sat looking through the windows overlooking the backyard. Her love for being outside in the open air near trees and water made her think of going to sit in the backyard.

The sunset was almost gone, the sky darkened to make way for the moon. As she looked at the river the lonesome moon lighted the night for miles beyond. The trees seemed to be growing from within the river, a dark jungle teeming with unseen, unheard life. Quiet from the day's noisy birds. She knew many little tiny lives were being fought for out beneath the brush and grasses. It was a silent night except for the soft roar of the Striver River flowing rapidly just beneath her windows.

Eula left by the front of the house, letting Santi know where she was going. Once outside, she could see a few flickering lights in the direction of the town. She walked slowly around the house to the backyard as she took a deep breath of the fresh, damp night air. She smiled to herself. Night sounds pleased her. She looked for a rock or some place to sit near the river. As she stood still, looking, she heard a meow and turned to see a small striped cat coming toward her. "Well! Now I feel safer if you are going to walk around here with me."

She moved closer to the river, slowly, watching the cat to see if it would follow. She thought the cat would know when the ground was too wet to walk on. She reached a tree stump, sat down on it, and a moment later the little cat jumped into her lap. She was going to shush him off when she realized the kitten was shivering from the night cold and let him remain where he was. She smiled as she felt it for wet feet and dirt. Satisfied, she pet the cat until it settled comfortably on her warm lap, purring.

"What's your name? Who do you belong to? You smell a bit musty, but you're a pretty little thing." As she stroked him, she relaxed and forgot him; her attention was taken by the silence and beauty of the night, the voice of the river. They sat that way a long time.

Trees take on different shapes at night, still beautiful, but different. The few clouds looked black and somehow a different beauty floated in the sky. The moon looked so close, big and golden-white. The night breeze became cooler and Eula pulled her light coat tighter around her as she held the cat to keep it from falling. She felt peaceful. Away. Separate. Alone. Good.

Thoughts of Jewel, never far from her mind, made her frown and she sighed deep from her heart. Tears were threatening to come when she heard sounds that startled her, the sound of footsteps filtered through the undergrowth. She turned her face away from the river, searching the darkness to see who it might be. "Probably Santi," she thought. "Surely not Madame. Damn!"

Then she saw the form was that of a man. "Not Santi nor Madame," she thought, "Maybe a hobo?" She became a bit alarmed. "I am in a strange place." She sat very still.

When the man reached near the water's edge he stopped and stood still with his arms folded across his chest. He stared up the river in the direction of the railroad station. He was a tall and slender man, not thin, but his chest seemed broad. A short-sleeved white shirt revealed the outline of full, well-shaped arms.

Eula Too sat still as she watched him. He hadn't seen her yet. "Damn!" she repeated soundlessly. "My chance to be alone for a while, gone. You can't even get away in Place! I miss that huge yard at home." As she slowly rose to leave, the cat, reluctantly, slid to the ground. The man, startled himself, turned to face her. "Oh! Hey, I'm sorry. Did I disturb you?" A smile changed his sad face, but it was still a sad smile. He spoke to her in low tones so as not to disturb the night. "I'm not a trespasser. I'm a neighbor. Mrs. Fontzl lets me walk through her yard to the river. I like to come here at night; it's a good place for thinking."

"He's a black man!" Eula thought as she stared at him. She said, "You did startle me, but that's alright. I was just going back in."

"Please, don't let me run you off. My name is Lamont Heavy and I live right across the street. Please don't leave because of me." He smiled again.

Eula liked his smile, but didn't really relax yet. She could feel the soft little cat rubbing her legs as she thought, "He is a nice-looking man."

He continued smiling as he spoke, "Mrs. Fontzl may never let me use her yard again if I run you away. And how is Mrs. Fontzl? I haven't seen her lately. I work late so much, I've missed her."

Weary, Eula relaxed in spite of herself. "I am so sorry to tell you, Mrs. Fontzl died early today."

"Oh, my God."

"Yes. I am here with her daughter, Elizabeth, to take care of things. My name is Eula Too. The funeral will be in two days, if you . . . The wake will be, here, tomorrow evening around five-thirty, I think. I planned to let her neighbors know so they can come. I was just tired today and . . ." She thought she was talking too much and stopped. "Well, anyway, now I have told you."

"I'm really sorry to hear she has died. I liked her. She was always nice to me." He moved closer to Eula. "I know how you must feel. Don't you leave, I'll leave. I know this is an especially good place to be when you feel sad . . . hurt or blue." After a moment he said, "I see little Toots has found you."

"Oh, is she a girl? Yes, she just made herself at home on my lap. Is she yours?"

"No, though I feed her sometimes. She doesn't belong to anyone. She's a scrounger; a survivor, so far. I have a . . . I had a dog." After a moment, he continued. "He died not too long ago."

"Ahhh, I am sorry to hear that. I love dogs. And cats too. I just love living things, I guess."

Eula could see him better now that he was closer. His skin seemed to be a coppery brown. His eyes were dark and clear, but tired. His lips were tightly grim in a patient but slightly haggard face. In general he had good features. His pleasant manners and grave courtesy matched the warm mellow tone of his voice. Her eyes lingered on his face as she finally answered, "Yes. It is restful here by the river. I like the sound of water and feeling the breeze on my face. Why don't we both stay? There's enough room and I won't bother you either. I'll just sit here a moment more, quietly."

He sighed, moving away from her, saying "I needed a moment of peace and beauty. You won't even know I am here either. I'll be leaving soon." He looked at her as she turned away, thinking, "She seems to have an honest open face. She has the same golden-brown coloring as Odearlia. A nice height. It's hard to see, but her hair is brushed back; looks nice. I only saw a flash, but her teeth looked even and white when she smiled that pretty smile." He wasn't thinking of her for himself. He didn't want to get involved with anyone, nor love again. "Wonder why I never saw her visiting Mrs. Fontzl before. She must have known her, otherwise why would she be so sad? Well, it's not for me to know. It's hard enough to keep Lona away."

He left quietly. As his footsteps faded Eula turned her eyes to the space he was leaving. It seemed to be more lonely by the river now that he was gone and she was alone again. It was still a starry night and she had wanted to be alone, but now it was a lonely aloneness.

Soon she went in, carrying the cat with her. She rinsed Toots off and rubbed her dry. Then she fixed herself a cup of tea and watched Toots eat the small plate of scraps placed before her. "I think you are far too graceful and dignified to have a name like Toots. I think I will name you Tobe, as in 'To be or not to be,' and you will be mine if no one else claims you. And a better bath is in order, Miss Tobe."

A little bit of her loneliness slipped away as Miss Tobe slipped into Eula's life. In her sleep, throughout the night, she felt with her feet for the little lump near the foot of her bed. She listened for the kitten's purr as it signaled its pleasure at not being alone outside in the cold night. Eula Too would smile and slip back into her slumber. Such a little thing with a purring heart was doing a big service. Once Eula thought, "I hope Madame will allow me to keep it." Then she frowned, thinking, "I am going to keep it anyway, no matter."

. . .

The next morning Eula found Santi and Jean getting ready for the wake, doing last-minute preparations for that night. She went to check on Madame, thinking, "I am so glad Santi is staying to care for Madame. She really needs someone to do all these things right now. And I better call Dolly and see what is happening there."

Madame tasted her breakfast, but had no appetite for food. She was peevish, and in a quarrelsome voice asked, "Where were you last night? You didn't come to check with me." Then her voice changed, "Never mind, I know you are tired. You've been doing so much." She smoothed her hands over the spread and asked, "Have you heard from Jewel?"

"No, she hasn't called me."

"She will, Eula. You know she will. Eula, will you let the immediate neighbors know about the wake and funeral for me? We don't have time to write, so we should call them. I'm sure these are the only people who will be coming anyway."

"I already thought of that. I like the fresh air out here; seems like country air. I want to get out of this tight, busy house. I think I will just walk to each house and let them know what time they can come pay their respects."

Madame looked at Eula strangely, "Why are you so sad? You didn't even know my mother."

Eula sighed, "You forget . . . I lost my own mother seven days ago."

"Oh, yes! Eula, I'm sorry. Yes, you go walk and get some air. And there are nice places in the back by the river. You can sit there and rest in peace."

As Eula turned to leave, she said, "Madame, I have adopted a little kitten. It's a girl and I named her Tobe."

"Oh Eula, what will we do with an animal to carry around? I think you should leave it here when we go. That reminds me, I'm really thinking of refurbishing this house. Bringing it up to standards I can live with. I may stay here . . . and never go back to the other house. It's too lonely there."

"What about all your friends? Your dinners?"

"I'm tired of them also. I'm tired of life, I guess. But I could really fix this house up beautifully. Take all the things I really love out of the other house and bring them here. I will die here, you know. I don't want to die there, or anywhere else."

Eula listened without a change in her expression, not saying a word.

Madame continued, "I could even buy some of the land along the banks of the Striver River. There is quite a bit of it following the highway. That is the only reason the wealthy haven't built there; too close, now, to us river squatters." She smiled, a little. "I know the banker. Went to school with him when I was beautiful. He likes me because I put huge blocks of money in his bank." She was thoughtful again. "I could build something more suitable in size than this house. I can sell that huge damn house that demands so much of our time. Have you talked to Dolly? What's happening there? Is Greta gone? Please see to that, for me, please, Eula. And dear, tell Santi or Jean to freshen up my coffee pot; I'd like a little more. Hot, this time. And maybe one of those pastries that Jean made. Jean is an excellent cook, Eula. Perhaps I can get her to work for me when I move here. I know Dolly won't leave her family that lays around on her, not even for me. She saved a long time to buy that house. Though I could build her another one here, on the land I buy."

Eula opened the door to leave, "I had planned to call Dolly later this morning when she has most of her early work done. I will tell Jean about the coffee and pastry. We are not paying her, you know, she is just helping the nurse, Santi. I think her husband wants her to be home, not working. Though I certainly plan to give Santi a bonus and give Jean a gift or money or something."

"Oh, Eula, you are so divine. You think of everything."

As Eula stepped through the door, she turned her head to Madame to say, "It's too late to let the kitten go. I already love her and I promised her a home. I'm going to keep her if I have to buy us a house. I like it here. If you build yourself another house along the river, I would like to buy this one." She waved her hand in farewell. "Alright, I'm gone to tell the neighbors now." Then she was gone, leaving Madame looking after her with wonder and some consternation.

Eula Too nuzzled and pet her new friend, Tobe the kitten, checked to be sure it had food and water, then shut the bedroom door. Then she went out the front door, buttoned her coat, pulled a scarf snugly around her neck, and started down the steps to begin the errand of meeting Mrs. Fontzl and Madame's neighbors on Dream Street.

She did not know in which house which person lived, but she could see Lamont Heavy working on the fence in front of his house. She took a deep breath when she reached the last step and started across the Dream Street.

*Now I am going to tell you the stories these houses told me as my mother makes her way down the block.*

# Chapter Nineteen

*

## Lamont and Odearlia Heavy, 904 Dream Street

About fourteen or fifteen years earlier, Mr. and Mrs. Heavy had been young, full of hope and a desire for peace when they married and moved to Place from the near Elysee City. Having heard about the need for teachers, they came for a good job and a home. Over the years, stress from the politics of their profession had dried the juices of life from Lamont Heavy and his wife, Odearlia. They didn't make much money, but they sacrificed and bought their house.

Both of them wanted a family, two children, a boy and a girl. They worked steadily to that end, but Odearlia just did not get pregnant. Lamont wanted Odearlia to stop work and rest. "You work too hard, baby. All that stress of people and rules are taking their toll on you, on us. Just quit! We'll make it!" Odearlia would smile and answer, "Lamont, you know we are already struggling to stretch our money as far as it can stretch. I can't stop work, honey. Don't worry, things are going to get better." Lamont heard the sound of what he called her split-level laughter; meaning there was more than just humor in it. There was disappointment and a little fear.

Odearlia was still smiling as she turned her face up to him, "I have a chance for a small promotion to extra work which would mean extra money. Miss Willing, the new teacher from England, wants it because she says she is alone and has so much time on her hands and nothing to do with it. She could try teaching that undisciplined class of hers." She sighed, "Old Douglas, our principal, likes her a lot. We are competing for it, but I have been there much longer. Besides, it is not even remotely in her field of expertise."

In the end, the school board gave the job to Odearlia based on her good record and work ethic. Then, at the height of her joy and success, Odearlia had an accident. She *accidently* fell down a steep crowded stairway she had stepped down thousands of times and was incapacitated with a back injury. Then there was no job at all.

Months later, on her release from the hospital, Lamont caught up with the doctor as he pushed his wife, in a wheelchair, to the front door. The busy doctor said, "Oh, she will . . . improve in time, but, as I've already said, I don't think there can be any more work . . . for quite a while." He smiled as he looked down into Odearlia's face. Then he remembered her often-asked questions. He slid his eyes down toward the papers in his hands, adding words that crashed on her like lightning strikes, "Odearlia, there cannot be any children. There is certain damage that cannot . . . Well, anything is possible, but you cannot expect . . . anything." His voice faded away. He hastily walked away with a hesitant smile at Lamont. His words ricocheted in the silent air around Lamont and Odearlia. Words like, "No children. Nor a normal life. Ever."

Odearlia loved her husband. She had been sweet, kind, and generous to him, always. She had not been a lazy wife. She had loved, still loved, the house they had sacrificed for and bought, together, and made into a home, together. She had loved holding him to her breast, taking his strong hard body into her soft warm body, offering him her womb. Her womb cried to be filled, to grow full from the seed of his loins. She would think of the nights in the past, "Making love with my husband, holding him, was like being wrapped in a warm safe cloud in heaven. I cannot be a wife again. He needs . . . more than I can be. And I love him so." Her eyes filled with tears and her soul filled with shame and disgust for herself.

Lamont took on a second job and worked carving frames for pictures and beds for one of the better furniture stores uptown. He also built window frames and stair banisters for a few building contractors. He could work on the beautiful woods at home, near his wife.

Odearlia was given the best medical care and medicine to help her bear the pain and inconvenience of her body. But during the next few years, painful arthritis set in. She almost gave up. She wanted to die. Without health, what could life be? She still tried to help Lamont in everything she could.

As time passed her thoughts helped her body grow sicker and, quickly, older. She was not able to do much more than leave a tidy mess behind her as she rolled her wheelchair slowly through their loving home. She was confined to her wheelchair first, then at last she was confined to her bed, with medicine bottles full of nearly useless pills and liquids surrounding her. Expensive on Lamont's income. Odearlia received no compensation at any time because, as they advised her, she had stumbled and fallen on her own responsibility.

Lamont was still healthy, could make love. Odearlia couldn't, though she tried . . . for him. He didn't want to hurt her, but she insisted on trying. They could do it but, though she didn't tell him, it hurt her, and because he loved her, he knew it did. Finally, making love was given up, but Lamont loved Odearlia and never went anywhere else for sex for a long, long time. When he did, at last, go into the city, there would be long intervals between his trips. This will seem strange to many people about a man and sex, but it is true. You see, it was not just her lovemaking body that he loved. It was all of her, Odearlia, that he loved.

Lamont would have had no problem to find a woman; he was yet a handsome man! He was not an overly religous man, but he went to church regularly, at first. Then, only occasionally because he could not usually find what the preacher was saying in the Bible. He knew his Bible well. He loved philosophy. He was a history teacher with a minor in philosophy. Being a teacher himself and a bit scientifically minded, he searched for truths. Now, when he went to church, it was just for the peaceful feelings he sought there in the place where the Lord was supposed to be.

He was grateful to Henry Lee for having a grocery store so close in the neighborhood. Henry was a little higher in grocery costs, but reasonable when Lamont thought of not having to go across town to a larger market after work when he was, often, so tired. He was also grateful for Henry Lee accepting telephone calls from Odearlia for little items she might need during the day. Henry Lee, a considerate man, would even lock his store doors and deliver the things.

Lamont paid the old woman, Mrs. Green, a friend to both of them from across the street, to look in on Odearlia throughout the day, when Mrs. Green was able.

The main disappointment to Lamont was not having any children to love and teach. Late in the warm summer evenings he carried Odearlia out to sit on their porch to watch the sunsets. They could see the river, here and there, between the houses across the street. He would look at the tops of the tall trees, listen to the birds, crickets, and other night sounds, and place his hand over hers, feeling some contentment. Still, he would think about the children they never had. Would never have. He was a full-grown healthy human man, so he thought about making love again too.

All Lamont did for years was *think* about making love. His life was full of work for pay and work for no pay other than the gratitude in Odearlia's eyes. After many, slow-passing years, he still loved Odearlia with all his heart.

During the last several years Mrs. Mary's son, Robert Green, had married, and he and his wife, Lona, had moved to Place. They now had two children, sons. They named the oldest Prince, and the second son Homer. Lamont liked the boys very much and let them spend time at his house learning all the things men teach little boys how to do.

Odearlia's heart, happy for Lamont, and at the same time sad for herself, would listen to her husband's laughter as they all worked on whittling small pieces of wood or flying kites in the clear sky. Listen as they played catch or mock football on the quiet street. Sometimes they went too far for her to hear, going through someone's backyard to the river and discovering nature things Lamont would teach them. She couldn't hear them then, but she knew her husband was happy and it would make her happy . . . for a while.

Robert Green's wife, Lona, the boys' mother, began to saunter across the street to join them, but Lamont discouraged her by saying, "Well boys, I guess I better get busy on some things I have to do." And they would leave, frowning and dissatisfied because they sensed what had caused the sudden change in his attitude.

Lamont liked Lona's sons, but didn't seem to care for Lona. He didn't like the way she looked at him or the way she made a very obvious difference between her sons. Anyone could tell she cared about her oldest son, Prince, and did not like her other son, Homer. She often called him "ugly" with light, cruel laughter. She hugged Prince often, but seldom touched Homer. Prince was like a poet or a dreamer, but he was also a liar and petty thief. Homer was not as clever and quick as Prince. Homer was a worker, honest and also a dreamer, but his dreams were more realistic because his life was. At that time they were very young. Prince was five and Homer was four years old.

The years passed in this quiet, uneventful way for Lamont and Odearlia. Times for them changed even while they remained the same. Then Lamont took an accounting job for four hours each evening three days a week about twenty-five miles away from Place. Odearlia urged him to take the job and not worry about her being alone. "You take that job, sweetheart. It's something you can do that won't be boring. It'll get you out of this house and it pays good money. Don't worry about me, I'll be alright. Lona likes to come over and have a drink and talk with me. I catch up on all the gossip!" She laughed, so he would be at ease.

Finally Lamont took the job, but he always made sure there was only enough for two drinks in the bottle he left for them. "This is not a bar and I don't want her getting drunk with nobody here but you. Be sure we put all your money and pretty things away 'cause you know she will steal them."

"She is not a heavy drinker, Lamont, and I always see that my money is in bed with me. She doesn't go anywhere in this house except the kitchen for the drink and back in here with me anyway. So rest your mind, sweetheart."

Odearlia wanted Lamont to be gone an extra little while. She had been practicing walking a few steps every day with Lona helping her. The steps were painful, but with a few pain pills, she could make the effort. She had been doing better. They slept together every night and she wanted to walk the five steps to the portable toilet Lamont had made her for their bedroom. She was about to achieve her dream: to go to the toilet alone. "A little more practice, that's all I need, Lord!" she would think to herself.

For nearly a year that worked out alright. Odearlia couldn't practice every day Lamont was working. Sometimes it caused too much pain, but Lona would still visit with Odearlia, have her drink, and talk about Mary Green, her mother-in-law. "She always watching me! She act like she got something precious in that ole beat-out house. She keeps her room locked! She always tryin' to make me go to that fallin'-down church of hers."

Odearlia would listen, understanding why her friend, Mary Green, wanted Lona to go to church. "It does not hurt to go to church. It's good for youngsters to learn there are some good laws in this world that are made with love; not like man's laws. Adults need to learn more about love also. There is too much hate in the world. They could meet nice children at church, Lona. They are growing up."

During the visits Lona would often say, in some manner, things like, "Odearlia, you are some kind of woman! You trust that man of yours off every evening for all these hours and you don't even know if he is really on some job! If I know men, and I do, that man is off layin' up with some young strong girl."

Odearlia would always shake her head, saying, "Lamont is a good man and if he can find some satisfaction . . . let him. I told you I cannot be a true wife to him."

"Yeah, but he shouldn't lie about it. I don't trust men. They just are no good. None!"

"I think you have a good man, Lona. Robert works steady and brings his pay to you. He loves his sons almost too much. He is good to all of you."

"Yeah, and his mother too! He shouldn't have to pay her nothin' to live in that ole house! That's his house, too! Now, this here house belongs to you even if Lamont was to leave you for somebody else. If Robert left me, I'd have to take my kids and get out! I'm tellin' you, men ain't nothin'!"

Odearlia would usually wave her hand and laugh at the ridiculous woman. "Where did you come from with all that bitterness in you? I think you have a good life with a fine family. You should pray you live a long, safe, happy life with them. You are blessed, Lona."

Lona waved that away, saying, "I don't know about living a long happy life with them. I ain't happy now, what makes you think I'd be happy five years from now?"

"Oh, Lona, I not going to let you wear me out with your thoughts. I think I'll get some rest now. It's so good of you to come check on me every evening Lamont is gone. I appreciate it. Just lock the door as you go out, as usual."

Those words of dismissal angered Lona. She could not resist saying a few last words as she prepared to leave. "Odearlia, you ever thought about Lamont's wishing you would die so he could have a free life and be able to live normal with a woman? I feel so bad when I think of you and him. I just know that sometimes you wish you was dead and loving could come to Lamont again. Natural like. I feel so sorry for you, and I really feel sorry for him 'cause he is a healthy man, kept back from life. Well, he got a life, even if it is full of medicine bottles and pills." She stood watching Odearlia for a moment to see the effect of her words. "But I feel sorry for you the most 'cause you got to live with all this mess." She went through the door with a smile on her face. "I'm goin'. The door is locked. See ya!"

Odearlia called out, "Lona, come back a moment, please."

Lona stuck her head in the doorway, "Yeah?"

Odearlia shook her head in sadness and said, "Lona, I like you because I try to understand you. But . . . don't come back to visit me again. You hear, dear? Don't come back until I send you word. And don't come then if you don't want to."

"Oh! Did I say somethin'—"

Odearlia interrupted her. "Don't think about it. You were being your normal, usual self. Just don't come back until I call you."

"Lord! I didn't do nothin'! Well, okay then. 'Bye." And she was gone.

Lona had said many things Odearlia had thought about from time to time herself. And now, she thought of them again. Over the next few weeks she thought of them again and again. And again.

Lamont came in that particular evening from the job he really did work—there was no woman in his life save Odearlia. When he kissed and hugged her as usual, he detected a tenseness, but thought it was from the pain. He loosed her from his arms, her happiest place, and stood up, looking down at her. "You need something, baby? You want me to get something for you? If you're hungry, I'll have your dinner ready in a few minutes."

"No, sweetheart. Lamont. I'm fine. You rest. I'm . . . I'm not really hungry. You just have a drink maybe, and rest. Don't worry about me anymore, today. Rest. You must be tired." Her mind did not believe Lona, but her eyes looked, searching for some sign of his being tired from having sex. Her thoughts conjured up pictures of him holding someone else, placing his body next to, inside of, someone else. Leaving his seed inside someone else. No matter how often she told herself whatever he did was alright because she could not help him, have sex with him, she was still a human being. A woman in love.

Odearlia kept her love pains in her heart, quietly. But the plans inside her mind were much louder. A voice whispered to her, even under Lamont's sweet, heavy arm laid over her breast as he held her in the night. "You are killing his life. He could be happy if you were gone. If you were dead, buried, gone. Give him a chance to live a normal, good life. He could have the children he loves and wants so much. Children of his own. Not Lona's children." (*Satan whispers things like that.*) And so her pain grew until she could not carry it anymore.

One day, after Lamont kissed her good-bye when he left for his evening job, the pain screamed inside her weary head. When she heard the car door slam, the motor start, and the car leave the driveway, she began to raise her body up to leave the bed. She was very careful as she grabbed the new cane Mrs. Fontzl had recently given her. She used the cane to slowly make her way past the portable toilet into the kitchen. Under the sink was a gallon can of gas the grocer, Henry Lee, had brought her. He thought Lamont had requested it.

She could not carry the heavy can, so a jar at a time, she carried it throughout the house as much as possible. She was getting tired and the pain was getting too severe to continue much longer. But she had one more thing to do; she must lock all the windows and doors. Front, back, and the door to the basement. She did not want anyone to be able to reach her.

"God, I don't like fire. I don't want to burn up. But I am tired. And, Lord, Lamont has got to have some life besides my life. The life I give to him. So you forgive me, please. Look in my heart and know that I am doing this because I love my husband. Him. Oh, I love him so."

She had taken a long, long time to get all the things done. When she finally got back in her bed, she lay just breathing for a few moments. Tears ran down the corners of her eyes, down the sides of her face to the pillow, as she struck a match and reached out to the pretty, fluffy, flowery curtains Lamont had bought her just a week ago. She had doused them good with the gas.

For some reason, they did not catch. She waited with her eyes tightly closed. Smelling no smoke, she turned her head to look up at the curtains. There was no flame. She lighted another match and raised her arm to reach the curtains. The curtains still didn't catch afire, but the gas was all over her hands and arms and bed. The flames leaped up from her arm to the curtains, then they hungrily licked down at the bed. All control was gone.

The flames were on their own now. They were in control. Devouring, seeming to relish every object they touched. The fire bolted, flew, leaped, gobbled until everything in that room was ashes. At the same time its hot fingers spread, reaching out casting its glow and feelers over and into the rest of the beloved house.

Mrs. Fontzl and Mrs. Mary Green had both called the fire department. They came almost immediately. Mary Green told them, "There's a woman in there that cannot move! Can't walk! She's right there in that front room!"

The flames had spread, but the front door was still visible. One man was trying to get to the door to smash it when Lamont drove up and saw the flames eating his house. His first thought was "Odearlia!" He ran to the door, pushing the fireman out of the way, thinking the door was unlocked as usual. "I can get in." But the door was locked, chained, and bolted.

"Go ahead! Break it down!" Lamont hollered at the fireman. "My wife is in there. She's an invalid!" The fireman smashed the door with his ax, leaping flames burst out of the door. Startled, Lamont jumped back. Immediately he took a huge breath and started into the doorway. The fireman grabbed the tail of his jacket, then the collar and would not let him go even when Lamont tried to hit him. "That's my wife in there! Let me go!" He was crying. Spit, mucus, and fear were flying from his mouth and nose.

Another fireman joined the first to make them both come away from the house. "Let the firehose do its work now! Let's see what we can do! We can't let you go back in there, sir!" And they didn't let him go back in there. He cried and shouted, "Odearlia! Mama! Get up and walk out of there! They won't let me come get you! Walk, Mama, walk! Come out!" She didn't walk. She didn't come out.

Three firemen had to pull, tug, and drag Lamont, who held on to the banister of the front porch, which was blistering from the heat. They finally got him away from the crackling, flaming house. He stood with shoulders bent and clothes blackened from soot and smoke, watching the black smoke surge, swelling like waves, rising to the sky from his dream house. Little by little the brave firemen were able to put the fire out.

The firemen saved most of the house, but not the front bedroom Odearlia was in. Lamont grieved, burdened by his loss. "My woman. Odearlia. My God, she is gone." He was discouraged, disheartened, and could see no reason for working or living. Robert Green made him stay with them for a few days. Old Mrs. Mary Green was home, but Lamont didn't like being there with Lona and no way to get away from her.

Lamont did not know the things she had said to Odearlia. Even Lona did not particularly remember them herself. Her mind did not plan, it simply reacted to things, most of the time thoughtlessly. He just did not like her coming around him to check to see if everything was alright. "Do you . . . need anything, Lamont?" There was no way to get away from her as he used to. So he asked Henry Lee to rent a space to him. "Let me sleep on a cot in your storage room until my contractor friends and I can make my house livable again. Won't be for long, man."

Henry agreed, glad for the company, because he had been a lonely single man for a long time. They became better friends and that was good for both of them.

Old Mary Green, sick most of the time now, didn't know why Lamont was so anxious to move from her house, but she had a good idea. Prince and Homer had loved having him at their house but, instinctively, they knew he didn't seem to like their mother and thought they knew why he had gone to Mr. Lee's store to live. Robert was so tired with work and his life. He didn't much like his wife, Lona, either, but for different reasons, and would never have said so. He thought Lamont just didn't want to be in a house full of women and needed to be alone to grieve for Odearlia.

Lamont had been living in his house again for about a year when Mrs. Fontzl died. He had lived alone, on Dream Street near Striver River, with his dog, Mate. Like the navy term "shipmate." When his dog died, he gave up. "Well, Lord, Mate's gone now. Another mate of mine gone. Everybody is gone now. What do you want me to do? Just be alone?"

The night he met Eula Too near the river, he was still grieving for not only his wife, and his friend, Mate, but life. He missed, wanted, and needed someone. He was that kind of a man. A man's man, but a woman's man, too. He knew the value of a mate. Togetherness. Every day he thought about his dead wife, Odearlia Heavy. He was afraid to think of the future too much. The future looked so lonely and so empty.

After Eula Too had spoken with Lamont for a moment reminding him of why she was visiting each person on the block, she asked about the lady next door to him, Mrs. Maureen Iris McVistin.

"Iris. She likes to be called Iris. She usually goes shopping on Saturday mornings. She isn't home in any event."

"Well, I'll just have to come back a little later on then. Well, it was good to meet you again. At least this time I can see who I am talking to." She was smiling at him when Santi opened the front door across the street at Madame's, hollering, "Eula Too, there is a telephone call for you!"

Lamont smiled, saying, "Eula Too! That certainly is a different kind of name."

"Don't you laugh at my name," Eula laughed lightly. "That name has a past."

"It must be interesting."

"It is to me," she said as she was leaving.

Eula thought it might be Jewel calling her, but it was Dolly. "Oh, hello, Dolly. How is everything there? How are you?"

"I'm doing alright. I just want to let you know everybody is cutting out. Rita was still a little sick, but she left to go home to her family yesterday. Melba is going to go home with Greta until she can decide what she wants to do. They're going to leave today. So, I'm just calling you to see what you want me to do."

"Oh, thank you, Dolly. Listen, you are remaining on the payroll until you decide you don't want to be. So when you lock up and leave, just come back every few days and check on the house until Madame decides when she is coming home. She might stay up here at her mother's for a while."

"That sounds alright with me."

"I'm glad Rita decided to go home. That house she was paying for should be paid off now. She was smart. Now she has someplace to go that belongs to her too. So, okay. Just let us know what is going on. Paul is still working so he will be in and out of his own apartment there in the back over the garage. I don't think he has a key to the house. He does not need one in any case."

"Alright, Eula. You all take care yourselves. I'll talk to you in a few days. Oh, by the way, if Jewel comes back, she has her own key, doesn't she?"

"Well, yes, I think so. I don't think she left it downstairs. But she knows your number and this number."

"Alright, Eula, see you later."

"Thank you, Dolly. Say hello to your family for me."

And they each said their good-byes and hung up the phone. Madame was resting after her breakfast, so Eula Too went back out to visit next door with Mrs. Mary Green and Lona Green.

# Chapter Twenty

*

## The Greens' Home, 905 Dream Street

Mary May Green, the elderly mother, had been born at 905 Dream Street, the youngest of three siblings. After their high school graduation her brother and sister did not remain in Placeland. "Ain't enough colored people 'round here! There ain't nothin' to do 'round here either, once you get out of high school! Don't nobody want to marry none of these people livin' 'round here!" They had made their way out into the world, moved to the large cities and made their lives.

Mary married her husband, Ray Green, at the age of sixteen. They had remained in her family's home because if she had gone away her mother would be alone, old, and ailing. Mary stayed behind in Placeland with her husband. Ray was a good, serious, churchgoing, hardworking man.

She had given birth to three children, a girl, Marion Rae, and two boys, Robert Ray and Calvin Ray.

Her husband worked two jobs, in this small, secretly prejudiced town, trying to survive and raise his family. The jobs finally gave him high blood pressure and a heart attack, literally worked him to death. Mary's children, now grown and gone, left her there alone. Marion moved to Elysee City to a job, Calvin followed for better choices of employment, and Robert, the eldest, went farther away to another big city. Marion came home often and the sons called home to check on her regularly and came for visits on some holidays. They loved their mother, but they were not ready to return to Place to live. Or "that Otherplace," they would laugh.

Mary May was now old and more tired from child rearing and hard work than she was from her years. She was only in her late sixties, but there had been too many ailments that could not afford to be taken to a doctor, and too many pains suffered in silence. Now, she was in pain most all the time. She prayed for one of her children to come home to live, to be with her, but she knew in her heart that would never happen, so she never asked them.

Mary May Green could make it to the little store and over to Lamont and Odearlia's house to check on Odearlia. Before she started back slowly to cross the street to her own house, she would stand at the front gate of Iris's house and ring a bell. When Iris heard it she knew to come to the door and answer her friend's ring. Lamont Heavy had put the bell there for their convenience.

They would speak back and forth a few minutes, then Mary would trudge on home, back to her bed. Sometimes, on better days, she would go to the swing on her back porch that faced the river. She would sit, watching the river flow peacefully past. Since everyone she had was gone, she would think the river was taking life away with it. She would smile with the river, thinking, "But, you do it so beautiful-like, ole Striver."

For a long time Mary didn't have much to do with the lady, Mrs. Milicent Fontzl, to the left of her at 903 Dream Street. A middle-aged woman who was "kind'a snooty" looking down her nose at everyone around her except Iris and the schoolteachers, Lamont and Odearlia. "'Cause they so educated, I reckon." But their daughters, Elizabeth and Marion, were friends.

Milicent had a decent education, but she had married a poor man who was not so educated. He had left her after their daughter, Elizabeth, went away. She had stayed there with the house rather than go back to her family, who had almost disowned her for marrying "beneath herself." Mary May Green didn't know all that about her neighbor, but she did not give much thought to Milicent anyway.

The house on the other side of Mary, number 907, was empty now, and had been for a long time. It had been a very nice, sturdy, large house in its beginning, and had some interesting people living in it.

But as time passed, children left Placeland and the old people passed, finally. The house remained empty and lifeless so long it had become a sad-looking house.

Her daughter, Marion, didn't get any farther than Elysee City before she fell in love and got married to a good man named Fred Bridges. He was a Jehovah's Witness, he meant his vows of marriage. They had two children, a boy, Fred, and a girl, Barbara.

Marion worked hard right alongside her husband and saw to it that Fred Jr. and Barbara got a good education. Her own earlier efforts to get one had not been successful. She knew education was what made the difference in this world, right after money. "We don't have any money, but we sure are going to get you all a education so you can make some money! And you are sure going to study God's word so you can live safely in this here world and make you some peace and happiness! No one knows more about all of creation than the Creator."

Their house was full of love and consideration. Their children grew up knowing things did not have to be miserable and unhappy in the world. You just had to watch your choices and not be fooled by life and the people trying to live it, or ruin it.

Calvin, the youngest, had been married for several years, then divorced. He had been single for several more years, but now he was thinking of marrying again someone he had known about a year. A peaceful woman, not too ambitious, not greedy nor a gossip. She wanted a good home and a good life. They were both good cooks. The future looked good for them.

Robert had never married yet. "He is too busy taking care of me, sending me money," thought Mary May. For the last several years she had been saying, "He needs to find someone to make him settle down and be happy. That boy is in his thirties, getting old, he thinks. Well, whomsoever he chooses, I will love them too!"

**O**ne day, watching the river from her back porch, old Mary May sighed as she thought of her late husband. "Oh, my Ray, I still miss you mightily. I ain't got to ask you to wait for me 'cause I know you ain't goin' nowhere. And the way my side and stomach been painin' me, I don't think I'm gonna be much longer foolin' 'round down here. Honey, I wish you could'a seen your grandchildren. I wish so many things, Ray. But mostly I wish you were here with me. Oh, God, I'm just sick. I ain't felt bad like this in my whole life. Let me go on in the house and take my pills. That doctor don't know what he's doin'! I ain't gettin' no better! Marion make me keep goin' back to that doctor, Ray. If he so smart why ain't I well? Why ain't you here, if they so smart?"

Several months later, Mary received a letter from her son Robert. He told her he was thinking of getting married to someone named Lona. The mother smiled to herself as she thought, "That is good. Robert is like his father. He is a good man and he will make a good husband."

Robert Ray Green was a good man. He was a hardworking man. And he was a thinker. He was thinking of marrying a woman he had met recently in a nightclub, a young woman by name of Lona Rich. Although he had met her in a nightclub, he didn't feel that was necessarily a bad thing. "Nightclubs don't mean what they used to mean, when it comes to women."

His new friend, Lona, did not like to talk about herself, so he still didn't know much about her several weeks after he met her. But Robert knew he liked her . . . a lot. At least the other men, his friends, did not know her in any "intimate" way. That pleased him. "I want my own woman. I don't want something everybody been jugging in before me." He grinned as he thought, "I'll get her to tell me everything I want to know, someday, anyway."

*I told you of Lona at the time of her birth. Now I will tell you all I could learn from her past. I will tell you, now, how she came to be on Dream Street in Place.*

## *Lona Rich Green*

Lona was left on the steps of Hopeful Orphanage when she was a baby. It was around the times of what most people call the Great Depression, but Lona was a "Negro" baby and, for her young, destitute mother, all the years had been a great depression. They took her in because they must, because they were hopeful.

She lived, no, stayed there several years and then a family, the Wilcoxes, showed up. The couple, married for at least fifteen years, had four children of their own. Times being hard and the husband unable to find the work he halfheartedly looked for (*he had undiagnosed consumption*), the couple decided to take in foster children so they could feed their own children. "Even get a little money for rent," he sighed.

Lona was one of the foster children they acquired. She had never been given a last name. When she was old enough to look at life around her and see what poverty had done to everyone she knew, even the social worker, it seemed, she took for her last name, Rich. "I am Lona Rich."

Lona Rich had learned to fight for her survival. She had grown up to be a dominating bully to the other children in the Wilcox house, except for the oldest male. She liked him. She stole extra food for him and shoplifted clothes for him, not for herself. Trying to buy love? But he didn't have anything to give her and didn't give her anything when he did have it. He "loved" her only long enough and good enough to give her a baby when she was thirteen or fourteen years old.

He was put out of the foster home, hesitantly, because they really needed that money. Lona and her foster mother tried to use a clothes hanger to abort, get rid of, the baby because the foster mother could not afford to lose another check. Their record with the agency was getting pretty bad and they might not be able to get another foster child. Besides, the foster father did not want the noise of a new crying baby in their dilapidated, drafty, rented house.

The abortion had gone all wrong and Lona had to be taken to the free hospital, much to the social worker's chagrin, because it was on a Sunday, her usual day off. A doctor tried to repair the damage done to her and she was sent back "home." Not too long after she returned to the house, she was up and able to do housework and start cutting school again.

The consumptive foster father of the house, knowing Lona was no longer a virgin, began to place his attention and his hands on her. After he had succeeded a few times, his tired wife looked and finally saw what was going on in her house. She hated Lona because of her husband, he hated Lona because of his wife's knowing, and Lona hated everybody. Lona Rich was sent back to the social workers. To the Hopeful Orphanage.

She was sixteen years old and was disliked or hated by the other children and some social workers, too. Lona, full of potatoes and stale bread again, took a good look at the life around her. After her breakfast one day she cut school, again, and walked downtown in the large city where she lived on the outskirts. She looked into the shining store windows of the best department stores, which displayed clothes and other artifacts for people from the high middle class to the very rich.

She walked slowly, hardly moving, staring at the rich designer suits, dresses, and gowns with their matching shoes, gloves, and handbags. She looked down at herself; her patched fifth-hand dress and hand-me-down sweater with the holes in it that she had not sewn together. She could feel the holes in the sole of each shoe she wore, and the lumpy cardboard under her feet she used to cover them.

Lona stopped moving and leaned against the plate-glass window displaying such extravagant beauty. She bent her head and cried and cried and cried. Passersby who noticed her just passed on by the "little Negro" girl. But at last one white lady in a fur coat stopped and asked, "What is wrong, young lady? Where is your mother?"

Lona turned her tear-filled eyes and running nose around to face the lady who smelled so good. But she didn't say a word, just sniffled and wiped her face with the sleeve of her ragged sweater. Lona was speechless because the fur, the fur, was so close to her. The woman thought, "Dimwitted, poor child," and gave Lona a dime. "Here little girl, buy something you like." Then the lady in the fur walked briskly away, with Lona staring after her until the fur turned into the store with all the brilliant beautiful things in the windows.

After thinking all that night, in the morning Lona went to the Social Welfare Department, where she had been many times, to see her social worker. She asked the bewildered woman, "Will you help me find a job?"

"Why, doing what?" came the reply.

"Working," was Lona's answer.

"At what? What can you do? You don't know how to do anything!"

"What you got? I want to work in a rich people's house."

"In a rich house? Why there? To be sure you will be paid, I suppose. Well, you still have to know how to do things. Can you clean a house good? Thoroughly? Do you even know what that means? Can you wash clothes? Wash floors and walls?"

"Yes, I can, even if I don't know what that word means."

"Well, you go home and let me see what I can do. How are you doing in school? Why aren't you in school? Do the Wilcoxes know you are here? How old are you now?"

"I ain't at the Wilcoxes no more. I'm sixteen, going on seventeen."

Well, the tired and not-too-mean social worker looked seriously at Lona, thinking, "Well, this is the first time any of these people ever came in looking for a job instead of a handout. She will be put off the state in a year or so anyway. I can call my friend at the employment agency and see if they might have something for a Negro girl somewhere." Then she smiled, remembering "Rich people's house," and thought, "She'll be lucky to get a job cleaning some factory restroom."

When Lona left the Welfare Department building she went to her school, looking for the janitors. She found them in the basement sneaking a smoke and drinking cold coffee. She said to them, "I want to learn to clean up things, so will you teach me how to do what ya'all do?" They laughed, but one woman said, "Sure. You can com' on right now and help me clean that auditorium if your teacher'll let you!"

Lona's usual quick answer was, "I already told my teacher." They knew she was lying, but her lie cleared them. The helpful janitress worked her good and hard. After three hours Lona was through with the cleaning business. She knew a little something about cleaning though. But she went home to think of something else.

Lona didn't know much about God, but she prayed to God, sincerely, "Please help me get a job, Sir, so I can get out of here and live a better life. If You do, I'll find a way to go to church. Please God. I don't know nothin' 'bout You, 'cept You s'posed to be good and kind and love everybody. But I guess I love You, too. I ain't got nobody else. So pleeeeasssse help me."

As it turned out, there was a servant in a rich man's house who had sickened and had to leave to go live with a poor relative. The live-in job was open for a Negro servant to clean, wash, iron, wax, polish, cook on cook's day off, and watch two children on their nanny's day off, for ten dollars a week with half a day off on Wednesdays.

Lona took the job, gladly. She was not worried too much about the pay. She had heard hard stories from her janitor friends about how severe, unsparing, relentless, and complex working for some rich white folks could be, but they didn't know where nor how she already lived. So, yes, she was glad to have the job. "I'll be able to add to my pay in a little while," she told herself. She even dreamed of having her own apartment or room away from her job. "Someday soon now."

Lona had half-learned her work before she started her job. She knew they would give her a beginner's break because she was so young. And she had seen the beginning of respect in her social worker's eyes as they talked about the job. She even broadened her usually weak strategy: Say the right things whether you mean them or not, and you will get by.

Within a month she had moved to her new job-home. She had two new uniforms, black with gray collars and a gray apron. They had to buy her shoes, but that was deducted from her pay. Lona didn't complain about it one bit.

The first month Lona worked so hard she ached at night. The head housekeeper didn't like streaks, smears, dusty corners, and stair banisters stoked her fires. Glass and mirrors that had the slightest smudge had to be washed, rinsed, and wiped over and over again until a thing was almost transparent. She was grumbled at, then fussed at, then threatened about. Lona became better at her job and more careful about where she left telltale signs of less energetic, lackluster cleaning.

She ate all her meals at work and did everything she could do there so she could save her money. Finally she asked to be allowed to live out and they let her. There was something about her attitude that made them glad to let her live some other place as long as she could keep up with their needs.

Lona did not have an apartment yet. She got a large front bedroom in a rooming house. In no time at all, she had some sheets, pillowcases, spreads, doilies, vases, pictures, curtains, towels, soaps, two fine place settings of dishes, a tablecloth, all the very best money could buy. Her room was as complete as she could make it. She even put an extra lock on her bedroom door. She finally had to give the landlady a key to the lock because the woman put her hands on her hips and said, "Ain't nobody stayin' in no house of mine and lockin' me out of my own rooms! So make up your mind, Miss Rich!"

Now she could concentrate on clothing for herself. She was a medium-size young woman, so she was able to fit in many things. She had scarves and stockings aplenty. She had big feet though, so she had to buy her own shoes.

When Lona thought she looked good enough and had a few changes in good-looking clothes, she began to go out to a few popular places at nights to show her finery off. She knew her employers would never see her in the clubs in those areas.

Now we know there were plenty men in those places, clubs and such. Lona would buy only one drink. She would smile and flirt a little with the bartender until he would give her the second drink. But by that time one of the many men who were speculating over this young, fresh, clean-looking woman had already stepped in to try their luck. What they could not know was that Lona's experience with that one baby, that one boy, and her foster father kept her from making the same mistakes again. She thought of sex, never love. But, so far, it was associated with physical pain, disrespect, and no love. She heard some terribly good stories told through liquored breath to her. She was reluctant. She thought of marriage . . . first. She did not know what she was waiting for but she knew she hadn't found it. She waited.

The time came, as it always does, when a man sat next to her, but not for the reason of seducing her. Or maybe he did have such a reason, but he never spoke to her, never looked at her. He was dressed as though he was coming from work. She heard someone call him "Robert." He seemed to enjoy his drink and convivial conversation with his comrades in the bar.

Lona stopped going to the few other nightclubs she usually visited, and soon was going only to the one where Robert might be. He soon knew it because she always headed straight to the seat nearest him. She thought it wasn't noticed, but the men saw how often she watched him when she thought he wouldn't notice. Soon they began calling her Robert's lady.

One night he came over to her. The bartender was fixing her a Tom Collins drink. "I'll take care that for the lady, 'cause I got something to talk to her about," Robert said, smiling at both of them. That night they became friends. The time soon came when one of them would rush into the club, eyes searching for the other, both faces bursting into a thrilled little smile.

Lona often felt warm, confused, and embarrassed. The heat of her body invaded her eyes. She flushed, blushed, and smiled up at him as he would throw a leg over the stool and plant his self there for the evening. He never went home with her or asked her home with him. If he hadn't become so serious about this nice-looking, clean, well-dressed woman, he would have tried. But his mother, Mary Green, had taught him manners and how to treat a lady. He acted like his mother had taught him, with respect.

One night Robert came into the club, smiling big as he reached Lona Rich. He said, "We having a little get-together party Friday night, and I wanted to let you know so maybe you could come. Be a little dancing and we could do a little hugging." Lona's smile in return was just as big as she agreed.

Lona went home to her room that night with her head and feet in the clouds. "People invited me out! I am wanted. And Robert personally asked me!" Her joyful anticipation was still there when she got up at five o'clock the next morning to go to work.

Next morning, as she stepped off the bus for her job, she was thinking of what she could steal to make her look really beautiful at the party. She had been on her job two years, and had taken so many things even she knew her employers were casting suspicious looks at her. "Well, that's too bad, cause I got to look good for Robert!"

Lona could not know her employers, the Howards, had had a meeting in their sitting room and discussed putting locks on their closet doors. Mrs. Howard was terribly upset. "I don't think we should have to put locks on doors inside our home. Certainly not!"

Because Lona had made no friends among the maids, cooks, or the housekeeper on her job, they would not tell her what they heard and risk losing their own place. "Why should we tell her? She is so smart, let her take care of her own self! If they fire her, we'll all be glad to see her go. I got a cousin who needs a good job like that!"

Mr. Howard, an old attorney, had set his cigar down and stroked his forehead, saying, "We don't really know just who is taking these little things. We can't accuse her if we have not caught her doing it."

The oldest daughter, her eyes glaring like her mother's, peevishly whined, "Little things? Twenty-something blouses and as many scarves! Even skirts, my new ones! And Leora's handmade shoes. I know everything I have . . . or used to have! And I can't leave my money lying around anymore either! I feel just like I'm in a prison. Who else could it be, Father?"

Mr. Howard thought of his daughter's idea of what prison was like and almost smiled. He had heavier things on his mind than skirts and scarves. But Mrs. Howard patted her favorite daughter's knee. "It all started, I think, about two years ago, soon after Lona began working for us. I know all the other help. They've been with us for some time. The clothes wouldn't fit them anyway, Everett."

He sighed heavily, "They have children, Mrs. Howard."

"Oh, Everett! Don't be absurd. They've been here for many more years than that Lona."

"Father, we don't have to wait to catch her, this is our house! And, mostly, my clothes and Leora's shoes, with those big feet of hers." She laughed softly and politely at her sister Leora's pained blushing frown at mention of her large feet. "You don't have a real lady's feet, Leora," her sister often told her. Her sister never mentioned Leora's brilliant green eyes and glorious golden hair except to say, "All that color makes you look so cheap, Leora."

Mrs. Howard covered her mouth with a handkerchief and tried to sob; she didn't like Lona's hips. Mr. Howard, who liked looking at Lona's well-shaped behind he had never tried to touch, cleared his throat, sighed, and said, "We will give her another two weeks. If you miss anything else, we will let her go." He turned to his wife, "You had better start seeking a replacement, just in case. Try a different service." And the matter was settled.

When Lona came in the next morning the die was cast. She could have bought a few new things with her own money, but she hoarded all of it except for her rent, and that was five dollars a week. She did not buy food, she brought it home. She did not buy many clothes at all, or perfume, or lotions, lingerie, underwear, or combs nor brushes or soap, stockings, nor anything.

She was too busy thinking about Robert and the party on that day to linger around cleaning the bedrooms and closets until no one was there to see her. She gave the idea up. Lona was thinking of how good her life was as she hastened from work. Of how much better her life would become over the years, now that she was making friends. "I'll never be alone or lonely again. Oh, Robert." She sighed, "I'll find something in my own closet . . . or go downtown and shop. I'm not going to spend my money though. Not even for Robert."

The Friday night finally came. Robert was happily preparing for the party. "This may just be *the* night," he thought to himself. He sent most of his extra money home to help his mother, old Mary Green, so he dressed in his best pawnshop suit, freshly cleaned and pressed, along with his pawnshop tie. His new shoes were polished to their highest. A new white shirt topped everything perfectly. He looked fresh and handsome.

Robert Green had thought long about the move he was making. "You are taking this girl serious, man," he said to himself almost in a whisper. He had watched Lona for some time. He saw she never went home with anyone or took anyone home with her. He knew she frequented the club for company, not money. Most of the single women were there for fun and money. "I know with times as hard as these are, that is the result of being poor and never having enough. It's like violence on the likes of some poor men and women. Colored and white. But there are no rich colored people I know of. Maybe a doctor or something. I don't have no education, but I respect it."

Then his mind, as usual, returned to Lona. "I might go back to some school and learn something better, like my sister Marion keeps after me to do. Marion would like Lona. She is so clean! And neat. She must be thrifty, or have a generous boss, because her clothes look like good clothes and she always look nice!"

Robert Green was not the type to fool around with women he thought were loose women, because of disease and the lack of cures for them. So he was lonely. He was thirty-two years old. A laborer who had learned carpentry by watching carefully. In school he had gone as far as the tenth grade when his father had died from overwork, from his two hard jobs as laborer.

Robert became head of the house his parents had bought. He dropped out of school and became a part-time, cheated laborer and a gofer. But he was able to help his mother, who was no slouch herself. She cleaned house, washed clothes, even helped to put a roof on a house once. She saved and spent wisely. She did what she had to do to feed and clothe her three children.

Robert left Place to find a better job, to be of more help to his mother. He left with everyone in his family standing on the porch crying. Old Mrs. Green had understood; she knew he was being cheated because he was so young and, maybe, colored. As the tears slipped down and dropped from her hard-set jaw, "Lord, he ain't goin' far, just up the road a way to that big city. Lord, take care my boy. He ain't no fool, but he is young. He know 'bout You though, don't he God? 'Cause I taught 'em all. You watch him for me, please.

"And what I'm gonna do about my Marion wanting to go away to college someday? And Calvin." The worry and work-worn Mary put her arms with the red-raw, callused hands around her other two children still standing on the porch beside her, still staring at the empty road in the direction their brother had gone. She thought, "Well, God, we'll talk about that when the time come. Meanwhile, I'll just keep doin' the best I can, with Your help. Thank You, Lord."

**R**obert thought Lona would be such a woman as his mother. That's why he had watched her so long before he made his move to her. He knew she watched him also. When he had sex he used condoms, but he wanted a clean woman so he wouldn't have to use condoms. "I just want to love her with nothing between us, that's all." He hadn't been going to the club so regular before he saw Lona there. Then he "wasted" his money again. "I should be sending this to Mama, but Calvin and Mary are helping her now, so . . ."

At last he arrived at the club to meet Lona. He checked the menu for the night. (He had already ordered pork chops and potatoes.) He smoothed the paper table cover, checked the mismatched table settings, then sat back, smiling slightly, and waited.

*Poverty is real. Reality. The misery, the hunger, squalor for many people, the filth and the cruelties of a society that loves the rich and hates the poor, some of themselves poor. All over the world, money makes all the difference in the world. The, almost, hopelessness of life. Even Robert Green's life. Some of the rich may laugh at the poor and their God, but they had better be glad the poor have a God. Without God, hatred and angry violence could destroy the world. As I know it will destroy the world's people. And I know, because of where I am, that he who loves the world, the love of God is not in him. For God hates what people do to one another. He says so in His Book. "He who loves the world, the love of Me is not in them."*

Lona came happily and hastily into the nightclub. She was smiling, looking for a crowd of revelers. But there was just the usual crowd and the usual sound of low voices and clinking glasses. Confused, and even frightened, she looked around for Robert as he turned to see her at the same time. He smiled as he stood and started moving toward her. Her heart trembled a bit as he held out his hand and she took it. He led her to his table.

She looked around the partyless room as she followed him. "Ain't nobody here yet? I'm the first one?"

"You're the only one besides me and our party is right here." He pointed with a grand gesture to the orange-papered table and pulled out her chair. "My mama taught me my manners, beautiful lady."

Lona was taking off her coat as she sat down and settled in the chair, thinking, "I don't know my mama, so I can't tell you nothing she taught me." She said out loud, "Well, what happened?"

He leaned near, still smiling at her, "Nothin' happened. It's my party and I invited you. Just you."

She smiled with delight. "Just me?"

"Just you. Disappointed?"

"No, no. I think it's nice."

"Are pork chops and pototoes nice, too? Because that's what I ordered for us. You want a drink first?"

"Yes," she smiled, tilting her head, "a Tom Collins."

He signaled the bartender, "Hey Sam, a Tom Collins for the lady and you know what I want." He turned back to her, "Then we'll have dinner. 'Less you want another one . . . drink."

"Robert, you must'a found yourself a gold mine!" she laughed intimately with him.

"You are the gold mine I'm digging for tonight."

Her laughter tightened to a smile, "What do you mean?"

"I want to talk to you. Just you alone."

She relaxed and shyly smiled again. This was the first time anyone had gone out of their way to do something, anything, so nice for her. So the evening continued.

"You know, girl, I really like you."

"You really like me?"

"Yeah. I been watching you, just like you've been watching me, and I like everything I see. Everything I can see, anyway."

"What do you see, Robert?"

"Well, your ways, how you carry yourself. You work, you're clean, and you're quiet. When you go home, you go home alone, far as I can see. You know, things like that."

"Well," she laughed softly. "I been watching you, too. I guess I like you."

"You guess?"

"Well, you know. I do like you. You're nice . . . and clean and you ain't too loud." They both laughed a little. "And you don't hang around on the streets. You work, too."

"Lona? Have you ever thought about 'loving' somebody?"

"Oh, I'd like to be in love and have somebody love me back. You know. Get married and . . . stuff."

This time Robert laughed, saying "Stuff?" He really was not sure he was thinking of marriage.

Lona laughed with him, lightly. "Stuff."

So they bantered as they drank, as they ate and watched each other. He kept putting quarters in the jukebox and, after their dinner, they danced, close. Finally, he suggested he walk her home.

Lona's fears and memories of the pregnancy and abortion came clearly to her mind. She liked Robert. She wanted to make love with him, "But not right now," she hedged to herself.

He walked with her and when they reached her house they squabbled, mildly, about his coming in. "Well, you can let me see where you live, your room."

"Well, I guess I could." She was nervous because the inside of her body was sparkling all the way from the top of her head down to her toes. She thought, "I know I will get weak for this man." She said,

"Well just for one minute." He smiled as he walked up the stairs and she let him into her room.

She flicked the light on. Robert looked around the room at all the lovely things; the lace scarves on the dresser, the perfume bottles and silver hairbrush and comb. He turned to the bed and saw the smooth, soft-looking sheets. He moved to reach out and passed his hand over the bedspread that looked like it cost plenty money. He realized he was standing in softness and looked down. The plush throw-rugs around her room! He took it all in; the fine draperies at the windows with the lace curtains. The precious little bedside lamps, the pretty feminine clock ticking away, the pretty little figurines such as he hadn't seen at any other woman's house . . . room.

Robert's thoughts stirred around in his head; this woman, young as she is, knows how to spend her money and she must save a lot to buy things like this! Talk about taste! Now he knew what the word meant! Her mama sure raised her right! In a low voice full of respect and awe, he said, "Girl, you have a beautiful room. I could sleep like a baby in a bed like that."

Lona laughed, nervously, as Robert continued. "But I don't mean tonight," he hastened to assure her. "I know you are a lady. I wouldn't ask you nothin' like that . . . right now. But I sure like you. I think I'm falling in love with you. So . . . you know . . . one day . . . we are going to sleep together somewhere."

Less fearful then, Lona let him take her into his arms. They kissed and kissed and kissed. Their lips still clinging as he led her out of her bedroom back down to the front door, opening it with one arm still around her and one hand on the doorknob. He knew he couldn't hold himself back much longer. His last words to her were, "Baby, Lona, I'm'a be seeing a lot of you, soon." With her head leaning on the front door frame, she smiled her good-bye a long time, even after he could no longer see her.

She slowly went back to her room, thinking, "I should'a let him. I should'a let him. I'm gonna marry that good man, Lord. Mmmmhummm, kissing like that! My goodness."

Still thinking of his kisses, she reached into a dresser drawer and pulled out a very beautiful, expensive nightgown; it was from Paris, France. She slipped it on, loving the feel of the silky chiffon, and lay in her satin-covered bed thinking, "I wish Robert could see me in this." She fell asleep still thinking of Robert Green. "I know he loves me. I'll be a good wife to him. Mrs. Lona Rich Green. My goodness."

Robert left her and went straight to one of his standby girlfriends. An easy one. He made sex to her, thinking of Lona. Later he went home to sleep because he couldn't stand to think about or touch any longer the woman he had had sex with. He dreamed of Lona's room, which he would soon sleep in, with her holding him. "I might marry Lona. Shit! I'm in the mood for some real love!"

Well, things come to this and things come to that and soon they were making love in Lona's room. They made love. They made a baby, too.

Between business affairs, family vacations, and students going away to schools, two weeks had turned into a few months. But it was inevitable, the time came when Lona's employers had another family talk about further losses and Lona. It was decided that on the next payday, two weeks away, she would be relieved of her job. "Why do we have to wait two weeks, Father?" Mr. Howard set his cigar in a crystal ashtray and looked at his daughter, whose ways he disliked. "Because I think it is best."

Within those two weeks Robert and Lona got married. A rush affair at the city hall. Robert paid fifteen dollars for a wedding band. "You will have a better one with a diamond in it someday." Now, he moved into that room they both loved. Suddenly, it was a small room. But it was full of delight, love, sex, laughter, and beauty.

Shortly after the marriage, Robert heard from his family in Place. His mother, Mary, had finally broken down from all her little ills and stresses she had survived during all the years of hard work and children, worrying and crying and striving to stay alive and pay the note and taxes on her house. The house had been paid for, but she had borrowed money for something. Something. There were so many things you needed to do to keep a house together.

She knew her sons would come together and help her, they always did. But Mary hated to ask. Her daughter, Marion, sent her money, but she had two children of her own with her husband. He was a good husband, fortunately, and did not mind her sending her mother money.

Mama Mary's illness was very serious this time so Robert decided he'd better go home to Place and see about his mother. "There is room there for my growing family, if it comes to that," he thought to himself. "But I know I can get a job if I have to stay there awhile. Times are better and I know everybody." He said to Lona, "I might be gone just a little while, baby. Anyway, it's a nice little town and we live on Dream Street. I won't be gone long. You'll be alright, you know how to take care of yourself. For a little while, baby." Lona looked dismayed, and it wasn't because his mother was sick.

Robert smiled at his still-new wife. "It's nice. You'll see someday. You'll love my mother."

He took a leave from his job and left a week before the Howards were to let Lona go from the job. He even borrowed some money from Lona, which put quite a dent in her "love" for him. "But, what the hell," she thought, "his mama owns a real house and it will be Robert's and mine someday. Maybe soon, if his mother is that sick."

So that is the way things were going.

A week or so after Robert left to go home, Lona went to work in the morning as usual. While she was on her job, the oldest daughter and an older aunt went to the house where Lona lived and, because they were white and rich, they gained access to Lona's room. Then they called the police and had a policeman wait as they packed their things in bags and boxes the landlady got for them. They did not want the sheets, nor the lingerie, nor anything she had worn; they would donate them to some charity. But they did want the perfumes, clock, drapes, curtains, lace doilies, figurines, bedspread, and everything they recognized and some they did not recognize. They carried it all away, taking it to their home and spreading it around the floor in the sitting room.

When Mrs. Howard saw they were through with their task, she sent for Lona to come to the sitting room and said, "You are dismissed. Please leave my house. Take only what you wore into this house. George, the butler, will search you."

Lona backed up when she looked into the glaring, angry eyes and the round open lips screeching at her as they were still unpacking all "her" stuff in the room. It was more than she could take. There was no answer necessary from her. The evidence was all over the floor.

Mr. Howard was not there.

Lona left in tears, with a diminished check squeezed tight in her hand and her mind boggled. Then she got angry. "They have messed my life up!" She forgot to be ashamed in front of her landlady. "How dare you open my door and let them in my room?!"

The landlady hadn't liked Lona ever since she had seen her dressing so grand all the time. She had often peeked in Lona's room and seen all those wonderful things and that made her jealous, and her dislike for Lona had grown. Now she was torn between her usual dislike for Lona and her understanding of the woman's circumstances. She also remembered that Lona always paid her rent, on time. She answered, "I always has a key made to every lock on my rooms in my house! 'Sides that, they had the police with 'em!"

Lona wailed, "Oh, look what they did! Took all my things. That old lady, their mother, gave me all those things! They don't have no respect for her and what she wants to do!"

The landlady didn't believe a word. She looked at Lona from the corners of her eyes. "They sure was some nice things. Maybe she give 'em back to you again."

"Oh, I'll never go back there again. No matter how much they beg me! They are liars and . . . stealers!"

In the doorway, the landlady turned to leave. "Sure was some stealin'." Lona looked up sharply at the old woman, then she stepped over the mess on the floor and shut her door.

They had left the sheets that were on the bed, but took the others from the drawers. "These are clean. Take them." Lona broke down in tears as she lifted last night's nightgown. They left it behind because it was dirty. Slowly she took her clothes off and picked up the nightgown again, holding it tenderly, loving its softness and knowing she would never be able to afford such for herself. She crawled between the sheets they left behind as "filthy" and cried herself to sleep. Her anger woke her up several times, then she would cry herself to sleep again.

The next morning, eyes red and swollen, she got up and called Robert. "I'm coming where you are. I miss you too much. I can always get my job back. They love me. I can get any job anyway. I miss you. I . . . love you, Robert. I can get a job where you are." She started crying again, this time from shame. Robert thought she was crying from loving and missing him. He was manly proud of that. He said, "C'mon, baby. Come where I am. It may not be much, but wherever my home is, that's where you should be too."

After he hung the phone up, he looked around his mother's house. It had always been neat and clean and nice, even if there was nothing in it bought firsthand except for what his sister, Marion, bought her. He rubbed his hand across his brow, "Now, though, Mama has been too sick. She don't have the strength to keep it up. Marion and Calvin are too far away to help."

The house had been let go a bit. A white neighbor, Maureen Iris McVistin, who lived on the corner across the street, had come over several times to help clean Mary's room or bring her something hot to eat, or just fruit, juice, or soup. Mr. Lee at the grocery store gave her credit when she needed it. He knew he would be paid.

Robert had come home to clean house, care for his mother, and look for a temporary job, all at the same time. He almost cried as he thought of what Lona would think when she saw his mother's house and compared it to her own deluxe room with all the beautiful nice things she was used to. "Oh, Lona, oh, Lona, you're gonna wonder what kind of man you married.

"And now she will be here on Dream Street in two days. Her rent will be up and she is packing, Lord." His distress was real, but soon he felt a little better. "I will hold my wife sooner than I thought. We gonna make love in my house now."

Robert found a night job so he could be with his mother all day when she was awake, needing things. With a lighter heart now, he went to attend to his mother's needs. "I'd better get some sleep and rest," he smiled to himself. "I'm glad she's coming. I need her love to help me through these days."

He blew his nose, stood up and went to check the noisy washing machine he had already fixed three times since he had come home. Washing was necessary to keep the sheets and towels ready for his mother. Ready, fresh, and germ free.

Old Mary could hardly get around when he first arrived. It seemed she had given up in a flood of tears and relief as soon as she saw her son and fell into his arms. His deep and gentle voice curled around the fears in her heart. "Thank You, Lord. Someone is here to see about me." Love helped her, rested her, and her health began to improve.

He had called to tell her when he got married and she had spoken a few words to Lona. She had been surprised, but pleased, that her son had found someone he loved and had done the right thing. She thought, "If you're gonna have a family, have a real family."

When Lona arrived on the bus she instantly hated the small gray town with slow-moving people, content with their lives. She had most of her clothes, one set of sheets, a few towels, and the nightgown. Nothing else . . . except two hundred dollars tucked in her brassiere. She kept it on her body at all times.

Robert's neighbor, a schoolteacher from across the street, Lamont Heavy, drove him to the bus station to pick her up. Robert thought she would have a lot to carry. When he saw the small secondhand trunk, two medium-size boxes, and her, he wondered about all the other things a moment. All thoughts fled when he held his lovely wife in his arms again. She had told Robert she was pregnant. Now Robert looked over her head, smiling at Lamont as his eyes tried to say, "This is woman's stuff, man, you know."

The Heavy family had a nice car so Lona felt better—a little. She was so glad to see her husband. She had thrown her arms around his neck and sobs of relief filled her breast, choking her throat as she held some of her feelings back. Her head was still full of the experience of being caught, losing everything she felt she had "worked" for, embarrassment with the landlady, and, finally, shame. She had felt so alone, again.

Now, sitting next to her husband, she was not alone anymore. And there was the rest of her family in her stomach. She thought, "I am a family, at last. The hell with the Howards!"

Lona went through another unhappy scene when they reached the Greens' house. Thinking, "Shades of the orphanage and foster homes." The house needed a little work, but it was not like either of those nearly loveless buildings. When she met his mother, Lona had smiled kindly at her, but she did not puff a pillow or touch her hand. One of her thoughts was, "She sure ain't going to be around long. So this will be my house and I will fix it up with the best of everything!"

As she unpacked in the room Robert had chosen and cleared for them, he noticed many things were not there. "Where are all your nice things, Lona?"

Lona sat down, winding up the clock that used to sit in her landlady's hall on a little chest. "Well, honey, I didn't want to worry you, with your mother so sick and all. But somebody got into my room, even with all my locks, you remember? And they stole all my beautiful things. I think it was the landlady, or some of her relatives, but I couldn't prove it. I called the police, but they had time to hide everything already. Anyway, I didn't want to worry you, and I knew I couldn't stay in her house another day more than I had to."

She sat the clock on a dresser as she jumped up to hug him. "Oh, honey, I missed you!" She nudged him to the bed and sat on his lap as she wound her arms around his neck. "So I quit my job and came straight to you, my husband." She looked around the room, frowning slightly, not enough for her husband to see. "We'll be all right. We're here together."

She kissed him hard but lovingly and placed his hand on her stomach. "We a family, honey." Actually at that moment she felt love for the child she was carrying, for the first time. A little amazed, she thought, "This is the beginning of my own family." She was not sure whether she was thrilled or not.

A few days later, Robert found a good day job in the construction business. He thought, "Now I can fix that house up and get it right again, now that Lona is there to take care of Mama." Old Mary even felt better since her son's wife had come and she was not alone any more. It was her nature to be a sweet and independent person. She tried to do most things for herself.

It was not long, perhaps two weeks, before Mary could see that Lona was deceptive and insincere. "She don't have to do nothin' for me no more. But everything she do for my son, her own husband, is just half-assed. S'cuse me Lord. Well, sometimes pregnant women are just that way."

One day, as she heated some cold soup Lona had brought to her for lunch, she said, "Lona, wouldn't you rather be working somewhere in one of those nice stores uptown? Before you start showing real good, I believe you could get a job easy. You can help your own self and start getting some things the baby will need. It'll be here before you know it, chile!"

Sitting at the kitchen table, Lona gave her a thoughtful smile as she mused over her cold cup of coffee, and the thought of going uptown. "I do need to get some things for this house. But I was thinking more of working as a maid or something in a . . . good house." She looked expectantly at old Mary.

Then old Mary said, "My daughter, Marion, is gonna be here in a few days. She'll get what I need. I'm feeling better now anyway. Did you know she is a minister? A Jehovah's Witness. They make you study so much, when you get through it all, you are a real minister. Can even officiate at anybody's weddings. She is very sweet. You will like my baby girl."

Lona closed her eyes and frowned, using her hand to shield her face. She thought, "Jehovah's Witness. I'm not going to like her and I don't like this marriage. Lord, I'm getting nothing but surprises. First this baby, then this house and this town. Now I'm gonna have somebody talking 'bout God to me day and night." She said, " Okay, MaMary. I believe I'll take a bath and go right out today and find a newspaper and some kind of job, since you are so nice to think of that and since you are feeling better."

Lona Rich Green went out to find a job and found one. Mr. Lee, at the grocery store, would have given her a part-time job cleaning up his store on weekends, but it only took a few visits to the store by Lona for Mr. Lee to know she was stealing. "Leave her alone in my store is not good." He hated to do it, but he had to watch Lona, carefully, when she came in. "She very quick," he thought. He could not tell anyone because he didn't want to hurt Mary Green.

In a few days Marion arrived and everyone was glad. She made a change in all their lives. They could relax. MaMary was going to be well taken care of and be taken to the doctor until she was all well.

Lona tried the rich houses first, but having no references and they having no real need at the moment, she did not secure a job. But they knew her husband's family, and said they would certainly keep her in mind for the first opening.

She finally found a job as stock girl at a small variety store. They paid little money, but it was better than "sitting in that sick house with sick chores to do and a minister, too! I can't stand that sister of Robert's to even look at me with her busy self!"

The doctor said old Mary Green needed to have an operation for a tumor. She had insurance, but it didn't cover everything. Everyone in the family had to chip in and help pay the costs. Calvin sent some money and said he was on his way. Marion tried to cover the balance needed because Robert didn't have any savings, but he did keep the house going with food and utilities. He was, also, daily bringing the house back to good repair. When Calvin arrived he started right in helping to repair his mother's house, the house where he had grown up. To Calvin, the house was beautiful and full of love.

Lona's two hundred dollars was hidden away and stayed that way. But she did like Calvin. She liked a working man.

Robert was thoughtful when he said to his wife, "If you stop buying all those trinkets from your job, we'd have a little to offer on the bill." She just looked at the floor as she said, "Them little ole things don't cost that much, Robert." Then, after a few moments, she asked, "Robert, does all this mean we are gonna have to stay here all the time? 'Til she gets well?"

"She is my mother, Lona. Wouldn't you stay with your mother if she needed you? And where would we go, right now? With you pregnant and neither of us knowing when we'd find work or where we would live?"

Well, he received no answer to that question. Lona just gave him an enigmatic smile and walked, slow and thoughtful, to their room. Later, she said to Robert, "I gave up a good job and my house to come here and be with you. And help your mother."

He looked at her strangely, "It was a room, Lona."

"It was our home, Robert. And now we're here and we got a baby on the way. If your mother dies, your brother and sister are going to take this house from us. We won't have nothing from all this trouble."

The bewildered look was still on Robert's face as he stood up and left the room, saying, "My mother is not going to die. That's why we are paying that doctor."

Lona watched him close the door. She had been counting on MaMary dying and her, finally and at last, having a real house that belonged to her. "I'd'a fixed this house up in here so beautiful it would have been a cryin' shame!"

When old Mary came home from the hospital her daughter wanted to take her home with her. "I'll feel better if I can see her and take care of her every day. I've got to go home to see about my family."

Robert thought it too soon for his mother to make a trip even if Elysee City was only forty or fifty miles away. Lona said, "Honey, we are both working and MaMary is going to need some special care."

Calvin said, "She can stretch out in my car. I'll drive her to

Marion's and Marion can drive her own little car home. Then, brother, I'll drive back here and help you finish some of this work on the house so when Mama comes home to stay, it'll be better. I can stay a few extra days because we have good substitute teachers. The principal and I are good for as long as I need."

That night, when they were alone in bed, Lona said to Robert, "You have a really nice family, Robert. You all make me think you really do love each other. You are blessed. All of you."

"Now this is your family too, Lona. We love you."

But Lona didn't believe that, not for one minute. Hidden by the darkness of the room, she cut her eyes at Robert. She didn't intend to be jealous, didn't even think about it, but she was jealous of Robert and Marion and Calvin. Envied them. She didn't like Marion, though Marion had not kept God in her face like Lona had thought she would. "Marion Bridges has everything she wants, her and her family, but she ain't going to end up with this house, no matter what she thinks. This house is for me and my child. My family."

Soon everyone was gone and Robert and Lona were alone in "their" home. The house was cleaned, repaired, spruced up, and Lona was working on the yard. Old Mary had peach, apple, and fig trees. "I like a yard. Have something to eat growing up all around you!"

In time the house began to be filled with little things from Lona's job. "To brighten it up a bit," she said. Robert, happy, laughed as he said, "Baby, all these things cost money. We better cut down on our spending."

Soon the store cut Lona's hours in half and she brought home less pay. Still, things kept showing up in the house: a vase, artificial flowers, face and hand towels, dresser scarves, pot holders, silverware, tablecloths, sheets, pillowcases, the types of things her store carried.

Robert was so glad to see Lona settling in, thinking that she was feeling more at home, his happiness shone all over his face. He could see his love growing inside Lona, his own child. "Mama is gonna be so pleased with me. I have just what she wanted for me! Just wait 'til she gets back home and really gets to see what kind of person Lona is." Love filled their house. His love for Lona. Lona's love for having her own house.

*Being an orphan had almost nothing to do with the way Lona was. The problem was never being loved by anyone, never being touched except for selfish touching and never being taught there was such a thing as "Love." Animals and babies can die without any signs of love. She had never even seen love. When she did see it, she didn't recognize it, therefore she didn't believe it. Robert loved Lona for herself; Lona loved Robert for what he was to herself. She knew how to call on God, but she didn't know God nor the Bible that tells humans about Love.*

It was when the new dishes began to show up, two at a time until there were six. Then came cups, then saucers. Robert began to wonder if Lona was stealing. He knew about stealing; everybody at school used to do it as youngsters, but no more. He shook the thought out of his mind.

Then, one day, soon after he had such thoughts, Lona came home saying, "I quit my job 'cause I had a few pains in the bottom of my stomach and I don't want anything to happen to the baby." *The baby was her hold, her connection to "her" house.* Robert exhaled a sigh of relief. If it was true she was stealing, and he was pretty sure it was, with the job gone, that ended that.

In her seventh or eighth month, Lona began feel a tenuous love for the child she was carrying. It occurred to her that this was *her* child, her family. When she rubbed her stomach now, she felt for the baby inside. She glowed a little and began to pray, by rote, that the baby would be healthy and smart. "He got a hard world to make it in, Lord." Naturally, she began to go shopping for things for the baby, rattles, clothes, and such. Lona felt a little happiness that went a little deeper than ever before.

Robert was a casual, but good, carpenter and he made a crib for "My boy!" He bought a crib mattress of blue with airplanes on it. Lona brought home the rubber mattress cover and little sheets, pillowcases, diapers, cute tiny shirts, booties, and dresses with little bonnets to match. "For my baby girl," she thought, as she lovingly put them away.

Robert was at work all day, so all the things were put away by the time he returned home, tired, hungry, missing his mom, and thinking of the new baby his mother would love. They were doing most of the things a normal, happy, expectant family would do.

The new baby came, a fine eight-pound boy. Robert was ecstatic and Lona was happy enough that it was all over. Robert wanted a junior, but Lona said, "I want my son to have a name with some class. A rich name." Robert felt his wife had been through a great deal so he said, "Okay, name him whatever you like, but his middle name has to be Robert." Lona agreed, but on the birth certificate she put "Prince Rich Green."

Truly, Lona loved Prince Rich Green, her son. She held him, staring at him for hours. She nursed him, holding him close to her breast long after he had finished nursing and gone to sleep.

Her husband worked all day, came home, and played with his son, Prince Robert Green. Then he trudged as he cooked his meal, fixed the baby's formula for the next day, straightened up the house a little, washed the pile of dirty diapers, showered, and fell into bed, asleep before his head hit the pillow. He was a proud father when he had time. But he was not such a proud husband any longer.

Robert had been born in Place; people knew him. He had friends and acquaintances all over town. Naturally, he learned why Lona had left her job—fired for stealing. Unhappiness, fear, and worry hit him throughout the days and nights like a little hammer tapping on his head without end. A child stealing; you can talk to them, teach them. An adult stealing, rather, Lona stealing; he couldn't talk to her. She argued with him, denied whatever he brought to her attention no matter what it was about. His heart wailed in his chest for the loss of the happiness he believed he had known. "What happened!?" he asked his mind and the sky.

When Robert realized that Lona was really a thief, his respect for her dropped with each new item coming into the house. Dropped down to the bottom of his struggle for a livable life. Respect is a barometer of love; the less respect, the less love is able to survive.

*From the vantage point of where I am, I have learned Love is a natural process, a necessity of life. It is why God said hold to Love, protect yourself by not doing things that cause respect to dwindle or fly away because when respect goes, Love goes with it. You can even lose respect for your own self. What is life . . . without Love?*

He tried to talk to Lona about stealing. About the gossip, their reputations, honor, lawyers, and jail. "They lyin' on me! These people in this little piss-ass town don't like me! Never did. 'Cause I have some class about me! I'm not stealing nothin'! You can believe me or you can believe those liars! I don't care who you believe. My child is going to have the best!"

When Lona realized that Robert knew the truth, a part of her relaxed. Illogically she thought, "He knows we're poor. Why would he act a fool about something stupid like that?"

Arguments began slowly, because Robert was weary and tired. But they grew, because his tiredness became a sickness. Sick of a dirty house full of cheap, pretty, stolen things. A kitchen with no hot food, just snack foods from the store across the street and jars of baby food. Tired of empty baby food jars and dishes caked with dried food left for him to clear away. "If you so worried about a clean kitchen, clean it," Lona would say as she walked away.

But he loved his son. "Nothing will make me separate from my son."

Their sex life dwindled. He was mind-tired, body-tired. Lona, rested, was always ready. So lovemaking was only sometimes, which Lona complained and whined about. The beautiful nightgown was worn out, often left to lie mildewing by the washing machine as Lona waited for Robert to wash the baby's clothes.

But on one of the "sometimes" they made the second baby.

Robert sighed some of his heaviest sighs. Double work for him. It was a shock for Lona. She did not want another baby, did not want to go through that again. Ever!

She gave birth to another boy. Six pounds, because he was full of snack foods, sweets, colas, cigarette smoke, gin, and beer. He was named Homer because that's what Lona wanted, a HOME. Homer Robert Green.

Lona was not working, so there was no layette for him. No fancy little clothes. He wore old worn diapers, stretched, torn undershirts, and booties with holes in them, ribbons gone. Lona did not hold Homer Robert like she had Prince Rich because she did not like him. She blamed him for her pain, and the tension and stress in the house they called home.

MaMary had returned home by then. She was old, but was pleased about her grandchildren and the house being repaired like new. She was perplexed by her son, Robert, and his frowning silences.

Robert was at work when his mother came home. Lona said, facetiously, to her mother-in-law (closest thing to a mother she might ever have), "Oh, MaMary, I'll move our things back to that little room in the back so you can have some privacy. I meant to be gone already, but you know, there's so many things to do when you have a baby to look after."

MaMary was her usual kind self, "No, honey, you all stay right in there. You all are young and need more room than I do. Them babies and all." So now MaMary lived in a smaller room at the back of the house. So life proceeded on Dream Street.

MaMary was nobody's fool. She saw the difference in the kind of care that was given to the two sons, Prince and Homer. She tried to make up for some of it by doing little things for Homer. She mended the torn shirts and bought a few new things to help his meager wardrobe.

When he cried like his heart was alone and wondering why, Lona seldom picked him up. After a while Homer did not cry for care and love unless his father was home. He was a quiet baby, lying on his back playing with his fingers or toes or staring at the ceiling at what was left of a dangling toy Prince had long since broken off, one that couldn't be reached even if Homer could have stood up. Sometimes when he did cry, MaMary would slowly go to see about him. Lona would tell her, "Don't pick him up, MaMary, I don't want him spoiled. He just cryin' 'cause he spoiled."

"I think he is wet maybe, Lona, honey."

"Well, the washed diapers ain't dry yet anyway. He'll be alright.

You go lay down and rest." Lona popped Homer on his little wet behind. "You better stop bothering your grandmother, boy!"

So MaMary didn't always know what to do. She didn't want the sad little boy whipped because she had tried to do something for him. She mentioned things to Robert. "Mama, I wish I could tell you something so you could understand, but I don't know why myself. I try to make up for it, but I ain't always here."

Homer's behind was covered in blister sores from wearing wet diapers too long. Now that Lona had to do some washing because there were too few diapers to wait for Robert to come dragging in, she dipped them in cold water a few times and hung them all over the bathroom. When they dried they still had old urine in the cloth and when a diaper was wet again with fresh urine, it burned the baby's skin like ammonia would do. Robert and MaMary put Vaseline on him every night. But it was sometimes twenty-four hours before Robert could apply it again, except on the weekends.

Lona would say to MaMary, "He's alright, MaMary. Let him alone. You go rest. You need to be getting well."

As the days passed MaMary's anger grew and it was getting harder to control, for her son's sake. "I am well," she would answer.

"Then you need to stay well, MaMary. I ain't gonna have your son mad at me if you get sick again."

"Child, I know what to do for my own self and for this baby. He needs—"

"I know what he needs, MaMary. You just let me take care of my own baby. You just rest, sweetheart."

And so it went.

Robert began sitting on the front porch in his work clothes, holding the baby Homer and drinking a six-pack of beer instead of eating. Homer would just turn his little round, heavy-lidded eyes up to his father, whom he loved with all his little baby heart and soul.

Later, Robert would walk the child down to the river to sit and look out over the whispering water. He would talk to Homer about the river, pointing out plants, insects, and animals. He wanted to take his son,

Prince, with them, but Lona always wanted Prince to stay with her. "Something down there on that ole dirty river can bite my son, or he might fall in. Leave him here." Little Prince wanted to go with them.

MaMary would go to the backyard and sit with them sometimes. Then she could hug Homer to her heart's delight. He came to know his grandmother and loved her.

After work and home chores Robert carried his son until he could walk, then they walked down to the river and sat watching it flow by, sometimes catching a fish or two and cooking it right out there on the shore. Robert always brought two fishing poles and two tomatoes to eat with the fish. "You got to have vegetables, son." Homer loved those times. He felt wanted . . . and he was loved.

One day when Prince was nine and Homer was eight years old, Robert came home from work, another backbreaking day behind him. Lona was now cooking the evening meals with MaMary's help. Robert sat down to rest a minute before going to take a shower. When he stood up he let out a tired heavy breath, then he frowned and dropped dead of a first, and final, heart attack.

The children hollered and screamed, crying. MaMary held her own heart as she knelt to look after her son. Lona ran to him to try to shake him awake. He didn't wake up. He was dead of a heavy heart and a sad, sad life.

His insurance had lapsed. He had used the money trying to go back and pay for things Lona brought home. The friends he worked with, black and white, took up a collection for the funeral and his family came from their distant homes and paid the rest from their scant money. It was barely enough, but his sister chose a nice, peaceful, grassy knoll near a running creek for his grave. If he had known it, he would have loved it. His family grieved, even Lona. For what was she to do now?

One thing she finally realized when he died: She had loved him. It shocked her a little. He had been her safety, he had loved her in the beginning. She cried . . . hard. She even held both her sons close to her then. "Well, he loved his sons. Your daddy loved you both."

At the funeral Lona looked around at Robert's family as she held Prince's hand. Though Homer was just on the other side of her, she didn't hold his. She told herself she wanted to comfort Homer, "But I just can't. Worryin' 'bout him is probably what killed my husband. And another thing, Lord, they ain't gonna make me move. I ain't leavin'!" Suddenly, at the thought, she screamed and cried, "I am alone with these two little children to take care of all by myself. I ain't got no job! [*sob*] Robert wanted me to stay home, here, and be a mother and take care our sons. [*sob*] Oh, Lord, we ain't got no place to go. Lord, what am I gonna do if they put us out?" [*big sob*] Some people looked at her as though she was crazy. Others just shook their heads and wondered what she was going to do, themselves.

After the funeral she spoke to Marion. "I s'pose you all gonna want me to leave here now."

"Oh, Lona," Marion's voice sad, "what would make you suppose that? Haven't you learned what kind of family we are?"

"Well," Lona sighed, "Robert gone. This is Robert's . . . ya'all's house."

"It isn't nothing but a house. You were his wife and you have his children. No one is going to ask you to leave."

Marion knew all the details of Robert's marriage because MaMary always told her, until she said, "I don't want to hear it, Mama. He made that marriage and he will have to work it out his own self. Everybody has problems. Life is not easy."

"Well, you and Fred seem to make it alright."

"That's because we try to do all the right things that make two people living together understand each other. We follow Jehovah's laws. One is to love someone as if it were your own self. If you both do it, it can work out. You need all the help you can get to live in this world. We depend on Jehovah. This is a hard world most of the time, even when it looks easy."

Now Marion looked at Lona, feeling sorry for her. She thought, "Some people make it so easy to dislike them, but they really don't know what they are doing. A person has to remember that. Though they sure can make it hard to keep remembering. I don't want to hate anyone, Lord." She said to Lona, "He is gone, but you are still my sister and Prince and Homer are still my nephews. MaMary is still your MaMary."

Lona looked at Marion wondering how much she could believe. Marion knew that, so she said, "We need you to stay here. MaMary would be alone if you left. She loves her grandchildren."

Lona sensed an advantage. She changed gears and games. "Well, if I have to leave, I can think of somewhere to go live. I had a life before I came here."

Marion, knowing Bible wisdom, followed Lona's game. "Well, you have to do whatever you think is best, Lona. Our children are grown and one is in college. Fred and I will not mind renting our house out and moving back here with Mama. Won't mind at all. Be good to be back home, resting by the river."

Lona backed away from that particular game, feeling for another one. "Well, Robert been paying the taxes on this house all these years. I s'pose it belongs to him and his kids, a little."

Marion smiled, "It belongs to all of us equally and that includes his children. It really belongs to Mama. We're talking like she is dead. She isn't, and she looks mighty well to me, even if she can't get around like she used to. That is why I'll clean this house before I go, then you can just rest and look after the boys. You let me know when you decide what you are going to do, leave or stay. Then we can make arrangements. In any event, we will pay the taxes from now on."

"Well, if you think I can be of some help around here, I'll be glad to stay with MaMary. I love her like a mother. The kids do too, and they don't want me to take them away from their father's home." Lona smiled as she said, "They want to stay right here by this river where their daddy used to take them. Just like he wants them to stay here."

When they left, Homer followed his aunt to their car where Fred waited. He loved them both, they were loving and kind to him. She smiled down at the bright eyes in his little brown face and said, "I ought'a take you home with us. You look just like your father!"

Homer wanted to say, "Oh, please, oh please, take me witchu!" But he didn't say it. He loved his mother even though he knew she did not love him. He knew that. But he believed his brother loved him. They were close when Lona let them alone.

Then his aunt Marion said as she handed him a paper, "Here, you take my address and phone number. Put it away where nice little boys put their secret things. We are just fifty miles up that highway. You are welcome anywhere I am. I mean that. I am your aunt and I loved your father, my brother. And I love you. You may need me . . . someday, and when you do, you just come on. I'm ready for you. When your mother asks you what I gave you, you just give her this dollar bill. We won't be lying because I am giving it to you. But put this paper away without anyone knowing about it but you."

Finally, everyone was gone. They did not leave any money with Lona. Marion had bought a few clothes and some shoes for the boys and stocked up a little food and milk in the icebox. She left all reserve money with her mother. (Robert had cut into a back wall in her closet and built a six-by-six-inch safety hold that could be covered so Ma-Mary's money would be safe from everybody.) Saying, "Mama, I think Lona will be getting a job. You let her, you hear?"

The next morning Lona told her children, "I'm going to get a job. Prince, you keep right on going to school. You need a education so you don't end up like your daddy. Homer, you check with that grocery store 'cross the street and see if they need some little help over there, cleaning up or something. Check with the paperboy and see can you get a paper route. Whatever time left over, you go to school. If the school let you do that."

Prince spoke, "Mama, I can go 'round the neighborhood and see if I can mow lawns or clean up backyards. Mr. Heavy will help me find something I can do."

Lona smiled and patted his head, "Baby, you just get your schoolin'. You daydream too much for hard work. Homer and me will see 'bout things to do." Then she left the house to go seeking employment. She looked, thoughtfully, across the street at Lamont Heavy's house as she walked away. Thinking, "Poor man, he's single now too. All alone in that big house."

Homer took a regular paper route and any other job he could find.

Prince began waking up early in the mornings, waiting for the delivery truck to rumble past his house. He began stealing milk bottles from porches in the last darkness of night.

And so it was . . . at 905 Dream Street in Place.

Eula Too had talked a long time with MaMary and Lona about Mrs. Fontzl's wake, the neighborhood, and raising children. MaMary said, "I am so sorry I wasn't more help while she was alive. I knew them ever since we first moved here. My daughter, Marion, will be down for the wake and funeral. You know, her and Elizabeth grew up together in this neighborhood. Marion will be so glad to see her old friend again. It's too bad it has to be under such conditions. But, sometimes, that's the only way you get to see old friends. You mighty lucky to have Mrs. Santi over there with you all, too. She is a natural-born good person, sweet and nice as she can be."

Lona didn't say very much, just looked at Eula Too. She was studying her like a book. She blinked when the telephone rang; it was Madame calling for Eula Too to come home. There was a slight smirk on Lona's face when she hung up the phone.

Eula Too left, saying, "I have been here too long." She laughed, embarrassed, "It's taking me all day just to go to four houses. Now I am hungry. I think I'll go home to eat before I go to the last two houses."

# Chapter Twenty-one

*

Eula saw Maureen Iris McVistin going up her stairs carrying grocery bags; she waved to her. Mrs. McVistin, her arms full, saw her and nodded.

"I'll go over there next," thought Eula, "I just want to grab something to eat first, and see what Madame wants." She went up the stairs of Mrs. Fontzl's house feeling pleased about the neighborhood. "This is a good neighborhood to live in. Everyone is so friendly and nice."

When she went to Madame's room she watched to see if Madame was feeling any better, thinking, "I know I still feel very low about my mother. You just wait, Mama, I'm going to be alone in a few days. For a long time, I think. I'll be able to find someplace where I can really think about what has happened to us. I didn't see you as much as I should have. Oh, Mama, I wish I had the chance to do it all over again. I wouldn't have left you there so long. Oh, Mama, I didn't know what to do. But I sure miss you, Mama."

She could see Madame was doing better. From the look of the lunch tray, she was able to eat a little more today. Papers were scattered all over the bed and Madame had a gentle smile on her face, a pen in her hand, and the telephone beside her. "Was something the matter, Madame? How did you know where to call?" Eula smiled as she removed the tray, setting it on the dresser to move later. She was glad to see Madame coming alive again. "What is all this? What are we planning now?"

Madame looked up at Eula with a tremulous happy smile. "I have decided I do not want my mother buried in that ole cemetery. I am making some arrangements to buy some land I know about that runs right along the river. I've been looking at it for years. It's full of trees and birds, beauty! I am going to bury my mother there."

"I think that's good, Madame. As long as you're satisfied. How much land is it?"

"There are four hundred acres available; nobody wants to build there. It's about four miles from town."

"You are going to buy four hundred acres for one person?"

"Well, I'll probably be buried there someday. I want you to take care of all that, Eula. But I am only going to buy two hundred acres."

"Is it expensive?"

"Good Lord, no. The original owner is dead and his children are dying to get rid of it ever since they inherited it."

"I want the other two hundred acres then."

"Why? Whatever for? You will be with me, here, in this house. I am going to have it renovated, refurbished. The basement can be made just perfect for you! With all the glass doors and windows facing the river. You will love it!"

Eula Too had been thinking of certain things for a long time. The words Earle had spoken to her on the ride home from their mother's funeral had been ringing in her mind. So now, she said, "Madame, I need to talk with you about something I have on my mind."

"Certainly, Eula."

"Try to understand, I—"

"And another thing Eula, I am putting our old house up for sale. I informed my broker today. We don't need that anymore. I can use some of the money for all the beautiful work I am going to do here." She looked seriously at Eula Too as she said, "I never intended to return here to live. But I am older now. There is nothing out there in this world for me. I'm too old to think about love and other such nonsense. We can have a good life right here. In Place." She picked up several papers, smiled, said, "Eula this place has grown; you will like it much more than I did when I was growing up and life was wide open in front of me." She hadn't meant to dismiss Eula Too, but she had.

Eula Too sat down on an old wooden chair, looked seriously at

Madame, and said, "Madame, listen to me, dear." Madame turned to Eula with a smile that still had pain lingering about it.

"Madame, I am not your daughter, dear. I am a grown woman now. I have worked for you, with you, for many years now. In fact I have given you my life and my daughter. I have decided it is time I take my life back for myself. I might have . . . have some dreams of my own. For one, I want to live my own life, not just yours."

"You work for me, Eula. Don't I pay you enough? I give you whatever I think you want. Isn't it enough? What is the matter? I thought everything was wonderful between us. It seems like a good situation to me."

"It is hard to put a price on a life, Madame."

"But I pay you. You make a hundred dollars a week! It is not my fault if you choose to help everyone that asks you. I have tried to teach you to think for yourself and take care of yourself."

"I make a hundred dollars a week and I help some people. I should be able to do that and still have some money to do other things I want to do. I don't work for you eight hours like Dolly, or three or four hours like the ladies upstairs. I work for you twenty-four hours, seven days every week for the last nineteen years, since I was fifteen."

"But, Eula, I helped you to—"

"You helped me, Madame, in order to also help yourself. Now, don't get upset. We are both grown women. You made four or five, sometimes ten thousand dollars a week, but I did all the work. It was your house, your building, your friends, but I did all the work. Greta was a servant you did not trust. You trusted me and I have proven you could trust me. I did everything and helped you do whatever you had to do. I even came to your dinners. Thank you for the lessons. But, now, I need money because I want those other two hundred acres of land that you are not going to buy. And I want a raise, please."

"A raise? Eula! Now that we don't have that income anymore! Why didn't you talk to me about this when the ladies were making money?"

"I'm talking to you about it now. Now is when I need it."

"You don't have any savings?"

"Not enough."

"Enough for what else beside the land?"

"For whatever I think of that I want that would be reasonable."

"How much have you decided I should pay you?"

"I have not decided on any amount of pay. I need a good-size amount of money because if I get that land I am going to want to build on it, live on it. Have a home that belongs to me. And Jewel."

"Eula, you know I have no one to leave my belongings to other than you."

"Ahhhh, Madame, I don't want you to die. I don't want to wait until you are dead to live a life of my own." She reached for Madame's hand, but Madame moved it away. She was adjusting to Eula Too's words. She had not planned on being alone, with only servants around her, in her old age. And she loved her money.

"Eula, are you in love? Have you met some man?"

With a puzzled look on her face, Eula sat back down in her chair. "No. I don't need to fall in love to want a life of my own. I am a young woman. Thirty-four years old. Life is still in front of me."

Madame looked, thoughtfully, at Eula. "I am fifty . . . in my fifties. I never . . . You are right, of course, Eula. I just never thought . . . you . . ."

Eula stood, leaned over Madame, and took the hand that had moved away, and held it tightly. "I am not leaving you. You are my best friend. I love you. You have been between me and the world in many good ways. You have become my family, you, and Earle and Jewel. I will never leave you. Do . . . not . . . worry . . . about me going away and leaving you alone. I am alone too, and where in the world would I go? What other place have I to be? I have planned for nothing. My life has been built entirely around you. You and Jewel."

"You mean, Eula, if you bought, had, that land, you would stay here? In Place. Near me, and work for me, with me, always? Be here?"

Eula hadn't thought that far ahead, but she said, "I am thinking of doing just that. I am thinking of living here, always. Near enough to you to take care of you. But I need some money, enough money to take care of me, so I will be independent."

"What is enough?"

"I don't know. You decide. But, I don't want it when you die, I need it now."

"I will tell you this, I will not decide about the money just now, but I will give you enough to buy those two hundred acres. They are only twenty dollars an acre, so that is forty thousand dollars right there! You will have to pay your own taxes though!"

Eula smiled, "My own taxes. Alright, Lord! But I still need some money. I have to live on something. We need to talk about more money for my pay."

The phone rang and Madame, agitated, answered it. It was Rita, crying on the phone. "My sister won't let me in my own house! It's in her name because I thought I would be protecting myself. Now, she won't even let me in the house I paid for. She called me a whore and said she would not allow her children to know me. Me! I helped her all her life. I paid for her education! And that house! Oh, Madame, what shall I do? What shall I do?"

"Rita, I don't know. Didn't you save anything of your own? You know that part of my life is over and I do not know how I can assist you now. Why not call one of your old gentlemen friends? They loved you!"

"They didn't love me. You know that, Madame." The tears were drying a little.

Eula took the phone, which Madame gladly let go. "Hello, Rita. Tell me what you told Madame."

"Oh, what the hell for, Eula? Nobody cares what happens to me. And it's too late to find my place in life now. There is no place for me. I'm sorry I called."

"Wait a minute, Rita. Just you tell me what the matter is." Rita repeated herself. "Rita, do you have any money? I know you have some money."

"A little. But not enough to find a place, a home for myself right now. And I am older than you are, Eula. There is no place for me, no place I would want to be, anyway. I guess I could get a job. A real job. But, right now, I don't know what to do. My sister," her voice softened, "my little sister, who I love, has really truly, deeply, hurt me. In my heart," her voice grew hard again, "and in my pocket." Despair and tears almost dissolved her voice. "I thought she loved me. I thought we were a family. People you could trust."

"It takes a lot of love to make a family. Do you have enough money to go to a hotel?"

"Certainly, but I won't be able to stay long. May I go back to the house? Dolly said we had to leave."

"The house is being sold, Rita. That part of our life is over."

Rita, crying softly, said, "My life can't be over. I'm not old, I'm not ugly, and I'm not ready for it to be over. I want to live. I don't even have a child. I need a place of my own to be in life. But there is no other place like Madame's house I know. It wasn't a whorehouse to me. It was a place where the same intimate visitors came again and again. They were the same. Not different, like whores."

"I am not going to argue with you about that, Rita, but what is a whore to you? No, don't answer me now. Just find a hotel and call back with your number. We will think of something. We might have to bring you here temporarily."

"I don't feel like coming to a funeral, but alright, Eula, I will. You do make me feel a little better."

"And Rita, any money that ever comes through your hands again, if you did the work, you need to keep your own money, your own self. I have to go. We'll talk to you later."

When she hung up, Madame asked, "Why would you have her come here? What can you do for her? She had her opportunities. She could have saved her own money and asked me to help and I would have helped her buy a house, with her own money, of course. I have no time for fools."

Smiling over her shoulder at Madame, Eula walked to the doorway saying, "That is why I wanted to talk to you today. You taught me not to be a fool." Madame smiled, faintly, in return. "Now, I'm going to get a bite to eat and finish my walk through the neighborhood. I have two houses to go."

"Which house are you going to now, Eula?"

"I saw the lady across the street going in her house."

"A white lady? That would be Maureen Iris. She's a nice lady, always neat, clean, and very quiet. Her husband was a nice man, too. He always had something for the kids. But, he died. It was sad." Madame shook her head sadly, in commiseration. "She and Mama were friendly. Iris has always looked . . . hungry to me. Like she was looking through a glass at something she wanted, but couldn't have."

Eula briefly shook her head, smiling sadly, said, "I'm gone, Madame Elizabeth." Before she left she went to her room and checked to see if the kitten, Tobe, had enough food and water. She sighed, satisfied when she saw Tobe curled up asleep in the middle of her bed. She went to finish her duties.

# Chapter Twenty-two

*

*A sad and lonely house, as I told you when I looked down upon it the first time. I will, now, tell you the story the house told me.*

## Carl and Maureen Iris McVistin, 902 Dream Street

Maureen Iris had been born in a small township in North Carolina to an Irish-Welsh mother and a Hebrew-English father. No one remembers how they met and fell in love, but both had just arrived in America by ship. The mother and her sister were traveling together, away from prejudice and poverty. No one knows from whence they came, nor how, but they were all poor. They came to America to make a fortune or just a better living: I will tell you, anything would be better than where they had been trying to survive.

It was probably on one of those cold, damp, and foggy, windswept-ocean times when, alone and facing unknown odds, that the two hearts came together in their fears and loneliness. Maureen Iris was the result of their hasty love. But love it must have been.

Maureen's aunt, a strong, redheaded young woman, had gone on to find employment. She separated from her sister because she had married "the Jew!" "Still and all," the strong sister thought, "she is my sister." So she tried to look in on her sister and bring her things, small things. Times were more than hard.

The young mother was sickly all during the time she carried the baby. Even at that time they were not sure she would live long. It was not, in the beginning, tuberculosis, but eventually poor medical care and lack of nourishment brought her to that devastating sickness.

Her young husband loved her and tried to care for his wife and child. But he had to work several small niggling jobs because his race and religion was used against him. Then, too, there was such competition among the poor. Trying to afford the room and medicines they needed for life took all the young man's time and strength. Finally, they were led to an old woman cook who rented rooms above her filthy café. She was paid to look after the mother and child while the father worked. The price included feeding them.

The world is full of liars and this woman was one of them. She took the hard-earned money of hard labor while giving the sick mother little more than thick soup remaining in a few bowls other boarders had left behind, too vile for even some of the tired hungry workers to eat. The father often went without food so his family could have a little more.

But the mother was strong in her heart; she nursed their baby girl with near-empty breasts pulsing with a thin stream of milk. Mother and child survived. They named the baby Maureen Iris. They called her Iris, because she was like a flower to them.

Later, when the mother was strong enough, she found a much-needed job in a cotton mill. At last, it wasn't long, she developed tuberculosis. She worked there, slowly dying, for five years. Her stronger sister worked there three years, then married a railroad man and moved farther up the East Coast.

The mother coughed through the nights even as her husband held her tightly to keep her warm in their drafty room, using a hot plate to give them a semblance of heat. Overburdened, weary, downtrodden by uncaring bosses. Cheated by his employers with short pay because he was a Jew; they said to each other, "He is a Jew! He has plenty money he has stolen from others hidden away somewhere!" The young husband gave up. His only friend, other than his wife, was money. And he had none.

He searched his mind and cast-off newspapers for something better. He walked away one morning after kissing his little daughter, holding her in his arms, feeling her rags. Rags were all he could afford. Most of his money, now, had been spent buying medicine for his wife to keep her up and working. They were poorer than poor, destitute and misused, lied to and abused. He was ashamed of himself as a man.

He found a decent job about a hundred miles away, for he had been well-trained in his old home. He was intelligent and quick with his hands. A year later he was returning to find his wife and child again. "At last, I have a good job!" He died trying to tell her, to take her in his arms and tell her they were safe.

He had never been a regular drinking man, but on this cold winter's night he drank a small bottle of whiskey to keep warm, to celebrate his job, and the nearness he felt to finding his wife. When he reached the town of cotton mills, he became excited, "This is where I left them! She works here!"

He would not spend his money on a room for the night. He thought, "I must save it for my wife and our child. This whiskey will keep me warm through the night." He crawled up under a rickety wooden front porch to rest and sleep a few hours. He took a long swallow as he planned, "Then I'll go straight to the mill and find her!" He slept, almost instantly, from his long walking, fighting the strong winter winds. During his sleep, the alcohol in his throat passage froze, his lungs, his body. He died quietly, unaware that his struggle with life was over. His wife and his child never knew. But God did know.

There was never any let-up from ignorant, uncaring supervisors on jobs in the mills. They were greedy in their ignorance and hunger. Love for their neighbor or even kindness to those as poor as themselves never entered their minds. In the end, the mother died also. She knew when she was dying. She died trying to take a breath between sobs, her crying for her child she was leaving behind among the wretched of all the earth. The liars, the thieves, the perverts, the murderers, the bosses. God did know that too.

*God does watch what people do to one another. He loves His creation. But God has a greater plan and His Will will be done, finally, in His Time, which is different from ours. God is still good, even when people don't think* so. *It is wise to learn His plan and get off that wide road that leads to a greater death than the death that is on earth now.*

The mother had a friend, Maggie. Maggie tried to stop the mill from taking six-year-old Iris and putting her to work at child labor to pay for her mother's debts, but was unable. For a year or so, Maureen Iris worked, standing on a stool trying to spool cotton. She lived with Maggie sometimes or slept hidden under some bench at the mill. Some other weary, caring soul always took her back to Maggie.

Maggie loved the pathetic child, so like herself, so in need. Maggie had taught herself to read a bit, though she could not write; never anything to write on to practice. Maggie knew an old railroad man who worked in the telegraph office. He sent a message of inquiry to all such men as himself that might know of the sister. After a few weeks they received an answer.

He then wrote out a letter for Maggie to mail the sister, who had married again. This time she had made a rather fine marriage. Barely eating and hating to leave Iris alone while she *had* to work, Maggie waited for an answer. "Oh precious Lord, what do I do with this child if they ain't no answer? I got my own little two to worry about. We are all hungry and ill-clothed."

At last, several weeks later, there was an answer and a few wrinkled dollar bills for a train ticket. As Maggie put little Iris on the train, she cried and prayed, "Oh, thank You, Lord, I don't know what You want me to do in this here mean ole world we got down here, but whatever it is, I'm'a do it, Lord! Watch over this child, please."

Maureen Iris's aunt, who had no children of her own, raised Iris somewhat begrudgingly. She never forgot Iris was part Jew, though she never mentioned it. She did not want her husband to know. She clothed Iris and fed her, and sometimes even loved Maureen Iris because she could see her dead sister in her niece's face. The dead sister she had not gone back to help.

The aunt was still a little frightened of life because of her experience in the old country and in America. She did not want her good husband to feel burdened by a child that was not his, and worse, a Jewish child. She forbade Maureen Iris to ever speak of her father. And she did not want her husband reminded that she, his own wife, had not given him a child of his own.

Iris was a reminder to her aunt of many menacing things from the past. Things she cautioned Iris about when they were alone. "Do not tell anyone your father was a Jew! Put all that out of your mind. You will have trouble if people know you are a Jew! I would have to send you away. No, I will not tell you why. Just forget him forever!"

Consequently, Iris grew up frightened and did not know exactly what she was frightened of. Her aunt often taught her in their little "talks" of the constant shadows of lies, hatred, and envy in the smiling eyes that would be around her. "And you are a Jew, too! A Jew and poor. All your life, until you have so much money they will be frightened of you! You need to get a husband as soon as you can so he can take care of you!"

Iris was sent to school and grew up a pretty young woman, auburn-haired like her mother, green-gold eyes like her father with the soft, clear skin of the Hebrew and Irish people. But she was always a little terrified. She could not explain it because her terrors were vague. She was bewildered and helplessly intimidated by people. She was, by nature, a gentle person, kind and caring with much empathy for others. She loved animals because they were helpless. Like she was helpless.

She never thought of lying, if for no other reason than she never did anything that made a lie necessary. As she grew older and was still an unmarried virgin, that, for some reason, embarrassed her. She had a great desire and longing to know "what men and woman 'do' when they were alone. What does it feel like to make a new baby? To have love." Of course, all these thoughts were kept to herself.

Her aunt said, "Your virginity will be a good draw for a good man." Iris was comforted, but still anxious. "Your reputation has to be known," Iris thought, "and who knows anything about me?" When she was around men, her anxiety inclined her to draw her narrow shoulders together, hunched.

Young men were attracted to her, but they did not remain at her side long. Some of them laughed at her as they said, "She is hysterical!" Anyway, hard as her aunt tried, Iris did not marry when it was suitable.

Her aunt would not afford her going to college. "You are a woman! What do you need to know? You just need a husband! Silly girl. You should be happier; I give you everything!" Maureen Iris became even more careful of her appearance. She hid her anguish, stress of her sexual repression, and desperation beneath "appearances." Iris's life was abysmal in her mind and, definitely, in her heart. Now, when she was alone, she began to escape in fantasies of another life, of love.

Love can do such strange things, if you have it . . . and if you do not have it. Ever since the cotton mills and even before her mother's death, Maureen Iris had dreamed of better things.

Now, in her aloneness, Maureen Iris turned to other living things. Vulnerable things of beauty. The birds living in the tree outside her window, calling out in sounds so clear and purely beautiful. She would study an ant crawling along the kitchen windowsill until it disappeared. Watch a spider accidently stepping from some shadowed corner of a room, "To go where?" she would softly ask the air. Her eyes would follow a bumblebee who wasn't supposed to be able to fly. "How will I fly?" she would whisper in her mind. She envied the butterflies wandering across her view, "You are so beautiful. How? Why not me?" She even built shelters in the winters for the birds; like the shelter of fear and solitude she framed against the constant winter in her life.

She loved moving-picture shows. Her aunt thought young people should not see movies, "with people in them who do all kinds of devilish things!" Her uncle sneaked her money so she could go to them. Or she sat on the bench in the backyard for hours, or, between meals, in her room all day in a trance.

*Now . . . history does not repeat itself so much as life remains ever the same. What have new inventions to do with the basics of life? Animal or human? Human beings remain human beings and riches or poverty, too much or too little, loneliness or boredom do their same damages. Only a fortunate few find the middle ground.*

Maureen Iris watched as her friends got married or went happily off to college, then came home and got married. Watched them go off to a future somewhere. Her aunt did not mean to be intolerant, foreboding, and threatening, but she was. Considered a "grown woman," Iris was compromised by her loneliness and her age. She was lonely for her mother, still. She was lonely for life, mentally, physically, and emotionally starved.

Satan is ever busy and Iris met someone who would never, to her face, call her hysterical or embarrass her. Would never tell her the truth either. To him, making love meant having sex. Sex in those times was not easy to come upon, and Iris's aunt had made her sensitive and vulnerable to kindness from strangers even while she was afraid of them. The man took advantage of Maureen Iris's aloneness. He did not make love to her, he screwed her.

In a short time Iris became pregnant by her suitor. He had promised her marriage but instead ran away, disappeared, chuckling at his cleverness.

Iris's thoughts were, "What can I do? Who do I tell? The police? Then everyone will know what I have done! They will know he didn't love me! Oh, God, I don't want to tell Aunt." But, finally, she had to tell Aunt.

Aunty thought of letting Iris have the child, putting her out for being a worthless, low woman, but decided she did not want that reflection on her. What would her husband say? She, finally, "knew someone" and hastened through her house gathering money from almost all her secret hiding places. She then hastened Maureen Iris across town to the obvious slums to the someone who did these things, and the abortion was performed, but it was not successful.

When they discovered Iris was still pregnant it was too late to try the abortion again. Iris suffered throughout her pregnancy from her aunt's constant harping on her mistakes, her foulness, the grief she had brought upon herself and her aunt. When the child was born it was given up for adoption. The husband fought his wife over such a solution, but the aunt did not give in. The baby was gone. Their house was full of reproach, bickering, and hostility.

Iris was in pain emotionally and physically. Her heart hurt with an authentic, true, agony of suffering. Despair and anguish filled her days and nights for longer than you can imagine. She dreamed of her lost baby. She dreamed, night and day, of a place she could go to be away from everything she knew, even from her kind uncle. "I don't know what I can do, but I need a place of my very own. Oh, God, some place for me, please."

Time passed, a year or so, and with it some of the emotional pain receded. Iris began to venture out socially again. It was considered by many people, mostly Aunty's friends, that Maureen Iris was growing too old to be unmarried much longer. They said so, out loud. They smirked, knowingly, as they whispered about the baby.

At the time Iris was twenty-six years old. "A blight on my life!" her aunt moaned, aloud. But the husband did not mind taking care of the gentle Iris. "She is a bit of peace in the house, that's to be sure," he told his friends, "but the poor girl needs a man of her own, if only to get away from her aunt!" He would laugh good-naturedly, "That's better than me. I can't get away!"

Time seemed to be passing swiftly. Little sad and lonely Iris heard the whisperings of her friends. More fear moved into her heart, into her otherwise empty bed, into her whole life. Her desperation to be wanted and loved began to dim the smile on her face and even the sweetness in her heart. Fear can do that to a life. She still had the youthful glow that can make almost anyone pretty, but, it was being whispered off her face by her "friends."

Over time Iris became very thin, with a drawn, fretful face. Then she met Carl McVistin at a church social dance. (The only kind her aunt let her attend.) She was trying to smile, as her aunt had told her, but her smile was like a slight and unhappy frown. Carl McVistin did not think she was the girl he would marry. He thought she was pleasant and, best of all, she was with a group of ladies, not with a beau.

Maureen Iris danced with Carl because she thought she should. When Carl returned and asked her to dance the second time, she could not believe it. A dim light began to glimmer in her mind. The idea!

"He likes me! Oh! He likes me!" She was not conniving, but also not dumb. She smiled up at him, not too much, but still a lot. The frown, for the moment, was gone.

Carl had been born in a town named Placeland, fifty miles away from there, and was visiting a friend in Elysee City on vacation. He was a nice-looking man in his mid-thirties with a pleasant personality and a patient, smiling face. His was a frail constitution in a healthy-looking body. He ate well, he slept well, but there were moments of weakness when the earth seemed to circle around his head. No doctor had as yet discovered a reason for the sudden weaknesses.

Carl was a hard worker at any job given him. He was, in fact, a plain, good man. He was in Elysee City hoping to find a wife and now he had met Maureen Iris.

Time she spent with Carl in the following days had brought a tentative grateful smile back to her face with the now pretty, passionate lips. He took notice that she was neat, clean, and thrifty. Two weeks later, when Carl's vacation was all but one day over, he had grown to know and even love the soft, gentle woman. In his own needs it was enough. Enough to propose marriage to her.

Maureen Iris accepted Carl with surprised tears in her eyes. Gratitude flooded her heart while a thank-you prayer to God flew from her soul. At last, she was not afraid to love Carl anymore. She loved him with all her grateful heart from the day he proposed. She did not make the mistake of making sex before the marriage. Nor did he ask her to make love. His experiences in Place had not been good ones. He wanted someone he could keep after making love to them.

In the throes of joy her aunt bought her everything she needed for the wedding. Her uncle proudly gave her away. As he walked her down the aisle in the little church, he whispered in her ear, "We will miss you, Maureen Iris. You have been a wonderful niece. This Carl is a lucky, lucky man! If he does anything to hurt you, he will have to answer to me!" She glowed under his implied protection.

She threw the wedding bouquet and a self-respecting smirk over her shoulder at her "friends." Then, joy of all joys, Carl McVistin proudly took her home to Place on the train that same day. She went to her new Place, gladly.

She tried to subdue her smile, like her aunt had warned her, "Be a blushing bride, Maureen Iris. Men don't know anything. He'll think you are a virgin." Maureen Iris tried not to hear her. They were not words for a new and blushing bride.

Her husband said he preferred the name Iris because she was like a flower to him. (Her whole body and face had changed, filled out and blossomed since she had known him.) Iris was in love. Her mind was daydreaming on the short train ride to Place. "At last! I will know what 'Love' is! I have finally found a place of my own to be. When my husband and I have children I will love them with all my heart and I will make Carl the best wife he could ever have in the world! Oh, God, how will I thank You?"

On their wedding night Carl was gentle. His own needs were more than sexual; they were the needs of a man who had also been lonely for something that was real. He had paid for sex in the past. This was not sex, this was his wife whom he loved.

He was tender before they made love and after they made love. He held her soft, starved-for-love body in his warm, strong, manly arms, close to his heart. Sweetness and affection filled their marriage bed. His mind sang the happy words, "I am a man. I have a wife. I shall soon have a family and get on with living a full and satisfying life. I am a man. I have a wife." He never thought to wonder if she was a virgin. Her body was tight, wet, warm, his woman, and wonderful to him.

Carl worked all the time he could as a bricklayer and cement finisher. They saved money. Then he found a lot with a small shack on it he liked. He brought her to see it and she smiled up at him because she didn't care where they lived. They bought the lot and he built a home at 902 Dream Street. And she found out more about being loved and wanted.

They did not live a big life, but it was a normal, good life. Iris did not work. Carl's only problem was stopping off to have beer or a bourbon with his friends after work. Iris hated the smell of cigarettes and liquor. She read about that in a magazine, and besides, Aunt hadn't liked Uncle drinking or smoking either. And she didn't like having to keep a dinner warm.

Iris had become a very exacting woman, everything in its place and on time. Carl wore her down even as she wore Carl down. But they "got along."

She got pregnant soon after their marriage because their lovemaking was so full of love. The baby was born very frail and sickly. It struggled for its life for several months but, pitifully and finally, the baby died.

Carl buried that one dream with that one baby and commenced to dream of the next baby. As the dirt was thrown over the tiny coffin Iris wondered why her body did not make a better, stronger baby. "Was it the abortion? Am I too old? Did the years dry out my mother lifeblood? Oh, why God? Why?"

They tried very hard. They knew it could happen any time. By now Iris knew she didn't have orgasms, or ever feel like Carl did when he made love to her. "Still, we made my one baby without me. We can make another." But they didn't make another that night or that month or that year. They didn't make another baby ever again.

After twenty-four years of living together in a good, but to Iris, sad marriage without children, Carl died from cancer.

Even though Iris knew he had cancer and cared for him with all her energies, his death was still a total shock that shook her life from its roots. Iris, then in her early fifties, was alone. In her mind she knew she would never find another mate. She was alone, again.

So she settled in to live without a man in the home they had built and paid for, without any children. Iris was, indeed, alone. She thought of the child she had loved and given away, every lonely night. She had hated her aunt a long time now.

She had lived on Dream Street many years and seen people, some renters, some homeowners, come and go. Iris had only a few nearly close friends. One of them was Mrs. Fontzl at 903 and the other was Mrs. Mary Green, who lived at 905 Dream Street across the street.

Her hair was gray but neatly kept by her own hands. She carried the plumpness of an older age. She dressed cheaply, but becoming to herself. "I only go to shopping and to church, anyway. Maybe I visit my friends now and then, if they need something."

Aunt was old and far away, widowed, but married again . . . for company. Alone, Iris's mind returned to her fears of other people. She thought of the shadows of lies or stealth in the smiling eyes around her whenever she went on her errands. Nights, alone in her bed, she listened for some threat to her life, some violence to break into her house that felt so empty of safety. She thought of her friends, old now, too. "There is no one now, God. Just You. Just me. Well. I have always trusted You." In her nights she would sleep with her prayers still breath-moist on her lips.

Eula Too made her way up the steps to the McVistin residence, raised the metal knocker and let it fall. Iris opened the door. She had seen Elizabeth arrive home and had seen Eula a few times in the past several days, so was not leery of her. She knew something must have happened to her friend, Milicent Fontzl. Her face saddened even more. "Oh, dear, has Milicent . . . passed on?"

Eula slowly nodded her head. Iris stepped back, opening the door wider. "Well, come on in." An old fat, gray cat was slowly walking toward the door. "Oh, don't let Comp'ny get out!" She picked up the grumpy, disappointed cat. "You must be tired; going around carrying such sad news." She motioned Eula to follow her to the sparkling kitchen where she put the cat down. "I'll fix you a cup of tea."

"I just had lunch, Mrs. McVistin, but a cup of hot tea sounds good."

Eula watched her as Iris turned the fire on under an old but shiny metal kettle and began to gather other things she needed. When cups, saucers, and spoons were set on place mats on the table (sugar, salt, and pepper were always there), Iris sat down, looking at Eula, waiting.

Eula saw an old Victorian-looking woman. Her plain dress was dowdy but clean. Her soft gray hair, rolled hastily, sat neatly, from long practice, in a bun on the back of her neck. Several strands sprang free on Iris's wrinkled forehead and around her ears. She held her body stiffly as she tilted her head, smiling at Eula. The sweetness of her expression amid the sadness she was feeling awakened pangs of sorrow in Eula's heart for the sadness all vulnerable people feel. And all people are vulnerable.

"Milicent has died. Now there is no one left on Dream Street but Mary and me."

Eula made herself smile, "That's not true, Mrs. McVistin. Mrs. Green has her children and you have yours. This seems to be a family street."

Iris looked down at her worn hands laying open in her lap. "Yes. I s'pose so. My . . . our children are dead," her voice faded, "or were never born." Eula could see that Iris was not used to easy familiarity with strangers.

"You live alone here, Mrs. McVistin, all by yourself in this big house? There must be three or four bedrooms and a large basement in this house. Don't you get lonely in this big house all by yourself?"

Iris blushed, embarrassed by the nerve of a stranger to ask such questions. Still, she answered, "Oh, I'm too old to make new friends or be lonely. Who would want to visit with a old lady like me? All wrinkled and gray and . . ."

Eula tilted her head, smiling as she said, "Your wrinkles mean you have lived, you have survived, and you have some wisdom." Iris, pleased at the words, blushed again. Thoughtfully Eula asked, "Do you sew? Do you like music? Do you have a television to watch? Oh, not those stupid serial shows, but things about geography and history? Television has some wonderful documentaries and discussions. Don't you think so?"

Iris almost fell backward from the barrage of words rushing, directed at her from Eula's mouth. She frowned, saying, "I don't have a television. I always thought it was made for two people to watch together." She smiled and Eula saw the sweetness again. "Carl, that's my dead husband, would have liked one of those things."

"He would probably like for you to have one for yourself." Eula could see that this could turn into another long talking visit, thinking, "I'm so used to taking care of everybody. I must stop that. But everyone seems so lonely here, why? They have each other, don't they?" After explaining about the wake that evening, Eula finished her tea and stood, saying, "I hope you will come to the rememberance for Mrs. Fontzl this evening. It will be around eight o'clock. I know she was your friend." Iris nodded as she fidgeted with her spoon and cup before she rose to follow Eula.

Iris followed Eula down the hall to the front door, subdued, yet excited by her visitor. She whispered "Eula Too" to herself, turning the name over on her tongue; the name moved smoothly. "A visitor."

In a low voice, Iris said to Eula, "You know, I . . . I am a Jew. I am Irish, but I am a Jew. I never bother people . . . because I don't want to be hated. Like . . . Jews are hated."

Eula turned back, stunned. She said to Iris, "Iris, anyone who would hate you for that is one of the biggest fools there are. They are shallow and ignorant people. Never pay attention to fools or let them determine your life. You seem a wonderful human being to me and I'm sure to Mrs. Fontzl also. God pays no attention to such people, such haters, and neither should you. Will you come? You must come, please."

Iris, almost weak from pleasure at words she had never heard before, said, "Yes, of course I will come tonight. Milicent was one of my best friends." Sadly she considered again, "Now I won't have no place to go when I want company." She sighed in mild distress. "Did old Mary say she was coming?"

"Yes, mam. She is coming to pay her respects also. So then, I will see you later. I have one last stop at the grocery store, then I can go back to help them get ready for everybody." She started down the stairs.

Iris asked a little anxiously, "Are . . . many people coming to Milicent's house tonight?"

Eula smiled up at her from the steps, "I'm sure just her friends will come, just like you are. And, Mrs. McVistin, I may be around here for a while, so please consider me your friend, too. Don't worry about anything. And don't be lonely. And we ought to look into a television for you." She laughed as she turned to step farther down the steps, "You can even lie in bed and watch things happening until you go to sleep." She turned back once, "Oh, Mrs. McVistin, do you need anything I can pick up for you from the store?"

Iris wanted to say yes so Eula would have to come back, but she had shopped just yesterday. She hesitated, then shook her head no. She hated to close the door. But she did close it at last, after the cat, Comp'ny, rushed out. She sighed, going back to her kitchen to clean it up. But for some reason, instead she sat back down at the table and smiled at the used cups and saucers and the sugar spoon resting on the tablecloth. She smiled at the little dish of sliced lemons they had used. She lifted her eyes to the ceiling and closed them, speaking softly, "Life? You have visited me."

Eula ran lightly back across the street to Madame Elizabeth's house. In the kitchen Nurse Santi and her friends Jean and Jerry were talking in low voices, laughing and working steadily. They had cleaned and arranged the hall and living room. Elizabeth had asked Jerry to move some of the unnecessary pieces of furniture down to the basement. "The contractors will be here next week to begin drawing plans for the work I want done up here first."

She told them, "If you see something you want, just let me know what it is and perhaps I can let you have it." Jerry and Jean looked at each other, thinking, "We don't see anything here that we need. Our house is full, honey." But they said, "Thank you."

Santi thought of several poorer people she cared for sometimes and decided there might be something from here they could use. "That is still worth keeping," she thought, "I'll look later when I have time." She knew Elizabeth would keep all the good, new things she had bought for her mother.

Eula breezed in, breathless from her little jog and from the heavy, sweet atmosphere of meeting Iris McVistin. "I'm on my way to the grocery store, do we need anything?"

Santi shook her head, smiling as she said, "Chile, we already bought everything we have to have, I think. We bought it uptown at the cheaper stores."

Eula frowned a little, saying, "Aren't the store people the same people who ran little errands and brought food for Mrs. Fontzl?"

Santi became serious immediately, "Yes, they are. I should have thought of that. We need to help them stay in business in this little ole neighborhood! Here, let me give you some money and you buy some things you might think we will use."

Eula answered, "Well, we have to eat after this night is over. Never mind your money, I have some. Alright, if you can't think of anything special, I'm gone. This is the last house, grocery store house."

Santi said, "I hear the grandchildren of the people who owned that vacant house are thinking of coming here soon. I don't think they will live here, they been gone so long. But it may be going up for sale. They have refused to put it on the market before."

Eula was leaving, "Well, I'm gone again." She turned back once, to say, "Oh, if Rita calls for me, tell her I really want to talk to her. Tell her to leave a number or call me back in an hour or so." She was thinking of all those rooms at Iris McVistin's empty house and of Rita's empty life.

# Chapter Twenty-three

*

## Henry Lee,
## 906 Dream Street

Henry Lee, the Asian grocer, lived alone and was lonely. He was not a good-looking man, though he was good-hearted. His had a short, plump, round body. Whiskers grew out of the most unusual places in the coarse skin on his smiling face, nostrils, ears, moles. He always smiled, lips stretched over clean, but yellowed teeth. His eyes bulged, probably from some thyroid condition, so he always seemed to be startled, staring at things and people.

Henry saw his future as a bright glow at the beginning of his move to Placeland. But, after spending all his savings, made in China for his passage to the land of gold, America, he found no land of gold here. He found only work that did not pay for much more than his store's replenishments and his everyday needs. He had to be frugal and thrifty.

When he first arrived in America, he worked for his wealthy cousins in their multiple businesses in Elysee City. He slept in a back room at his cousin's house for which he paid rent. They did not cheat him because he was family, a cousin, but they begrudged him. They laughed at him, privately of course. As part of a large family, he did not expect to eat alone or sit alone and pick his teeth. He expected to do these things with them, his family. Times were always confused; they were busy or they had appointments . . . or dates. They were friendly, but they were distant-friendly to him.

He had country ways to his city cousins, old-country ways that were embarrassing among their city friends. His staring eyes made the ladies nervous, even when he smiled at them, showing his yellow teeth. He was also not very fastidious. His eyes staring in childish wonder, he would ask his cousin, "Who can waste such water for one body to bathe in every day?"

So they were eager to help him make new plans in America. "Then," they whispered among themselves, "he will leave, away from us."

In their soft voices, they offered him the suggestion of a grocery store. "A very profitable venture, wise, good cousin. Americans love to eat," they smiled. They offered him financial assistance . . . and a condition: They must help him by choosing the place for the "profitable" store. His honest, hardworking heart was grateful to his American family.

So he had borrowed their offered money and he let them "help him" choose the location. They, wanting distance from his country ways and staring eyes, had chosen the town of Placeland for his place of business.

There were not many Asians in Placeland for Henry Lee to choose friends among, or especially a wife from. He was not good-looking or sophisticated enough, nor physically handsome enough, to have brought one from the city. Besides, he did not particularly like the smooth, dancing friends of his female cousins, nor their madeup faces. Nor did he like the way they spent money. Not stranger's money perhaps, but still, anyone's money.

Henry Lee was a hard worker. He liked pretty women and pretty things, but his eyes were full of canned peaches, catsup, salt, pepper, and such. The dream of his own store. His eyes glowed when he thought of it. "In America!"

Henry Lee was medium height, medium fat with a good appetite, and medium intelligence for counting money and ordering stock to refill his shelves. In his little store, the smile remained on his face almost all the time, even when he was alone. To him, his life was good; he had achieved a wish. He was not a big dreamer, so his store was indeed a fulfillment.

But . . . the dream of all dreams!, he wanted a wife. "A wife. And my own children to come after me." He did not want to lose any of the small money his store brought in, so he wouldn't close the store to go back to find a wife in the city. Instead he wrote letters to his city relatives, which they meant to answer, but never got around to. For a long time, he waited to hear from them.

A year or so passed with no word from them about his wife. So he decided to write to China. On a trip to Elysee City to buy supplies and visit his busy relatives, he inquired of other casual acquaintances about the procedure to acquire a wife. Back at home behind his empty little grocery store in Place, he thought about a wife many mornings as he sipped his cup of hot water with a pinch of sugar stirred in. Armed with his new knowledge, he decided to write a letter to China.

He smiled in pleasure as he looked his letter over. "Is a good letter! I will have a good wife! Better than a greedy American wife!" He mailed the letter after much patting of the envelope. Then he went back to work. To wait. He worried a little, about the cost, the money to be paid for a wife. Still, with much anticipation, he waited to hear word of his wife. He saved all his money.

Each morning, every time the mailman passed, he hurried to his mailbox. But, always, nothing but bills came. He would sigh and go, dragging his feet a little, back into his store. Lonely and longing.

Every day, he waited in his little store that was empty of Asian company. Every night, he waited in his bed that was empty of love and a wife. His eyes, which may have slanted with the beauty of the Asian, bulged with patient impatience. "I am growing older," he thought often. He waited a long time. He did not give up; he still rushed to the mailbox every delivery day. One day, one night at a time. Two or three years he was alone, anxious, and . . . waiting.

### *Ha*

China has always had many, many poor people. In fact, most of the people were poor. This is true all over the world, for that matter. In the 1920s and '30s (and before) there were millions of poor people in America too. The war in the 1940s changed things for many Americans, but still there was great poverty in much of China. There were many farmers in China, and all over the world, who made their living from the land. Depended on the land to support their families.

Earlier, I spoke of Ha's birth to you. I will tell you more about it now. Ha was born in a small Chinese village and grew up surrounded by poverty, among the others of her village. Before Ha was born, her mother had given birth to five babies: two sons and one daughter had died soon after birth. Two sons had lived. The mother working in the fields and poor nutrition were the cause. The midwife had used only local herbs for medicine.

Ha was born at a time when her father was frustrated by government tax collectors and small bands of bandit warlords taking sometimes the few coins he had made on the food he had grown to feed his family and pay taxes. He was poor, frustrated, and wearied.

Sons were reasons to rejoice because they had strength to help their family. Girls were mouths to feed who would marry and go off to another family to help their husbands.

When Ha was born, sometime around 1933, the father did not want to keep her alive. He wanted, he needed, another son. The mother fought for her only daughter to live. "My beautiful girl-child." The household, in the small, square two-room hut with a kitchen that held the woodstove that cooked their pitiful food and kept them warm in winters, was a gloomy place, with the despair poverty always brings. But the mother had the rich gift of humor that lit up her family for small moments.

That is why she named her daughter Ha. "You will live, my little Ha. We shall laugh at life and you will survive!"

Ha had never known anything but poverty in her home and the homes of the neighbors, so the only thing she dreamed of was food. As she pulled weeds, following her mother hoeing in the fields, she would daydream of bowls full of noodles. "I would like to eat until I am so full I shall burst!" So she filled her eyes with the trees, birds, sky, and clouds. Ha loved clouds most of all. "They are soft and they change shapes and when the sun peers through them, they look like heaven must look to the gods."

She also loved the river not too distant from their fields. Its name meant River of Good Harvest. Ha could stare into the gentle flowing waters for hours, seeing the reflections of the clouds in the sky and watching as time moved her little world.

Ha could have been a happy child. Her disposition was good. She had good common sense and love in her heart. She learned this love from her mother and her two brothers, who often spooned to her bowl of meager portion some of their own food when the eyes of the father were turned away. If he caught them he would say, "She is a girl! She does not need the strength to work this poor piece of land, such as it is, you do! The land is all there is between us and starvation! Do not waste good food and strength!" And he would send Ha away from the tableboard.

Now . . . the father would have been a kind father, but poverty had dried his thought, love, and laughter. Blowing it hither and yon to wait in some dark corner of his being, waiting for some moment when he could feel lighter of heart, and laugh between his heavy despairing sighs.

Still, Ha grew up in some ways content and loving the beautiful land. Her mother taught her chores to do in the field and depended on her for seed chores and weed work. They grew corn, cabbage, turnips, carrots, and rice. The entire village grew rice near the river's flooded paddies. Ha knew all the seasons. Spring and summer were for planting work, summer and fall were for harvest, heavy bundles, and burning heat. She knew, as her mother did, the ache of all the body's muscles worked to get something from the soil. The cold winters were for corners near the stove where she could sit and play with her favorite little rocks in the dim house. She loved the frozen river she saw when she went with her mother to the village market to barter for their needs. Her mother stopped on the return home to leave a little gift for good harvest at the small altar of the gods, set in a niche, along the way. The Confucian temple was in a larger village. Ha gave respect and love mixed with fear to the gods, just as her mother did.

There was a teacher who traveled in a rickshaw to the nearby villages to write letters or read those received from some distant relative. Ha was always near, listening, longing to know what the characters on the paper meant. She swore in her heart, silently, "I shall learn one day. I will! I will learn to read." She longed to ask the old teacher a question or two, but the elders of the village always moved her aside. She was a child and . . . she was a girl.

By the time Ha was twelve she preferred working in the fields to staying in the gloomy hut. She was only happy in the hut when she helped her mother light the fire and cook the rice gruel with bits of meat her mother managed to get sometimes. They laughed together around the stove. At something or at nothing. They were happy together. Ha also loved going to the river with her mother.

Often there was a young man there, Ling Woo, tending his father's business. Ha looked at him, he glanced at her, but he saw her and looked for her each time he went near the river. He made up excuses to take his father's cattle near the river to graze, just to be able to glance at Ha. He liked her name and he liked her. In time they exchanged a few words, then more words, more often, all in common good manners of the village. They fell in young love.

Ha's family had several chickens the mother would not kill for meat unless it was a very special holiday. She needed and used the precious eggs in barter for the bits of meat or some other special thing she wanted but did not grow on the land. They had a lean cow for light plowing and, after they sold the calves, rich milk made from their own grasses and the multitude of greens near the river. For a while they had a pig, but it was stolen one evening before they could bring it into the hut for the night. The good mother cried, the good father cursed himself soundly. He silently searched, with his eyes, the entire village and a mile around. The pig was not recovered and there was no money to replace it.

Each season came for its purpose, always bringing its problems with it. The family was used to fighting with all their strength for their lives on the land. So when the drought came, they readied themselves to withstand it. But it lasted three years. Ha's family suffered greatly. They and the whole village were starving.

The good father did not know what to do. "This worthless land! I pay rent to a heartless landlord and have taxes to pay to a useless government! I am a worthless man. We are in the agony of starvation and I can do nothing!" His wife would lead Ha back to the river where everything was bare to search for one little something, a blade of grass, a leaf, bitter greens to boil and make soup with.

One day one thin and starving son said, "Honorable Father, I must go. I can no longer stand to see the faces of hunger on the ones I care for. I will seek to find a way to help my honorable family in all this distress." The father did not want his son to leave, but he said, "Go, my son, there is nothing to stay here for at this time. But watch to see when we will be able to make the land give us succor again. Come back and let your old good mother, full of tears for your departing, know you are well." They had not heard from the son, but they believed they would.

There was a man who, several times a year, passed through their village in a wooden cart drawn by a tired horse. One evening, he rode near their farm. He was a very pleasant man with courteous and coaxing ways. But he did not try to sell them anything. He knew the times, he knew the village was poor. He simply asked for a drink of water knowing that, at least, they would have that.

He was not a rich man, but he was plump from much food, and dressed well and warmly. As he drank the water, he looked around the farm at a small shed. He handed the half-full bowl back to the father, saying, "I see you have a place where I might put my horse safely for the night." He hurried to say, "There are thieves about in these poor times and I do not want my wagon and horse out on the roads." He did not mention his fear for the prosperous look of himself.

Knowing there would be some payment for the courtesy, the hungry old father welcomed the stranger to the small shed he sometimes used for his cow. The man said smoothly, "Good! That is settled. I will pay you for your courtesy to a stranger."

The old father, trying to save face, said, "No, you cannot pay me. You are a lone traveler with no relations here. May the gods smile on both of us if we treat each other well."

The old mother had been listening, now she stepped forward, which was an insult to the father because he was the head of the house. She said, "Yes, kind sir. We will take the pay. We are a poor family. Everyone knows of the time of droughts and no food." She took the money, a few small coins, from the man, who respected her for it. As she handed the coins to her husband, she said, "We have nought to offer you for a meal. We are eating water soup."

The man reached into his cart, reluctantly, not wanting anyone to think he had anything to steal. "Well, and see here, someone just up the road gave me these grains for gruel, a handful of rice, and a few dried peas. You may have them, good mother. We must help each other."

Ha had been sitting outside at a corner of the hut watching a nest of ants scurrying around sticks and rocks, surviving. She often watched birds seek food, and even spiders as they wove webs to catch their meals. She was fascinated with the energy of life and hunger.

The man ate the meal of rice and peas, all the family had, under the eyes of the agitated mother who resented the ingredients she was forced to use, which she had wanted to measure out in smaller quantities. She took her bowl of food outside to sit and eat in quiet. Ha, holding her bowl of food with her face in the steam of it, followed her mother out.

The man had noticed Ha. Though she was thin, her hair was black and long in braids that fell down a straight back to her thin hips. Her skin was not so smooth, but it was thin and fine. The glow of youth was dimmed, but the man decided that was from her poor diet. Her clear dark eyes were the perfect shape of an almond with long black lashes and a shining clear white. He decided her bones were strong and well-shaped, even though there was not much flesh on them. "She could be a great beauty. More likely she will be misspent and wasted here in this desert of farmland." And so he ate and so he thought.

The stranger began to speak to the father of the uselessness of female children. He spoke of his own (he had none) he had managed to give to a good family that (he laughed) wanted a female to raise for a good husband. "I'm glad she will be happy and content with many children in her life." He looked down at his bowl, empty now of even the little he, in his mind, had tried to find fault with. "Has your good wife taught your worthless daughter to cook such food as this? If so, you are a rich man!"

And so they talked.

Later that night as the good father and mother lay on the pallet, he told his wife, "The stranger has offered us food in exchange for doing us the honor and favor of taking Ha to a rich and kind home that will marry her to a good, rich man."

"Liar!" the mother screamed in whisper. The good mother did not believe the man or her husband. She refused to let Ha go. They argued all the night. The father almost crying, "He will give us a bag of beans!"

"A bag of beans?! For my daughter? You will not sell my daughter, old man. She is my child. I bore her from my own belly. You may not sell her!"

But he knew he was the man and he said, "Sell her I shall, old woman. She is worthless to us. A bag of beans will nourish us and our son in these times. If you were a good wife and mother . . . and she a good daughter you would both take this gift the gods have sent us!"

But the mother could not let go her daughter. She threatened to leave him, to even poison him. "I will not let you sell our daughter." When the mother realized the father would have his way at any cost, she went to her daughter's pallet. Ha had been listening to her parents talk as had everyone in the small thin-walled hut.

She reached to hold Ha in her arms and console her, but Ha spoke first. "Do not cry my good mother. You shall eat for a little time; maybe until the drought is over." Ha lowered her voice more, "And I will wait a moon or two and then I will run away home to you."

The strong, but beaten mother cried softly, "Listen little flower of my daughter, my precious Ha of laughter, we worked hard for you to live. Now we must work hard again. You will be in the world of men. They are not all like your father or brothers. They will fear the gods. You must make yourself ugly so they will not like to look at you. You must look, oh, let me think, foul and disgusting. Unpleasant, snotty, and dirty. Oh," her mother wailed, "I do not want them to want you, to take your innocent flower self and hurt and ruin you."

Ha tightened her hold on her mother as her own eyes filled with tears, but she stopped herself in order not to hurt her mother more. Her mother quieted enough to say, "You must have boogers hang from your nose, snot upon your lips, and an idiot's grin upon your face. And do not answer in ways to show your mind. You must keep your soul in some secret place into yourself. Remember to know, there are no friends for you. You will know when you ever find one. Until you know . . . love no one. Trust no one . . . lest you suffer from it. I pray I would go with you. But I cannot. Your brother, your father, my husband." Her voice stopped on a sob.

Ha held her mother close as possible. "I will come back little mother. There is no place to keep me from you. No one. You will tell my hoped-for betrothed, Ling Woo, I have gone. We have secretly agreed we would marry one day. Tell him I shall not be gone long and I will keep myself chaste"—she blushed in the dark—"for my husband. Oh, do not worry, my mother, I will be careful. I will survive. You and I have agreed forever, I will survive. And return."

The good mother sighed, saying, "I will hold you for this night, my little flower petal. I will not sleep on your father's pallet again for a long time. I will sleep in your bed so I may smell your presence. I will hold you now, for as long as I shall."

Early the next morning the man handed the poor farmer father a small sack of five pounds of beans. Ha was set upon the cart holding a small sack of the things she would take with her. The exchange was complete. The wagon lurched away over the hard, rocky road as Ha looked back with tears in her eyes and a booger stuck to the side of her nose. At the last her chin was held high in determination to survive and return.

The poor father went into his hut and handed the bag of beans to the poor good mother. She raised the bag above her head and hit him with it across his face. Beans flew scattering everywhere, settling over the little kitchen. He loved his wife, but he cursed her roundly and went from the kitchen. Still in tears, she got down on her knees and picked them all up, carefully. "I shall cook these for my son."

The peddler's destination, this time, was Hong Kong. He knew, among many other things, the value and cost to certain people there of a young, lovely, untouched by the world, though thin, girl-woman. He was old, in his forties, and had a more than decent home and a healthy, greedy wife.

The man was kindly and after a time Ha's sorrow dimmed and the wondrous landscape of China filled her eyes and mind with awe. The golden-green hills, the purple-green-black mountains in the far distance, the silvery streams, the black-gray and red-brown rocks of beauty. They ate simple but good food bought from the vendors along the way.

The man urged her to bathe, wash off, in some stream they passed. She pretended to, after demanding in her thin voice, "You go away. Let me be alone." She never put a drop of water on herself. She saved her boogers until the one on her cheek, nose, chin, or lip dried and fell off. A little moisture on the saved booger would make it stick to her skin again.

When he began to tell her to move closer to him on the cart (after all, his wife was far away), she began to smear her feces on her legs beneath her long robes or on her wrists, like perfume. The man would ask, "Why do you stink so? Move away! You smell of offal. You must wash yourself more! How will I recover my investment that is feeding your family? Who will want you if you smell like an outhouse or a beast?" Then Ha knew there was no family waiting to treat her well.

As the villages turned to towns and even small cities, she began to hunch her shoulders, bend a bit like an old woman. She did not talk to the man nor anyone. She thought of some of her mother's words, "Your outside may change, but your soul remains the same." Her eyes searched the few little villages they now passed through.

As they came closer to the city the crowds grew thicker, faster moving. She saw people selling wares and food from carts. So many shops and stalls! with all kinds of curious, colorful things in them! "I would never dream there was such a world!" Streets were full of the smells of all kinds of foods; her mouth watered with desire for them. The man wasted no money; if he bought anything he would eat three parts and she would get one part, if any. Mostly she had noodles and gruel. She was constantly amazed at the wonders of the world. She remembered more of her mother's words, "There may be a miracle waiting for you."

When they crossed into Hong Kong strangers were indeed strangers. She wished her mother was there to tell her about these things. "Oh, I miss my good mother so!" The curiosity of her eyes and mind overflowed. "People living in boats on water! Clothes hanging out to dry, cooking fires on the boats!" The beauty of the coast was beyond all imagining. Ha opened her mouth in astonishment, wonder, and fascination. She forgot, sometimes, to be sad and ugly.

The man, who was no fool, said to Ha, "You! I know you are not stupid. I say this to you, you may like it or not. I am an old man. You had no trouble from me. But now, I will sell you. If you continue with this game from demons, you will end in a worthless house with common fools or the wretched poor who would sell their mother to a leper. Now, see, you have gained a little weight from regular eating. If you clean yourself and comb your hair, and you will look as the first time I saw you. Clean and a little good, you may go into a good rich house . . . and marry a rich husband!"

Ha did not believe what he said about the rich husband, but she knew he spoke the truth about the kind of house he would sell her to.

She said, "Take me to your house. I will be a good servant to your wife." But the man laughed, saying, "My wife is older than I. My wife would not let a young female such as you live in my house that she did not choose herself. No, I cannot afford to keep you. You are business. You must go where I take you." And take her he did. He stopped once that she could wash up behind the screen of a vendor of water and hot towels.

The plodding wagon slowly made its way between the huge moving crowd always in front of them that filled even the entire street. Ha watched the life flow of the great city. People turned, twisted, and curved, stepping their way around or over anything in their way. Talk, talk, talk carried on the winds filled the air to the sky. Ha heard her first music. Startled and amazed at sounds accompanied with words coming through the air between the constant talk.

Ha thought of Ling Woo, the boy she loved, and her mother; wishing they were there to see the different world. She forgot her plan to watch the streets so she could find her way out and back to her mother's hut again.

The man pulled his cart through the crowd to a safe place near a two-story building decorated around its door with false gold leaf and marble-looking narrow columns. Around the door were many shining good-luck symbols. He knocked and, after a moment, the door was opened by a plump lady dressed in a neat green silk kimomo with her hair brushed smoothly back over her ears. She looked at the dusty travelers and her smile disappeared.

The man spoke his intentions, she nodded her head briskly and motioned them in, saying, "It is early. Wait here." Her eyes slid over Ha then rolled to the ceiling in mild disgust. She left them, returning soon with her eyebrows lifted, gesturing for them to follow her.

Ha stooped as they followed the woman. Everything in the house overwhelmed her. It was all imitation grandeur, but it looked real to Ha. She had never been in such a grand house.

They were brought into the presence of a painted old woman, Madame Wu, with a face of dried skin, hard black eyes, and a grim mouth that tried to smile, but did not. She looked frankly at the man, then frankly at the girl as she spoke a few words. She moved only her hands as she spoke. Her body was still as a wooden image.

The man spoke to Ha, "This is the venerable Madame Wu. We are hoping she will be your new mistress." He turned to Madame Wu, saying, "Venerable Lady Wu, see, look what I have brought you, a lovely, beautiful young girl fresh from the good country lands."

Madame Wu turned her lips down as her eyes slowly moved over Ha, who stepped back, hugging her shabby bag close to her body.

Madame Wu sneered, answering (for she knew they were bargaining), "A country turnip you have brought me, foolish one, to wake me so early and waste my time."

The man laughed, "Ah, but you turn turnips into princesses, honorable and generous one!"

"I do not do magic, I am no magician."

They talked now with voices rising and falling in supplications and refusals. In a short enough time they had almost agreed. The man urged, "She has a good strong, young body. Well made, as you can see. What more can you seek?"

Now Madame Wu's lips almost parted in a smile for her own wisdom. "First, I want the beautiful one. If she is not beautiful, she must be strong. If neither, it may be one who can do housework. Maid work, for those she can never be."

The man opened his arms, "Then she is perfect in all three."

At last it was settled and Ha felt a hard tug on her shoulder. She turned to see the lady in the green kimono. The man said, "Ha, you will follow this kind lady, please. Her name is Orchid."

Now Ha hated to leave the man she had grown to trust a little, but Orchid gave her a not so gentle push and Ha's body followed the lady without volition.

Orchid was not too cruel a person, but she was not kind at all. She was not worried for herself; she thought she pleased Madame Wu too much to fear for her position. To Orchid, Ha was a dumb country girl. She did not care enough to treat Ha too unkindly, but she did not treat her kindly either. She treated her as nothing, something of no value at all.

Ha was given a maid, Old Ma, and a small but satin-shiny room. Old Ma prepared her for her future, to meet with gentlemen. She was taught how she must entertain them. Old Ma shouted at her, "You make them laugh. You, onion-head, make them be happy." She would push, nudge, and slap Ha when she was displeased with the way a lesson was progressing. On many occasions Old Ma would grab Ha's arm in her hard, long fingers with the piercing fingernails and twist her soft flesh, leaving blue, green, and purple marks there. Ha tried to please her; her fear of Old Ma was always aching in her mind.

But, Old Ma or not, Ha managed to make herself ugly when Orchid, Old Ma, or some other overseer could not see her. She could not use the feces because she feared losing her place of living in the strange Hong Kong with its many strange peoples. She would slip the boogers on her face near her nose when she was left alone with a man. Finally, the men did not choose to spend their money on her. They waved their arms and hastened away to ask for some other favorite. Within a month the satin robes were taken away, replaced with cotton ones for a maid or kitchen helper.

A year passed, then another, as Ha stared into space or out window openings, trying to see another future beside the one with Old Ma. Ha worked very hard at all hours. She slept and ate in a room with three other women who had no reason to be jealous of Ha, but looked down on her because Old Ma did. They treated her as nothing also. They lied to her, playing jokes that often got her into trouble. They were hired to work and so were paid for their work. Ha was not paid. Old Ma told her, "Madame Wu already pay for you!" In time Ha was taught to shop for food and allowed to carry small sums of money to pay for things Madame Wu had not arranged to be billed. Ha worked very hard at all hours.

Sometimes some lonely, beautiful woman, whom men welcomed into their arms, would think of a sister or cousin back home and would give Ha things, some of good value, but all pretty. She had learned to watch these things carefully, secretly hiding them, or they would be stolen in the blink of an eye.

One extremely beautiful and favored woman, Lily, had also come from the country. She took a special liking to Ha and talked to her when her work was over. She was a dreamy woman; Madame Wu encouraged her to smoke opium. One day as she was gazing dreamily at her ceiling and Ha was performing some task, Lily asked Ha, "What do you want most from life, little Ha?"

Ha had her own dreams by then, "I want to read books."

In a surprised voice, Lily asked, "Not money? Just reading?"

"More than anything, except freedom and my mother."

In a slow voice that sounded to Ha like it came over waves of heavy air, Lily said, "Well, little Ha, I cannot give you freedom or your mother. But I shall teach you what I know. Buy a book for first learning when next you shop, and bring it to me. Tell them I request it from you." That was in Ha's fourth year of hopelessness.

Lily requested, no, demanded that only Ha serve her, planting seeds of hatred among Ha's coworkers. Ha did not care, and Madame Wu wanted Lily to be as happy as possible so she did not care either. When Old Ma complained, Madame Wu said, "Shut up, old fig. You do not tell me anything to do!"

Ha persisted in her learning to read. She would learn a little and would practice the characters when she was alone in Lily's room and Lily was in the "working" parlors. Lily was the only friend she had or talked with then.

Old Ma had studied Ha long and hard and thought she knew something she could use to separate the two friends. She had no good reason to separate them, but some people do not like to see happiness or contentment.

Old Ma said to Ha one day, "The cornstalk-girl who cleans the courtyard is such a fool she cannot even do it right. I must find someone else to tend the gardens and such." Ha volunteered for some part of every day and was given the job. But even in this separation Ha remained Lily's servant and continued the reading lessons. Old Ma had only made Ha more happy. "I can learn to read and still be outside, in the sun, with soil and small animals!"

Ha's duties now included cleaning the courtyard. It was seldom used because most everyone slept during the days except the kitchen workers. The courtyard had several small trees as well as two large, beautiful trees. A pear tree and wild cherry tree were planted near the small fish pond. In season there were many blossoms and the yard smelled delicately sweet. Ha had missed the pungent smell of the earth.

Under Ha's care and from her own seeds, many flowers bloomed in their time, some only at night. Ha loved her work. She spoke to the neglected little gods sitting in a forgotten niche, "You are giving me so many happy things, reverent ones. Please let no bad things come down upon me." She placed many beautiful sweet-smelling flowers or leaves before them every day to show her appreciation.

Madame Wu knew most, but not all, of what went on in her house. She did not know about the courtyard work because she never moved that far from her room. Ha thought she would be pleasing Madame Wu, but whenever she came into the presence of the old Madame, Madame Wu turned mean and hateful eyes on her. Ha would complete the task that brought her there and flee from the sight and feel of those eyes.

Except for Lily's room, inside the house Ha's hunched shoulders were more pronounced from her fear and caution. She bathed and changed clothes when going to Lily's room, but everywhere else in the house she smelled faintly of feces. Old Ma wanted her to leave the house, but Madame Wu retorted, "My cash paid for her! She will earn my money back to me! She will stay and work until you die or anybody die!"

Madame Wu could not think of her own death. She paid an old Asian priest to say many prayers for her to go to heaven and she made a few gifts each to many gods. She would not give the holy men much money, because she did not trust them. "They do not know. I am a heavenly woman. I will not be cheated."

Ha continued to do her work as she dreamed of freedom. "I know there is someplace for me. Another place, not this one. I will run away as soon as I learn this city and know my way. I will! I will! Leave this place and go home." But she had heard of the "Revolution" in China and knew that many things had changed. Many people were newly poor and many people were more poor. "I will find my mother and Ling Woo and make a place for us somehow." Oh, her worries were many and her answers were too few.

Ha's courage grew and she began to sneak the newspapers and a few bits of quiet paper money some sleeping women had in their rooms. She would smile when she saw their rich, false jewelry thrown about. They wore their true jade and precious stones at all times. They knew thieves; some were thieves. She read all she could find to read and saved the money to send to her mother.

Now, there came times when old iron-face Madame Wu would have a public secretary write the few letters she had to write. Ha would fold the quiet paper money in an envelope and mail it to her mother, never knowing if it was intercepted or not. She usually took the mail on her shopping days, so her envelope was sent with Madame Wu's mail.

Also, Ha made many casual friendships as the months turned to years. When she went on errands for some special delicacy, she might pass the crowded train station and markets with people spilling out into the streets. She loved the marketplaces. The air was full of the smell of all different kinds of foods. She would buy for the cook crabs, mussels, seaweed, shrimp, carp, and many types of fish, pig's feet, and ears, beef, and many types of vegetables.

The narrow winding streets of parts of Hong Kong served all types of people and seemed to have millions of shops and vendors all with different things to smell, taste, or see. It was like being at a very huge, busy carnival. The streets were always as packed as they had been on the first day she arrived in Hong Kong.

By the time Ha was nineteen years old she had tasted many things and knew many shops and streets. It was around 1948. She could read fairly well and could even write as well. When Madame Wu found she could write well enough for small matters, this was added to her chores. This made Old Ma, who was getting older and suffering more arthritic pain, very jealous and revengeful.

Ha did not allow herself to become attractive. She still smelled most of the time, but she was intelligent and was more useful in other ways to Madame Wu, who had grown used to her being unwanted by men. She had even forgotten why. Every once in a while when she noticed the face, hair, and skin of Ha, she wondered why she was not "working." Then she forgot why again. She did not crave money so much anymore, she craved the gods to love her. "Still, I must take care of my business the gods have given me to do."

Around that time Madame Wu purchased a young woman brought to her from India. The woman had tried to fight her captors, but was overpowered and brought to Hong Kong. She would never tell her name, so they named her Rose because of the deep rich color of her cheeks. She was very beautiful and . . . different. She cried most of the time, but Old Ma gave her special drugged food to eat and so she performed her duties. The men adored her, but not in a good way. Drugged, and therefore careless, she became pregnant.

Her stomach was five months full before it was truly noticed. Madame Wu said, "It is too late to take the seed away. She must bear the rotten fruit. She means too much gold for me to get rid of her. Let her have the child. We may give it away, or . . . perhaps we can raise it to seven or eight years," she thought a moment, "or even five years, and we will gain a good bit of gold for it. Some of these debauched men like little children . . . to fondle."

The child was born a girl. They did keep it. Taken from the mother, who died before the babe had completed its emergence into this sickening world. Someone who did not want to be so bothered handed her to Ha, "See that the child is fed, clean, and quiet. Above all, quiet." Ha named the beautiful, ugly little female Maheema Do. She had discovered, she hoped, an Indian name. She did not know what it meant. Then, to make herself closer to the child, she added the name to her own. She became Ha Do.

She kept the child with her at all times when the baby was not asleep. No one cared, they were glad. She cleaned the courtyard while the child breathed the fresh air and slept in the shade of a full and blossoming tree. Ha grew to love the child and think of her as a sister, or even as her own child. But Ha had never known a man.

As the Old Madame slept one day Ha went to her rooms to collect some mail to be sent out. She scooped up all the mail and hastily left so as not to awaken Madame Wu. Ha was already out of the house in the street sorting the mail when she discovered one envelope that was not for mailing. The letter had been opened and the stamps were strange to Ha. She did not know what to do; she did not want Madame Wu to be angry with her. She knew about "U.S.A." and was naturally curious. She decided to continue on with her errands and replace the letter when she returned home. "I hope Madame does not miss it while I am away."

During her business she had to say good-day to many of her acquaintances. She was passing just such a one who was American and had lived in Hong Kong for many years. He spoke her language. Quick as a second Ha decided to ask him about the letter.

He welcomed Ha and took the letter to read. He laughed a little as he handed the letter back to Ha. "Someone is seeking a wife to come to the United States, Ha. This is his fifth letter. He wants an answer to his letters." He smiled as he asked, "Is it for you, Ha?"

"What place in America, kind gentleman?"

"Someplace called Placeland. He says he will pay the money necessary for a good wife."

"I will ask Old Madame. See if she will send me. I want another life."

The man smiled sadly at his little innocent friend as he said, "Madame Wu will never let you go. You are too valuable to her, Ha. I understand people do not get to leave her very often. Why don't you answer this letter yourself? You would like America, and what will you gain in the job you have now?"

"But I cannot write American. I do not have the money to travel to that place, that village."

"He says he will send the money to you. Listen, Ha, I can write the letter for you and mail it. I will also see what it takes for you to go.

When he sends the money you can then go." The man grew a little excited and that frightened Ha a bit.

"I . . . I do not know." But the excitment infected her. "Suppose I do not like him for a husband?" She thought of Ling Woo, "He is probably married now. The Red Communists have taken the land. He will never come to Hong Kong to find me."

The man was thinking his own thoughts, caught up in the event that had broken his own opium hell from the night before. "You may not be able to get a passport though. So I will tell him to marry you by proxy and then you will be an American and you can go to him."

"Suppose I do not like him for a husband?"

The man shook his head, "Then you prefer to stay with Old Madame?"

"But I do not prefer that. I prefer to go to America. Go to get very rich. Come back to get my mother."

"You will have to decide that, Ha. The only part I can help you with is the letter."

"Do the American people speak Chinese as you do?"

"Some do. Many people are American Chinese, but they speak both languages."

"What is English? Speak it for me." He said a few words for her. "You should try another life, Ha."

She laughed gaily, saying, "That is an ugly, strange sound! I will never be able to speak such a language!"

"You will, Ha. You are a smart one."

So they wrote the letter together. Right there and then! Ha forgot about the time in her excitement. She was thinking with her mind as her heart was begging for life. "I may have a strange husband in a strange land, somewhere in the whole world for me. I will go to America. I will be rich and make another farm with my mother and my strange husband! I will give him many children and we shall be a family who owns land." The letter was signed "Ha Do," and mailed with her friend's return address on it.

· · ·

Ha's heart often gave her thoughts of her life with her family, with Ling Woo, of the past. She missed her old family, but now she realized she was not happy in the past. Now, she wanted some contentment, if not happiness. "I cannot go back to my old village now. China is Red and I do not know where my parents are. I receive no answer from my letters. I need a place of my own. A place I can rest and feel joyful." Then she would forget to think of the American marriage and America in the steady rush of her duties.

Ha was still the caretaker of Maheema Do. They slept together. She did not want to leave the child behind. Maheema Do was a child who would play with her colorful scarves or the occasional toy given her, quietly sitting in one spot, never running about and shouting. Ha noticed Old Madame Wu often looking at the beautiful three-year-old child when she was near. There was an ugly gleaming light of greed in Old Madame's eyes. Old Madame would reach out to touch the child like she was feeling a piece of market meat for tenderness.

Ha would frown, thinking, "I must find some way for the child." She began to stop Maheema Do from playing near Madame Wu's rooms. Saying, "This little mouse must not bother busy people. Come, naughty turnip, sit by the kitchen where I can see you get into no things." So while she waited for her life to unfold, she watched another life, planned many plans, not knowing what or how to do what she needed and wanted to do. She also began taking Maheema Do on some of her errands.

The man, Henry Lee, in America was ecstatic when he received the long-awaited letter. He sent the money with a brief letter to let the marriage-broker (the American) know he had a "poor" grocery store but could take care of a wife. In time, with the help of friends they were married by proxy. Ha, nearly frightened out of her wits, made preparation. "My name will be Ha Do Lee?"

Weeks before the appointed day, Ha read the instructions she was to follow, written by the American friend, many times over. With

Lily's secret help she had decent clothes to wear on the plane flying to America.

When everything was ready and the time came, Ha stole the child. She simply walked little Maheema Do out of the Good Luck doors. The streets were crowded, as usual. She picked up the child, holding the little body to her own small body and walked to the place the American had told her. She was shaking with fear and trepidation. She got in the arranged taxi, someone the American trusted, and went to the busy, crowded airport where the American waited with her for her plane to leave.

She sat on the plane marveling at the never-ending sky. Maheema Do sat on her lap. Her American husband did not know she was bringing a child, but she did not worry. "If he will not accept her, well I will just get back on this plane and . . . Well, he can not put me out, I am his wife!"

Ha was on her way! Thoughts flew around in her head. "I am on my way some place where I will certainly be happy. I have a husband to look after me. I will work hard and be sure he likes me well enough. I will give him many children. Look! I have given him one daughter already! He will protect me and Maheema. I will have a place for me in my life now."

And so, she flew to her future in America.

I will tell you this, Henry Lee could hardly contain himself. He told everyone up and down the street, beyond the corners of his block even. "My wife, she is coming from China. I am a married man! Oh, she is beautiful and young. She loves me."

Henry Lee had waited almost four years for this answer to his prayers and his letters.

# Chapter Twenty-four

*

When Eula Too entered Lee's Grocery there were a few people there. By the time she had finished her own shopping she was third in line, so she waited her turn. As she waited, she watched the busy little Asian woman bagging groceries. The man stood by the cash register, waiting for her to finish. There were other things he could be doing, but he waited for Ha to do them.

Eula could see two children sitting in the room connected to the store. Their heads were bent over books so Eula decided they must be studying. Eula smiled as she turned back to pay for her things. She told Henry Lee and his wife about the wake that evening. Henry Lee looked at Eula with wide eyes while Ha shook her head and looked at her with sad eyes.

Henry said, "She a very nice lady. I know her long time."

Ha said, "Death is always too sad. Too bad. We never talk a lot. She kind'a mean lady sometime, but she alright to me. My name is Ha Do Lee."

Eula Too smiled at Ha, saying, "Well, I hope you come. You know it's just across the street. There will be some food and punch, you know, the usual things. The nurse, Santi, is running the kitchen so everything should be good."

Ha smiled a tired smile, "I know Santi. She is very nice person and friend. She help me with my children." She turned her head with a baleful look into the other room where her children were studying. She turned back to Eula, saying, "I will come."

Henry Lee made a big smile of sorrow for Eula, as he said, "We cannot come, maybe. We have sorrow for her, for everybody, but we have much work to do here. We bring flowers." He was pleased with his new thought and his face brightened. "Yes! We will bring flowers at the funeral!" Satisfied, he leaned back on his heels waiting for some agreement or approval.

Ha said, "I will come. Bring my oldest children. They are in school." Now she spoke a little slower. "They go to school and teach me English-American, Maheema and Goa Do, my daughters." Ha was proud. She cast a quick, side look at Henry Lee. "We have . . ." she looked down and put the last item in the bag, lowered her voice as if in defeat, "plan."

Henry Lee dismissed the word "plan" with a wave of his hand. He did the butcher's work in the mornings; Ha worked the whole store most of the day except when she stopped to cook. He spoke up, proudly, "We have sons also. They home from school. They in other room studying. Books! I want more sons!" He smiled, "More sons!"

Eula sensed a certain tension but smiled as she picked up her bag of groceries, and said, "Good! Perhaps they can help you do some of your work today and you both can come. I'm glad you will come, Ha. They told me your name was Ha. I think that is a beautiful name."

"Thank you." Ha frowned, "My husband, Henry Lee, say sons should study, not work. Daughters for work. But I can come see everybody, her daughter, tonight. I like daughters." Ha smiled when she spoke of her daughters, her face made suddenly beautiful. There was pain there and a flicker of hopelessness, but hope remained there also. Even wisdom was there, and contained energy. She was still a young woman in her early thirties. Eula Too liked Ha Do, her open face and smile, almost instantly.

As Eula Too walked "home" her thoughts were of Place and all the seemingly unhappy people here. She looked sidewise at Lamont Heavy's house, looking for him, and there they were! He was sitting on his porch with his new dog at his feet watching her. Lona was there with him also, leaning against the porch rail. When he saw she was looking his way, he waved his hand at her, saying, "See you later, Miss Eula Too."

Lona watched her walk toward the house then said, "I think I'll go on home and get ready for the memorial. See you later." Lamont raised his hand a bit in farewell, saying, "Yeah, okay." Lona called out "Eula Too!" and ran across the street to catch up with her.

Lona smiled as she reached Eula, saying, "How is Elizabeth taking things? At least she knew her mother was sick, so she knew she had to die. It wasn't no surprise." In lockstep they walked the short distance, Lona passed her house and stopped with Eula in front of the Fontzl home. She tilted her head as she looked into Eula's eyes and asked, "Are you married?"

Eula, bemused, thought it was just idle chatter of small-town people. "No, I'm not."

"But, I heard you got a daughter."

"I do have a daughter. She is in college."

"Divorced, huh. Is your man-friend coming here to be with you in all this?"

"No. I don't have a man-friend, as you put it, Lona."

"You don't?" She didn't wait for an answer. "I got one." She turned her head and looked in the direction of Lamont. "He is mine." Lona was still smiling, but Eula clearly understood her meaning.

"That is nice, Lona. He seems to be a nice man. Didn't he just lose his wife a year or so ago? I think I heard that—"

Lona interruped her, "Yes, he did lose his wife, but I am going to be his next wife. We already decided we love each other."

"Well, that is really nice. Two people who love each other—"

With a smile, Lona cut her off again. "I'm just telling you because you are new around here and don't know about things, so I am telling you, he is taken." She laughed, strangely.

"Good, Lona. Well, I better get on in here and see what else I can do to help. It will be time soon." Eula walked away as she finished speaking. Lona looked after her until she reached her steps, then she turned to see if Lamont was watching Eula also. He was. She frowned and called his name, "Lamont!" Then she smiled at him. "See you later."

. . .

The house was ready for those who wished to come pay their respects to Mrs. Fontzl and her daughter, Elizabeth. Everything was sparkling clean or new. The table was set in a fine linen cloth and old cut-glass and crystal bowls of punch and dishes full of many appetizing foods, enough to feed fifty people. Bottles of scotch, bourbon, and vodka for those who wanted drinks.

Madame Elizabeth sat in one of the main chairs near the window. She looked splendid in her rich and simple black dress and pearls. Eula shook her head sadly as she looked at her, thinking, "She has grown old in these few days. She is taking this very hard."

Madame was thinking. "My mother is gone and now," she looked up and smiled mournfully at Eula, "Eula will have some land to build a house on and she will leave me also. I will be all alone." She turned to look through the window again.

Santi was tired and had gone home to check quickly on her husband. Jean and Jerry, kind, loving friends to all, were looking to see if there was anything else they could do. Earle had arrived and settled her things in Eula's room. She was looking for Jewel. Eula was looking for Jewel. She had not told Earle anything yet. Eula waited, almost willed, Jewel to come. She turned to the front door and sighed as the first guests arrived.

Old Mary was being helped in by her daughter. She helped her to a seat as Elizabeth stood up, opening her arms and sighing, "Marion! Oh, my friend. Let me hold you hello." The two old friends clasped each other, with Elizabeth resting her head on Marion's shoulder. They murmured to each other and sighed together. When they parted Elizabeth pulled Marion to the chair opposite her. "Oh, Marion. Stay here. Talk to me. Oh, Marion, I had forgotten I have you too."

Marion laughed softly, "Oh course you have me. I've missed you, Beth."

"Oh, I've missed you so much. I think of those old times we shared together. Now I have Eula." She turned her head to look for Eula, who was standing in the doorway, a gentle smile on her face, happy for her friend. "Eula, come here. I want you to meet my very first friend!" Eula smiled at the both of them, glad someone was there to keep Elizabeth company. Elizabeth turned back to Marion.

Marion patted the hands still holding on to hers, saying, "You never have to be alone; that is why God is always there for the choosing. But, good, I'm glad you feel better."

Eula was thinking of Rita. She had spoken to Iris about using one of her rooms for a "dear friend," Rita. She had called Rita again and Rita was coming. "I have a little something to do then I will be there. Not so much for the funeral, but because I am not comfortable alone." Eula sighed, thinking, "Too many years of being looked after."

Lona was coming through the door holding Prince's hand, pushing Homer ahead of her. She wore a black dress, the same she would wear to the funeral, "If I have to go." Now she thought, "I hate all these signs of death." She spoke, "Go on, Homer, get out the way." Then to Prince, "Come on, honey, I know you don't like coming, but I bet they have some good food, sweets and all. That's what they do at wakes; they eat after they pray." Lona sat with Prince on the edge of her chair and Homer on the floor at her feet.

Santi came in with a few other people she knew. She told Elizabeth, "Here are a few people that helped me serve Mrs. Fontzl. They wanted to come give you their condolences."

"I'm glad, Santi, I didn't know she had friends and I'm glad." Then she turned back to talk to Marion, huddled in quiet conversation.

Several other people came, including Iris and Ha with Maheema and Goa Do. The youngsters made their way to each other, talking quietly, stifling their young laughter. Eula was pleased Iris and Ha had come. She seated Iris comfortably and placed Ha in a chair close to one for herself. She was intrigued with Ha. "We will talk later. I want to hear about your plans." Ha turned a questionable look on Eula and gave her a small smile. Eula touched Ha's shoulder lightly and moved on.

There were about twenty or twenty-five people there when Lamont came through the door with a look of respect and grief on his face. He walked over to Elizabeth and bent to murmur a few words. Marion smiled up at him and asked, "Get me a glass of water, would you, Lamont? Or some of that red punch."

Elizabeth quickened, "Yes! but let's have a real drink. There is bourbon, scotch, or would you like vodka? Marion, I know just what I want. Do you like Champagne? Oh, does your church let you drink?"

Marion leaned back and laughed, saying, "I can do almost anything normal, in moderation, and I don't want to be drunk anyway so that works out just fine. I would love some Champagne. Beth, it is just like you to have such a high-class drink."

Elizabeth laughed and waved for Eula. "Lamont, you do not have to serve us. Eula will help us." Eula waved for someone else. Jerry opened the bottle and brought it in an ice bucket with four glasses, chuckling as he said, "I'm going to have a little glass of this myself." He set the fourth glass on the table with the bucket.

Lona's eyes intently watched him with the Champagne, her eyes narrowed on the remaining glass. "I would like to have a glass of that myself, Jerry. I don't care for punch or none of the rest of that stuff." Jerry poured and handed her the glass with a smile at Prince and Homer. "You kids get some punch and cookies."

People were eating, drinking, and talking softly. There was no music. This was not entertainment. Lamont had not allowed himself to look directly at Eula Too since he had come in. He felt silly and didn't know why he should. "I'm usually relaxed. I must be catching something." He had a drink of bourbon over ice. "Maybe this will help. I know what it probably is, all this grief. I'm tired of death near me. But, you have to pay respects." Then, after avoiding looking at Eula, his eyes sought her out.

Eula, briefly, wondered why he did not say something to her. Then her attention was caught by something else. Then both of them looked up at the same time, and into the other's eyes. She wanted to look away, but couldn't. He did not want to look away, and didn't. They did not mean to feel anything unusual.

To Eula it felt like every cell in her body decided to change place with another one. Everything inside her moving swiftly, softly. She took a breath and it was cut in half by another breath she hadn't meant to take. Lamont was stirred. His knees and thighs were stirred. His brain felt a little tilted. He wanted to move his eyes but, at the moment, could not. When he could break the questionable spell, he blindly sat his drink down, stood up, and walked over to Eula Too, who had not moved her eyes from his.

She had to consciously make an effort to take her eyes from his. When he reached her, he leaned over to her, whispering in her ears. "I am not being vulgar. I'm telling you the truth. We have just fucked." Then he walked back to his seat, picked up his glass, and looked into her eyes, which had not turned away.

Eula could not help looking aghast, but her heart was pounding, pumping blood a hundred miles a minute. Immediately her body moistened, her breast came alive with unused emotional thrills. She made herself turn her head away and immediately went to her room to look out of the window and think. Instead, she lay down and stared at the ceiling, thoughts swirling in her head. "This must be what those men came to buy from the ladies." Her hands moved down her hips, "Can you buy this?" She turned on her side, "Oh, God, what have You given people to deal with? I don't even know that man."

Lona had seen them. She watched the entire thing. Her eyes filled with envy and jealousy for Eula and resentment for Lamont. She wanted to leave and make Lamont miss her, but she knew he would not miss her; he would not even know she was gone. She decided to stay to watch him. To watch Eula Too.

Earle had seen it also, and after a moment she smiled, and followed her sister. When she opened the bedroom door she saw Eula lying on the bed. She did not preamble, "Is he married?"

"Who?"

"You know who!" Earle laughed. "You know just who I'm talking about. That handsome man with the eyes! that just made some kind'a love to you. That's who!"

"I don't know what you are talking about," she smiled at her sister.

"But that is his girlfriend sitting in there. The one with the two little boys? Her."

"Eula, that is not his girlfriend. If she was, if she see you all look at each other again, she will sure know she ain't his girl no more. Get up from there and go back out there and protect your interest!"

"I'll never look at him again. Do you know what I felt? For the first time?" She hugged her body, "Oh, Earle, girl, how can you live with something like that?"

"Honey, after while, you can't live without feeling like that. C'mon, I'm going back out there and help. Say, where is Jewel? I'm gonna tell my niece off when I see her."

"She may not come, Earle. She has gone. She said she was gone for good. She called me a liar about the rape. She sounded like she hated me."

"Where has she gone?"

"Back to school, to college."

"If I know that greedy little heifer—you know I love her—but if I know her, she will be back because she is going to need some money."

"She is getting married. To a doctor, she said. She said she won't need me any longer and will not be back."

"Sister, let me tell you, don't you let that child worry you. She will be back, and it won't take no long time either. Don't worry about it. Rest while you can, 'cause she coming back. Probably with some new shit for you. Get up from there! C'mon, let's get back out here around people and life."

Eula slowly stood up, "This is about death."

"Life is about death, Eula. Of many things, many times." Earle took a deep breath and said, "I was going to wait to tell you, but I am going to be getting married myself."

"Oh, when Earle?"

"Soon. Because I find I am a pregnant lady." She smiled, saying, "I love him, Eula. We've been together a long time. He is behind me one hundred percent in whatever I do. I'll have an art exhibit in about two months. He arranged that too. He doesn't mind that I go play music whenever I want to, and he even goes with me when he is not working. You know he is a musician. Plays the bass fiddle. Real good, too. He loves Martin Luther King. Whose kitten is that, Eula?"

Eula shook her head, still reeling, overwhelmed, with all the feelings she had just experienced. "That is Tobe, she does not have anybody to look after her, so she's mine. Don't let her out. I'll take her out for some air later, when everybody is gone. This day is getting to be too much for me. I hope no one says anything else to me about anything."

Her eyes immediately looked for Lamont, who was talking to Old Mary Green. It was only seconds before his eyes found her again. Lona's eyes stayed on them both. Earle's watched Lona now and again, when she wasn't watching the door for Jewel. They would all make it through the evening.

Eula did manage to talk to Ha for a minute. Poor little Ha had no friends in Place. No one to talk to. She liked to visit Henry Lee's family in Elysee City, where she would be surrounded by Chinese, but still, even there she had no friends. One man bothered her when she was around the family, a cousin who was handsome and knew it.

The cousin was tall with smooth black hair and smooth, soft-looking skin of a beautiful golden bronze color. Ha often felt his gaze upon her and was made uncomfortable. She was not happy with Henry Lee; he was not her dream. He was not Ling Woo. But Henry Lee was good to her. He had allowed her to keep Maheema Do and he provided for her. But she did not intend to give him more sons.

Henry Lee's lovemaking was not lovemaking. It was a rush to feel, to crush without cruelty, to grab a breast, not gently fondle it, to find a hole and rush, with lustful glee, to fill it.

His cousin was always sidling close to her, brushing her hand, her foot, her clothes. He was handsome, but she did not want him. The one she wanted was Ling Woo, but she thought, "He is probably married to someone else now."

She did not like the way the relatives laughed at Henry Lee either. Right in front of him! And he would laugh with them, because he did not understand the joke was on him.

Ha loved all her children, but she worried over the females more. "They need me more. My sons have Henry Lee. They got this store." When she talked with her daughters she told them, "A very wise person, named Lily, my friend, told me many times, you must have a plan. Even more than one plan. So we must make a plan. You must go to school, study, study, study hard. When someone hands you the paper that tells you your self is worth money from the brain, we will be able to do our next plan.

"I am American citizen now, with your good help. When you finish in college, make money, first we go India, find Maheema's family. If not possible, we leave Maheema in good place to find husband like her." She smiled at her daughters looking up at her. "And you, Goa Do, you going to marry rich Chinese college man. Take care of you very good. And me, I am going to school, maybe to college, too. I get paper to say Ha Do, me, can take care herself very good from now on." And so they planned. The girls loved their father and their brothers, but they never asked what Henry Lee was to do, they always pictured him and his sons with the grocery store.

Eula sat next to Iris to chat for a little while. "Are you alright, Iris? Can I get you anything?"

"Oh, I'm fine, Eula. You know I really enjoyed your visit earlier today. I hope you come again, soon. Well, I guess you will, because your friend, Rita, is going to be there. That will be nice. I'm glad you asked me. I like colored people, we will get along fine."

"Oh, she is not colored, Iris. I'm sorry I didn't think it was important enough to mention. She is white. In any event, it would still have been alright. I wouldn't have anyone there I didn't think you could get along with."

"Well, good. Either way. I love Old Mary and young Marion too. I often think of what your people have gone through, Eula. Sometimes I feel so sorry for you all."

Eula smiled at the little lady, "Thank you, Iris. And I am sorry for the things you have suffered and gone through. The things all human beings suffer from those who have the power, and just from life, I guess."

Iris sadly asked, "You mean because I am mixed with Jewish blood?"

Marion, just passing by them, lingered, hearing Iris's question. She put her hand affectionately on her shoulder, and said, "Iris, who gets treated well in this world? No one. Black, brown, yellow, red, or white. Look, you are white, what has that done for you? I know people think Caucasian people have it easy, but there are plenty white people starving to death and living in hovels in this world. Right now. And if being rich is so good, why do some of them commit suicide? The reason God is so important to us is because God treats us equally. God is the only one who does. We all have a difficult time of it. The rich try to make money make their life easier, and it does in many ways, but they suffer in many ways too. In fact, it is harder for the rich to find a true friend than for the poor."

Iris opened her mouth to answer, but Marion raised her hands to stop her reply, saying, "Remember, God chose your people first. The Hebrew people had to be special for God to do that. Never mind other people. You can't count on other people's brains working right. I want you to start loving yourself. Life is not all race. It is love that matters! You are loved, I'm telling you! Learn more about God's ways. Don't let this world keep messing with your mind." She hugged Iris's shoulders, then she was off to check on her mother.

When people started leaving and everyone was saying their farewells, Eula looked down at Homer, still sitting on the floor. She liked the sad, open-faced young man. He had been very quiet, as his mother bade him, and he had taken only one cookie and one cup of punch. Eula took a large napkin and filled it with cookies. Then she had a better idea and took a large paper plate and filled it with chicken, cake, and a slice of sweet potato pie with flaky crust. "Here, this is for you and Prince. Enjoy it." Eula looked at his clothes and made a decision, "Why don't you stop by one day and we can talk about a few little jobs around here where you can make a few dollars?" Homer's eyes brightened as he nodded, smiling up at her.

She smiled over his head at Lona, who was staring at her with a strange look. Eula stopped smiling and became serious, her eyes asking a question. Lona changed the look on her face. She smiled at Eula. "Thank you for everything." She grimaced, "I looooved the Champagne even though I only got one glass of it."

Eula laughed and looked over at Madame. "Hold on a moment, Lona. I'll be right back." When Eula returned she handed Lona a bottle of Champagne wrapped in a paper bag. "Now you can enjoy the whole thing."

Lona looked surprised as she took the bottle. She looked around to see if Lamont had seen what had happened. She was going to invite him to share it with her at his house. He was helping Old Mary Green make her way out. She stepped over to him and showed him the package. "I don't know why she gave this to me. She must mean for us to share it together. She thinks we are lovers." Lona laughed as she said, "I'll bring it over later on tonight and we can . . . share."

Lamont rubbed his head as he answered, "Ah, not tonight, Lona. I have something I have to do. I'm sorry about that. And don't worry, I'll have to straighten her out about that lover business."

As Ha was leaving she plucked Eula's sleeve and waited for her attention. Eula turned, smiling at her. Ha said, "Thank you for invitation. This is first time I'm invited to join community group. I serve Mrs. Fontzl and her daughter and all neighborhood for eight years, but this is first time. Now I see how American house look inside."

Eula took her hand and Ha pressed it warmly in return. Eula said, "You have an American house right here on Dream Street. They come in all styles."

Ha slowly shook her head. "No. Henry relatives have American house, but they are Asian. Mrs. Fontzl is white lady and you are black lady. Theirs more pretty, so this is different to me." Eula could tell Ha wanted to say something more to her. "What is it, Ha? Is something wrong?"

Ha was thinking of her old friend in Hong Kong, Lily. She liked Eula Too, who reminded her of Lily. She decided to trust her. Ha leaned in close to Eula, saying, "I save one dollar every day since I am in America. Someday I will pay for college for Maheema and Goa Do," she blushed, embarrassed, "and for me. I go, too."

Eula pressed the hand she held still more, "Ha, if you like I can help you find some ways that education is free or less expensive. Your daughters must already know some ways."

"They very smart. I always like to learn. Want to be . . . independent."

Eula lowered her voice, "Are you planning to leave Henry Lee, Ha?"

"Oh, no. Henry Lee bring me to America. Otherwise I not have good job in Hong Kong. No education. I do not leave Henry Lee. I work to pay for person to work, help him in store, while I go school and go see America. Also, go home to China and see mother, bring her here."

"Good. I will help you." Eula wondered why she offered such help when she already had so much to do. She thought, "I don't care. I like her!"

At last, most of the people had gone, except for Marion, who was huddled with Elizabeth. They were still talking steadily and softly together. Night had fallen. Jean and Jerry were helping Santi clean and settle everything in the house, then they too would leave. Earle was lying down in the bedroom. Everything was quiet except for the low voices of Marion and Elizabeth.

Eula thought, "I think I will take Tobe out for a little fresh air. She's been cooped up in that room all day." And so she did.

# Chapter Twenty-five

*

Eula was sitting on the stump near the river's edge watching Tobe investigate and jump at mysterious shadows. She laughed at the kitten, glad to have someone to laugh with.

She had relaxed watching the steady flow of the Striver River with the moon shining on it. The sky was full of stars with only a few slow-moving, beautiful black clouds. "It is good not to hear any sounds except those of nature." That was when the sound of footsteps crushing undergrowth and sticks came on the breeze to her ears. She started to turn to see who was coming, then decided not to. She sighed and thought, "I don't want company."

Then she heard his voice, "I thought you would be out here. I hope you don't mind if I join you at my usual place." When she didn't answer, he continued, "I'll be very quiet. You won't know I'm here."

Eula smiled to herself, because she could *feel* he was there. She said to herself, "It's magic. Just like Earle said." She said no word.

He thought a moment, hesitated, then asked, "Did I . . . insult you when I spoke to you earlier today?"

"Did you mean to?"

"No. No, what I said was how I felt. I knew it."

"You don't know me. And making love can't be that easy. For anybody."

"Certain kinds of lovers . . . find it easy. It was just the feeling . . . your look gave me."

She turned in the direction of the voice. "But, we are not . . . lovers."

He smiled even as he frowned. "I guess I have so much love inside me that it just spills out sometimes. It's been so . . . long since I have felt anything like that. When I saw the look in your eyes, well, I just let myself go and . . . when that happened I just felt that is what we had done. It was . . . good. Just the look felt good."

"What do you mean, Lamont, it has been so long? Making love? Don't you have a woman friend? Isn't Lona your friend?"

"Yes, we are neighbors and friends. That is all we are." He raised himself from his kneeling position, standing up. He ruffled his dog's neck a moment, then, very slowly, moved closer to her.

"Please don't come any closer to me, Lamont. I don't mean to be rude, but . . . I don't know what I felt today. I'm a little afraid of myself right now. My mother just . . . Madame's, ah, Elizabeth's mother . . . See, I'm feeling particularly vulnerable right now and I don't want—"

"But you do. I just know you do. Do you have a man . . . friend?"

Perspiration appeared just beneath Eula's nose and in the crevice of her breast. She reached for Tobe, who sprang away, playfully. "Mr. Heavy, that is personal. What are we doing here talking like this? You don't know me. I don't know you."

His voice lowered, husky with unexpected desire. "I want to. You can." There was only silence after his words disappeared into the night breezes. After a few moments he spoke again. "Eula Too, I know I am being forward, maybe too aggressive . . ."

Frightened of her feelings, Eula said, "I really don't feel like talking. I don't feel like any company. I don't really know what you are talking about. I've never had a man friend. I've never *fucked* as you said to me. I've never . . . I've never . . ."

He was standing beside her when she burst into tears. Tears of a weary, hungry, exhausted heart. He knelt down and placed his arms around her and just held her. She did not pull away, instead she buried her face in his shoulder. He let her cry for a while, then he gently put his fingers on her chin and turned her face up to his and kissed her. He kissed her (*my father?*), a warm, moist, long, soft, gentle kiss. There was no tongue, just warm, soft lips. She melted deeper in his arms, and she did not pull away.

After he slowly removed his lips from her lips, wet with her tears, he looked down into her face and his heart rejoiced. Rejoiced! "I am happy, however foolish I may be. I am happy."

Eula's thoughts were, "Oh God, I don't know this man. How can I love this man? But if it is not love, then what am I feeling? I never felt this way with any man before in my life. I don't want to be a fool." She looked up at his face and thought, "I will not be a fool." She loosed herself from him, hating every movement that separated them. "I'm sorry, Mr. Heavy. I didn't mean to do that."

He laughed softly, saying, "Girl, I want to be with you when you do mean to do it." Then he grew serious. "Eula Too, I won't put my hands on you, again, if you don't want me to. I'm sorry if I compromised you, but I couldn't help it. And will do it again. As soon as you . . . say it's all right."

She started away from him, her face turned away. The woman did not know what to do with herself, her face, her arms, her body. She was halfway across the yard when, in a low voice, he called to her. "Eula, you have forgotten your kitten, Tobe." She stopped, turning to him as he brought the kitten to her. He said, "Please, do not forget me that way."

Eula held the kitten close as she rushed away and into the house. She went to her room, dreading to have to talk to anyone. She wanted to hold his kiss and live it over and over. Earle was asleep on her side of the bed. "Good," Eula thought. "Now I can hold him in my mind and think of what all this means."

**L**amont walked with his new dog after he left Eula. Walking and thinking. Restless. When he finally turned into his gate, Lona was sitting on his porch waiting for him with the bottle of Champagne in her hands. He did not want to see anyone. He had just lived a kind of dream, a hope, and he wanted to hold it quietly all the night until he saw Eula again.

"Oh, Lona, Lona, Lona. What are you sitting out here for? We just talked at Mrs. Fontzl's house. What do you want now?"

"I just thought we could have a drink and talk. We can talk about your new girl, if you want to." Lamont started up his stairs with a heavy sigh. As she rose to follow him, she asked, "What is wrong with me, Lamont? Don't you like me anymore? You don't even know that woman. I saw you through my back window when you were holdin' and kissin' her."

"So? I think you are . . . nice, Lona. We've never had any problems. Personal problems. Because we don't have a personal relationship. You need to build a life for yourself without counting on me. What I do is my business." He reached for the bottle. "I don't want any Champagne. Gives me headaches. I'll open it for you to have some."

When she held a glass of the sparkling wine in her hand, she sat stretched out on one end of the divan. She took a sip and looked at him speculatively, "I saw her, Eula, out there a couple times today."

"Good."

"But you don't know what I saw. I don't think she is the type of woman you would like, Lamont. She is not a clean woman."

"Why would you say that? You don't know that woman."

"Because," she took a sip of the Champagne, "because I saw her throw a dirty used Kotex into the river. Twice today. Somebody must have been in the bathroom in the house, because she changed them right there outside where anyone could see her." She took another sip.

Lamont winced as the image came involuntarily to his mind. "Oh, God, Lona. I don't believe you. And so what? What if she did? A whole lot of things go in that river."

"I just wanted you to know what kind of woman you were liking, that's all. You are my friend. I know how important cleanliness is to you, being a very clean woman myself. I can't stand nothing dirty 'round me!"

"Lona, Lona, I have to get to bed—"

Lona interruped him, "I bet you do. You know, Lamont, I need a man. I know I am a better lover than she is." The frown on his face made her change her attitude. Now, she frowned and asked, "How long do I have? What time is she coming?"

"Let me tell you something, Lona. You don't have a single thing to do with my life. I do not let my friends, or aquaintances, run my life. We, you and I, have never had or done anything together and I have no intention of starting anything with you. So, finish that glass of Champagne like a good friend and go home."

"I didn't know you were so hungry for somebody. I been trying to tell you that I could be a good wife to you. You already love my kids."

"But, not you, Lona. Not you." He did not want to hurt Lona and he did not want to leave her alone in his house while he went to bed, so he just opened his front door and waited for her. Lona was humiliated as she walked onto the porch but he had not humiliated her, she had done it to herself. He shut the door softly.

After a quick shower, he patted on cologne for the first time in a long time. He did not brush his teeth. He wrapped up in the covers and stretched out in his bed. With a smile on his face, he tasted Eula's kiss until he drifted off to sleep.

*My gift of knowing what people are doing and thinking is shrinking. Matters fade and disappear from me quickly now. That means my time to be born may be near, and I will know nothing when I am, at last, born. I will not be able to talk when almost all my knowledge has evaporated. So I must be quick!*

**T**he following morning Jewel was ordering flowers to be sent to Madame. "I don't have time to go to Madame, but I want that lady to know I love her and she is my family. Now that her mother is gone, there is only me. And, of course, my mother. But I am all she has too, so everything will end up in my hands." Then she went back to the apartment where she was living, part-time with her fiancé-lover. It was only part-time because his mother would never have countenanced anything else for the son she and his father pampered. But Jewel was already pregnant; she did not know it.

. . .

Meanwhile, Rita was waking from a boisterous night with a very rich young man she had met in her grand hotel. She had needed to be held . . . and was. He left her with a set of twins, but, of course, she could not know that yet. After a bath and a good breakfast she began to prepare to leave for Place, to join Madame and Eula. She sighed, thinking, "Well, life, where are we going this time and what are we going to do there? The name of the town is Place, and that is just what I need, a place!"

Earle woke up and had a very good breakfast with Santi, whom Madame had employed to stay on until after the funeral. "I'm going to need a maid, Santi. Would you think about it and help me find someone? Eula does not know anyone here, so I need your help." Santi agreed.

Eula Too woke up and just lay there, thinking, feeling, wondering. About life. Her life. About Lamont. She did not trust her heart to tell her what to do. "Surely this is not the way *love* happens. Surely you must have to know someone a long time. Know how they are. Know if what you feel is really real. Oh, God, I don't know what to do with myself. I feel so . . . so . . . unusual. So good and so bad at the same time. But I want to feel, again, the way I felt last night when he kissed me. Oh, I want to be kissed by him again. But ohhh, no! I don't want to see him. I am so damned embarrassed."

When she, at last, got up, showered, and dressed, she called Iowna Hart. "It will take you at least six months to pack to move, so start packing. In six months I am going to move you . . . wherever I am."

When she and Earle were alone in the room, Eula said, "Earle, you would know the answer to what is on my mind. You see, I think I really like . . . someone."

"That man, Lamont, at the memorial last night? The one I saw you locking eyes with?"

"Yes. Him. Lamont."

"I like him too, Eula. I'm glad you finally like somebody! Girl, you need to love somebody! I know you have to be careful about that, but he sure seemed like he cared about you."

"But, Earle, doesn't love take more time than two or three days of knowing someone? How can you love someone in such a short time? It is probably just an infatuation."

"Then take your time, Eula. Take your time to see. But if you think life can be good with him, don't let it get away."

"Earle, my mind tells me—"

"Eula, your mind may be your palace, that's good and fine. But you better fill the moat around your mind. Fill it with love, honey, and maybe have all the wonders and joys of God's creation. Love, real love, can give you that. If you let your mind talk you out of it, you'll be living in your palace all by yourself."

"Your mind can talk you into it, too, Earle, and be wrong. How can you find love at a funeral?"

"Love don't care where you are, Eula, and don't always come when you call it. It comes when it comes. It's part of life, and life is the game that must be played if you are alive. Eula, you are almost thirty-five years old now. How long you think you gonna get away without paying some dues? You are too old to be so empty. The thing you know how to do best is count money. You better learn something about love before you get old and ugly and nobody offers to teach you anymore!"

Then they laughed and hugged. Earle was happy something was about to happen for Eula besides Madame's business. Eula was happy but frightened, confused, and uncertain because she didn't know that was the way love was sometimes; frightening, confusing, and uncertain.

Eula Too sat looking out the windows at the riverbank wondering if Lamont ever came there during the day. Her heart sent thoughts to him, "Come on over here, where I can see you." She was happy with her thoughts. She thought of the night to come when she would take her kitten, Tobe, and go out by the river again. "Well, at least I know what I'll be doing tonight." But, she didn't really know.

. . .

Iowna Hart had been sitting in her worn easy chair waiting for death to come take her. "I'm tired. There is nothing else. Eula Too keeps sending me money and I don't know what I would do without it. But I'm really getting too old to keep living and accepting her help. I might as well get on 'way from here." Little tears rolled down her wrinkled, dry cheeks as she pressed her lips firmly together to keep from crying her thoughts out loud. "Oh, God, I been here on this earth all this time, almost for nothing." Then the little phone, that never hardly ever rang, rang, with Eula's call, and a little piece of Iowna's heart lifted up. A breath of life made it to move with hopes, with love, again. A few hours later she had several lists of what to keep and what to give away. A new beginning was rushing to her heart, making it come alive, filled with new hope. It was already full of love.

Mr. Burnett was in New York surrounded with his problematic family he loved so much. He was a wise old man and kept his financial business to himself. He could relax and enjoy the family love given to him even though he knew it was because of the hope that he would pass his money and apartment on to them. He knew the thieves and the plotters in his family; he understood and loved them all. He had his private thoughts; his choices were already made.

Burnett was not going to the funeral of Madame's mother. "I didn't know her mother, she didn't know me. Why carry my almost eighty years anywhere that is not a happy place? I've given enough of my life. I'll call her, because she is my friend. But, now, she has our intelligent little Eula Too with her. I know she is well taken care of."

That same night Earle helped Eula dress to look good but as though she really hadn't tried to look especially good. Then Eula sat near the windows petting her kitten, looking at the sky waiting for it to darken so she could take Tobe out. And see Lamont. She wondered if he would come earlier, before she went out and posed herself for him.

Lamont was, indeed, planning to walk his dog and go over near the river. Near Eula Too.

Lamont was on his way out of his front door when he saw Lona backing up the car. At the same time he heard her call out to Homer, he saw that Homer was moving something out of the driveway for his mother and was still in the driveway. He saw Lona back the car out, too fast. The car hit Homer, who fell to the ground without a scream or a word.

Lamont rushed down his steps, hollering at Lona to stop the car. He reached Homer and felt over his thin body for broken bones. Lona stood over them, looking down, gasping, and covering her mouth. "I think we can move him, Lona! We better get him to the hospital to see a doctor!"

"I don't have any money for a doctor. We can take him in the house and if he rests awhile, he'll be alright. C'mon, Lamont. Bring him on."

Lamont picked up the lightweight body of nine-year-old Homer and started across the street to put Homer in his car. "I'll take him myself."

"Well, if you gonna help me pay, we can go in my car. Saves time." Lamont hesitated. Lona said, "C'mon, Lamont. We don't have time to argue! That's my son!"

Lamont agreed and stretched Homer out in the backseat as he talked to him. "Hold on, young man, we're going to get you some medical help. You'll be alright." They would be at the hospital about three hours.

Eula had been sitting on her stump by the river for more than two hours. At first she settled Tobe near her and moved her body in many different ways to be sure Lamont saw her in her best light and look. When she got tired in that pose, she would find a new one, always looking about, casually, to see if he had come. "Is he seeing me yet?" Normally she would have simply enjoyed her rest by the river playing with Tobe. But after hours of that strain and stress of trying to sit the right way and look beautiful too, she was weary of the whole thing, and it was getting cold.

She got up to go into the house and as she turned to go up the front steps, Lona drove Lamont and Homer into the driveway next door. Eula forgot herself, stopping to look for a moment until she realized she was staring. She caught herself up and pranced up the steps, through the front door, which she slammed behind her. She went straight to her room, but she did not cry, she was too angry. She could not stay in her room; she went back to the front of the house to look through the windows to see if Lamont was going home.

The doctor had said Homer would be alright, and he was able to walk. Lamont was bracing Homer's walk up the steps when Eula saw them. She thought, "He is going in with her!" She went back to her room, flying past Earle and Jean, who were talking in the kitchen, without a word, and shut the door. She lay on the bed and glared at the ceiling, then the windows, until Tobe slid into her empty arms. Then her glare softened to a sad, disappointed look into space. "I'll never think of him again. I can't live here. Madame will just have to find someone else. I am not the one."

Lamont did rush around to the river, but naturally did not see anyone. He sat on their stump awhile, but Eula did not come out. "Damn! It's too late!" he thought. "That damn Lona! Poor Homer. I ought to take him and raise him myself." He looked up to Eula's windows. "Come on out, girl. Come on out here to me." After a moment, disgusted, he thought, "She must think I'm crazy! A fool! Well, I guess I am. How can a woman like her even think of somebody like me?" At last, he got up, walking slowly back to his home, thinking, "I won't bother her again. I'm not going to be anyone's fool. I should have stuck my tongue down her throat! She might be out here now! But, no, I treated her like a lady. I want Lona to stay out of my face, and I am going to stay out of Eula's face. Get back into myself. I was doing alright with just my little trips up to Elysee City. I'll just stick to that and stay to myself. In fact I think I'm going tomorrow night. I'll pay my respects at the funeral then go on up to Elysee. I don't know how I ever dared hope about anything anyway."

**R**ita arrived in her fashionable clothes with many expensive luggage cases. Eula took her directly to Iris's house, cutting her eyes, inconspicuously, at Lamont's house as they crossed the street. Rita, stumbling in her high heels, asked Eula, "Are you sure this old lady is all right with me being there? Does she know . . . ?"

"No, she does not," Eula answered. "There is no reason anyone should know. It is only your business. She just thinks you are a visitor to Madame's, we call her Elizabeth here, and are staying for a while. This lady has no relatives, no family, so you will be a welcome guest in a lonely house."

Iris's eyes were almost wide enough to walk into when she met the glamorous Rita. Rita took a good look at the soft, motherly Iris and hugged her, getting her fur in Iris's nose and eyes, saying, "Oh, Miz Iris, I am so happy to be here with you. Thank you for letting me stay. I do not have any . . . close family and I need a Mama. We can play family."

After Iris had shown Rita to her best bedroom, she took Eula aside, saying, "How can such a rich lady stay in my house? I know she is used to much better than this! She won't want to stay here." But Eula, smiling, assured her, "Iris, I'm sure Rita will be more than pleased to stay here with you. It may be for more than a few nights though, until she finds another place." When Eula left Iris was making tea and setting the table with Rita's help.

**T**he funeral went as scheduled. There were the same people there, except Lona didn't come. She said, "I have to stay at home with Prince, and Homer might as well stay home with us and not get in anybody's way." Lamont came, sitting in the back of the church as the minister spoke about someone he had barely known. Madame would have been hysterical, but Eula had a doctor give her tranquilizers. Mrs. Fontzl was buried on the new acreage with a grand tombstone. It was a hard time for Madame.

Eula had seen Lamont enter, but she had not seen him leave. She meant to "almost" ignore him to let him know she did not care about him. When the funeral was over, Lamont was nowhere in sight. Her heart felt like it fell to the bottom of her breast. He didn't come to Madame's house after the funeral. He didn't call. He didn't come to sit by the river (where she waited for a while).

When Earle was getting ready to leave for her home, Eula was haughty with her. "You are so smart, Miss Earle Mae! That man didn't care for me at all!" She mimicked Earle, " 'Let myself goooo. Fall in lovvveee.' Well, don't give me any more advice about love!" But the sisters hugged when they said their farewells. Earle said, "I'm going to one of my favorite bookstores, Marcus Books, when I get home and send you some books about love. Everybody suffers a little. I don't believe he don't care for you!"

The day finally ended. Everyone was tired. Santi went home, saying she would check in on them now and then. Jean said she would also. Other than a temporary housekeeper-cook Santi had found for Madame, the house was almost empty. Eula fell asleep in her bed, Tobe curled at her feet, as she looked out of her windows up at the sky full of stars. She refused to look down near the river to see if anyone was there.

*We can only assume what Lamont Heavy was doing. I can't tell.*

# Chapter Twenty-six

*

*We know my time is short. I can not tell you everything; some things you will know for yourself. But if I am to tell you more I must be frugal with my words.*

During the next month Rita discovered her pregnancy from her last night at the grand hotel with the gentleman of her own choice. She thought of an abortion; she did not want one. "I am too alone to get rid of my own family."

She and Iris had become very close. Rita playfully called Iris Moms and Iris called her Dear. She discovered a sense of place in this house, a new life of her own. It irritated Madame, somehow, when Rita told Madame of this.

Rita and Iris often went out to eat in fancy restaurants or to the picture show. They even drove to Elysee City to get Chinese food or see an exhibit at a museum. Iris noticed several prosperous-looking men following Rita with their eyes; they were interested in the mature, sophisticated woman. They thought she was with her mother, which added to their respect. Iris was proud to have people think of Rita as her daughter.

Rita and Iris would browse for interesting hours at the museum and bookstores. Iris was so thrilled with her new life, sometimes she could not sleep at night. She lay in bed thinking, "I am living. This wonderful woman has brought me life."

One night, soon after Rita's discovery, they were watching television together. Rita reached over and touched the older lady's hand, saying, "Moms, I need to tell you something. You know I am old enough not to be a virgin." Iris nodded, blushing a bit as Rita continued, "Well,

Moms, I had a close friend before I came here for the funeral . . . and I believe I am pregnant."

A soft "What?" from Iris.

Fear made Rita's heart lurch as she thought, "Will I be forsaken again?" She sighed and said louder, "I believe I am pregnant."

Iris took her hand quickly, saying, "Oh! That is wonderful, Dear. Oh, that is wonderful. You are blessed. Have you told the father, your friend?"

Relieved, Rita smiled, "No, because I don't know what I should do about this baby. And when I do know, I still might not tell him."

Iris loved Rita and didn't want to lose her. She said, "It is none of my business."

"Yes, it is, Moms, because I don't want to leave this life I have with you."

Maureen Iris smiled in her heart as tears filled her eyes. "Well, if it is my business, let us keep the child. I always wanted a baby . . . in my house. It will be our house. Our family."

Rita hugged her in gratitude, feeling washed clean from her past, hoping there was a future in her future. Iris felt gratitude to Rita for giving life to her life.

Iris asked, "How will we provide for everything? A house is not all we will need."

"I don't know, because I have very little money. But I will take care of everything somehow, Moms." She sighed, "I'll get a job. Just let me worry about that. We'll just let the baby be born and watch it grow up and give us back all the love we will pour on it . . . him? Her?" They laughed in their happiness. Rita began to wear her thin cotton Parisian dresses and such to the store and around the house. Iris planned to sew maternity dresses when the time came for them.

Rita's character grew, the edges to her personality softened, blurred, and faded. Laughter was at the ready to her lips. Her honesty came forward. Her capacity for joy was so large, so eager, and she was daily filling her mind with good books and beautiful things; filling her body with nourishing foods Iris bought. "I have nothing to fear here. I can feel things, good things." And she loved the child growing in her womb. She went looking for a job. First she tried the banks. "I can count money!"

Madame was speechless when Rita told her about the baby. Jealous a bit. But she thought, "I have Jewel. She is mine."

Ha loved the books Eula brought to her. She, Maheema, Goa Do, and any interested family member sat reading every evening. Henry Lee was made nervous by all the reading. "We can find some work to do in the store." Ha always answered, "The workday is over, Henry Lee. Now we rest, eat, and read." He would go away mumbling to himself. "I will write a letter to that matchmaker and tell her what she sent to me!"

The books Eula brought led to more dreams and possibilities. The girls dreamed of travel. Ha wanted to go back to China and see about her family and . . . Ling Woo. "The heart must have love to fill its belly!" She still wrote letters to the address her mother had given her, but received no answers.

Maheema wanted to be a doctor and go to India. Goa Do wanted to work with animals as a veterinarian or be a beautiful model. "Or write books!" she said, "and I know I can, Mama!" Ha loved the words "mama" and "mother." She delighted in the sound of her children calling her. Henry Lee always called her honey-darlin' as he fumbled over her body. But she wanted to be called darlin' by someone who loved her not for her work, but for herself. "I want a deep love all to my heart." She would sigh, "One day, maybe."

As usual, Lona watched everyone in the neighborhood, but particularly Lamont. She watched for Eula through her river windows at night. Hatred and envy seethed in her sad, ignorant, pitiful heart.

She would look around the house thinking, as usual, of the day it would be hers. "Then I will have a home of my own. He will want me then! He thinks I ain't got nothin'. He'll see. Somebody gonna want me! I'll sell this house and go 'way to some city where more people are and somebody is gonna want me! And Prince will have a real home! Lamont ought to be the one. I know I could make him happy. I have tried to show him ever since Robert died on me!"

She even said to Marion on one of her visits, "If you know so much about the Lord, why is it some people get everything they want in life and some people don't get nothing? Not only never get rich, just never get a way to buy anything they want?"

Marion answered, "What do you want? Money is not going to make your life happy. Your husband may be dead, but you have two wonderful children. Love is more important than money. All you talk about is money. If you learned about God, you would know more about life. Attitude is important, too. What do you think life owes you? What have you done for life? Your own life? There is no life without some wisdom, some sense. No life without God. God gives you true hope in a world that seldom gives anybody anything. Who are you counting on? People? Chile, you better wake up. Life is a struggle on this earth whether you have God or not, but if you don't have God, and you believe in all the glitter and false promises the world offers you, you end up paying more than you can afford, every time."

Lona thought Marion was a fool. "Always talkin' 'bout God! He ain't never done nothin' for me! Didn't even give me a mama!"

*Lona was healthy and able. Many things were there in life for Lona to choose, but she could not see. Her pain from the past was in the way, blocked her view of life. In this hard world you have to fight and struggle for your place in life. But fight with kindness and consideration; don't destroy your bridges, you may need them. Build them up. Make yourself strong. No one else can. Don't count on anyone else to do it for you. Money can be wonderful, but it won't buy you life. May help keep you healthy, but it won't buy you health. I'm going to try to remember that for myself.*

Old Mary Green, usually strong, came down with a strange sickness. She was becoming weaker and always tired. She stopped working in her garden and was forced to go to bed early in the afternoons. Some days she could not get up at all.

Marion came to see about her, and was there when her mother vomited one day. Marion looked at the mass of green mucus and wondered, worrying about her mother. She went to the kitchen, took an empty jar and scooped some of the vomit in it. She took it directly to the doctor to have it examined for some allergy or whatever it might be.

Marion stayed a few days, and her mother began to feel better. The doctor called her the day after she left and told her, "Your mother must have ingested some poison while she was out working in her yard. Or it must have gotten into something she ate. I'll send her some good medicine to stop the damage. See that she takes it, because it is vital that the poison is stopped." Marion got right into her car and drove back to Place to her mother's house, thinking hard all the way.

Because of her Bible studies Marion knew humankind and their needs very well. She suspected Lona was capable of doing whatever was necessary to be sure the house was hers. She did not mince words when she spoke to Lona. "Lona, I know you were my brother's wife, but I think you better find some other place to live."

"This ain't just your house, Marion. This house is goin' to belong to Robert's kids, too! They s'posed to live in their father's house!"

"Their father is dead. My mother is alive and she is going to stay that way as long as she can."

Lona snapped her head around to Marion, then looked quickly away. She said, "She can stay alive. I'll help her. I didn't give her nothin' to poison her!" *Marion hadn't mentioned poison.*

Marion tilted her head, saying, "Lona, I don't intend to argue with you. You are going to have to move. I hate to see my mother's grandchildren leave, but you have to leave and I don't see how they can stay without you."

"You going to give me some money to find a new place? I ain't got no money to move with!"

"I'll give you a few weeks to prepare. I will be here every week and

I'm going to hire someone to come in and cook for my mother. You don't have to do anything for her anymore."

Lona tried to look as though she did not understand. "Why? What have I done? Why we got to move? This is their home too!"

In a voice filled with finality, Marion said, "They will inherit their part. They can come back then. But I want you out of this house, and right now. This is my mother's house and my house. You have to go. Take two weeks, but leave here you must. God help you."

**M**adame was settling into her new life. She called in interior designers and landscapers and began work on the house on Dream Street. She even brought real sand in to pour in the backyard on the riverbank. She had a few new trees planted, half grown already, all different and beautiful.

One day, during this time, Eula's hurt heart stopped its nervous fluttering, her mind calmed. She avoided Lamont. She only saw him now and then, coming in from his job or working in his yard. Sometimes he worked with the contractors on Madame's house. Eula would leave then and drive to Elysee City to go to the Black Images bookstore or the Black Bookworm store. It was the first time she had such bookstores to go to; she had read almost all Madame's books. She watched the riverbank from her windows at night, always. Looking for Lamont.

They had knocked out walls so Madame's bedroom, guest room, bathrooms, dining and sitting rooms were larger and full of furnishings brought over from her old house, which had not sold yet. The kitchen was modernized. Everything was becoming beautiful. The basement was almost completely rebuilt. Eula was gradually moving into that apartment. The sand for the riverbank was the last thing.

One evening Eula opened the glass doors facing the river and went out with Tobe happily following her. Madame didn't particularly like Tobe and would not allow her upstairs, so Eula kept Tobe near her.

She left only a night-light on and went to sit on the stump she had insisted they leave. She spoke to Tobe as the growing kitten padded a pebble about. She had been there about an hour, entranced by the murmuring water flowing past. When she heard the sound of steps coming toward the river, her heart hoped, and yet dreaded, it was Lamont.

Even as she told herself she would not turn to look, she turned to look. She watched him come closer to her, still keeping a distance as he stood near the river, looking at her. Her heart pounded so. She was blushing and flushed from his sudden nearness, feeling the violence of her heartbeat.

He was angry and hurt. He stood silent, looking at her. At last she said with a faltering voice, "Hello."

Lamont was thinking that perhaps he had moved too much, too fast. "I don't know this woman and she does not know me either. I let my need for someone fall on her shoulders. It must be a burden to her." Aloud, he said, "Good evening." Noticing the cat, he said, "Come 'ere Toots!"

Minutes passed as he continued thinking, "I don't feel like taking up any more pain. I take things too hard. I better stop before I am really hurt. Why should she like me? She is a city girl, used to better things. I must have lost my mind. I can see too many disappointments and too much pain in my life if I let myself love her. But, I see just as much pain, maybe, if I don't try to keep her." Aloud, he said, "How are you, Eula?"

"Alright. I guess. You?"

"I guess I'm alright too." There was no sound except the murmur of the river for a few minutes. Then he said, "I wanted to see you." He looked up at the sky. "I thought I might walk back here . . . and see how all the work we did came out. How you liked it."

"Oh, I love it. It's very nice."

"Good." Silence, except for the waters that wouldn't be still. "Any little part I worked on, I thought of how you might like it, and did it as well as I could."

"Ooooh, thank you, Lamont, but . . . I'm not sure I'm going to live here."

He stepped closer to her, asking, "What do you mean? You are leaving? When? How long are you going to stay with . . . before you leave? And where are you going?"

Eula's heart gladdened at the sound of distress in his voice, but she cautioned herself, "Don't forget Lona. You don't know this man, Eula." But she said aloud, "I mean . . . this is not my house. This is my job. I'm finally understanding that."

"But," he persisted, "you said 'leave.' "

"Well, yes. I want my own."

Lamont thought of his house, which could be hers. Suddenly it was not good enough to him, but what could he do. He was thinking and forgot to say anything. The moon had paled, the water grown darker. The sound and scent of the trees was changed.

Eula spoke again, "I have some land now. Two hundred acres on River Road. I want to build a house for a friend of mine and then, one for myself.

"A friend? You bought two hundred acres of land? Here?"

"Yes, an old schoolteacher who has been my friend a long, long time."

His heart relaxed a little; scents and sounds returned. "Who is going to build it? I can help."

"I have to plan that out, Lamont."

"Let me help you, Eula. I can only work in the evenings and on weekends, but I will be glad to." His thoughts were, "Don't break my heart, Eula."

She said, "I would appreciate that, Lamont. But I have to plan it all out, in my mind, what I'm going to do. I'll be glad to have any help."

His voice lowered, "But, not mine?"

"Yours especially. What will your girlfriend say?"

"Which friend would that be, Eula?"

"I was thinking . . . You mean there is more than one?"

"One what, Eula? I have many people I am friendly with."

Her voice lowered, "I was thinking of Lona."

He laughed softly and his arm struck out at the air, "I never think of Lona, except as Mrs. Green's daughter-in-law."

"I find that hard to believe. She is always at your house . . . and the other night."

He stepped closer to her, saying, "You believed that? That Lona and I had something together?"

She breathed, "Yes."

Encouraged by her voice so full of feeling, his voice lowered, filled with need, "Did it matter to you? Did you mind? Care?"

Eula didn't answer right away. He waited. She said, "You kissed me. I thought you . . . oh, never mind."

Lamont knelt down, resting on one knee, careful not to come too close to her. "Just tell me like it is, Eula, like you feel in your heart. I need to know." Tense, he waited for her answer.

Her voice was so low he almost could not hear her, but he did. "I've never known a man close before, in my life. I'm a woman who is alone. I have a daughter in college, but I don't mean that. I mean, I'm alone." He could see her swallow. "After you kissed me . . . I know it's foolish, but I needed to be kissed again. Held again." She kept her eyes down. "For the first time in my life . . . I want a man."

"A man?"

"But I want one who . . . understands that love can be painful . . . and who will not hurt me."

Lamont sat back on his heels, he was very near her now. "Oh, baby, baby." He moved to kneeling on his knees as he said, "I've been thinking about you so deep and so much. I can't rest my mind. I can't sleep. I knew I didn't know you, like people know each other for a long time, but still . . . I felt you. I knew you. And I wanted you."

"Wanted me?"

"Want you." Silence. He moved still nearer. "Eula, let me touch you. Let me hold you?"

She held up her hand as if warding him off as she said, "Why should you care for me and not Lona? Or someone else? This is where you live. You know everybody."

"Because you are you. Lona is Lona and everybody else is everybody else. I . . . love you."

The past weeks had cost Eula. She felt a deep well of sorrow in her soul. She had never met, let alone understood, love, this new emotion she felt. When Lamont reached out to put his arms around her, that deep well filled with all the joy her soul had begged for. Her emotions spilled over and covered both of them like the wings of a huge, magic, beautiful butterfly.

The hand she had lifted to ward him off, almost reached out for him, but she caught herself and was still. She could hear him breathe, feel the heat of his body, feel his nearness. Her heart was pounding sweetly, even as the nerves of her body were going crazy and responses were racing through her body. She could feel every strand of her own hair on her head.

Lamont touched her arms. She leaned toward him slightly. On his knees he moved through the sand and placed his arms around her, holding her close, close, close. Her breath stopped with feelings that overwhelmed her. She wanted to cry and laugh at the same time. They stayed that way, listening as the river rushed by full of life and the leaves of trees rustled. The breeze caressed their caress. Then he lifted her chin so her face was inches from his. As he looked into her eyes, he slowly closed his eyes and kissed her softly and long.

In this kiss his tongue slowly entered her mouth. Eula's lips accepted it, touching it with her own tongue. Love passed back and forth through this opening in their bodies. At last he pulled her up and pressed his body close, close, closer. But he made no move to suggest going further. He decided, "This will be a slow, exciting, good time of making Eula love me." Eula was thinking, "I love him. I love this man."

They talked more before he left and she went inside her apartment where Tobe had gone in and was asleep on the bed. She cried out softly, "Oh, Tobe! Tobe I'm in love. And he loves me. I must be with him. I won't let anything separate us now."

. . .

Madame had casually walked back to the windows facing the river. The moon was so bright she did not turn on the lights. She was smiling at the way life was turning out for her and Eula when she looked down at a slight movement below on the river's edge. She saw Eula and Lamont. She saw how he held Eula. She saw what she thought could hurt Eula . . . and herself.

The next morning after her breakfast, Madame called Eula up on the intercom. "Eula, would you come up when you have a moment? I have something important to discuss with you."

They talked. Eula was to go back to the old house, which was sold and in escrow. "Take care of things there and see if you can get Dolly to work here in Place several days a week." Eula asked, "But, Madame, what about your agent? Can't he handle all that? And we can call Dolly."

"The agent cannot do it as well as you. You know all the personal things I need. Besides I want those last few things on my list sent here within the next few weeks. That escrow will close soon. And Eula, I've had the escrow check made out to you, because of taxes. I would have to pay too much, my attorney says. You will not have to pay as much. As usual, like always."

Eula took a moment to think. Money. "How much do you expect to receive?"

"Perhaps half a million. Pretty good price. That broker is a good one. I will pay you a little extra for your work."

Eula had already been thinking about it, but waited a moment to say, "I can use some of it to build Iowna a little house on my land."

Madame hesitated, "Well, I don't know . . . I don't think . . ."

"Oh, Madame, why should we disagree about it? You use me and I don't disagree with you. Now I want some things, why should you disagree with me? You have more money than you will ever use anyway."

But Madame turned away, saying, "We will talk about a little house for your friend, Miss Hart. I suppose she is quite old now. She should be near you. Save you time from going so far to check on her."

Eula smiled, saying, "I'll need a few days to get ready."

But Madame disagreed again, "Paul will be here tomorrow morning to pick you up. He could not come today."

"What is the rush, Madame?"

Madame sighed, saying, "You have to take care of business when it is ready, not wait until you are." Madame waited a moment then said, "What is it you are doing with that . . . that man across the street? He is nothing, just another poor man."

"I like him very much, Madame. I don't know what we are doing . . . right now. But what is that to you?"

Madame didn't answer that, she said, "He is not a gentleman. He is too familiar with you. I hate familiarity. He is an unidentified object. We don't know him. I don't like you being so friendly with him so quickly. There is something . . . not good about him. And I don't make rash judgments, you know. What I am telling you is from many years of my observation and experience."

"The thing is, Madame, I must see for myself."

"You have become like your new friend the cat, Eula."

"Cats are very clean, very graceful, and very smart."

Madame smiled, not sweetly, "And very sneaky, as you are becoming."

Eula smiled, not sweetly, "Why are you so contradictory? You speak so well of your past love, and how much it meant to you, but you do not want me to know love."

"Because I am most interested in your happiness. You know almost everything I have is yours."

But Eula persisted, "I have been with you many years and not one year gave me this type of happiness. Now, I have someone I want and you don't like my choice. You always do as you please, but I cannot? Almost everything I have is yours, for that matter."

Madame sighed. "What have you said to him, Eula?"

"You want my private thoughts, but you are afraid someone else might want money." Now Eula sighed, and shook her head.

"I know what I am doing, Eula. Don't you love me? Aren't I your best friend? And Jewel's?"

Eula looked at Madame, realizing again that Madame did love them, but found her happiness in being able to exert a certain power and make a certain impression on her loved ones. Madame had expected to control Eula and Jewel in Place. Weary and annoyed, Eula thought, "I will do what I will do." She said aloud, "Don't worry me about my life, Madame. I am a grown woman and I intend to be happy." As she was leaving, she turned back at the door, saying sadly, "This man has made me happier than I can ever remember being. More happy than money. Isn't the happiness I want important to you? I will not give him up." She turned to leave, saying, "I will be ready to go on your errand tomorrow, as you wish."

Madame's words followed Eula down Madame's beautiful hall. "Your words are a fool's words, Eula."

Later that evening Eula talked to Lamont. She told him her plans. He suggested they take a ride to see her land. "If you show me where you want your friend's house to be, while you are gone I can get some friends and get started on it. Get a piece of paper and draw the plans for the house." Eula drew a replica of Iowna's own house with an extra room for a guest and a small library. "I intend to order all kinds of new books for her. I'll send them to your house to store. I'm going to bring all her favorite things out of her old home."

"Good! Well that will give me something to do while you are gone."

There was a long stretch of river road along Eula's land that was marked by red flags. Eula looked over all the various shades of green trees on her land; the bluest sky, the majestic hills just beyond the Striver River were beautiful this time of year. They heard a rooster crowing far off in the distance. Eula smiled in pleasure, saying, "I remember that sound from many years ago, at home."

Lamont whistled in amazement, "I like to hear roosters crow too. But this is beautiful, Eula! But, how did you all get all this done in such a short time? It usually takes months for surveyors and escrow to work all this out."

"Madame . . . Elizabeth has many friends with power. Her money in the local bank ensures she gets what she wants when she wants it. She wanted to bury her mother on this new land and so she did." She pointed as she said, "You know she owns the land on the other side of that flag way down there." She looked at Lamont, saying, "I know you want to ask why this side is mine, so I will tell you. I've worked for her almost twenty years. She paid and I saved."

"It's a beautiful piece of land, Eula. Well, now that I know where you want Miss Hart's house, where is your house going to be?"

"Well, I want to be on the river, so it will be up the road a little piece, close enough to watch over Iowna Hart. Where do you think we can build it?"

Lamont tilted his head, smiled, and asked, "We?"

Eula looked up at him, "Well, what do people do when they . . . say they are in love?"

Lamont's laughter, so full of relief and joy, sounded through the silence of the forest. "They get married and go home across the street!" Eula joined in his laughter. Later, Eula said, "That is too close to Elizabeth. I need to have a telephone separate us."

*Of course, they kissed and held each other closely. I think I know who my daddy is now.*

**W**hile Eula was gone, Madame learned that Lamont was working on the land. She arranged for Lamont to come check some of the work done on her own house. Madame greeted him warmly, leading him to the kitchen to look at a cabinet that had nothing wrong with it. She persuaded him to have a drink. He shrugged and accepted, curious about this aging beauty who controlled his woman's life. After several minutes of casual conversation, Madame asked, "What do you think of my assistant, my friend?"

"I think you are very fortunate."

"I didn't ask how fortunate I was, I asked what you thought of Eula."

"I think she is very fortunate."

"Do you know much about her?"

"About as much as has been possible."

"Oh? That much?"

"We are friends. I think a great deal of her."

Madame laughed softly, "She can be a 'great deal.' A wonderful person to know, though . . ."

"You hesitate."

"Well, I don't know you very well, only that my mother thought well of you."

"She was kind to me."

Madame nodded her head. "Mothers can be very important. I wondered if you knew Eula is a mother? Her daughter, Jewel, didn't come to the funeral because she did not want to see Eula, her own mother. That may be because I practically raised Jewel myself. She loves me. Eula was always . . . too busy for her child."

"If she did not come to the funeral, I wonder if she didn't care to see you either. She sounds ungrateful."

Madame changed direction. "Eula was never married. She was an unwed mother. I took care of her. She has never left me." Lamont waited, wondering where this conversation was going.

After a thoughtful moment, Madame continued, "I saw that you were becoming friends and I thought I should speak with you about Eula so you will not . . . make plans including her. Eula seems very nice . . . and she is, but, also, she is not." Lamont raised his brows in inquiry.

"She seems to have no real love in her, not even for her own daughter. She is not always . . . moral. She wanted to abort the poor child, but

I talked her out of that horrible idea. And she can sometimes turn the truth around until it is no longer the truth, it just sounds like it."

Lamont leaned forward and asked, "You mean she cannot be trusted?"

"You might say that, Mr. Heavy. She would not be a good . . . the right person to fall in love with or plan a life with."

"You have decided that for her? You trust her. Even now, she is gone about your business."

"No, Mr. Heavy, I was thinking of you because my mother thought so much of you. I may seem to trust her. I care about her and her daughter. I worry about her . . . she can be very violent . . . she has a temper she does not always control. All in all, that does not auger a good, safe relationship for you. You would not be happy with her."

"Thank you, Miss Fontzl. I will take your advice in the good intention with which you give it to me. Again, why are you helping me? Like this?"

Madame smiled warmly at him, saying, "You were kind to my mother. She would want me to offer protection to any friend of hers. Also, I haven't thanked you for helping her. When is your next vacation from school?"

"Thanksgiving will be a week, I guess. Why do you ask?"

Madame smiled and leaned toward him, placing her hand over one of his, "How would you like . . . No, I would like to give you something special! Mother said you liked to visit by the river. How would you like a long vacation cruise along any of the great rivers? Amazon, Nile, Mississippi? I would like to give you that as a gift of appreciation from my mother. You can even have the ocean for a choice."

Lamont stood up to go, saying, "I will think about that. I certainly will think about it."

"One last thing, Mr. Heavy, I think you should know; Eula was raped once. I'm sure it wasn't necessary to rape her, but it was a horrible rape, a violent rape. Her sexual organs are torn and scarred. You may never be able to have sex with her. And certainly have no children with her. After her daughter was born the doctor said . . . well, I won't speak of that. But think carefully about what you do. Do not cause yourself more regret. You have already lost one wife."

After Lamont had gone, Madame thought, "If he listens to me, he is not good enough for Eula Too. I hope he believes me . . . because I cannot lose Eula. I will not lose Eula."

Thoughts of Eula crowded Lamont's mind. "Eula, Eula, Eula! When I am around her I am immediately excited, though she always seems to hold me at a distance, in some suspense. I have never known a woman like Eula, a child-woman." He looked down at his body and was ashamed because his body was hard; he laughed it away. "Why does she owe her life to Elizabeth? Does she really owe anything? How much power does Elizabeth have over her? Lord, I married Odearlia very early. Until she was sick a long time, I did not know many women intimately. It has always been like women were under glass that blurred their reality. You get only a distorted reflection. Then you have to filter that through all the things, perhaps lies, other men say about them. But, I'm not a kid, I'm a man, and I'll make my own decisions."

It concerned him, a little, that Eula had no real profession like Odearlia; no work she loved. "I have never even seen her do housework!" He cast that thought aside. "I have seen her concern for children, for Homer and Ha's children. Where is her daughter? What is it that I don't know? What I do understand, if the story about her rape is true, is that if, no, when, we make love, I will be very slow, very sensitive to everything she feels. I will not leap upon her sweet body and ride like a speed demon. I don't want her hurt again. I love her. Lord, I love me some Eula Too!" He laughed softly, saying aloud, "Help me, Lord!"

While she was away, we know Eula Too was having her thoughts also. She was distant from any helper at the house, except Dolly, so she held her thoughts to her breast like a secret, a precious treasure. When she thought of Lamont a warmth spread all over her body, all over her future.

She thought, "I wish the people on Dream Street were not all so sad; Lona, Old Mary Green, Rita, Iris, and even little Ha. In spite of their laughter. Under the laughter, sometimes I feel their sadness. But, me? I do not intend to be unhappy if I don't have to! I'm in love with Lamont Heavy and I want him to love me! Lord, Marion, bless her heart, sure talks about You and Your purposes. I'm glad You are love and that I might have a little piece of it. I want You and Marion to forgive me, but Lord, that man makes me warm all over, fills me with life, and I want to make love with him. Let me have him, please, Lord? I don't know nothing about how it feels to be a woman with a man. I want to know. Don't worry, Lord, we are going to be married if I have my way. I'm making a new body, a new day, and a new life! If I can, Lord. With Your help. If I can I sure am."

# Chapter Twenty-seven

*

*Now, I must hurry if I am to tell you these things. I may not be able to tell you everything, in my rush, but I trust you will know everything anyway.*

Lamont had used the passing weeks and the drawing Eula had made for him. With the help of his friends, the adult-sized dollhouse was almost completed. Sliding glass doors faced the river and huge windows were on each side of the small living-dining room that held the fireplace and Iowna Hart's bedroom. He worked, spending his own money. "I don't care," he told his worried mind, "I love Eula and I hope I love this old lady friend of hers too."

Finally, Eula Too had taken care of all Madame's business and had the check in hand. She had sent Madame's remaining items and some of Iowna Hart's things ahead. When she returned she brought Iowna Hart and her brother, Tommy, with her. "She can sleep in my room until her house is ready and Tommy can stay with Lamont until he gets settled. Lamont will help him find work and I will help him find a school for what he does."

Iowna had sadly kissed her old home good-bye even as she beamed with anticipation of new joy in her changing life. "I won't be alone anymore. And I don't feel so old anymore either! I hope there is room for a little garden for me to plant a few things!"

Eula took the feeble Miss Hart out to show where her new house would be. Miss Hart clapped her hands in joy. "My own little house and all that land to garden! Oh, Eula!" She was laughing with joy through tears. "And I can sit out here on my own porch and fish! Oh, Eula, Eula! Dear Eula! I have a new life with fish and a river in it! I'll get my strength back; you watch and see! Gonna be flowers all over this place!"

When Eula saw all the work Lamont had done, she loved him more. "Damn! This is a wonderful kind of man! The kind to love." She didn't say that aloud.

Eula went to the bank to deposit the check. The check was for four-hundred ninety-three thousand dollars. She put two-hundred thousand into her own checking account and two-hundred ninety-three thousand in Madame's account. The banker came out to meet her and was surprised she was a colored woman. He started to ask her, "When did you make . . . How does it come about you have such good fortune?" Eula Too answered, "You know it is not good business to discuss my business, but we can discuss yours. Will our money be safe here?"

# Chapter Twenty-eight

*

When next they were together, Lamont asked Eula to tell him about herself. She told him about her parents and how she loved them and why she left at age fifteen. He sat back listening intently to the woman so important to his life. She told about the rape and the resulting pregnancy and Jewel and how she would not have survived without Madame's help. She didn't tell him about all the ladies because Rita now lived with Iris in Place.

He leaned forward, putting his hand on her, and told her, "That's enough." She gave him a wry look and said, "That's all."

Then he told her about his life and his joy with Odearlia. His pain, sorrow, and now, his joy with her. He had already thrown Elizabeth Fontzl's words out of his mind.

Iowna lived in Eula's apartment while waiting for her house to be finished. "I could live in it while they finish it! There is only a little left to do!" But they wanted to carry her into a completed house with all the things she loved in it already. They even carried and unpacked boxes of books and a brand-new record player–radio combination for what Eula could find of Iowna's old favorites.

They made plans for themselves. A contractor had started on Eula's house. Lamont wanted Eula to come live at his house while hers was being built. She would not go. Tommy was staying there and Homer stayed most nights at Lamont's because his mother did not like his early rising hour for his delivery job.

Lona wanted, encouraged, any connection to Lamont. His house might be someplace to move to since she had to leave MaMary's.

Eula was eager, but shy, afraid she would make a fool of herself if they made love. In the nights, she trembled with her own desire, but said to herself on a breath, "Not yet, not yet. Oh, Lord!" Lamont thought he understood, in spite of her age, now, what the rape had meant to Eula, then. He slowed himself, but he was looking for a way. "I need to find a decent, gentle way to make love to my own woman who is going to be my wife. Isn't that something?!"

*I am getting weaker, my time must be near. I must make haste.*

Eula was uncomfortable sleeping on a davenport in her apartment. She had tried sleeping upstairs in Madame's guest room, but she didn't want to listen to Madame talk about Lamont and why she should not be with him.

On the day they moved the old bedroom set made by Iowna's father into the completed house, Lamont suggested she stay the night there. Eula said, "Oh, I'd love to, but it's so far from everyone, I'd be out here all alone. I'm not ready to be alone in this place yet." Lamont's heart skipped a little beat as he mused, "Well, I could stay with you until you go to sleep, then see you are safely locked in from the inside."

"Lamont, I can't ask you to do that, you need your rest, too."

"I'll get it. Right on this couch where I can hear the sounds of the river. You know I'd love that."

Eula looked at him, strangely, "I don't know if we should."

"Girl, you know by now, I'm not going to worry you. I don't mind waiting. I'd rather wait until your house is ready anyway."

"Our house," Eula corrected him. He smiled, "Our house."

She relaxed, "Well, alright. I can fix a nice dinner and we can sit out by the river as long as we want to with no eyes watching us."

"Why don't we catch our dinner? I keep a few fishing poles in the truck for Homer and me."

Eula laughed happily. "Good! Let's do it!"

Lamont laughed softly with his woman's happiness, saying, "And I can kiss you. I love the feel of your lips when we kiss." (*I loved that they loved.*) Shyness made her blush as she said, "Oh, Lamont, you know I love it too."

And so it went. Electricity had already been turned on for the construction workers. Lamont went to his car to get some records he just happened to have in there. Music by Dinah Washington, Gladys Knight, Billie Holiday, Ray Charles, Arthur Prysock, Al Green, and Smokey Robinson. He told her, "One special record I want to play, but I am saving it for our wedding night." He also brought in a bottle of good wine he just happened to have.

They laughed and talked as she cooked rice and sliced some homegrown tomatoes and green onions. Playing house. He set everything he had up and opened the wine. Then they went out to fish for their dinner.

They cast their lines and sat talking. Kissing now and then. Hands and lips lingered. Their hearts were full of the joy of being alive and being together. They caught a few fish, enough, and when that was prepared they made a table near the river out of a piece of plywood. They ate, talked, and laughed.

As it grew later, after a few glasses of wine, serious kissing began. Eula pulled back, thinking, "We are out here all alone and I am not ready. I want a good bath, a beautiful nightgown, and perfume for him. I better stop this kissing before I can't help myself." He was careful not to get too excited, but it was hard for him to continue holding himself back. They stopped the kissing and, embarrassed, they mumbled words to each other as they cleaned up. "Well, it's getting cooler out here anyway," he said. "Yes, and we don't want to catch cold," she said. She scraped the food from the plates into a bag as he took the plywood to put away.

On the bank of the river Eula leaned over to rinse the plates before taking them into the house. Her feet slipped on the wet, gooey mud and she tumbled into the river headfirst. It was shallow in that spot, but she didn't know that, so she screamed. Lamont came running. He tried not to laugh as he pulled her from the river, but even Eula was laughing in spite of her fright and the few sore spots she could feel.

He carried her in his arms into the house, asking, "Are you hurt? Did your body hit any of those rocks?" She was dazed, still a little frightened of deep water in the darkness and what could have happened. She was grateful he was there and wound her arms around his neck. Then she pulled back, saying, "Oh, I'm getting you all muddy, too!"

"That's not important," he told her. He sat her down, saying, "You better take off those clothes or you really will come down with something." He laughed, "See if you caught a fish in one of your pockets!" They laughed together again as Eula said, "Better not be nothing caught in my clothes!" But she rushed to get them off her body.

"I'll get a fire started in this fireplace," he said, "and run a bath for you. You wrap yourself in one of those blankets and lie down until your nerves are settled from the fall." She did as he told her.

When the bath water, full of foamy kitchen soapsuds, was ready, he went to get her. He wouldn't let her walk; he insisted on carrying her. "You wait until you have calmed down and are steady. I don't want you to fall in that bathtub." So she did.

After he sat her gently in the bubbly tub of warm water he told her, "I am going to bathe you." She looked up at him, startled, and started to say, "But I . . ."

"Just do like I ask, Eula. I know about these things. You don't even know if you are really hurt or not, yet." She closed her mouth, still looking up at him. He continued with a gentle voice. "Now, lean back and let the warm water soothe you. I'll start with your arms and back." He got down on his knees, bending over the tub and gently began to rub in long gentle strokes her arms, then her back. It relaxed her so much she forgot to be uneasy and tense about her naked body.

His gentle hands slowly moved, tenderly, from her back and shoulders to her breast. It took a moment for her to realize his hands were softly, like silk, smoothing over her breast and stomach. She sighed and closed her eyes. "What is there to fear from this man?"

He saw what had happened in her mind. He smiled with relief and appreciation for her trust. His hands moved from her stomach down her legs to her feet, which he took a few extra moments over. He was enjoying himself. He knew it was soothing his woman.

His soapy hands moved up to stroke clean her legs, her calf and thighs, her hips. Eyes closed, she was relaxed, her body almost prostrate, sliding deep into the tub. He leaned over her and with one arm lifted her body a little and stroked her buttocks clean. Her body tensed a little; then relaxed again.

He said in a gentle voice, "Eula? Baby, I'm going to wash all of you. You do not have to worry. I love you. You are already mine. We have already fucked, baby, you remember what I told you. So just relax now." Eula knew these were dangerous things. She told herself, "But, we are going to be married."

She felt his soapy fingers soothing private parts of her body. He gently pushed one thigh over and, taking the soap, rubbed the lips of her vagina with it. Then he put the soap down and washed the same place. Eula wanted to moan her desire for him aloud, instead, she slowly turned her head to the side and lived her bath. She felt his fingers inside her, rubbing ever so tenderly, so lovingly. When he removed them, she wanted to say, "No, no, don't." At the same time, she didn't want to say, "No, no, don't." She was struggling with herself when she realized he had stopped. His hands were gone.

He was letting the bathwater out and rinsing her off with a showerhead. She was sparkling clean, relaxed, and refreshed when he finished toweling her dry. She looked at him, in wonder, as he carried her in his arms to the old homemade bed and placed her in it. Laughing softly he said, "I know a whole lot of love has been made in this old bed." Eula looked up into his eyes, questioning. He smiled down at her, saying, "Now, you will feel better when you wake up. I'll be on the floor near the fireplace." Then he was gone. And she was safe. Safe from what? From herself, it would seem. She loved him more. For his tenderness and his patience. But her body was wide awake and yearning, yearning, yearning. Wailing in the silence . . . for more love.

She finally dozed off to sleep listening to the music he was playing softly in the next room. During the night she woke up, cold. She got up and looking into the other room, she saw that he had fallen asleep and the fire was out. She knew he must be cold also. She gently shook his shoulder, waking him. "Lamont? Wake up, honey, and come in here with me. It's cold. The fire is out."

He turned sleepily to her, saying, "I can make another fire. You cold? I can . . ." He tried to wake up and rise, but Eula told him, "Leave the fire out. We will both be asleep and can't watch it. Come in here with me. It will be warm in there."

He looked at her a minute, then followed her lead. She rushed to get under the covers. He smiled, half asleep, and got under the covers too. They formed themselves into spoons, and fell almost immediately back to sleep.

Eula woke first the next morning. She lay there feeling his weight next to her. Then she realized his arm was flung over her hip, his hand cupping her vagina. Just covering it, holding it, while he snored lightly over the top of her head. She lay still a long time, just feeling more of her new life. She smiled as she thought of the years to come.

Then, unwanted, her fear stole into her mind. She slowly removed his hand and crept from the bed. When she was dressed, she sat outside on the little deck, thinking and waiting for him to wake. When he was up, he didn't mention anything about sex or love. He just smiled and looked content, even a little smug.

**S**oon Iowna Hart was moved into her house. She had made friends with Dolly instantly. Dolly had even slept downstairs with Iowna sometimes and they played gin-rummy, talked and laughed about life together. Neither had had an easy time in life. But Dolly promised to come visit and even stay a few days a month with her. "I'll get some peace, and even fish a little. Ain't had time for that in years!"

Iowna settled, jubilantly, in her own little house. She was surrounded by her own comfortable, old furniture and shelves full of old and new books. "Even a phonograph! And windows, windows everywhere! God You are good to me. Please, bless Eula. Bless everybody." Her heart was so full, she felt like crying. Homer often came to help her do little things around her house. He liked being around her, was even learning to like books.

Eula began pushing for her own house to be finished. She was scared, but she wanted to finish making love to her man. She thought constantly of that bath. Her brother was living at Lamont's house and she would not even think of going to a hotel. "Not me! We need to be married!"

Lamont was pushing everybody working on the house, including Tommy. He wanted to make love to his woman. Be married! Be a husband again. He thought of that bath and the feel of her body often; no matter what was on the top of his mind, that memory was always at the bottom, waiting. He carried the marriage license folded neatly in his wallet.

Eula always refused Lamont when he asked her to stay at his house, but she began looking at it as a place to be married and live until her house was finished. In the meantime, she stayed in her apartment at Madame's.

**M**adame could see that Eula was spending quite a bit of money. Naturally, it came up in their coversation one day. Quite casually Madame said, "You mentioned you had put some of the check from the escrow into your account, but you didn't tell me how much."

Eula answered, "Oh, I'm sorry. I gave you all the papers. That check was for four-hundred ninety-three-thousand dollars. I put two-hundred ninety-three in your account and two-hundred thousand in mine."

"Eula! Why did you? How could you take so much?" Her voice hardened, "Of my money?"

"I need it, Madame. I have two houses I had to build, and I have a few other things I want to do."

Madame shook her head, saying, "What made you think you were entitled to that much of my money? You've been paid, regularly."

Eula leaned toward Madame and smiled a little indulgently,

"Madame, my dear friend, I have given you so much of my life, myself, my mind. No regular check of two-hundred-fifty dollars a week could pay for it."

"It is what you accepted."

"I would never question you, then. I question you now."

"It is too late to question, Eula."

"It is never too late between friends, Madame."

"Friends?"

Eula smiled again. "Friends. Practically relatives. You had, and still have, my life. My life, my daughter, my everything. I do not even know the half of what you have done with me."

Now Madame smiled. "For instance?"

"The taxes. I never declared anything because you told me you took care of it. I don't know what kind of record I have with the Internal Revenue. I never cared, because I trust you."

"So that is what you are going to hold over me so you may keep that two-hundred-thousand dollars."

"Madame, I hold nothing over your head."

"You would threaten to inform . . . report me."

"I would never report you to anyone about anything. I never have. I love you. I am your friend. You have been my friend. My best friend. You cannot pay me for what I have given you and I cannot pay you for what you have given me." Eula tilted her head, smiling, "Besides that, you have a lawyer to keep you from problems."

Scornfully, Madame said, "The profession of lawyers sharpens the brain by narrowing it. All he wants is my money also."

Eula was silent a moment, then said, "Rita is going to have a baby."

"I know. She is a fool. She is planning to support it by visits over here when I start having my dinner guests again, which will be soon. I am lonely here. You are always off with that man or your house." Then Madame sat silent, looking at Eula, trying to read her mind.

Eula read Madame's mind. "I will not be able to come to your dinners. You know I never liked to. Why not invite Rita? She is perfect! Oh, not in the old way, but as a guest."

"They might want to . . ."

"Well, let one or two do it once or twice a year for ten-thousand dollars. They can well afford it. She is a good, clean, beautiful woman. She can support herself and the baby that way."

With a strange laugh, Madame said, "I might not want even you to come as a guest. Your clothes. You do not dress with style or class as I taught you. You need to pay attention to your clothes."

Eula laughed in return, "Clothes? For what? For who? I used to dress for your life. Now I dress for mine."

Madame sighed, "I told you that man would make you lose your mind." In the answering silence she sighed again, and said, "In any event, when it comes to Rita, I do not want a whore at my table as a guest." She sighed, looking thoughtful, "Well, I could use the spending change though; now that you have taken what I would have had. Rita is like a piece of false jewelry. She could be an ornament at my table though, pretty, but of no value."

"I have never found Rita to be false to me or you," Eula voiced. Disgusted, she moaned, saying, "Oh, Madame, does no one ever finish paying you? Let her keep it all. She has a home with Iris. She has responsibilities now. She can be an advantage to you as a good guest! Let her keep it all. She is not interested in being a . . . whore."

Madame leaned forward, her smile was gone as she said, "If I listen to you, I will lose money in every direction from every source! I have responsibilities! I do not have an Iris. I am alone!"

Eula stood up to leave, "Listen . . . I am your friend. As long as I live. You never have to worry about being alone or sick by yourself. Rita can be a very good friend also. Someone you can really talk to. No one in this town will understand your thoughts or have your memories to share like Rita will. I don't think of Rita as a whore. But you have taken from her for years, now let her keep her own. Be glad for the friendship! Count your blessings!"

Indignant and infuriated, Madame stood up from her silken chaise longue in her beautiful bedroom, "I'll have to count my blessings! There will be no money to count!"

Eula left the room, saying, "Remember what your friend Marion says. You can't take that money with you. Leave some love behind you when you go, instead of all your money. I'll always be here for you, but there are some other people around here who could be here for you, too! You are so smart about money, why not be smart about love! That old man you had is gone. Get some new loves beside me, because that is just what I am trying to do for myself!"

Madame looked at the space Eula had left behind her for a moment. Then she walked through her house. It contained every luxury she could ever dream of, Aubusson carpets, Persian carpets, French tapestries. She had original paintings; some that should have been in a great museum. Brilliant chandeliers from France, Spain, and Belgium. Gleaming silver from England. The best of Limoges and priceless porcelain from China sat in gleaming antique wooden cabinets with glass fronts. All to serve her guests and herself.

She went to the river end of her house and the apartment she had built for Eula. Now it had lofty windows that looked down on her private park. There was a garden of trees and flowers, sand spread beside the flowing river. This small sitting room was carpeted with a lush, velvety brown, like chocolate. The walls were covered with an apricot-colored raw silk. The few chairs were covered in chocolate-colored velvet. A few lime-green or pale lavender silk-covered pillows were thrown about.

She sat in one of the soft chairs and, placing the tip of her finger between her teeth, thought about herself and her life. "The monotony of this almost rural life will bore me and settle on me like a fatal disease. I even hear roosters crowing in the distance some mornings." She smiled grimly. "My years seem to have gone slowly, like dead leaves falling from a tree. But they have, still, gone too soon. My youth, my beauty, has faded away. Fading more quickly every day. I am without love. I could never love one of my guests; on the contrary, I seldom like them at all. I am even without hope. Perhaps my Marion is right; what is important aside from love and hope?"

She turned her head to look through the windows at the sky. "Eula hates me now. She can no longer understand a strong mind that is right! She should leave that man, Lamont, alone. He will take all the peace and comfort, the true love, from her life.

"People are so fickle, so tasteless. They are stupid; that's why they are poor. You have to cajole, coax, flatter, or fill them with fear, blackmail, or fool them and threaten them to keep them from making mistakes that will harm you. Oh, Eula, Eula. Oh, somebody!" The tears that were about to fill her eyes, dried. "But not just anybody."

Suddenly, she felt old, old, old, with a sense of a lonely, empty old age. "I am not even as old as my mother was when she died." Madame yearned for her old emotional anchors. "Where is my lover? Where is Barnett? Where is Eula going to be? My youth was my anchor once. I was the center of my existance. I am still the center . . . but, I see, it is not enough." She smiled sadly. "Well . . . even queens die. Who can quarrel with Time?"

A tiny seed of hatred for Lamont Heavy found fertile ground at last and, slowly, began to thrive.

Eula had called Tobe and gone to sit by the river. She was thinking about all the sadness in the life around her. "How can I be so happy and everybody else, except Marion, has some problem they can't seem to solve, God? Madame, Iris, Lona, and even Old Mary Green a little bit lonely. Ha is frustrated in her life, her plans; saving a dollar a day to help her children and herself. Lord have mercy.

"Rita needs money for her new life and her baby. She's still a beautiful woman, a more mature beauty. She looks better, if anything, because she has beauty in her heart. She'll probably get married . . . someday, if she wants to.

"But what about now? Money or loneliness. Everybody needs something. And I have to think of Lamont and me, too. I better go count the money and see where I stand. I might even give some of it back to Madame since it bothers her so; money she will never think of again." Eula sat thinking for a while longer, then, calling Tobe, went in her apartment to count money.

Eula called Earle to tell her that she would soon be getting married. Whatever Earle said, my mother's answer was "I know it!" She tried to call Jewel, as she had, often, in the past few months, but was told this time that Jewel was no longer living at college. Eula hung up the phone perplexed and worried for a moment. Then she thought, "Jewel is alright, because I know Jewel would let Madame know if she needed anything or anything was wrong."

She had been feeling so good, and now, she was tired all of a sudden. After several minutes thinking about Jewel, Eula thought, "She must have married that boy! That doctor! And I don't even know him. Or his family. Oh, dear Lord." She felt like crying, but didn't. Her good feelings were returning. "I have too much to do right now. I'll think about it later."

*Something is going to happen soon. I feel it. I am getting weaker. I must hurry to finish my story before I am unable to continue.*

# Chapter Twenty-nine

*

When Eula emerged from her apartment onto Dream Street she had such a pleased, warm look she actually glowed. Her eyes shone with a little excitement. She looked up the street of embattled dreams with a lingering gaze on Lamont's house as she walked to Lee's Grocery.

As usual, Ha was working, stocking the shelves. She looked up at Eula and the frown she wore changed to a smile as she said, "Hi! Good morning!" Henry Lee came to stand by his cash register, frowning slightly at Eula. He didn't like the time his wife took away from work to talk to this "too much talking lady."

As Ha came away from the shelves, Henry said, "I already told Mrs. Green daughter, that Lona woman, she don't come in no more. She all time steal. Send Homer. But, now, that Iris lady, she always buy cat food, but now she steal cat food today. What's the matter with people?"

Ha looked at the floor, embarrassed. She said, "She never do that before, I don't think. I know Lona steal. I did not know old lady steal. I don't stop her. She be too ashamed. I will tell Rita. She will pay when she knows."

It only took a moment for Eula to realize why Iris had stolen.

Ha turned to her husband, "Go have your tea, Henry Lee, please. Take a break. I am here." When Henry left, mumbling, Eula reached across the counter, touching Ha's hand. "I have been thinking of all the things we talk about, about your plans, Ha."

Disheartened, Ha said, "Oh. Plans."

"Yes, Ha, I have an idea you might think about."

"You been thinking of me, Eula?"

"Yes, Ha. Now listen. This is just an idea. I know you save one dollar a day or a week toward college for your daughters because Henry saves for your sons, and you want to go to school or college for yourself. Yes?"

"Yes." Ha sighed, looked toward the opened door at the back of the store, and picked up a can to put on the shelf. "Oh, I never get to go. Just a little dream. But my girls get to go. I save some way."

Eula's face was full of her smile as she said, "You might. Suppose you had the money for the girls . . . or most of it? And suppose you went to school every summer while they work in your place in the store?"

Ha listened very carefully, her eyes searching Eula's eyes for even a wisp of her dreams, some sign of the reality. Eula slid an envelope across the counter until it rested under Ha's shopworn hand. Ha frowned as she looked down at the white envelope, then quickly, back up to Eula's eyes.

Remembering her own beginnings, tears brimmed in Eula's eyes as she saw the disbelief, confusion, the fear that it might not be true, or it might be true, in Ha's face. Ha's fingers slowly curled around the envelope.

Eula said, "This is a gift from Madame Elizabeth Fontzl. There is ten-thousand dollars in there. Four thousand for each girl's start. Take your one dollar savings and go, yourself, to summer school, or junior college. Your girls can prepare you. They cost very little. Go until you find what you want to do. Learn more English. Have your dream, Ha." Ha began to smile as her fingers curled tightly over the envelope and slid it into her pocket.

Eula continued, "That will leave two thousand dollars for you to go home to China to see about your mother. I will talk to Madame Fontzl. She will be glad to use her friends to help you get through Chinese political issues. Shall I tell her you said alright."

Ha lifted the envelope from her pocket, opened it, saw the money, and quickly put it back into her pocket. "You tell truth!"

Eula's face became serious as she said, "Yes. I tell you truth. And Ha? Madame is getting old . . . and lonely. When you have a free minute, if possible, go over and visit with her. Take her a little plate of some special recipe you have. Sometime?"

Ha's face shone with wonder. "My mother. I can find my mother." She bent her head to look at Eula and faintly smiled. "You do this, Eula Too. I know you! But, no matter, no matter. I go to see Madame lady and take friendship to her."

Eula shook her head, saying, "Good. Madame Fontzl made this possible." They talked a little longer, then Eula left. The last words she heard were, "My girls; they be very happy and not so much scared anymore. Thank you, Eula Too."

Eula passed Lamont's house on her way to Maureen Iris McVistin and Rita. They were outside working in the yard, the big cat laying on the porch contented and lazily watching them. Both of them smiled at Eula in welcome. Rita, suntanned and healthy, spoke first, "We are planting small trees that will have blossoms. We are going to make this a beautiful wild garden!"

Eula, glad to smile again, said, "Well! It looks like you are at home here."

"I feel that way."

Iris spoke up, "And we are going to have a baby!"

Rita, looking a little worried and embarrassed, said, "I am going to look for a job. A receptionist. Or something like that. That's about all I know I can do. I'm in my early forties now."

Eula said, "I'll soon be thirty-six. Life can be just beginning for both of us. That's why I dropped by to see you . . . both." They waited. Iris asked, "Shall I give you all some privacy?" But Rita answered, "No, dear. You are my family." She looked in Eula's eyes, questioningly, as she said, "What would I not want you to hear?"

Eula spoke, "No, it's not private, Iris." She looked at Rita. "I'm glad you plan to keep the baby. When you go to work, you already have a grandmother to keep the baby for you."

Iris spoke up, "Rita is like a daughter to me. She is the loving, considerate person I want my daughter to be. But, I don't think she will stay here long after the baby comes. She is too beautiful; someone will marry her and take her away from me."

Rita just shook her head no without saying a word for a moment. Then she said, "This is our home as long as Moms will have us. I don't want to be alone again. I want to stay here."

*I could see there were two babies nestling in Rita's womb.*

Eula said, "I want to help." They looked enquiringly in Eula's face. She continued, "But I need a promise from you." They asked "What?" in unison.

"I need you to let Elizabeth be the godmother or aunt. I need you to visit her, Rita. Keep up with her a little. See if she is lonely."

"Oh, I'd do that anyway, Eula. Are you going away?"

"I may be getting married. My life will change. I won't be living there with her." The old woman and the middle-aged woman smiled for Eula's joy, then frowned for Elizabeth. They had both been lonely for long times. Iris thought Madame would survive; Rita knew she would survive.

At first, Eula spoke slowly as she handed a white envelope to Rita, saying, "Well, we want to give you this."

Rita took the envelope, looking into Eula's eyes as she opened it and took the check for ten-thousand dollars out. She looked down at the check, not understanding what it meant, then at Eula with questions, hope, and gratitude so deep it was humiliating to Eula.

Eula reached for Rita's dirt-covered wrist as she said, "I had a thought . . . if you would like to hear it." Rita nodded so Eula said, "I know how expensive it is to have a baby these days and now you want a new job. If you take care of yourself real well while you are pregnant you could go to school. You know, take typing, shorthand, or even start nursing school, if you like that better. And you know how you like to wear hats? You made your own a few times when you couldn't find one you liked in the stores." Rita nodded, smiling. "Well, you could take millinery classes. I've seen hats you threw together that were gorgeous. Start your own business! This would be enough money to get you started, a year or so. Throughout the hardest times. I know it's not much, but it gives you a chance to breathe and plan. Both of you seem happy here together."

Rita burst into tears and pulled Eula into her arms, saying, "Thank you, thank you, thank you, my friend."

Eula held Rita, but said, "No, no. Madame! You must think of Madame. If she has a dinner or something, please try to go when she invites you. This is from her."

"I know it is not, Eula. At least I can't believe it. But, I understand, and don't worry. I will do everything I can to help. I'll make her an auntie. That will give her something to do. And I'll go to her dinners if she invites me; that will give me something to do, if they are not too often. I will be a mother, you know. That takes time."

As Eula crossed the street to go to Mary Green's house, Iris said to Rita, "Isn't that something. A colored girl! Giving you something like that! Why, I never would have believed it of those people."

Rita looked at her a moment before asking, "How many colored people have you known, Iris? I can believe it because I know kindness does not come in colors. Some people who have been the meanest to me have been white, just like us." She turned her head to look toward Eula. "We didn't even tell her we were in need. She knew because she thinks." She bent down on her knees to work again. "Don't even say 'those people' again, Moms. Think of what Marion told us, life is a matter of human beings. All humanity alike."

As Eula crossed the street to go to Mary Green's house she saw Marion getting into her car. Eula's heart was full of emotion, even as she thought about Madame. "I'm doing this for you, you ole bat! I told you I love you! And you wouldn't have done a thing but let it sit somewhere in a musty old bank vault."

She called out to Marion, "Hello there. You coming or going?"

Marion turned, smiling, "Hello Eula. I saw you over there talking to the ladies. How are you? You are always moving. You keep yourself busy. What is this my play-brother, Lamont, has told me about you and him? You all getting married!"

Eula blushed. "Well, yes, we are talking about it. And since you brought it up, I can ask you about it. Sometimes I don't know what to do. I don't really know him."

"Do you love him, Eula?"

Eula looked at Marion seriously and said, "Yes, I do love him. At least, I feel in my heart that I love him."

"Well, Eula, where else are you waiting to feel it? I'm'a tell you something girl, Lamont is the only other man besides my Fred that I would ever think of marrying. I mean that! When Lamont loves, Lamont loves hard. He doesn't mess around and play with any feelings."

"He certainly seems to be a good man."

"Lamont is a good man. Now, you know I get my information from the Bible. I am going to tell you, you would have a good husband and marriage, and a good life if you keep other people out of your business. The first thing Jehovah did was make a man and a woman. To start a family! A family is important, girl. And if Eve hadn't let Satan into her business the entire world would be different. All he used was one word, 'not' as in 'you will not' surely die. People's mouths, words, can ruin your individual, private world."

Eula was listening so intently Marion continued. "Life is a very important, fragile thing. Every day you are building your life with things you run into every day. Satan is busy, works all the time. You have to guard your happiness. Build a fence around your home and a mental fence of wisdom around your mind. Life does not play. It is not a game, Eula. Life is dead serious. You can only laugh when you know you are protected wisely with your mind. You can relax, and still keep your guard up, you know. I do. That is why, much as I hate to see my nephews go, Lona has to go, has to move."

"She is moving? Why? A job? Mrs. Green will miss her grandchildren, and Lona was company to her. She will be alone if Lona goes."

"Honey, Mrs. Green is my mama. I never will leave my own mother alone, if I have to take her to live with me in Elysee or we have to move back here." She frowned as she said, "Lona has problems. It is necessary she go. I am not saying this to you for gossip, but I just told you, you have to stay on guard. Even with the most unseemly people. Lona tried to poison my mother because she wants this house and is afraid somebody will take it away from her. It will never be her house; it may belong to Homer or Prince. So, you see, Lona has to go. She says she is not taking Homer." Marion started getting into her car again.

Eula put her hand on her shoulder, saying, "But . . . I came to give you all something. Just a little something to help in some way. I want people to check on Madame . . . I always call her Madame, I mean Elizabeth. Check on her when I get married because we are building a new house. We won't be across the street."

"Oh, Eula, of course. I will always be close to Elizabeth. And if we move back here, she and I will be over the fence again." She laughed, her eyes twinkling. "You don't have to give us anything. But what were you going to give us?"

"Well," now Eula was ashamed it was so little, "five-thousand dollars. Just to pick up any loose edges."

Marion laughed joyfully, saying, "Oh, Eula girl. That is so good of you to think of us like that. But I tell you what would be nice. Give it to Lona instead. Maybe she can put it down on a house of her own. Then no one will be in danger of losing their life over a house. She will be so happy!"

"You would tell me to do that, even though you think she was going to poison your mother?"

"Eula, all people are flawed. Something's wrong with all of us, some more than others. When you do not have God you are at your weakest. He gives you the wisdom so you can avoid spending your life in some prison, physically or mentally. The Truth does set you free! Listen, I don't hate Lona, I feel sorry for her, but I cannot let my pity blind me to the danger of her mind. She is a liar, one of the most dangerous things on earth. Look at the condition this world is in! I know, a lot of people lie, but I don't trust them either. Lie to me, lie on me; I'm afraid of those people and I avoid them. I'm certainly not going to leave my mother with one. No, give it to Lona. She deserves a break in life. That gift may help her see some good in life. Go on, go on and tell her; she could use a kind word of hope now."

Eula shook her head in wonder at Marion and thought, "She practices what she preaches."

When Eula rang the bell the door was opened by Homer, his eyes bleary with tears. Lona was not far behind him, her face was hideous; her eyes bulged and mouth contorted with teeth bared like an animal. She glared at Eula as she shoved Homer aside, saying, "And what do you want? I saw you out there! Probably talking about me!"

"We were."

"I know it! Everybody in the world must know I'm leaving!" She turned to walk away, talking, "She thinks I tried to kill MaMary to get this damned house!"

Eula was alarmed, but tried not to show it. "Where will you go?"

The woman, Lona, just gave up. She was on the verge of crying, but trying not to. "Who knows? Who cares? That's why I'm only taking one of my kids. I have to find a place and a job."

"Well, you will, Lona. You're young and you are able."

"I don't need advice."

"Yes you do. You need everything."

Lona turned abruptly to Eula. "You got him, didn't you? And he buildin' you a house out there on that land. A house! Like the one he got across the street ain't good enough." She threw herself into a chair. "So that's all settled. Well, maybe I can rent his house when I get a job; if it's still empty then. I'm gonna get a job. I can't pay much rent right away, but Lamont likes Homer. I know he don't want him without a house to live in."

"I don't know, Lona, but I have a proposition for you."

Lona immediately looked suspicious and wary. "What? A proposition?"

"Yes. I have seven-thousand dollars to give you. *But*, number one, you have to take two-thousand dollars and go to school. Sign up today or no later than tomorrow morning. Find one. What do you think you would like to be doing, in say . . . a year's time?"

"Are you foolin' with me?" Moments passed as Eula waited in silence. In a softer voice, Lona said, "I like doing hair. Cosmetological, I think. There is a college in Elysee. I guess. Prob'ly one wherever I go live."

"Then go to cosmetology school." Eula thought of Marion's words about God and pitying humans. She also thought of Lamont's house that would be empty, but put that out of her mind. She said, "I'll help you find a small place you can rent for six months while you learn. Let MaMary watch your kids for you free. In six months' time you can be an apprentice in some shop in Elysee City. Then, when you do that, I will give you the remaining five-thousand dollars to put down on a house for yourself and your children . . . maybe in Elysee City."

Lona was quick to dream, "My own house!"

Eula smiled with her, "Yes. One you bought yourself and no one can take away from you. A home for your children and you. But, I was hoping you would let Homer stay here with Lamont; that would give give you more time to concentrate on your studies." Lona broke down and cried. She had snot and tears flying. Her heart was heavy, but it was happy, too. Strangely, she liked Eula even less. Behind her happy thoughts was this one, "She sure is a fool. Can you 'magine a fool like that? If Homer stays here, there is still a chance for me with Lamont." She smiled at Eula. "Oh, yes, he can stay. I need to know he is alright!"

It was a Friday. Lamont always went directly from his teaching job to work on their house. He kept clothes and other necessary items there. He usually took Homer with him from school because Miss Iowna Hart went over his homework with him and gave him extra lessons. But Lona had kept Homer home on this day. Eula always took their dinner out to them in the evenings. Lona said Homer could go with her this evening when she drove out to the land. How could Lona say no?

After talking to Lona, Eula went home to Madame's. Her heart was light, she was feeling good about life, the neighborhood, and herself. She showered, dressed, and went upstairs to help Dolly put together a nice meal for three. In her happiness she went to Madame to hug her, give her some sign of her love and friendship. After all, Madame had made all these things possible.

Madame was looking a few shades happier when Eula entered her bedroom. She looked up at Eula with a smile, saying, "I have heard from our Jewel." Eula's heart wanted to feel lighter, but was not sure how. She asked, "How is she? What did she say? What happened at school? Is she married? When is she going to call me? Her mother?"

Madame waved her hand in a sign to calm Eula down. "She is coming here. Soon. Sit down, I have to tell you something." Eula sat and began to worry about her daughter. Madame smiled and said, "She has had a baby. She does not want to stay with her husband. She says he is . . . boring. She is bringing the baby, here, to . . . us. Then she is going back to college to finish. She will get a divorce, of course."

Eula sat back in the chair and softly moaned a sigh. So many things rushed to her mind, she shook her head to try to clear it. "She is coming here? To you?"

"To us, Eula."

Eula was speechless for several moments, while Madame tilted her head and looked off a thousand miles in her mind. Eula watched her, watched her thinking. She knew what Madame was thinking. She thought of her daughter, Jewel. Then she thought of Marion's words from the Bible. At last, very thoughtfully, she told herself, "You have a life now, Eula. You have a man who loves you; who is building a house for you right this minute. Waiting for you. Thinking of your happiness. You will be thirty-six soon. Do you want twenty more years like the last twenty? Do you even have twenty more years to live? Do you want that man?" She answered herself, "Yes, I do want that man."

When she stood up, she smiled at Madame, who was aglow with her own thoughts. She said, "Madame Elizabeth, whatever you decide will be fine with me. I know you and Jewel will decide what is best for the both of you. You are alike in many ways. Me? I have a new life I intend to live. If you all can live with me, I will live with you. I'm not living *for* anyone again. Just remember, my dearest friend, the baby will be my grandchild. Mine. And I will be here watching over it."

Then she went to take the food Dolly had prepared for her, and left the house. She got in her car and honked for Homer; he ran out smiling and jumped in the car, glad to go.

*I wish I could tell you more about Homer, but I don't have time.*

As Eula drove along the tree-lined river road, she thought of Jewel, until she turned off the paved road onto the dirt road on her land leading to her house. It was getting dark fast and Homer had noticed the clouds gathering in the sky. "Miss Eula I believe we're gonna get some rain tonight. You can still see, but it's getting too dark to work much."

Eula looked up at the sky and said, "Well, you can take your food over to Miss Hart's. You don't have to go to school tomorrow anyway. You all can work."

Then they were at the wooden shell sitting on the circular concrete foundation of her house. Some of the rooms had been closed in right after the roof had been put on. It had electricity because of the easy access to the river road, but the water line had not been completed yet. It looked beautiful to her. She could see, in her mind, the way it would look one day . . . soon.

She dropped Homer off at the cut-off road to Miss Hart's and hurried on to the house. Well, to Lamont. She could see a few little lights and hear the table saw as she drove up and parked. Now she could hear his music. "Always has his music." She sat still, full of her thoughts for a few moments. She put the thoughts of Jewel aside as she climbed out of the car and gathered the packages, their dinner. She stopped to listen for a moment. Eula liked the sound of the roosters and the mooing of the cows in the distance. She could smell the rain in the air.

At last she went into the house, where the kitchen was going to be, and put her packages down neatly beside a hot plate on the makeshift plywood table. The framed dollar was hanging on the bare wall. The kerosene heater was lit, heating up the space around it. There was no wind, so it was not really cold.

She found Lamont on his knees trying to set the wood he had just cut. He looked up, smiling, then laughing in the pleasure of her company. She knelt down beside him and put her arms around his neck, while she laughed in the pleasure of his presence. She squeezed him extra tightly. He leaned back from her, gave her a look deep into her eyes, with a secret smile of appreciation on his warm lips.

He set his tools aside and stood up when she let him go, saying, "I have something I want to show you, baby." She smiled and asked, "Something for the house?" He smiled back, saying, "Everything is for us first, then the house." (*Oh, my daddy, my daddy, my daddy.*) They laughed that silly, foolish laughter people make when they are in love.

He led her to the light then opened his wallet and showed her the marriage license with their names on it. As he placed it on another little makeshift table, they smiled over it at each other. Then he reached into his carry-all and took out a Bible, laying it beside the marriage license. He smiled at her again, she smiled back with a tentative question in her smile.

He kissed her forehead then started taking his tool belt off as he said, "I'm really hungry. You going to eat with me?" Eula relaxed and nodded. He put his hand on the back of her neck as he said, "It's going to rain. It's nice out here when it rains through the trees. You ever take a shower outside in the rain?"

Eula opened her mouth in a round O, "No!"

"Well, baby, I like to shower outside, so . . ."

"Lamont, we can't go around getting naked in the wide open outdoors."

"Baby, there is no one out here but us and Miss Hart, and she is not coming over here!" He laughed. "If she does she can join us. Let's eat, Eula. Before we shower." He laughed again when she blushed.

They ate in the darkened moonlight with one little candle. They managed many times to touch each other, lean over for a brief kiss, another smile, and much laughter was shared between them. (*My parents*.)

When the rain started, Lamont stood up and started taking off his clothes for his shower. "Did you know that all the sun that shines on this land is ours? That all the rain that rains on this land is ours? Ours, Eula Too." His warm laughter softly tumbled out of him. "I guess you better stay here with me tonight, unless you want to go over to Miss Hart's warm little house where I bathed you that first time. Tonight we are going to give each other a shower."

"Oh, Lamont, stop that foolishness."

"First, you rub the soap on, Eula. Then you rub and wash it all over your body, well, my body. The rain rinses it all away then you wrap yourself up in a warm towel and get under some warm blankets and you have the best sleep you ever had."

"Lamont, I'm not going to get naked in front of you."

"Why not, baby?" He leaned back, lazily. "I have seen every part of you; I have even felt every part of you." He leaned forward and grasped her thigh. Electric currents darted swift and warm from his hand through Eula's body. Still she shook her head, no. He got up, turned the music low, took her hand, and pulled her to the table where the marriage license was.

"C'm 'ere, stand close beside me." She did. "Now," he continued, "I have my hand on this Bible, you put your hand on it, too." She did.

He said aloud, looking toward the heavens, "God? Jehovah God, I am taking this woman to be my wife in front of You. I will love her and honor her all the days of my life." He turned to Eula, "Now you say it."

Eula had her hand on the Bible, now she raised her eyes to his, saying, "God, Jehovah God, if that is Your name, I will take this man to be my husband. I know I will love him and honor him all the days of my life I live."

"Now, we can kiss, Eula, and we are married tonight, until we can go to some minister and get married in some conventional way.

Alright? Now, let's go take that shower. We got a good rain coming down now. Don't worry about being naked, it's too dark to see all your secrets anyway." He finished undressing and turned the music up.

Eula was more than touched by the brief ceremony. She blew out the candle and took her clothes off. Laughing, she followed him outside into the rain. She tried to see his body and she could, a little, but it really was dark. So she relaxed. She soaped his body as he soaped her body. Laughter, always happy laughter. They scrubbed each other, played around in the rain until, finally, they spread their arms, letting the rain rinse them clean.

Lamont took his woman's arm, pulling her into the sound of music in the open-air house. He took a fat towel from near the heater and wrapped it around her. "I'll dry you, Eula, you dry me." They dried each other to slow lovemaking music.

He got immediately into his little flat mattress roll-up bed and pulled the covers back for her. She said, "Lamont, I better go home. I didn't plan for this to . . ."

He looked disappointed and very concerned. He looked at his woman and said, simply, "Don't go." When she hesitated, he said, "Stay. Stay here with me." That record by Etta James started playing. It was all about "At last, my love has come along." (My, *my*.)

My mother didn't really want to leave. She looked back and forth at him, at the ceiling, at the floor. Then, very nervous, she looked through a wall without sheetrock at the rain pouring down on the dark forms of trees, branches waving in the wind and rain. She fumbled around with her clothes a bit, then tightened her lips and said, "Alright, but I will only stay a little while, Lamont."

My father smiled a little, to himself, raised the covers, and welcomed her into his arms.

She was glad to get under the covers where it was warm and so cozy. Where he was.

*And I started packing to leave this place for that other place. Gathering all my little seeds together, for everything I might need on Earth: heart, lungs, liver, kidneys, ears, eyes . . . oh, all those things. I wanted to be completely ready to go when the time arrived, when my chance came.*

*I know what I said about Earth way back in the beginning of this story. Oh, I've seen so much. I know you can come to Earth, excited about really living and doing things. Dreaming your dreams. Learning how to make your dreams come true. Failing from time to time. Winning now and then. I also know, when you get here, people in Life may try to, can, beat your body, smash your dreams, twist your vision, annihilate and consume your psyche, snare, purchase, end your life, or use love to break . . . your . . . heart. Oh, all of it. I did not see much Love on my journey. Some, yes, but there could, should have been more Love. Humans are too much alike to find so many reasons to hate each other, to kill each other. But I also know with wisdom Life can do you right if you do Life right. If you learn your lessons and wisdom from the Master of all creation, Jehovah God. I will do my very best not to forget that. My very life shall depend on it.*

My father folded my mother in his strong arms. He wanted to laugh aloud, he was so happy. Holding her close to his heart, he said, "You are my everything, Eula. My ever-ry thing." She smiled inside her ardently hungry heart. "At last, my love has come along."

They kissed some of their long, warm, wet kisses. When he leaned his warm body over hers, she squeenched and made a little moan of fear. But her body, full of need, just as his was, rose to meet his.

Their damp, warm bodies pressing tightly, his strong, long arm reached out and brought back a small jar. In a small voice, she asked, "What is that, Lamont?" He answered in a soft, husky voice that had a smile in it. "Some Dixie Peach hair oil. A little of this and you won't feel even imaginary pains, baby." He gently, tenderly rubbed some on, and around, her private place. They started that hot wet kissing again. He took his own good, slow time. Her body opened like a ripe, sweet peach. He entered, melting, dissolving in the moisture of her body. Eula Too, my mother, said "La-La-La" and "You" so many times, trying to call out my daddy's name, it floated outdoors, throughout all the trees and rain. I knew what my name would be—Yulala Too Heavy.

*I'm not sure what happened after that. I was rushing, battling, fighting my way to life. My father was full of seeds, all trying to beat me to the place I needed to be. The struggle in Life begins.*

*There are many things I did not get to tell you; things you might want to know. I want to know them also. Time slipped away.*

*I know Dream Street is full of dreams; some may come true. In the end, to me, the people in the houses on Dream Street became like a family. A family of human beings. As all human beings on the Earth are a family.*

*I'm wondering what this Place is going to mean for me. I'm wondering if I will remember that nothing and no one is permanent or perfect but Almighty God. I'm wondering, when Time starts slipping through my life like sand, will I have sense enough to know the Place for me. Please, God, help me have some wisdom in my life, make some sense of my life.*

*I'm wondering if you and I will meet, dear listener.*

*I must go now. Can not speak anymore. I am . . . going. Gone.*

# Acknowledgments

*

First, I am thankful to my editor, Janet Hill—a great editor I have been so fortunate, so blessed, to have. I learn from her because she is generous with her time, knowledge, and consideration. She is one of the best editors I know. Tracy Jacobs, you deserve special mention. You are, also, kind and considerate. Working with you is easy.

I really wish to thank everyone at Doubleday/Random House who has anything to do with my books. I find you all considerate people who try to understand what a person wants and needs; then you try to make it possible.

I want to reach back to Peternelle van Arsdale and when I said "she has my head." By those words I meant I respected her excellence. She is professional and deeply involved with what she does. I was going through menopause, and she had to suffer me. Forgive me, Peternelle. I appreciated you then, and I do now, more. I want to thank Sharon Elise for her huge help to me. I love her. Much love and appreciation to my friend Rita Hogan of New York.

A special thanks to you, the readers. Believe me when I say I love you. You have been with me, truly, and I deeply appreciate you because you like my work. I am honored and grateful that you do. God bless you all!

I thank God, Jehovah God, for allowing me to do what I love: play paper dolls in a book, exploring real life.

A heavenly new collection from
beloved storyteller J. California Cooper

# WILD STARS SEEKING MIDNIGHT SUNS

*by J. California Cooper*

J. California Cooper's powerful short story collections, including *The Future Has a Past* and *Some Love, Some Pain, Some Time*, have attracted a large and devoted audience. Her evocative new set of stories proves again why she is a master of this form, as she explores the mysteries of the human heart and the longings of ordinary folks in an endearing and enthralling style all her own.

"Cooper's stories beckon. It is as if she is patting the seat next to us, enticing us to come sit and listen." —*Ms.*

AVAILABLE APRIL 2006 WHEREVER BOOKS ARE SOLD • WWW.DOUBLEDAY.COM

# ALSO BY J. CALIFORNIA COOPER

## FAMILY

J. California Cooper's storytelling has earned her frequent comparison to Langston Hughes and Zora Neale Hurston, but she has proven hers is a wholly original talent. In this wise, beguiling, and beautiful novel set in the era of the Civil War, Cooper uses her deceptively simple style to paint a haunting portrait of a woman named Always, who was born a slave, and four generations of her family.

Fiction/Literature/0-385-41172-3

## THE FUTURE HAS A PAST
*Stories*

There's Vinnie, an overworked single mother who sacrifices her own needs to her children, until an old flame returns with an offer she can't refuse. A happily married mother laments the fate of her beautiful friend, whose naivete has deadly consequences. Luella, who feels destined for a life without romance, is left her mother's modest inheritance and her luck appears to change, but much differently than she imagined. And Irene confronts her womanizing boyfriend with information that will bring him to his knees.

Fiction/Literature/0-385-49681-8

## IN SEARCH OF SATISFACTION

On a once-grand plantation in Yoville, a freed slave named Josephus fathers two daughters, Ruth and Yinyang, by two different women. Ruth is born to a hardworking mother and seems destined for a life of material poverty that is enriched by family. Yinyang, Josephus's daughter by the alcoholic mistress of the manse, weaves in and out of spiritual awareness. In seeking their legacy, the daughters pull each other, their families, and their neighbors into a vortex of emotion.

Fiction/Literature/0-385-46786-9

## THE MATTER IS LIFE

The various men and women—some good, some wickedly twisted—in this exuberant collection of stories confront, cope with, and celebrate each seemingly tiny detail of life. Cooper's characters are plainspoken and direct: simple people for whom life, despite its ever-present struggles, is always worth the journey.

Fiction/Literature/0-385-41174-X

## A PIECE OF MINE

This extraordinary debut short story collection reveals ordinary people caught in their individual thickets of want and need. In "Say What You Willomay!" an arrogant city slicker learns the hard way which feminine virtues really matter. A mistreated wife gets sweet revenge from beyond the grave in "$100 and Nothing!" In these and eight other tales that have the essence of parables, Cooper's characteristic themes of romance, heartbreak, struggle, and faith resonate.

Fiction/Literature/0-385-42087-0

## SOME LOVE, SOME PAIN, SOMETIME

In the stories of *Some Love, Some Pain, Sometime*, we meet Darlin, a self-proclaimed femme fatale who uses her wiles to try to find a husband; MLee, whose life seems to be coming to an end at the age of forty until she decides to make a new life for herself; Kissy and Buddy, both trying and failing to find someone to fit them until they finally meet each other; and Aberdeen, whose daughter Uniqua shows her how to educate herself and move up in the world. These characters and others offer inspiration, laughter, instruction, and pure enjoyment in what is one of Cooper's finest story collections.

Fiction/Literature/0-385-46788-5

## THE WAKE OF THE WIND

Set in Texas in the waning years of the Civil War, *The Wake of the Wind* tells the story of Lifee and her husband, Mor. When Emancipation finally comes to Texas, Lifee, Mor, and their extended family of other slaves set out in search of land they can call their own. At once tragic and triumphant, this epic novel is a penetrating look at the challenges that generations of African Americans have had to overcome in order to carve out a home and a future for themselves and their families.

Fiction/Literature/0-385-48705-3